Ripples

Lia Cooper

Ripples

Produced and printed by Stillwater River Publications.

Visit our website at
www.StillwaterPress.com
for more information.

First Stillwater River Publications Edition.

ISBN: 979-8-950131-07-3 (paperback)
ISBN: 979-8-950131-08-0 (hardcover)

1 2 3 4 5 6 7 8 9 10
Written by Lia Cooper.
Cover & interior book design by Ken Paquette
Published by Stillwater River Publications,
West Warwick, RI, USA.

Ripples

Part 1

Chapter 1

Mia heard the familiar ringtone; adrenaline surged. She fumbled for her reading light and squinted at the clock. *One a.m. This ought to be good.* Her mind immediately flashed to Jimmy, and she tried to calculate the time difference. Her brother was one of the few people to call at that hour, usually collect, in either one of two conditions: a drunken blackout or bragging about his latest sober kick. And if he were on a really good bender, he'd often drop off the face of the earth for up to a year and then come crashing back in as if he'd never left. If cats had nine lives, then her brother was definitely part feline.

Despite her psychotherapy profession, Mia had little tolerance for his alcoholic dramas. Despite herself, she loved him deeply. On the outside, they couldn't have been more different. He lived without rules; she had too many. She was dependable and regimented to a fault; he was neither. He was who he was, without shame. She, on the other hand, was nowhere near as transparent.

Despite their differences, they were bound by tragedy they couldn't escape. *I guess it boils down to how we learn to lick our wounds, wrap them with whatever vices work for us. Our defenses against our pain are more than complicated.* She knew this first-hand. *Jimmy pickled his in booze.*

If she were honest, she'd admit her shame and resentment toward him. He was a constant reminder of the past she had all but wiped out.

"Hello," she grumbled.

"Hello, is this Dr. Capaldi?"

Mia sat up slowly. "Yes, it is."

"Ma'am, I am sorry to bother you at this hour…"

Dread swept over her as she braced for tragic news regarding Jimmy. *Goddamn drunken idiot. Please let him be okay.* She'd been expecting this call for a long time. She tried to remember the last time they'd spoken and held her breath.

"You're one of the family members of Mr. James Capaldi, Sr?"

It took a minute to register, and then relief flooded her heart.

"I'm sorry to inform you… He died of natural causes at the RI Department of Corrections earlier this evening."

The man continued, but Mia only heard bits and pieces. *Natural causes… My father's dead, Jimmy's alive… How do I want the State to handle the burial…*

When the caller noticed she hadn't said a single word, he asked her to take down the name and number of the state's mortuary and call them in the morning.

Mia sat, phone in hand, staring at nothing in particular. *My father's dead; dad's dead…* She waited to feel something, anything. *I have to call Jimmy. I feel relief; that's a feeling.* She let it wash through her, allowing her shoulders to drop back in place and her breathing to return to normal. She was overwhelmed with such a rush of relief, it felt like her heart would beat out of her chest.

She loved her brother despite his impairment. Although she felt anger toward him, she felt the hurt of abandonment more. Mia wasn't surprised by her lack of emotion at the news of her father's death. In her heart, she knew the sad truth: her father had been dead to her for years.

She crouched beside her bed and reached under until she felt her fingers brush against stiff cardboard. Lifting it onto her bed, she took a deep breath and started leafing through the envelopes. She scanned Jimmy's most recent letter for his phone number and punched in the digits.

She used to keep his info in her contacts, but it changed so often that she couldn't keep up. Her stomach dropped when she heard the all too familiar recording, "The number you have reached…"

Hanging up, her relief quickly turned to the familiar mixture of disappointment, annoyance and shame. Dealing with Jimmy was always the same. Mostly, she tried not to deal with him or anyone from back home. She pitched the letter back into the box and let her eyes linger.

Lying beneath the stack of letters and cards were vivid pieces from her past. Memories from *before*. The before memories were colorful, bright, and blissful. She could look on them without pain. It was the ones from *after* that kept her from returning. She worried the after-memories would eventually swallow her whole.

She'd left Rhode Island over twelve years ago as Marianna Capaldi. She'd since reinvented herself as Dr. Mia Capaldi, never looking back. She'd tried to forget the young, grief-stricken girl who'd boarded that plane all those years ago. She'd been so distraught after Robert that her Auntie Rose sent her to California to live with her Uncle Joe.

Frenchie, her dog, stared at her with the annoyance and attitude only a puffy French could give.

"What?" she grumbled. "It's like tracking down a homeless guy?"

She carried the box into the kitchen, dropped it on the table, and walked to the refrigerator. She craved the sedating effects of alcohol. She rummaged through the bottom shelf, pushing around a package of Oreos and other items until she found the cold bottle of Pinot Noir in the back. She fumbled in the drawer for a wine opener and pulled off the cork with a pop.

On tiptoes, Mia reached into the upper cabinet for a wine glass. Standing, she sipped and thought about Jimmy. *It's all about sedation for him.* The traumas from her past had left her with unbearable nightmares and anxiety. But with time, the unbearable became bearable, and she was down to a script for Trazodone to sleep. *When was the last time I took it?*

Only two people might've known where he was: Auntie Rose or her cousin Joanne. She didn't dial either of their numbers, knowing her aunt would call her shortly. Aunt Rosie was also on the list. If Mia were honest with herself, she needed to delay the sympathy and compassion. She couldn't bear it. She didn't need it. Instead, she dialed Rory.

The two had been best friends since their freshman year of college. She loved Rory more than anyone—well, except Mr. French. She had gotten Frenchie as a going-away-to-college present from her Uncle Joe and his partner Peter. She loved her little fat-headed Bichon. She didn't know what she'd do without him or Rory.

"Tell me it's not morning already."

"Ror, sorry about the hour. I'm supposed to be calling my brother, but I…"

"Your brother? Why? What happened?"

He knew of their estranged relationship, a little about his drinking career and how upset she had been when he hadn't shown up for her graduation.

"Mee?"

"I got a call from Rhode Island. My father died."

"Oh, honey. I am so sorry."

The line was silent until she finally exhaled.

"I'm coming over."

She wanted to blurt the truth, her truth, but she knew no words could ever truly capture what had happened or her jumbled feelings. She wanted to tell Rory that her father had already been dead to her—that if she sounded any sort of way, it was only because she'd thought it was about her brother. But by the time she found the appropriate words, it was too late. Rory had hung up and was on his way.

Chapter 2

Mia heard Rory's sports car zoom up her street in record time. She felt a comfort she couldn't name. She could always count on Ror; she liked that about him.

Greeting him at the front door, she said, "Ror, you didn't need to come over, but thank you."

He gave her a bear hug, then released his hold to look her in the eye. "You alright?"

She nodded.

He smells incredible. She watched him stroll in, looking like he'd just stepped out of Vogue—white tee, sweats, sandals; even his stubble looked good. She patted down her wild curls and tightened her scrunchy.

How does he wake up looking like that? She was amazed that he'd remained oblivious to his own looks; he was probably the only one.

"Here, these are for you." He handed her a bag of biscotti and eyed the glass of wine in her hand. "Sure, I'll have one."

She placed a glass in front of him, sat down and smiled toward the bag filled with her favorite, chocolate.

"Thank you."

He poured himself some wine. "You can freeze them. What did Aunt Rosie say?"

Of course, Ror thinks Auntie Rose was the one who called. "He had a heart attack." *Natural causes…*

"That's too bad, so sorry."

She shook her head, unable to stand the compassion his face wore.

"Ror, listen. When I got the call, I felt… relief." She exhaled her explanation without guilt and watched his olive complexion.

"You told me he'd been sick, and even though you hadn't been in touch, you still didn't want him to suffer."

She didn't remember telling him that.

He patted her hand. "I get it. I'm glad it's not your brother, too…maybe this will change things between the two of you; maybe he'll actually turn his life around now."

Mia was less than convinced. There'd been a time when she'd wanted nothing more. She could still hear him, "Mare, I got ninety days! This is it this time; I can feel it. I'm doing good now, you'll see. I'll come out, and you and Ror can show me the sights."

It'd been over ten years, and he still hadn't come out for a visit.

Rory's face broke out in a grin that highlighted his features. He grabbed her hand and squeezed. "Hey, you feel how you feel. Besides, if you weren't a little fucked up, you'd be bad at listening to nut-bags all day."

"You're not wrong." She attempted a half smile, more than grateful for his presence.

Rory had been more of a brother to her than Jimmy had been capable of his entire adult life. She reached for the bag in front of her, remembering the last time she'd seen her father alive.

It'd been late summer of 1988. The air was still, almost wet—in typical New England fashion. Rob was dead, like her insides. Auntie Rose thought Mia should visit her father before she left for San Francisco. She didn't have the will to fight with her, even on a good day. And she hadn't had a good day in what felt like forever.

Rory leaned over and scooped up Frenchie in one swipe. Half of Rory's face was blotted out by a giant puff of white fur. He moved it aside to see her.

"Can I do anything for you? Flight plans, calls, cover patients, whatever?"

She snapped a biscotti in half and set the rest in front of her.

"I need to decide what I'm going to do." She dunked the cookie in her wine.

"What do you mean?"

She watched the line on his forehead deepen. "Mee, you have to go; don't be stupid."

"I don't have to do anything. I'm not canceling my patients..." *for him.* Her patients depended on her. She didn't want to let them down.

"Scott and I will cover for you. You need to go home and be with Aunt Rosie, your brother."

She stared at him defiantly but knew he was right. Dread slowly started creeping up her spine.

"Do you think Jimmy knows?"

"Not from me, he doesn't. His number's been disconnected again, I tried." She eyed the box still out on the table. She absently reached for the twisty tie off the counter and began rolling it between her fingers.

"You think it'll send him off on a bender?"

"He might already be on one. Plus, he hasn't spoken to our father in years."

She knew he was probably thinking about his own estranged

father. Before moving out West, Rory had "come out" to his old-school Italian parents. His father disowned him on the spot. Soon after Mia met Rory, his father died. They never had a chance to mend their relationship, and Rory was devastated. A few years later, his mother sold off the family business, leaving Rory with a hefty inheritance. He understood the complicated layers of loss. It was one of the threads that bound them.

"What's in there?" he asked, nodding to the box.

"Letters, cards, a few pictures from… when I was young." *Why didn't I put it away?*

"Show me something from when you were young and cute."

She rolled her eyes. "Really?"

"Come on, I've never even seen your dad."

"Alright." She knew better than to fight with him. She dug under the letters and lifted out a Polaroid picture. "Here's one."

She was around five years old, sitting on his shoulders, wearing a yellow bathing suit and a huge toothless grin. *We must be at the beach or somewhere with water.* She smiled down at him like he was God, her hair a mass of wild curls.

Mia's mind tried to conjure the moment, some feeling from it, but there was nothing. *I was part of a family then.* Sadness crept through her body at the thought. *Was…*

"He was a big guy," said Rory.

"He was." She stared down at the picture.

She remembered riding in Auntie's car. They turned onto Reservoir Avenue, almost there.

"Hey, I'm sorry," Rory said, bringing her back to the moment.

"Neh, I barely knew him." *As an adult.*

His thick brows lifted toward hers as he rubbed his beard with one quick swoosh.

Forget it; I'm not going.

Rory's emerald eyes flashed concern, then understanding. He sat forward, holding Mr. French asleep in a ball on his lap.

"Mee, you should go. Maybe it'll be good for you to see Auntie, your cousins, even Jimmy. Who knows, it could be therapeutic? Scott and I can handle your patients. Maybe you should take a short vacation afterward."

"I don't need a vacation." She felt annoyance pulse. *Is he kidding me?*

"I just thought you'd already be there. Would it be that bad?"

That bad? She started compiling a list but looking at him, her annoyance melted away. She knew he didn't fully understand. She felt a pang of guilt over leaving out whole bits of the truth, especially to her friend. Rory was one of the few people who knew anything about her past.

Long ago, she'd told him her mother was killed during a botched robbery while working in a diner. Jimmy ran away to the army, where he took up drinking. Mia sought comfort by running to Jimmy's best friend—her virtual cousin—for love. Her father had left her and Jimmy in the care of their "aunt," unable to deal with his grief or them. *Maybe both.*

She'd been telling this version of her life story for so long that it sounded authentic. All these years later, she still couldn't bear to fill in the blanks—even for him.

My father sat behind the glass, phone in hand, waiting. He didn't look like the hero from my childhood.

Sometimes, telling the whole truth was overrated.

She placed the picture back into the box and shut the lid tight. Her mind wouldn't stop. She saw herself at eleven, watching as her mother's casket was sealed shut.

She tried to swallow, but there wasn't enough saliva. Her stomach dipped, and her heart felt a familiar pang; the past began to swarm. She tried to count her breaths. *1… 2… 3… 4… 5… 6.* She started straightening odd papers as she felt her hot, angry tears begin to swell. She tried to fight, stay in control. *I'll allow tears of relief that my brother's still alive—the drunk jerk he is—a few of shame for my family secrets. But I won't shed one tear of sadness over losing a father who caused so much pain. Forget that.*

She planned to call her aunt in the morning and explain that her schedule wouldn't allow a return home. They could have a memorial service without her.

She sat back down, twirling the end of the napkin in front of her.

She swallowed her feelings, pushing her thoughts aside. She buried them as she'd done for years. Done straightening, she drained her glass and tried to reclaim a sense of order, inner calm. Her mind tried to imagine the colors of a sunset, the feeling of her face being tickled by the sun like the little girl in the picture. When it didn't work, she reached for her empty glass.

Rory refilled her glass and topped his off. "Here's to the one we do need." He winked.

They clinked their glasses. She swirled the wine, then took a long sip to gather her thoughts and rein in her emotions.

Through the murkiness of her past, Mia heard the phone.

Chapter 3

"Hello."

"Marianna, did they already call you?" her aunt's voice boomed, strong yet soothing.

A feeling of disappointment shot through her; old expectations die hard.

She mouthed, "Auntie Rose." The alcohol had started to work its magic, and she felt a disconnect from herself that was more than welcome.

Rory grinned and lifted an eyebrow. He could obviously hear Auntie Rose from where he sat.

Despite herself, Mia felt her heart smile. Auntie Rose's loud voice came straight out of her childhood.

"Hi, Auntie… Yes, thank you. I'm fine."

"I think he'd like a private service. We'll make it dignified, simple. Like the man."

Mia's stomach took a dive. For a minute, Auntie choked with emotion. Mia felt for her, remembered they were once close friends.

"This must be hard for you," Mia consoled. She twisted with

guilt. She had adored the father from *before*. He'd been her idol, her favorite in every way. It was the man from *after* that'd lost her respect.

Auntie laughed her hardy laugh, uncomfortable showing emotion. "He was a dear friend to me. Both your parents were."

Mia remained silent.

"So, when can you get here?"

Mia's stomach sank. She stammered nervously as if she'd reverted back to twelve.

"Y-you should probab-bly plan something without m-me. My schedule is so crazy lately, t-this week alo—"

"I hear that, but your patients will understand… How could they not? Clear it and call me to let me know which day you'll be here." Auntie was done with the discussion, subject closed. Mia watched as Rory tried not to smile and shot him a snide look.

"It'll be so good to see your face out here again. It's been way too long. The girls will be excited to see you, too. It'll be like a reunion… It's hard to stay in touch; everybody's so busy. We still miss having you here, near us."

Mia hadn't done her part to keep up with her aunt or cousins. After her mother died, they treated her like one of their own. She felt a small piece of truth dislodge and bob to the surface; after Robby died, being near them became unbearable. In trying to save herself, she'd stayed away from them. She pushed the truth back down, but her guilt remained.

"You could probably use a vacation by now, anyways. Last time I spoke to Rory, he said you'd been working too many hours."

She eyed him.

"What?"

Auntie Rose and Rory talked a few times a month. It'd started back when she and Rory were roommates. Rory filled

Auntie in about Mia's life so Mia didn't have to. It worked. Mia found their relationship endearing, sort of mutual and sweet. But at that moment, it was on her last nerve.

"Have you spoken to Jimmy yet?" Auntie Rose asked.

"Nope, I tried, though."

"Listen you… I admit he's a pain in the ass, but he's doing better now. Living and working with a friend out in Scituate… for a while now."

"I'm glad." *Gold star for him.*

"Maybe this will bring you two together again. Your parents would want nothing more than that. They loved you kids more than anything."

"I know," Mia recited automatically, but an old confusion settled in her gut.

"Ok, it's late there. Tell Ror hi for me. And let me know the day."

Just like that, she was gone. Auntie Rose took a place by storm. There was no negotiating with her.

Mia hung up and groaned something to Rory about her aunt being impossible. He enjoyed her annoyance a little too much for her taste. He offered to call the airlines, and this time she let him. As he made the call, she escaped to the bathroom. Going back felt surreal.

She yelled to him, "Not until the end of the week." She needed to see her scheduled patients the next day and call the rest to explain.

Chapter 4

"The reservation is complete," Rory said. "I booked you a one-way ticket back to Rhode Island."

She felt panic rise in her chest.

"You can always get a flight home within 24 hours, practically any time of the day or night."

She knew he was right but didn't like being forced to return. Her father had no right to expect anything from her.

They hugged, and Rory headed home.

Knowing she had to work in the morning, she brushed her teeth and got back into bed, but her mind wouldn't stop spinning. She tossed and turned as snippets from her past spun like tired bits of tape. With the news of her dad's death, her old wounds resurfaced like the harsh rip of a band-aid from an open wound.

She lay there thinking about her mother and Robbie. Whenever she was alone, they were never far from her thoughts. She kept them close like her own private set of guardian angels. Her old confusion about her mother's death began to nag away. Was her father's involvement truly an accident? If it was, why hadn't he fought harder? It didn't make sense; it never had.

He was either guilty or too much of a coward to deal with his own grief. What kind of a man abandoned his children after their mother died? *Probably not an innocent one.* When her father was arrested, she was told it was an accident. She believed him; she needed to. She could still hear his words, *"Marianna, it wasn't meant for her… I would never hurt her on purpose, you know that. I loved her more than my own life."*

He'd adored her mother; she knew it was true. Her reality had already been rocked; not believing him was unthinkable. The details didn't matter; her mother was dead. But after so many years, she still found the story confusing. She tried to push her thoughts away, listing the patients she needed to call tomorrow and the other things that needed to be done.

She hated how vulnerable and alone she suddenly felt. When her mother died, Rob had been her saving grace. She missed him something awful. She padded back out to the kitchen and stared at her empty wine glass. She filled a glass with water and then headed back to bed.

Even with sedation, or maybe because of it, her brain returned to thoughts of Rob. She urgently craved being near him. *He would know just what to say…do.* The old loss felt like an ache ripping through her heart. She squeezed her eyes shut, imagining his warm body near hers. She could see his bright eyes shining toward hers, could almost hear the nuance of his gravelly voice in her ears. Thoughts of them together brought a warm comfort, enough for her to drift off…

The familiar scene flashed. The angle of his leg was all wrong. The swoosh symbol on his lone sneaker lay illuminated under the streetlight. *Who's screaming like that?* She covered her ears. She bolted upright in bed, wiping her tears with the back of her hand. These reels of film were old haunts. She hadn't missed them. With her heart still beating out of her chest, she glanced at the clock, 6 a.m. Her fear got her moving.

The sun rose through her oversized bedroom window. She showered and dressed in her typical casual way—loose-fitting khakis and a black sleeveless turtleneck. It was early October, and the mornings and evenings had already turned cool. As an after-thought, she grabbed a thick, cable knit sweater in light pink and pulled it over her head. *I have a million things to do before I leave...* Her brain fought to finish the sentence. *For home.*

Her father was dead. She imagined the devastation this news would bring to someone else. How their day, their life, would be altered forever. She inhaled but kept moving.

Today will be scheduled, productive, and busy, just the way I like it. She exhaled in small b-b gun sounds, then called to Mr. French, "Let's go, you gorgeous hunk of fur. Hurry, we've got work to do."

She decided they'd take her old, comfortable Baby MG. Despite her mood, it was nice convertible weather. Rory gave her a lot of shit for keeping the old thing, but she loved its navy exterior and worn-out baseball mitt-colored seats.

The sun was up when she pulled into the long office complex drive. The practice sat on six acres of prime real-estate with the Sierra Nevada on one side and Lake Tahoe in the back. The view was spectacular, other-worldly. She pulled the car up to the gate, and Frenchie jumped to attention with both paws on the dash as he saw Joe, the security guard, approach. He was a handsome, older man with dark curly hair and golden-brown eyes. They had a harmless flirtation that Mia wouldn't allow to go further, another invisible scar from her past.

"Morning, Joe. How's everything?"

"Doc C., never better. You're here nice and early today...

Something different?" He smirked and threw a small bone onto Frenchie's seat.

The gate swung open.

"You look pretty in pink."

She rolled her eyes and pulled the car forward. They had played out this same scene nearly every day for the past several years. In the rearview, she watched his familiar face grin beneath the mirrored sunglasses.

Chapter 5

Mia and Rory had built one of the most prestigious wellness day spas in South Tahoe. They combined traditional psychotherapies with activities like hiking, skiing and biking. Rory specialized in the positive effects of exercise on mental health and mood as a physical therapist/trainer with an MD in sports medicine. Mia was responsible for talk therapy, though she sometimes exercised alongside long-term patients if needed.

Their program was tailored to each person. Patients had the option to participate in group workouts, group therapy, and even share meals together. Loneliness and trauma were by far the most common symptoms they shared.

For some, work was a dreaded place they had to go, but not for Mia. Her office was her refuge, her retreat. Simply being in the space filled her with familiar comfort. From the time she could remember, the work ritual had always helped her feel a much-needed sense of internal control and purpose.

She walked toward the oversized bay windows and let her eyes sweep the space. Her small but elegant mahogany desk sat against the wall, accompanied by her neatly tucked-in upholstered chair in a delicate floral print. The desk was nearly empty except for a day planner, a pen holder and a beautiful bouquet of mixed flowers, always seasonal.

The other side of the room functioned as the sitting area with a love seat, two overstuffed chairs and a rocker. The overstuffed cushions were a muted sea-green color she found calming. A few pillows had been scattered about in bolder, deep plums and violets with fringe—Rory's idea. Several chenille blankets were folded and draped over the edge of the sofa.

Mr. French jumped up to claim his favorite spot on a corner of the love seat. *We all have one.*

Mia's office always smelled nice. She admitted this was more for her own comfort than her patients. Being fall, the space smelled of spiced apples and pumpkins. Along with the view, she loved the built-in bookshelves that expanded the entire back wall from floor to ceiling. Many of her books were old friends she had taken refuge in throughout her career. Everything from the classics like Salinger's *Catcher in the Rye* to the newest self-help books to novels to every reference book her profession had to offer. She'd been so busy she hadn't been able to read much for pleasure.

Only one section remained bookless. She used a small middle shelf as a coffee, tea and hot chocolate bar. She offered snacks in a basket and fresh fruit and a built-in fridge directly beneath. She knew sharing a warm drink, maybe a treat, could be a soothing ritual.

Looking out over the tree line where the sky and lake seemed to kiss brought Rob to mind. *He loved nature…* For a minute, she could smell his musky scent. She inhaled deeply, trying to capture it, but the scent was fleeting. She felt her stomach dip with an old disappointment.

She checked her day planner, recounting the intimacies of the stories her patients had entrusted to her. She frowned with concern over leaving them. She'd start her day catching up on paperwork and then call patients to let them know she'd be away for a week or so. The uncertainty gnawed at her.

Glancing at the flowers in front of her, her mother's face materialized. Her eyes were crystal blue with a shine as though they were smiling, and her skin had a bluish tint. Mia hadn't seen this image in a long time. Every time she did, it left her troubled, nauseous. It was how she imagined her mother looked right before she took her last breath. Then it was gone, poof.

She ruminated for a minute and wondered about her mother's last thoughts. *Did she think of me and Jimmy? Was she scared?* The night she died, the light left Jimmy's eyes; he was never the same. *I guess none of us were.* As time passed, his self-destruction and fury built up like a cigarette tossed into the wind during a long drought.

She wondered if he even knew about their father. *Is he having the same reaction?* Her heart felt mixed. *"An accident… Not meant for her."* Accident or not, she wondered if her father's thoughts had been haunted by what he'd done, if he saw her face, too? A small piece of her hoped he was tormented over what he'd done.

She thought about how trauma never left a person's psyche, and her questions began to tumble and spin. She dug back into work, deliberately pushing her thoughts aside.

An hour later, a soft snore escaped from Mr. French, still asleep on the sofa. He looked so peaceful and content, a state she could only imagine. She sat, pen in hand, knowing she had more work but couldn't focus. Annoyance washed through her. She looked up with a start when she heard Liz's voice from the other side of the door.

"Dr. C., you in there?"

Mia forced a smile and tried not to sound as cranky as she felt. "Yes, I have some news, Liz."

"Be right in, sugar."

Mia watched Liz enter her office, smiling wide with more than affection. She epitomized the stereotypical southern grandmother, equal parts strong and kind. Liz had worked for Mia and Rory for almost seven years. They'd met her at their favorite place, Sunsets Tavern. Liz had waitressed there for a bit after escaping her abusive husband. She was nearly six feet tall with beautiful, chocolate-brown skin.

"Dr. C., you feelin' alright? You look pale," she drawled in her buttery southern way and touched Mia's forehead.

"My father, who I've been estranged from, died."

"I'm sorry to hear that." She engulfed Mia in a hug. Her fleshy skin smelled sweet and clean.

Mia fought off a wave of emotion.

"I leave tomorrow. I shouldn't be gone more than a few days, a week tops."

"You shouldn't be here today; I'll start calling patients for you."

"No, I can call them myself in between appoint—"

"Don't be ridiculous, I'll call them. You don't need to bother with anything else." She eyed her sternly and then headed out the door.

Mia and Rory agreed that the place wouldn't run as smoothly without Liz. Her southern charm calmed even the most anxious patients. Mia took a deep breath and stared back down at her charts. She felt a dull thumping behind her temples. She checked her watch and decided she needed a cup of coffee.

Rory usually stopped at Pickles Café on Tuesdays, so she headed down the hallway to his office. His door was open, and she could hear he was on the phone. She nodded as she entered his office. He pointed to a large cup sitting on his desk.

Rory's office was part gym, and he wore his usual workout gear: a black Under Armor shirt and baggy sweats. His body was sleek, tight and lean. Rory was a bit of a health nut concerning food, especially compared to her.

He smiled and slid a cream container toward her, mouthing, "Muffin?"

Thank God for Ror. She poured in the cream and added three packets of sugar, stirring it with the end of his pen.

He mouthed, "Gross! What the fuck?"

She half smiled and pretended to ignore him. Her head fully throbbed.

She broke off a piece of muffin and put it back down. *Chocolate swirl, my favorite.*

She whispered, "Thanks," and started to leave.

He held up a finger, "Wait."

Reluctantly, she sat across from him. She tucked a strand of curls behind her ear. Her stomach growled, but she had no appetite. She eyed his desk calendar. *October.* She tried to remember the last time she'd been in Rhode Island in the fall. She feels Rob's warm hand on hers. Leaves crunch under her feet, and she can smell candy apples and doughboys. Rob winks down at her, "Have some."

Rory's voice brought her back; the caller was distressed. Mia sipped her coffee as the word *pain* tumbled around in her mind. Pain was their business. The young athlete on the phone was new to recovery. He was craving narcotics; it had only been a month. Mia listened as Rory offered various strategies to help his patient fight his cravings.

Her mind returned to walking through the Scituate Art Festival with Rob. The day was cool but bright. The air smelled like a fireplace. She took a giant bite out of his dough-boy. He smiled wide and leaned down to kiss away the extra sauce on her lips. She's in love with him. Her brain jumps ahead to July. A quick, familiar dread sweeps through her. She sees herself curled up on Auntie's back porch, stoned and still in bed.

We do anything to stop pain, even if it's temporary. She preferred physical pain any day. She sat on the edge of the chair and rubbed her temples.

Rory finished his call. "You sleep at all?"

"Like a baby," she lied. "Got any drugs? I have a vicious headache."

"Liar, you have luggage under your eyes," he said, handing her an Aleve from his desk drawer.

"Whatever." She took the pill and got up to leave. "I gotta go; Jackson will be here any minute."

His phone rang again, and he answered with a quick, "Dr. Defusco here." He mouthed to her, "You still up for tonight?"

"I'll be there."

It had been a long-standing tradition to meet for dinner and farewell cocktails before travel at Sunsets Tavern, right up the road, overlooking the lake.

Rory winked and rolled his eyes at the caller. He motioned "drinking" with his water bottle.

"You have problems," she whispered, shaking her head.

Mia walked back to her office, her thoughts completely on her patients. Many were wealthy men and women—some coupled, many divorced—a few were even famous, but they weren't all local. Some only came to ski in the winter or vacation in the summer, returning for an emotional tune-up.

It didn't matter how much money they had; she knew they'd trade it all for happiness, peace of mind. Most of their patients had issues with mood, substances or relationships; some had all three and more. She forced her focus toward her charts.

"Doc C., Jackson's here."

"Good, send him in, Liz."

Jackson positioned himself in the rocker directly across from her. He was a highly regarded surgeon whose five-year-old daughter had recently died of a heart attack during an emergency appendectomy. He was on leave due to his grief and recent panic attacks and was racked with guilt that he wasn't there during the surgery.

"She'll be fine," he told his wife. "It's routine, done all the time."

He'd been emotionally paralyzed by the incident. Being unable to work had only compounded his upset. Mia met with him twice a week to work toward lessening his guilt and help him manage the intrusive images spinning in his mind. The insidious black veil of grief hadn't loosened its choke hold.

Sitting in the rocking chair, his face wore the mask of someone who'd spent their night battling demons. The pallor of his skin and the luggage under his eyes told her he'd lost. *At least last night.* She inhaled deep, knowing he was in for a long road.

"You want to tell me about your night?"

He sat forward and began describing the images that'd haunted him.

Mia bore witness to his story and sat with him in his sadness. Education aside, she understood. She knew what it felt like to suffer loss, to be haunted by grief. She knew despair could suck you deep into its blackness, where you never thought you'd see the color of the sun again.

She could still see the men in their official black suits nod respectfully. First, her mother—ashes to ashes—then Rob—dust to dust. Buried alongside the dirt and worms was a piece of herself. Her fragments of sadness sit just below the surface, giving her empathy the finest education can't teach.

Instinctually, she knew what Jackson needed from her. She held up her eternal mirror of hope and shone it toward him.

"I can't get her face or the empty look in my wife's eyes out of my head. I don't think they'll ever go away." He lowers his eyes, something she's learned he does when trying not to cry.

"It's normal to feel responsible for them, but none of what happened was your fault."

"Tell that to my wife. She can barely look at me." A tear trickled down his check and dripped onto the floor.

This is progress. It was the first time he'd cried in front of her.

"Everyone grieves differently; that's what makes it so hard for you as a couple, as parents."

"It never should've happened." He shook his head and wiped his eyes with the back of his hand. "And now I can't stop seeing her lifeless body on that table."

She waits for him to finish—silence her greatest tool.

"I'm being punished by God for not being there for them… and I deserve it."

"Jackson, you're not being punished. Your brain keeps replaying these moments because what happened was tragic, awful. No one expects a five-year-old to die, but we both know that life is unpredictable. It was an allergic reaction to anesthesia you couldn't have prepared for. It's traumatic and devastating for everyone involved, especially you, her father."

"I've had patients die before. I didn't feel like this; I could still work."

"This wasn't some patient; this was your daughter."

He shakes his head as more tears slide down his face. "I'm sorry. It's not right, it's just not."

"You're right, it isn't."

"I don't understand either… Any of it."

"You don't understand because it's illogical. You're struggling to make sense of something that doesn't make any. It's normal to be heartbroken." She hands him the box of tissues.

"Will it ever go away? Seeing her like that?"

"Probably not. But it won't feel like this forever. You're doing all the right things. Eventually, the images will lessen."

She spent the remainder of the session pointing out every

sign of progress, as small as it may have seemed. He gladly accepted each kernel of hope.

The session was long and excruciating for them both. She explained her upcoming unexpected absence, and he said he understood, but she saw fear flash through his eyes. Racked with guilt, she reminded him that Scott would be available.

The rest of the day was filled with back-to-back patients, the way she preferred. But that day, their sadness and unspoken fear spoke directly to her, uncomfortably mirroring her own.

Sara, one of her afternoon patients, was barely eighteen. She was tall, blonde, pencil-thin, supermodel-pretty. She was dating a handsome college freshman who seemed to adore her, her grades were near perfect, and she'd had a shiny new sports car sitting in her driveway on her sixteenth birthday.

At a glance, she seemed to have it all. But things aren't always what they seem. She had been coming to Mia for five years. On the inside, Sara was intensely lonely, having internalized the unloving adults in her life. Her parents were divorced, and she virtually never saw her father. She lived with her career-driven mother, who viewed her only daughter as an obstacle that often interfered with her work schedule. She showered her daughter with things but was emotionally unavailable.

Sara suffered from bouts of depression and had attempted to gain control and esteem through food. Her mother had brought her to treatment because she was "Skipping meals." Sara knew the unspoken truth. She was unwanted, in the way. Mia nurtured her, a role her mother had resisted from the beginning of her daughter's treatment, despite Mia's efforts to draw her in.

Some people shouldn't have children. Sara cried silently when Mia told her she'd be away for their next appointment and they'd need to skip a week. Mia knew she was the only parent Sara had. She told her she could call if needed, but her words sounded tinny, even to her own ears.

Mia shut Sara's file and heard a soft tap on her door.

"Here's your flight information." Liz handed her a piece of paper. "I printed it out for you. Tuck it in with your luggage so you don't lose it now."

"Thank you. What about a list of numbers for Rory and Scott?"

"I already gave Rory the list of your more sensitive patients."

"Thanks, Liz. I'll see you and Ror in a little bit, then?"

Liz eyed her watch. "Umm."

"I won't be much longer."

She twirled her pen between her thumb and pointer finger as she replayed her last session.

Cara was a twenty-two-year-old college student with a tragic story. She was a local girl who'd grown up in Squaw Valley. Unlike Sara, she had no money but was rich in family love. She had worked at the Shop and Save to support herself but quit. She was smart enough to land a full scholarship to American University, pre-med, but to the dismay of her family and long-term boyfriend, she dropped out after her first semester and broke up with her boyfriend. They were deeply disappointed and more than confused. She was too ashamed to tell them the truth. She let them believe the course load had been too demanding.

When Cara's finals were over last term, she'd met up with friends to celebrate. She ran into a handsome pre-med student she'd seen around campus. After a few drinks, she left with him "to party." The following day, she woke up in a rest area with fragmented memories and torn clothes. She blamed herself, believing she should've known better than to leave a nightclub with a virtual stranger.

A year later, her PTSD (post-traumatic stress disorder) symptoms were so severe she couldn't even stand to be in the same room as a man, let alone be in a classroom led by a male professor. She couldn't forgive herself and refused to involve her family in any part of her treatment. At the end of the week, she was being transferred to an all-female inpatient treatment facility until she could stabilize her suicide ideations.

Mia's abrupt absence couldn't have come at a worse time. *I'm abandoning her.* She promised to call and check on her, but her promises felt hollow. Her sad truth hung in the air; her allegiance lay more with her patients than the father she was returning home to bury. Her mind pushed against the old memories from *before*.

Finally, finished with her last note, she slid the file cabinet shut with a thud. Waiting for the elevator because she was too drained to take the stairs, her head filled with her patients' stories. For a moment, she absorbed every bit of their sadness. She exhaled, slowly counting her breaths.

The shadows of her past loom. She knows she can't avoid going home any longer. As the elevator door shuts behind her, she thinks about the *other* box still beneath her bed. The messy *after* memories. Her fears swirl.

Chapter 6

The fresh air hit her like a much-needed slap across the face. She scanned the nearly empty parking lot and let Mr. French do his business before ushering him into the car. *I don't care what Ror says about my old jalopy.* The car had been part of her new life, the *good-after*. Rory fell into the *good-after* category, too.

She turned up the radio loud to drown out any lingering thoughts. Frenchie was already half asleep on his seat.

"We're really going back, boy." A wave of panic hit her in the gut.

He shot up one ear, feigning interest.

"I hate the east coast. Stupid old architecture, ivy league schools; it's uptight, Mr. Frenchie, not dog-friendly at all. You'll see. Oh, and wait until you get a load of the weather. Already bitterly cold and dark, for months on end."

Her ancestors must've been self-abusive and suicidal with those depressing winters. The long, dark months reminded her of her mother's death and the beginning of her unimaginable traumas. Even living in Tahoe, she moved to a satellite office in Sacramento during the winter months. Trauma never really goes away when the anniversary dates keep coming. She made a list of all the other inconsequential things she hated about Rhode Island, knowing they weren't about anything other than her pain.

Once on the highway, her stomach twisted with every truck that passed, remembering the sound of her father's rig pulling up to her childhood home. She and Jimmy played catch in the circle with their cousins when she would scream, "Daddy! Daddy's home!" She flung her baseball glove and raced toward him, pigtails swinging behind her.

"Marianna, there's my girl." He gave her a scratchy kiss and swung her up over his head.

Coming back down to him, she hugged him tight and breathed in his familiar scent; outdoors, Listerine and cigarettes.. A mixture of awe and love washed through her. *Everything's right again; daddy's home.*

The familiar sign for Sunsets Tavern brought her back to the present, her eyes scanned the autumn display adorned with colorful, giant pumpkins and dozens of mums in rich purples, yellows and orange in front of violet and brownish plumes of ornamental grasses all atop a giant haystack, her angst continued to grow, it reminded her of home. Despite herself, Rhode Island's landscape was spectacular this time of year. She found Rory and Liz sitting at their usual outdoor table far from the bar. They handled enough loneliness and alcoholism at work anyway.

The place was jam-packed with people, and Mia wasn't feeling up for a crowd. Honestly, she never was. Mia leaned back in her high-top cushioned chair and let her eyes sweep the outdoor deck. Behind Ror sat rows of docks, she could hear the water lapping back and forth, the sound rhythmic and soothing, it made her want to close her eyes. She inhaled and exhaled slowly, taking in the varying sized boats tied beyond. She let her eyes linger a moment on the snowcapped mountains, their outline even at night seemed to tuck in the space giving it an intimate feel. The tables sat upon tan decking rimmed with small white twinkle lights wrapped around the railings. The umbrellas were folded down for the evening, but propane tanks were scattered about every third table for warmth and ambiance. The small tea lights flickered softly in the crystal jars that sat on each table aside mini purple mums. A jazz trio in the corner played softly and rhythmically, and her shoulders started to drop. She hadn't realized they'd been so tight. The giant outside fireplace flickered softly against the back wall and the breeze smelled sweet like sunflowers and honey reminding her why they loved the place so much.

Rory and Liz shared a pitcher of Sangria, already a-glow. Liz's accent had thickened, and Rory eyed the band's lead singer. She didn't judge them; she'd worked later than intended. She sat down and reached for a platter of fries, suddenly starving.

Linda appeared to take her drink order. "Dr. C., the regular?"

White wine's not gonna cut it.

"No."

Rory and Liz exchanged brow-raised glances.

"Tonight, I'll have a Ketel One martini. Extra dirt, please." She usually avoided hard liquor but craved every ounce of sedation.

Rory threw a worried glance her way. "Glad you could join us, my friend."

"It's not that late," she defended as she rolled her eyes. She let her hand rub the rich fabric beneath her.

"It's almost nine, Mee."

"I needed my charts in order."

"I was just telling Liz how hot east coast men can be." He winked at her.

"Oh, God."

"Wait," Liz interrupted. "Let's make a toast. To the men on the east coast, may you get good and laiiiiid."

"Oh, my God. How many pitchers have you had?"

They cracked up laughing.

"Guess I'm on the wrong coast." Liz smiled.

"Doubtful," Mia mumbled.

They often teased her about her lack of interest in men. *I try.* She had the occasional one-night stand; she was human. She even tried to date a few but was busy with work and wasn't interested in the guys she met. *They're not Rob.* She brought her gaze to the giant pine next to Liz.

She knew they were intentionally teasing her, trying to distract her from her impending return home. When Rory drank, he did one of two things: he turned sappy or extra outrageous. *Tonight, he might be both.*

She took a long sip from her drink and played with an oversized olive before popping it into her mouth.

"How's your head?" Rory asked.

"Much better now." She readjusted her curls behind her ear.

"Good. What are we going to do without Mr. French?" He scooped him up and kissed his furry head.

"Oh, stop it. You'll miss us both."

"Nope, just him." He smiled and squeezed her shoulder as he stood.

Her jaw dropped as he strode over to the band.

Oh no, I'm not quite relaxed enough yet. She placed her drink down and smiled despite herself.

Together, Liz and Mia watched as he pulled off a jazzy rendition of Ain't No Mountain High Enough. Mr. French wagged as Rory sang to him. The words seemed meant for Mia; by the song's end, she had a lump in her throat. The audience went crazy. He could carry a tune, but it didn't hurt that he was also very charming and good-looking. Rory took a quick bow. He stopped the waitress on the way back, no doubt sending the trio some drinks.

Rory flashed his beautiful pearly whites and sipped his drink. “And that’s how it’s done y’all.” He leaned down and whispered in Mia’s ear, “And you know I mean it, too.”

“I know.”

The waitress placed a club soda beside Mia and turned to Liz.

“The nice gentleman at the bar wants to buy you a drink.”

Liz blushed and smiled over her shoulder. “Thanks anyway, sugar.” She turned back and laughed in her big, heart-felt way. “No more for me. I won’t be able to walk, let alone drive. Glad to know I still got it, though.”

Liz was the first to leave—usually Mia’s M.O.

She hugged Mia. “Send my love to your family. And you behave yourself out there now. Don’t you listen to us.”

Mia’s heart tightened at the compassion. “I never do.”

Watching the interesting mix of strangers dancing and socializing was refreshing. She wasn’t responsible for any of their pain.

The night air had cooled, making it feel more like late October—a prelude to what came next. Small flutters of dread prickled through her system at the thought of winter. It represented so much loss. She munched on the appetizers she knew Rory had ordered with her in mind—spicy fries and buffalo wings. She ordered a decaf coffee for her nightcap and thought about how many nights they’d spent there.

“Here’s to the one we definitely don’t need.” He clinked her mug.

She played with the edge of her napkin.

“Hey, you weirded out to go back?”

“Yes. It’s been a long time.” Her mind spun with thoughts

of her mother, of Rob. She couldn't believe they'd been gone for so long.

"I wish I could come with you."

"I know me too. Just take care of my people for me. And could you pop in to see Cara Saturday? This weekend will be hard for her. She feels comfortable with you."

The bartender announced last call.

"And make sure Scott lets Jackson sit in the rocker. It soothes him."

"We'll just medicate them all until you come home." He pretended to drool on himself.

"Stop it." She half smiled, trying to contain her worry.

"Mee, we got it. They'll all be fine; I promise."

"You're right; I know they'll be ok." The drink had slowed her brain to a more normal pace but only slightly dimmed her panic.

Rory walked Mia and Mr. French to their car.

"I can't believe you still drive this old thing."

"I know, I know."

"And just for the record, I know it's hard, but I think you're doing the right thing going back."

"I know, I know. Who was that on the phone before?"

"The future ex-Mr. Defusco."

"No, really?"

"Naw, just lining up a late-night booty call; you should try it sometime, Mee."

She shot him a look but stayed silent.

"I'm kidding; I met someone."

"Alright." She laughed but noticed he had a strange look.

"Hey, don't knock the booty call." Rory hugged her tight. "Good luck."

A piece of her didn't want to let go. "I'll call you when I land. Please take care of them for me."

"Naw, they're all getting a script, even me, just for fun. Come on, I'll follow you home before my next stop." He grinned wide. "I know you're feeling no pain."

"Me?! Says the one who sang with the band."

She pulled out of the parking lot and saw Rory talking on his cell in her rearview. A feeling of safety washed through her, and she wished like hell she could bottle it.

Chapter 7

Mia sat on the plane feeling irritated and tired. Dread filled her brain, and her headache had returned. *I can't believe I'm going home.* Mr. French snored under the seat; like everything else that morning, it annoyed her. She glanced at her watch, wishing she were at work. She let out a long breath. *Fuck.*

A passenger with a familiar accent settled in beside her. She silently cringed and squeezed her eyes shut. *"Yuse guys." Ulch, not a Guido.* Where she'd grown up, Guido's were little Italian men who wore gold chains of saints, pinky rings, dress shoes with sweatpants, and way too much cologne.

Mia cracked one eye open. *Dark hair probably gelled. Tan, probably fake.* His body ate up the entire space. *I'm sure his name ends in a vowel.* He adjusted his pennie every other minute. *I'm not in the mood for this. Not even a little bit.*

She felt herself stiffen as he tried to fit in the seat beside hers, surrounded by his cologne. *Wow, he smells nice, clean.* She tried to pretend she was resting.

"Hi, my name is Tony. Most people call me T, though."

Course they do. Clean scent or not, if he calls me sweetheart, I might scream. Please, somebody, shoot me right now. "I'd rather not call you ever. Now, go away. Go. Scoot." With her head back and her eyes still closed, she simply nodded.

When Tony stepped onto the plane, he hoped like hell nobody was in his row. Being a guy his size, he'd learned to request the bulkhead or aisle. Otherwise, he spent the entire time leaning sideways. He'd spent the weekend in Reno bonding with his mafia cronies, pretending to be one of them. He hated the Nevada heat and thought gambling was for losers. *Fucking dirt bags.* The undercover charade was more than old.

Tired, he reclined his seat to shut his eyes and turn off his brain. As he inhaled, he was assaulted by the smell of stale smoke and booze. He glanced at a red-faced, sweaty, middle-age dude. The stench oozed out of his pores.

Tony's mind replayed the previous night. Costa had gotten the guys VIP passes to an elite gentleman's show after dinner. In actuality, it was a high-end strip club with girls who were barely legal. Though dark, it had an old country club feel, almost classy. The smell of booze and cigars hung thick in the air.

Watching the predatory looks on the faces of the guys he'd been hanging with for over two years made him feel sick. It was the same look he'd seen on rapist psychopaths way too many times. The countless prostitute and stripper stories he'd heard over the years began to surface. For most, it had been a bad luck of the draw, running from fucked up families into the arms of guys who used them. *That life will make anyone need an altered state.*

Costa's men stared at a blonde. *Must be new.* The scumbags could all smell it, and Tony watched. The girl was tall and slender, with giant guns too big for her frame. His adrenaline pulsed as the guys at the next table pawed at them. She winced as some nameless middle-ager pulled on her nipple and winked at his buddies. *What the fuck? Where's the bouncer? Touching's a no.*

A big dude Tony could've dropped appeared and whispered, "Eyy, easy with the goods. We don't usually allow touching." He sleazily took in her body.

The big guy watched as the middle-ager slapped her ass, keeping his hand in place too long as he put a Benjaman in her purse. She moaned and pretended pleasure. When she turned away from them, Tony noticed she had the prettiest curly hair hanging down her back. *What's she doing here?* He silently exhaled his disgust.

When Shades, one of Costa's nastiest boys tugged on her hair, Tony stood and feigned interest in an older brunette, afraid he'd kill one of them on the fucking spot as they drooled and touched this poor lost girl. She was young enough to be any of their daughters.

He knocked into the asshole bouncer *accidentally* with the edge of his shoulder. He had the urge to hurt somebody bad. The bouncer nodded and backed up. *Pussy… All I need's an excuse.* He went to the bathroom to calm down and then waited at the bar. The guys came out looking like pigs. *Gross, no fucking shower will ever take it away.*

A passenger bumped Tony's arm bringing him back to the moment.

The woman in the window seat was small and dark-haired. He introduced himself, and when she didn't answer, he assumed she was sleeping. *She smells good, sweet like a green apple.* He scanned his surroundings and then stretched his legs out as far as they would go to try and relax.

He heard snoring coming from under her seat. He saw a cage but couldn't tell if it was a cat or a dog. He noticed her purse lying unzipped on the cage. He glanced toward her and noticed she had the nicest hair. It fell onto her shoulders, all wild and whirly. He pulled his eyes away, thinking of the young blonde. The purse bothered him. He Purell-ed his hands and leaned back in the seat.

Pretending to sleep soon became real for Mia. When she finally opened her eyes, she needed a few seconds to orient herself. She rolled her neck back and forth and winced. A feeling of dread swept through her body, reminding her she was headed home.

She glanced to her right and found herself staring into the greenest eyes she'd ever seen. She watched his serious face lift into an easy grin, his eyes crinkling at the edges. He wore his hair short and neat, no gel. He didn't look anything like her tired brain had conjured earlier. She hardly ever found dark-haired men attractive—Rory didn't count. She automatically compared him to Rob's shaggy blonde hair, blue eyes, and lanky shape.

About an hour and a half into the flight, Tony heard movement beside him and looked over.

"Morning." His eyes darted to his watch. "Actually, afternoon."

She only nodded.

"I'm Tony, T for short."

Her eyes were light blue, almost clear. They reminded him of the water in the tropics. She barely wore any makeup, and her lips were pouty and full. She half smiled, and he noticed a dimple in her chin. He felt his stomach twitch. She reminded him of Spring-time. *How corny.*

He glanced down at her open bag. "You should really zip that, tuck it away."

"Right. I fell asleep, wasn't feeling so great." Mia zipped the bag and folded an article face down on her lap.

"Dangerous, never know who's flying these days." He watched as she pushed her hair away from her face and imagined his hands tangled in it. He forced his eyes above her head, out the window. The snoring returned.

Her lip pulled upward. "Meet Mr. French."

"And what do you go by?"

"I'm Mia."

He nodded and chuckled once. "Mr. French from *Family Affair*? That's great. I like your name, furry guy." Tony turned his gaze back to her, thinking she was too young to remember the show. "Mia. That's a different name. It's pretty." *Like you.* "Where you heading, Mia?"

"Boston."

Her leg bounced, and by the look she was wearing, Tony thought she was either sick or afraid to fly.

As the flight attendant approached, he whispered, "My new friend here's under the weather. She's gonna need a cup of hot tea, maybe with some Buca, please." He turned toward Mia and nodded. "It does the trick every time. Is that okay?"

She seemed relieved.

"Boston's a nice city. I'm going home to Rhode Island."

She reached for her purse when the flight attendant returned.

"Please, I got it. It might help you feel better."

"Thank you." She twisted off the cap and took a long sip before adding the rest to her tea.

Returning from the bathroom, Tony noticed her leg movements had almost completely seized.

"Mia, are you heading to Boston for work or pleasure?"

"Some boring conference."

"That's too bad. Boston's a nice place to play and hangout, especially this time of year. Is Mia an Italian name?"

"Yes."

The way he pronounced Mia sounded funny to her ears, almost familiar. *It must be his accent.* She remembers Robbie's voice calling her, "Marianna! Hey, Marianna!" as they played rundown in the front yard on Tweed Street as kids. His face was sweaty and red. Her wild hair was braided, but whirly ringlets stuck out around her forehead.

The memory jumped to the falls in Scituate. He was a serious young man, and she was madly in love with him. He was down on one knee, doing the worst Romeo impersonation ever.

"Marianna, Marianna, where are forth you?"

"What?" She giggled uncontrollably. "What the hell was that?"

"Ey, I'm trying to tell you I love you, like Romeo." His voice was deep; his blue eyes shown up at her.

"I love you, too."

He stands up and kisses her. His lips are soft but urgent. The kiss is long and sweet. She can still remember what his mouth tasted like—Big Red, his favorite gum. They were in love the way only teenagers could be: honest, desperate, and raw.

Tony's voice brought her back to the moment. "I got it."

He passed her the article that had fallen somewhere in between them. His hand brushed against hers, and she felt her heart quicken.

"Thanks."

He nodded and ran his hand through his short hair.

She reached for her tea, comforted by its warmth.

"Can I ask what you do you do for work?" He nodded toward the article. "Trauma, The Body Keeps Score."

"I'm a psychologist. My practice is in Lake Tahoe, south side."

"We all could use one of those from time to time… You like your job, Mia?"

"I do, very much." *It's who I am.* She couldn't imagine doing anything else.

"Lake Tahoe. I'll bet it's pretty there. Scenic, huh?"

"It's beautiful."

He seemed to study her for a minute before dropping his gaze.

"What about you, Tony? What do you do in Rhode Island?"

"I'm partially retired, you could say. I'm an investor, but still sort of involved in a few businesses."

Partially retired? He's got to be in his late thirties, maybe forty, tops. He's in better shape than most men decades younger. The flight attendant interrupted her thoughts, offering snacks and a drink. She ordered a glass of wine and selected a packet of cookies and pretzels to snack on.

"So, what kind of conference thing you got going in Boston?"

"Actually, I'm not going there for work. I'm visiting a friend." She started leafing through her pocketbook, looking for nothing in particular, wondering why she had lied about her trip. She offers him a piece of gum.

"Is that a hint?"

"No, of course not." She laughed.

He looked down at the magazine on his lap, and she scanned her article for a few minutes. Something about Tony reminded her of her father *before*. He seemed familiar.

Still looking at her article, she blurted, "My dad used to bring me to Rhode Island all the time when I was a kid."

"Get out… He's from there?"

"Yes, born and raised."

"Where'd he grow up?"

"In Johnston."

"I'm from a town right near there. I'm from the Hill, Federal Hill. But now I live in North Providence."

She felt old layers of loss resurface. The feelings were sharply visceral, the kind that made you want to hold your stomach and breathe until they passed. She exhaled slowly, silently counting each exhausted breath.

"Ey, sometime when you visit your dad, you guys'll have to eat at one of my restaurants for lunch or something."

She continued to count her breaths.

"He doesn't still live there."

She nodded. *Dad would have liked him.* Sadness crept up her body. Her shock was wearing off, and she was surprised by the weight of her feelings. She needed to move, so she reached for her briefcase to organize her papers.

"No, he died." She remembered the strange man's voice telling her the news; his words sounded funny to her ears.

"Oh, I'm sorry."

His eyes softened as compassion flashed across his face. Her throat constricted with emotion.

"Don't be silly. How could you've known? It's fine." A familiar sadness settled in her chest. She fought to reign in her emotions. She just wanted the plane ride to be over. She reached for her wine and drained the remaining drops.

He nodded, back to his magazine.

The overhead speaker announced that they will be landing at Logan Airport soon.

Thank God. Eager to get off the plane and the hell away from the big guy, she neatly tucked her emotions away. Giving him a curt nod, she excused herself to the ladies' room.

There was severe turbulence for the remainder of the flight, but Mia remained unaffected; it was nothing compared to her internal struggles. She stayed busy collecting her things, reviewing her papers, and scanning another article.

Finally, the plane began a slow, bumpy descent. The city lights sparkled through the blur of the weather below. Once on the ground, she waited impatiently for the plane to stop. Getting off suddenly felt urgent. She had the anywhere-but-here feeling, a nasty mix of panic and claustrophobia. *Breathe in and out.* She turned to Tony and couldn't help but notice the way his shirt tugged across his biceps.

"It was very nice talking with you," she surprised herself by saying. "Thanks again for the drink."

"It was my pleasure. I hope you have a nice time visiting your friend."

The plane stopped, and Tony let her out into the aisle.

"Ladies first." He looked over at Frenchie's crate. "Good meeting you, too, Mr. French. You need any help?" he asked, gesturing to her carry-on and crate.

"I have it, thank you," she kept her eyes on the ground.

Chapter 8

Stepping off the plane in Boston, Mia's emotions burned the back of her throat. She was that much closer to Rhode Island. Her past circled her brain and landed on the reality that she'd come home to bury her father. She reached the ladies' restroom and quickly stepped into a stall, welcoming the solitude.

For a moment, she felt his death as a loss. The contradictions spun, stopping at her heart's center. When he was alive, she'd resented him, couldn't keep up any pretense of a relationship. Now, there would be no chance for a relationship ever again. Death, the permanence, the finality of it always stung with the same intensity. She never knew the man in jail, but she remembered the man he used to be. She'd miss that man.

She looked in on Frenchie, still asleep and medicated. She wished she were.

The airport was crowded with travelers. Mia headed over to Gate C25 for her connecting flight. The crate felt awkward and heavy, and she was glad to set it down for a few minutes while she dialed Rory.

"Hey there, Doc C.," Liz answered. "Rory is in with a patient."

"I just landed in Boston."

"Have you seen the forecast yet?"

"The weather forecast? No. Why?"

"They must've mentioned the weather on the plane."

"Maybe." She thought back to the awful turbulence. "I don't think they announced anything… Wait. Maybe there was some talk about rain, but frankly, I wasn't listening that closely."

"I hope you make it out today, but staying overnight wouldn't be that bad, either… Besides, the service isn't until the end of the week."

"What? Overnight; why?"

"The entire east coast is having hurricane winds and torrential rains. Sugar, they've been closing airports up and down the coast for hours now."

How oblivious am I? "Are you kidding me?"

"No, darling, I'm sure not."

"It's October!"

"It sure is an inconvenience. Maybe you can do some indoor sightseeing; check out some of those fiiine boys."

Mia's mind flashed to Tony. "It's a major inconvenience." She rolled her eyes and exhaled deep. "Just tell Ror I called."

"I sure will."

Mia made her way over to the long line of disgruntled passengers.

"I realize it's an inconvenience," the flight attendant started. "We're going to put you on the next flight out just as soon as we get word. We don't have those times yet. You'll be compensated for your room. Meals are not included."

"Fuuuuck," Mia mumbled under her breath. "No hotel in Boston's going to allow Frenchie."

"Ey, we meet again," Tony said, quietly coming up beside her.

She gave him a half smile and glanced toward the lines. *I don't have the energy for this.* "I don't think the hotels here are going to take dogs, even a small one."

He leaned in close and whispered, "I won't tell if you don't."

His breath smelled clean and minty. Her stomach did a mini flip. She was surprised at her body's reaction to being near him.

He stepped in the line to her left and approached the reservation desk. He was polite but brief. The attendant seemed extra friendly, but he didn't seem to notice.

Mia stepped up to her own reservation attendant and began to explain her doggie dilemma.

The attendant smiled blankly. "Pets aren't permitted at any of the local hotels here. For an additional fee, your dog can be crated. He'll arrive at TF Green Airport sometime tomorrow or the next day."

Mia's not sure which was more grating, the lady's blinding white teeth or her robotic voice. She decided it might have been a tie.

"Tomorrow or the next day!? We're only an hour away from Rhode Island. I can rent a car and drive him there, for Christ's sake."

"I'm sorry, Mrs. Ca-ca-palo. You'll have to go to ground transportation for a car rental but with the weather…"

"Oh, forget it." Mia lifted Frenchie's crate and walked away, leaving Tony and the other noisy passengers behind.

Mia walked through the airport tired, frustrated, and aimless. Feeling an internal heaviness, she sat down on a window ledge and tried to talk herself out of the funk she was sinking into. *I'm going to be fine; just focus on right now and try to chunk things down.* Didn't she instruct her patients on this cognitive behavioral strategy eight million times a week? It all sounded like bullshit.

Struggling to get over herself, she tried again. *Big deal; I'm delayed overnight. I don't want to go to Rhode Island anyway.* She exhaled slowly and counted the empty seats around her. She'd counted ten when she lifted her gaze and noticed a young girl sitting alone. She was pretty with short blonde hair, barely a teenager. She looked like she was waiting for someone. She held a yellow stuffed Tweety Bird. Mia scanned for a parent or a suitcase but didn't see either. Her eyes caught the stormy weather beyond.

She felt her mind rewind to the day she and Jimmy waited for Uncle Joe outside at the airport. It was a gray and rainy day in San Francisco—it comforted her. Since their mother's death, Marianna hated the sun. Its brightness and warmth felt wrong to her.

"Mare, Uncle Joe's smart like you. You should stay there, maybe." She watched him flick his cigarette, exhale. "Put those brains to use, help people, maybe teach kids." Tears leaked from her eyes, "I'll be here for you no matter what, we'll always be close, doesn't matter where you live." He pulled her into him, and for a moment she felt his warmth fill her heart. He was still in there. Relief trickled through her body, maybe she wasn't all alone.

Without knowing why her memory hung onto it, she remembered the Zeppole she had eaten for dessert. She could practically taste its creamy center, the sweet, powdered sugar.

Mia felt a tug at her sleeve. "Excuse me, senora. Lady, are you sick?"

"What?" Mia asked.

"You okay?"

She started, then brought the man and his airport security uniform into focus.

"Yes, I'm fine."

She unfolded her hands from her stomach and stood up.

"I'm okay. Thank you for asking."

She glanced back toward the girl, but she was gone.

Thinking about Jimmy and that long ago day; it was the last time she felt held by him.

Chapter 9

Mia craved solitude, something fierce, but was hungry and needed a drink. She headed into T.G.I. Friday's and ordered a hamburger with spicy fries and a martini. *Let's get right to it.* She chose a back booth, absolutely not wanting to be bothered. She stared at Mr. French, imagining him crated overnight. *It's ridiculous. He'd never make it. He doesn't even know he's a dog. I'd never make it, either.*

The lack of sleep and stress of the trip had taken their toll. *I've got to get a grip. Okay, breathe and sip. Just relax a little, then go back, book a room, and sneak in Mr. French. "Ey, I won't tell anybody."*

"Sorry, lady, we don't allow animals in the restaurant. Board of Health."

"Animal? What animal?" She draped a sweatshirt over Frenchie's crate and threw a fifty on the table.

The guy nodded and returned to his tasks.

Forget this whole Rhode Island thing. As soon as the weather breaks, I'm going home. I'll just tell Ror I've changed my mind. Maybe I'll tell him the whole truth… He'd understand. Let Jimmy attend the service without her. Would anyone even notice? Annoyance mixed with something else tugged at her heart; she still hadn't heard from him.

She inhaled deep, then let out a good, long breath. She took a bite of her burger and a long sip from her drink. It burned all the way down. A few minutes later, the alcohol took effect, but she didn't feel any better emotionally. She scanned the crowd when the waiter approached. She shot him a look.

"Miss, there's a gentleman at the bar who would like to buy you a drink."

Mia raised her eyebrows and looked across the bar to find Tony lifting up his beer. Her heart stuttered and jumped a beat, then she looked down away from him. *What is it with this guy?* She felt a hint of embarrassment and annoyance wash through her. She'd lied and acted out of sorts on the plane. *He's a stranger, Mia; you owe him nothing.* Unexpectantly, he towered over her.

"This is for the lady, if she'll have it," he said, setting a drink down on the table.

She exhaled her annoyance slowly. "That's not at all necessary."

Tony nods at the bartender. "Mia, I made you feel bad about your father back on the plane, and I'm sorry."

"Naw, I was being overly sensitive. Not your fault."

"Here, I thought you'd need these." Tony handed her a white envelope. "After you stormed off, I noticed you left it. I figured you might need a room, seeing as how your friend never showed." He eyed her questioningly.

"It's a long and very complicated story."

He smirked and waited for her to explain further.

"Wait, they let you walk off with my papers?"

"They didn't exactly let me. I booked two rooms under my name. The room charge can be transferred. I thought you could take care of it when the dog was already inside."

She hesitated. "You didn't need to do that at all."

"Listen, Tony, I've been acting out of sorts all day. I'm nervous about going home; I haven't really spent any significant time there since I was a kid. I'm actually from Rhode Island, too."

"You don't have to explain anything to me. I was thinking, though. We're stuck here, you and me, for a while. Let's get bumped up, like in Rocky I."

Mia bursts out laughing. "Bumped up?"

"Yeah, have a few drinks. You and me. We got tonight; who needs tomorrow?"

"Okay, Bob Seger. Is that what they're calling it back in Rhode Island? Bumped up?"

"Naw, that's my line. Just made it up. It's good, huh?"

"Not bad, actually."

"Mia, what do you say?'

There was something about his tone, the way he watched her, that was incredibly inviting.

"Listen, I appreciate the offer, Tony, but as you've seen, I'm not very good company today." *Damn, his eyes are nice.* She saw something flicker across them. *Disappointment? Not my issue.*

"A drink or two, a little food, that's all. It could be a nice distraction?"

"A nice distraction." God knew she needed one. *Absolutely not.*

Their eyes met briefly, and she averted hers.

"Okay." His voice was quieter. "I can respect that. Hope your trip goes well." He gave a slight nod and a reassuring smirk.

She had the strangest feeling. It was familiar, but she couldn't name it. She sipped her drink and set it down carefully.

"Thank you for the offer. When I finish here, I'm going to end this very long day by calling my partner Rory and then getting some sleep."

She was exhausted but knew she wouldn't be able to sleep.

Her cell rang.

"Speak of the devil."

Chapter 10

Mia woke with a rush of adrenaline. There were only a few flights to Providence, and she didn't want to miss hers. *Let's get this over with.* She smiled at the sight of Mr. French curled up in a ball. She got ready to head out, and as she stepped outside, her shoe brushed against a card near the door. Her lips curled upward as she read Tony's name and number.

The note was simple, the handwriting precise.

Mia, if you have any extra time while visiting Providence give me a call. I would really enjoy your company. T

She tucked the card in her bag and kept moving.

Less than two hours later, she and Mr. French were dropped off in front of the Westin Hotel in downtown Providence. The night before her father's funeral Auntie Rose had insisted Mia stay at her house, and Mia had agreed, feeling obligated, but the thought of staying at Rob's house without him felt more than strange to her. She pushed her mind away from thoughts of him.

She slid the key in, grateful her travel had finally ended. *I need a quick shower and a change of clothes, bad.* She let out Mr. French and watched with amusement as he did his usual yoga moves before jumping onto the bed to assess the place.

She turned the shower on full blast. She hoped like hell it would rinse away her fear. She stood under the hot water for a few extra minutes, trying to get a plan together. *Call Auntie, let her know I arrived. The service isn't until Friday.* She rubbed at her neck, rolling her head back and forth; she didn't know any of the details.

She threw on a pair of blue jeans and a pink turtleneck, scrunched her hair with a towel and assessed herself in the mirror, avoiding her own gaze.

She sat down on the edge of the bed, exhaled her breaths and silently counted. *One, two, three…* She walked over to the oversized window to take in the city below. She felt a familiar churning in her stomach.

"Come on, boy. Get your sweater and your leash; we're going out for a late lunch. We certainly can't sit here all day. I'll call Auntie on the way."

She walked out into the brisk air. *This is exactly what I needed.* It was the kind of fall afternoon where the sun was still warm, but the air was cool and smelled like leaves and apples. Mr. French nosed the breeze, and she smiled. She exhaled long and deep watching him.

As they walked, she found herself thinking of Tony. *"It's a nice time of year to hang out in the city."* He'd meant Boston, of course, but he was right; it was a nice time of year to be in any New England city. She'd enjoyed his company. He was different than the men she typically met.

She was wowed by the Providence Place Mall and Water Place Park; so much had changed. Her eyes moved up the street until she spotted the State House. Her breath caught in her throat. The last time she'd been there, Robbie had talked her into skipping school.

Mia pulled herself away from the painful memories, walking so fast that Mr. French did double time. She hadn't been close to anyone since Rob. *Keep moving.* She knew she'd always be indebted to him. He'd saved her, but reliving the pain was useless.

Thinking about what they'd once had left her with a heavy feeling in her chest. She exhaled deeply, trying to ignore it, but her chest felt tight. Her thoughts were never far from him. *They may never be.* Sometimes, she could still feel him, smell his familiar musky scent. For a few precious moments, they walked together. He took her hand in his.

"Hey, Robbie, can you believe I actually came back?"

"Uncle Jimmy adored his little girl; you did the right thing."

She picked up her pace again.

"Mare, it'll be okay, you'll see." He squeezed her hand tight.

His hand felt warm. She turned toward him, knowing he'd make her feel better, but he was already gone.

"Wait." *Uh, I hate that; I'm not done yet.*

Her brain automatically went to him for comfort. *Old habits die hard.* She let out a sigh and slowed her pace. She couldn't believe twelve years had gone by.

"Frenchie, Providence looks like a real city now."

He peed on a blade of grass poking out of the concrete.

"Not impressed, eh boy? When I was a kid, there were barely any attractions down here at all. This city sure looks different."

As she passed familiar places from her childhood, memories played like reels of film.

When she was eight, her family attended a Johnny Cash concert. She and Jimmy had felt like the luckiest kids alive. Their parents seemed so happy together. *How could one event alter so much?*

They approached Federal Hill, the little Italy of Rhode Island. It held such special meaning for her; it was where her dad was born and raised. Jimmy Capaldi, Sr. was a tough guy from "The Hill." When he was young, he was tall with broad shoulders, dark curly hair and ice-blue eyes. These were the only features they shared.

He always had a Lucky Strike dangling from his lips. He was a good-natured, likable guy, but if you crossed him or his family, a very different man emerged. *How he loved his family and this place, though.*

She took a deep breath and felt an old confusion begin to tumble around. *He's actually gone, too… Forever. Death is such a weird thing. Where do people actually go?* She watched a leaf float in the breeze and land on the street. She thought about Robbie's love for nature.

He'd had a theory about death. He thought people came back again and again through nature. Throughout the years, this thought had always given her hope. Back home, she would look out over the mountains or lake and think they might be out there, in the water or the breeze. *Maybe they're now one of the creatures—a part of it all.*

It could be; it was plausible. She wanted to believe, but doubt always seeped in. In the rare moments when she allowed herself to believe, she felt closer to her mother and Rob. Sadness and fear pulsed through her, reminding her why she was back. She fished out her cell.

Chapter 11

"Minelli's Diner"

"Hi, Auntie."

"Marianna! I mean…" she paused. "Mia. Me and Sal were just talking about the service. We booked St. Rocco's for 9—figured it was closer than St. Mary's—then we'll come back here for brunch. Got quite a spread planned."

The reality was that her aunt didn't want to step foot back inside St. Mary's. That was where both her best friend and son were buried.

"Makes sense. I'm sure you'll have plenty. I want to help with whatever I can."

"Don't worry; I got Sal here. The girls'll be by tomorrow afternoon. They can't wait to see you."

Guilt washed through her. "I'll be by tomorrow. I can't wait to see everyone. I'm walking to The Hill now with Frenchie, figured we'd grab an early supper and turn in. The time difference is a killer."

"Be careful walking up there; it's different than before. Everything is."

"I will."

"Hey, I talked to your brother; told him you'd be here by the week's end. He said he'd come by after work, said he tried calling you."

A mix of emotions passed through her. *Bullshit. Liar.* Her aunt would never give up hope of them being close again. Mia didn't blame Aunt Rose. Her brother was the type of guy you wanted to believe—he even believed his own lies.

The last time she'd believed him was when he promised to show for her doctoral graduation. Later, he'd said something came up at work. She felt annoyance fill the old wound. *Great, alert the press.* She never thought she'd feel this way, but she didn't want to see him. She hoped he'd pulled a no-show; it certainly was his M.O.

She stood under the entrance to Federal Hill. *Maybe I should've just eaten at the hotel.* She courted indecision for half a minute. The aroma of fresh garlic and spices smacked her right in the face, and she inhaled deep.

"You know what, Frenchie? I don't care if I fall asleep in my pasta and beans. I'm eating right here." She tried to remember her last meal. She'd been so busy with travel she hadn't eaten since dinner the previous night. *Tony.* She felt the stir of an unknown emotion.

She passed Angelo's and felt nostalgia so strong she thought about sitting on the curb. She wrapped her arms around her waist for comfort. *I'm alright.* She kept moving toward the restaurant. Despite her words of encouragement, an old feeling pierced her stomach and heart simultaneously.

Images of her family spun. Her mother, tall and blonde, was just gorgeous; way too pretty to be a mother of two. Dad walked close by. He was the protector, big and strong. Mia and Jimmy had run up ahead, glancing back when they reached the door to their favorite family spot.

"Hurry up, or we won't get our table."

Their table over-looked Atwells Avenue, perfect for people watching. They would speculate on the lives of the people passing by, always agreeing it was better to be them. The kids would toast their grape juice, pretending to drink red wine.

Mia and Jimmy had been so close back then. It was hard to believe that she barely knew her own brother. *How did it happen?* Out of the multiple answers that swirled, the simplest was that death changes everything. As the layers of truth washed through her, she could almost see the guys in white jackets with their snide smirks. "We've been waiting for you, Marianna."

Her fear carried her forward, and she forced herself inside the restaurant. *Fuck it. If today is the ultimate crackup day, I'll be admitted on a full stomach, God damn it, and a nice glass of Chianti.* She took a deep breath.

"This is for you, mom."

The restaurant represented warmth and safety to her as a child. She used to dream about it after her mom died. They'd completely refurbished, and the changes were amazing. Dark wooden tables draped with cranberry-tinted, freshly starched linens had replaced the cafeteria-style tables. Each table had a fresh sprig of greens and a beautifully colored mum. Crystal tea-light holders burned dimly, adding to the ambiance. Cream-veined, terracotta-colored European marble adorned the floors and the bottom half of the walls.

Sinatra crooned softly, and beautiful pictures of Tuscan landscapes and stenciled urns rendered the place absolutely gorgeous. The restaurant was packed.

"Hey, lady, we don't allow dogs in here."

"I'm sorry, I forgot."

Frenchie wagged his tail daintily.

"You want me to tie 'em out back?"

The music, the incredible smells wafting through the air, it all became too much.

"Maybe next time, thank you."

With the fresh air, her heartbeat slowed, and blood returned to her face. She moved down the street, counting her steps for a while.

She spotted restaurants that were like landmarks in the city. Joe Marzilli's Old Canteen, Camille's, and Andinos. No matter how many years had passed, some things had stayed the same. This gave her a small comfort. She looked up and down the street, scanning newer places. Mediterraneo, Zooma, Sienna and Providence Oyster Bar. *Maybe I'll pick one of these places to eat. No past associations.* She still felt nauseous.

She headed toward the fountain in De Pasquale Square and decided to sit. It was packed with people from all walks of life; it felt good to be among them. She spotted a quaint café, unsure if it was a restaurant or just a deli. The sign read Venda Ravioli. *I don't care at this point if my dinner is just a sandwich. I have to eat outside.*

"Whataya think, Mr. French? Maybe I'll get prosciutto and sharp provolone with roasted peppers, but only if they have real Italian hard rolls. The 'nice hard ones,' dad used to call them."

Frenchie sat with his regal, puffy head raised, people watching as he wagged his tail.

A young boy approached the fountain and threw in a penny with all his might. The boy closed his eyes to make his wish. His innocence made Mia smile.

"Mommy, why is that dog wearing that?" he asked, pointing at Mr. French.

A Christmas present from Rory, he sat in a bright red Coach sweater.

"It's silly, isn't it?" She loved the raw honesty of children. They gave no bullshit or obnoxious defenses.

The boy grinned wide and nodded in agreement. He pulled his mother to the other end of the fountain, begging for one more penny.

Auntie and the cousins are going to have a field day with his sweater.

Mr. French sniffed the air above his head.

"It smells great, huh, boy?"

A small place called Dolce Vita caught her attention. Several impeccably dressed men waited outside the restaurant. Their suits looked imported, expensive. She couldn't tell if they were politicians or mobsters—it was Rhode Island. The white guy in the back looked familiar.

No way, it can't be. She looked away. *He does own restaurants in Providence, Mia… And he lives here.* She got up to leave, starving for an early dinner.

Chapter 12

Tony and the guys had just finished lunch and headed downtown for a business meeting. He couldn't wait for the afternoon to be over, exhausted from a sleepless night thinking about his case and the woman from the plane. He hoped she'd gotten the card slipped under her door; he couldn't really do anything else. *Maybe I'll run her name.*

"T man," Bobby spoke. "What you think about switching it up?"

"Why not? It's all the same to us."

Word was, there was a big deal coming in from Jersey. Apparently, the guys found a better rock and roid connection.

"Gonna make a killin'," Bobby continued.

Yea, make a killing off lost street punks. It made him sick to stand by and watch. *For now. Be patient; not that much longer. We almost have enough to bury 'em for good. It'll be worth it, then.*

Bobby patted Tony's back, and Tony grinned sideways in return. *He really isn't a bad guy; this life is all he knows. God, listen to me making excuses for this guy. I can't believe it's been two years.*

I swear I'm done with this scummy undercover world after this case. I must be getting old.

His thoughts returned to Mia. She was gorgeous, but there was something else about her that he was drawn to. His stomach sank. He wished he'd asked her out last night. He knew she'd never call him.

As they passed the fountain, he saw a puffy dog in a silly get-up, and his heart jumped. He looked up, and there she was.

"Hey, guys, I'll catch up. Ey, Mr. French, is that you?" He patted his head. "Fancy sweater. Doc, nice surprise. I see they got you on a flight."

"I had to fly standby. It's my own fault… after yesterday's tantrum."

"You had an excuse."

"No, I acted like an ass."

"Caught a nice day today."

"Yes, couldn't resist. Figured we'd take a walk, eat a late lunch, see the city; it's been a long time."

"How's it going being back here?"

"It's fine."

"You got my note? Didn't wanna leave without saying… something…"

She looked away.

He slid off his glasses and tucked them in his shirt before they finally made eye contact. He wished last night had gone differently but thought he'd like another shot.

"Things have certainly changed in the city," she said, breaking the silence. "Just this street alone."

"Strange to be back, I'll bet."

"Frenchie and I are going to eat and then continue… sightseeing, I guess you'd call it. I'm thinking of eating there." She pointed toward Venda.

"Good choice. Tell Pasquale I sent you, that we're friends."

Her foot danced up and down. He raised an eyebrow her way, and she laughed, settling her foot.

"Okay then." She stood. "Nice to see you again, Tony."

He was about to ask her for her number but realized they weren't alone. He slid his glasses back on, noting the guys waiting for him to make an introduction. In the afternoon sun, she looked sexy and natural. He could tell the others had noticed, which evoked a strong impulse to protect her. He didn't want her anywhere near them, especially Costa.

He played it off and mumbled, "Gentlemen, say hello to Dr. M and Mr. French. She's an old family friend."

Mia glanced at Tony.

"We didn't think Iannucci was eva gonna introduce us," teased one of the younger guys.

"Hello." She eyed Tony and his friends.

"Yea, Tank man, what's up with that?"

From behind his shades, Tony watched as Costa stared at her. He kept his face in check, but his entire body stiffened.

"Did I overhear you're sightseeing, Doctor?" Costa asked.

"Sort of. It's been a long time since I've been— "

"It's late; we should go, guys. We don't wanna keep anyone waiting, right?"

They looked at Tony, then each other. Tony glanced at his watch and nodded.

"Me too," Mia added.

Tony leaned down and pecked her on the cheek.

"Wait, you live around here, sweetheart?" Costa asked.

Tony hoped like hell she didn't respond truthfully. *The less he knows, the better.*

"No, I'm just visiting for a bit. Nice meeting y'all," she said in her best southern drawl. "Bye, Tony. Good seeing you."

Costa tugged at her hand as she turned to leave. Tony felt the urge to smash Costa's face in but forced a half smile.

"Well, Miss. Southern Belle, I hope our paths cross again. You ever want a guided tour, I'm your man."

"Thank you, sir, but I won't be in town for long." She eased away.

"Enjoy your day, Doctor." He winked and sleazily touched the inside of her hand with a card while he whispered in her ear, "In case you change your mind."

"We should go."

Costa leaned over to pat Frenchie, but he let out a slow growl.

That'a boy.

"He's protective." She tugged at Frenchie's leash and walked away.

"Afternoon," Tony yelled. "Tell your family I was asking for them."

She didn't respond or look back.

Chapter 13

Once inside the deli, Mia looked down at the card in her hand. *Anthony Costa, President. President of what? Body disposal?* Thinking of his name, a sick feeling worked its way up to the back of her throat. *Johnny… No, Gian Costa. The guy mom supposedly had an affair with. Was this guy his brother, cousin, son?* She stuffed the card in her purse. *Old sleaze-bag. What's Tony doing with those guys?* She felt a hint of disappointment but pushed it away. *"I'm in business; partially retired, really." My ass.*

At the command of her stomach, she pushed her thoughts aside. In front of her sat gourmet dishes straight from her childhood: veal and peppers, pasta and beans, broccoli rabe, fried calamari, tripe, escarole and beans and snail salad. Above her hung dried sausage and rows of cured green and calamata olives. The hunks of cheese practically made her drool. *Wow, I haven't seen this kind of food since I was a kid.* The meat cases were filled with round chunks of salami, spiced hams, hot capicola, and Parma prosciutto.

"I think we've entered food heaven," she whispered to Frenchie.

He drooled while licking the case directly in front of him.

"Oh, I forgot about you, boy." She stepped out of line to tie him out front.

A small man appeared next to her.

"Hi, I'm looking for Pasquale. Tony Iannucci sent me; we're friends."

"Welcome, that's me."

Mia looked down at her dog.

"No-wa, don't-a worry. Leave-a the dog; he must be a hungry, too."

His accent warmed her heart. He was a short man in a white apron. He beamed with a kind smile.

"Hi," he greeted Mr. French as he handed him a piece of cheese. "It's-a okay?" he asked, looking back at her.

"Yes, thank you. I haven't seen this kind of deli since I was a young girl. My father used to take me shopping at Vito's on Broadway. He grew up just down the road. I haven't been back here in a long time."

"Oh-a. Vito retired, nobody want-a run it for him. You visit your father now?"

"No, he died. I came back for his funeral." His kind expression fills her with unexpected grief. There's something about admitting aloud that somebody has died; each admission makes it seem more final. She remembered feeling this way about her mom and Rob but didn't expect to feel this way about her dad. Pasquale touched her arm.

"It's-a alright, I know-a. I lost my wife last Spring." He handed her a piece of cheese. "It's an import from Italy."

"I'm sorry," she said, embarrassed by her emotions with a complete stranger.

"Ain-dona-be, it's-a worse if you a don't feel. Eat the cheese; it'll make you feel better."

"Delicious. Sharp provolone is my favorite." His kindness felt like a band-aid. "Thank you."

He dismissed her gratitude with a bat of his hand. "Is there anything you don't-a like?"

"No, everything looks great."

"I'll fix you a plate. Follow me."

"Really?" Emotions caused her lips to curl.

"You-a go get some wine from next door. Wine make you feel better, too. Tell them it's for Pasquale."

On her way outside, Mia glanced back to see Pasquale feeding Frenchie a piece of meat. She tried to purchase a bottle of Chianti next door, but the man laughed when she told him it was for Pasquale.

Re-entering the deli, the tables were filled with couples trading forkfuls of food or families with young children. A pang of something gnarled inside her. Pasquale waved her over to a small, private table in the back overlooking the courtyard.

He took the wine from the brown bag and poured it into small juice glasses. "Bon appétit."

They clinked their glasses.

"Start with the escarole and beans." He grated fresh parmesan over her bowl and pushed crusty bread toward her. "You dunk?"

She nodded politely and excitedly dug in. Escarole and beans were one of her all-time favorites. Growing up, her father did most of the cooking when he was home. She'd often request this dish upon his return. Many days, she'd enter their house to the smell of roasted garlic and olive oil. The flavor mix of mushy white beans and sweet greens was the best. *So many of my memories of him are interwoven with food.*

Pasquale re-appeared after a while to check in and take a quick sip of wine.

"This is great," she told him as she finished her bowl of soup and two large pieces of bread.

He beamed at her approval and empty bowl. He brought her a small dish of gnocchi, small round pasta made with potato done in a simple tomato sauce with just a hint of fresh basil. The smell of the sauce was divine. The pasta was accompanied by a side dish of sautéed broccoli rabe and sausage. While she ate, she looked out the window at the beautiful day, her mind fuzzy from the wine. Placing her fork down, she was full and a little buzzed. She touched Pasquale's arm.

"That was the best meal I've had in years. Thank you."

"Grazie. Your dad would approve?"

"Very much so."

"Tell Anthony it's been too long. Come back when you're hungry."

"Thank you."

She tucked a hefty bill underneath her napkin but couldn't put a price on what his compassion meant to her. She headed out past the courtyard, and with the sun almost completely faded away, the temperature had dropped. She shivered, reminded of how much she hated the cold. She crossed her arms over her chest to keep warm.

"You're lucky you have a sweater on, boy," she told Frenchie. Her thoughts drifted back to her wonderful meal with Pasquale. Between the huge meal and the homemade wine, she was beat. She was more than thrilled when she finally rounded the corner and saw the familiar sign for the Westin.

Chapter 14

"We've had one hell of a long day, Mr. French. I'm spent." She slid her card into the slot.

Frenchie went straight to his water bowl and lapped up every drop before collapsing on the bed.

"I'm jealous, boy. I wish my life were that simple." She peeled off her jeans and sneakers and pulled on a pair of sweats. She laid back on the bed and noticed a blinking light on the phone. She hit play.

"Mrs. Capaldi, please call the front desk; we have a delivery for you."

She called, and five minutes later, she opened her door to a young man wearing a dark blue suit.

"For you," he said, smiling.

Baffled, she accepted the beautifully wrapped fall bouquet. She closed the door and quickly retrieved the note tucked inside.

"Sorry for my business associates' bad manners. It's not every day they get to meet a young lady like yourself. I wondered if you'd like to have coffee sometime before you leave.

I believe you already have my cell."

Tony.

She placed the flowers next to the bed and couldn't help but smile. *That was nice of him. Coffee.* She laid back on the bed and thought about calling Rory to get an update on her patients. Her eyes felt heavy. *Just a couple minutes.*

Frenchie moved closer to her. Fragments from her day replayed. The happy couples in the bistro—she stroked her dog's back. Costa—she pushed the name away. Eventually, the memories swirled deeper and deeper into blackness.

Robert and Mia were on his bike. Their favorite spot by the falls. Robert down on one knee. The two making love in the grass. Suzy Q's for ice cream. Screech of metal and people screaming. Mia running to the corner. A tangle of metal and limbs bent in unnatural ways. A single Nike sneaker down the street.

Bang, bang, bang.

Frenchie barked wildly. *What is that?* Mia awoke to someone banging on the door. She pushed herself out of bed and realized she'd been crying in her sleep.

"Miss, it's security. Is everything okay?"

"Yes, yes. I must've fallen asleep with the TV on. Sorry; I'll lower it."

"There was screaming; you're okay?"

"Yes, yes, I'm fine. Those silly shows. So sorry to bother anyone." She wiped her tears and opened the door a crack, sure not to make eye contact.

"Thank you for checking on me. I appreciate it, really."

He glared at Frenchie, still going nuts.

"Shhh." She closed the door, pausing briefly on the other side to count her breaths. *One, two, three.* She felt shaken and embarrassed. She walked to the wet bar, reached for a water and drained it. She took a few more deep breaths and then sat back down on the bed. She thought about calling Rory. *It's too late.*

She walked back to the wet bar, opened a small bottle of wine and sipped, returning to the bed. She wished to see Rob's face one more time unbruised and handsome, like at the falls. *Before.*

"Come on, boy. Come up here."

He jumped up and nuzzled against her body. His warm, furry body felt comforting and silent tears streamed down her cheeks. It'd been a long time since she'd had this dream. It was still vivid, even after haunting her for years. She waited for the wine to calm her nerves.

"Mare, it's gonna be alright." She tried to relish every good moment they'd ever shared. *Damn.* It was increasingly hard to remember after such a long time. *He'd be turning forty this year.* She couldn't help but wonder what his face would look like. Would his hair have changed color? She tried to imagine his aged, handsome face until her mind blurred with the effort and the wine.

Chapter 15

Mia awoke to Frenchie whimpering by the door. *Oh, my head feels big and sore.* She reached up to her thumping eyes. She felt like complete shit between the time change, her dreams and crying. She glanced back toward the door and managed to drag herself up.

"Sorry, boy. You have to go outside, I know. Get your leash."

He wagged daintily, and she hurried him outside. Standing on the back sidewalk, she watched him relieve himself for three full minutes. Guilt burned her cheeks.

"I owe you. Extra biscuits and lunch is on me."

Once they returned to the room, she dropped him two biscuits and eyed the empty wine bottle. *"A hundred miles of bad road."* Her stomach sank; it was an expression her dad had used. Seeing the flowers, she made a mental note to call to say thank you but decline his offer for coffee. *I won't have time.*

Her mind returned to her father's sayings. Her mom always thought they were corny, but she and Jimmy thought they were hilarious, the ultimate. Jimmy once told his third grade teacher she smelled like a "French whore." Of course, she was stunned.

Mean Mrs. Bocook didn't share our sense of humor. Their mom was called into school, and Jimmy got in big trouble. Their dad had been on the road, but when he came home, she told him the entire story.

The kids pretended to sleep but listened to every word from their bedrooms. To Mia's relief, their dad shared their humor. Their mom's voice rose a little with shock but after a pause she laughed, too. Jimmy was still scared, though. Dad's mood ran hot and cold with him. He lucked out that night. Their dad was much easier on Marianna; there was no need to "toughen" her up, but he was constantly worried about Jimmy "going soft." An image of Jimmy asleep on her bedroom floor as a young boy crossed her mind, his dark blond hair hanging loose around his full face. His chest moving up and down with his breath. Her eyes kept landing on his purplish, swollen lip. She remembered Rob sneaking in that night placing Jim's baseball glove quietly next to his pillow. They had silently locked eyes, but they never spoke about that afternoon at the baseball game. She hadn't been there, but was told Jimmy "back talked" daddy.

Her stomach tightened. *I might actually see him today.* As an adult, Jimmy's contempt for their parents had gotten worse, practically devouring him. Mia could still hear the bitterness in his voice during those awful late-night calls. Drinking only made it worse. Depending on her mood, she screened his calls. He was too much to deal with.

She understood his sadness and grief about their mother's death, but she didn't fully understand his anger. Angry toward their dad, accident aside, sure. *Why did he hate mom? Wasn't she the victim?* She'd gone over these questions so many times. *He shot her.* She still couldn't say it out loud. *He didn't mean to. That's the part that's supposed to make me, us feel better. It never does.*

There was a robbery. Their dad had been away at work but came home early. He showed up at the diner to surprise his wife.

He tried to protect her, but things got muddled in the pulse of danger. There were rumors that Costa and his boys had been there earlier that same night, and maybe they'd come back to rob the place. He tried to protect her, but things got botched.

I hate him for it, and I'll never forgive him. She knew it was wrong but couldn't help it. Costa's name circled in her brain for a minute. She couldn't imagine her mom cheating on her dad. *It's crazy.* How could Jimmy believe that? The thought made her want to physically hurt him. She hated thinking about her brother; it always felt the same.

Slowly, she stripped down and looked at her reflection in the bathroom mirror. Her conflicted thoughts swarmed, and she let them. She turned on the shower as hot as she could stand and closed her eyes. She scrubbed her hair and mapped out a game plan. There was no getting around it; she needed to go to the diner. Caren and Joanne would be there.

Her gut churned. Guilt. *It's been so long.* The polite story was that she'd fallen out of touch with them when she moved out West. She tossed the truth around. Seeing them was always too hard; they reminded her of Robert and all that she'd lost. She wasn't proud to admit it, but she had avoided them like the plague right from the beginning. It was selfish but true.

After Rob died, the phrase hung–*anywhere but here.* She had to get away from everyone. Between her mother's death and Rob's, the pain had been too great. She had to get away from his family and the hell out of Rhode Island.

Her cousins had taken such different paths than her. It seemed like their pasts were the only thing they had left in common. Throughout the years, Auntie had tried to keep Mia updated. Jo married a trucker named Frankie and moved into a trailer park somewhere out in Chepachet. Last Mia heard, Jo had left him and stopped smoking—pretty incredible, given that Jo had been a burnout and sold pot for a while.

Caren, poor, beautiful Caren, was still with Jay, a local she'd been involved with on and off since grade school. He turned out to be a real mean, abusive drunk. A few months earlier, Auntie told Mia that Caren had taken out another restraining order against him. Sadly, they had two young children, and she was pregnant with their third. Last she'd heard, Caren had moved back to Tweed Street to get away from him. *What a mess.*

All of their lives changed after Robbie died. *How would things be different? One thing is for sure: if Rob were alive, Jay wouldn't be hitting his baby sister. I'm surprised Auntie hasn't tried to kill him herself. Or maybe she has.* Mia let out a nervous giggle.

Even after so many years apart, Auntie Rose and Mia were still close. *She's like a second mother to me.* She and the girls had helped her with all the girly things, and Rob took care of the rest. Her aunt had always had a special thing for her—even before her mother died. The other kids teased her about it all the time, "You're so special." Mia denied it, but she knew it was true. Auntie had always treated her like she was one of her own.

Auntie helped Mia remember the special things unique to her mom. She loved pink, hated olives, and smelled like Dove soap and Halston perfume. Mia conjured her mother's face, feeling a strong need to remember her and Rob. She and Auntie very seldom talked about Rob, though, as if his death were off-limits. Maybe it was just too painful to lose a son.

Leaving conditioner in her wild hair, Mia stepped out of the shower and grabbed a large bath towel. She couldn't believe how cold it felt. *Oh, get used to it.* She imagined Rory calling her a wimp. *I should call him.* She calculated the time difference. *He'll be in with patients already.* She decided to leave him a message. She couldn't wait to tell him about "The Hill." It was a place like something out of the movies. She searched in her suitcase for a black sweat suit. *This'll keep me warm.* She slicked her hair back and threw on her favorite pink pumas. She smiled, thinking of her mother.

Her eyes glanced at the flowers sitting next to the bed. *I need to call Tony.* She pulled out the card and dialed his cell.

"Iannucci here."

"Hi, Tony, it's Mia."

"Hey, glad to hear from you. How didcha like Venda?"

"I loved it. Met Pasquale and had a great meal."

"Yea, great little place."

"It is. Listen, I just wanted to thank you for the flowers, they're beautiful. You didn't need to do that."

"I wanted to. Glad you like them."

"Well, thank you."

"You're very welcome." He paused. "You done with memory lane yet? I was hoping you'd need a distraction by now."

She giggled. "I'm about done with memory lane, but there's this thing I have to attend tomorrow, and then I'm heading home.

"That's too bad. If your schedule changes, call me."

"I will. Thanks again." As she hung up, her stomach squeezed. *Maybe if something changes, I'll call him.* She grabbed Frenchie's leash and sweater and headed out the door. Once in the elevator, she dialed Rory's private line.

"Hi, this is Dr. DeFusco," his message began.

"Hey, Ror, it's me. Just want to say hi. Me and Frenchie had one hell of a time on The Hill yesterday. You'll never believe this story. Call me later. I'm going to Auntie's now; wish me luck. Bye."

Walking outside, Mia turned toward the main bus station. *I need coffee.* She spied a coffee shop on the corner of Westminster and Washington, directly across from the bus station. Still tired from last night, she ordered a large coffee with extra sugar and extra cream. The girl working the counter chomped her gum with attitude as her eyes widened toward Mr. French. Mia ignored her bad manners and threw several dollars down on the counter.

"Sorry, Frenchie. I told you Rhodey isn't dog friendly—or even people friendly for that matter. Don't mind her; she probably rides a broom."

The bus was nearly empty. She peered out the grimy window as it maneuvered past the freeway onto Plainfield Street and thought of Auntie Rose. Mia was both excited and anxious to see her. Her aunt was something else. A smile tugged at her lower lip. *Always was.* Her body pulsed with each passing mile, dipping and twisting at the new influx of memories.

Robbie's funeral had felt like an exercise in human fragility. The attendees tortured her with their sympathetic smiles and cringy pats on the arm. They all chatted, perfectly fine to keep on living. Auntie's strong hand comforted the shoulder of one of Robbie's teachers. Mia had simply wanted to be left alone. And the one person she needed was drunk and vacant. After the funeral Jo went out back where Jimmy was smoking. She got in Jimmy's face about drinking too much. He stormed out and never came back, not even to say goodbye to her.

The screechy brakes of the bus brought it to a halt. Mia got up absently and pulled at Frenchie's leash, but out on the sidewalk, her feet felt glued. She stood directly in front of a restaurant. *Did this place always look so run-down?*

"Frenchie, we may have to break out in a run any time. Get your paws ready." She laughed nervously and contemplated renting a car for the weekend. "Let's go, boy."

Mia paused at the local school yard, watching the children at play. *God, Thornton Elementary. This is where it all happened around here.* Looking through the fence, she could almost see herself running hard toward her mother, her eyes shining, face aglow. It was their ritual. Her mom would wait for her by the fence and act surprised when Mia nearly tackled her.

"I didn't even see you," she'd tease as she kissed her forehead.

Mia would beam. As a child, she wanted to be like her mom so badly. She would make her mom stand behind her in front of the mirror and put her straight, blonde locks over Mia's dark, wild hair.

"Marianna, you look silly."

"I wanna look like you and Cousin Caren."

"You look exactly how you're supposed to. Besides, I'd love to have your curls." She plucked a curl, making boingy noises as it bounced, and they'd both crack up laughing. After she died Jimmy and Rob stood right here waiting for her. Jimmy, "hey kiddo, how was school?" Mia gave a shrug. "Are you ready for the Johnston High dirt?" "Joey D's dad got arrested for drunk driving, his buddy Traf couldn't even get him out of it, he practically ran over the fuckin cop. I looked toward Rob "nope he's not even exaggerating." "Wow, that's crazy." Rob, "and Marcy from up the Pike, near the apple orchard is with child." "Wait, I thought she and Chains broke up?" "They did but apparently it happened before." Jimmy, "or maybe she was doin someone else?" Mia, "Wow." "Yup." they chimed in unison "fuckin crazy stuff," Jimmy shook his head in disbelief." After a while, Mia began to look forward to the three of them walking home together, and hearing all the high school dirt was strangely distracting, almost fun, and best of all united them. As the weeks ticked by, Rob would often appear alone to walk with her. Jimmy's absence was palpable. When she asked Rob where her brother was, Rob made excuses for Jimmy, he had to work or do some chore; sometimes true, but eventually she stopped asking and Rob simply told her Jimmy had gone off to be with his new partying friends.

A school bell chimed bringing Mia back to the moment, the children on the playground lined up like little soldiers and then disappeared from the school yard.

"Come on, Monsieur Frenchie. This whole memory lane thing is getting old."

"Need a distraction yet?" He's got no idea.

Chapter 16

Outside on the curb, Minelli's looked as if time had stood still. A shiver pulsed through Mia's body. She deeply inhaled, trying to muster the emotional strength to enter. *Here goes.* She smiled tightly, entered the diner and quickly sat at the counter. She froze when she heard her name.

"Marianna. Hey, hi. Is that really you? You're all grown up now."

Mia followed the voice behind her but couldn't place the older woman. Her heart thumped wildly. She scanned the place, still waiting for her aunt.

"Your aunt's been waiting all morning for you. She'll be right back; went downstairs to get something. So sorry to hear about your father."

She forced her shoulders down and let her eyes sweep the people from her past. Some of the patrons looked familiar, like long-forgotten characters out of a book—her own childhood drama. Time had passed with the usual signs, but she still remembered most of them. For an instant, she saw them as they'd looked when she was a kid.

"Marianna." Her old name echoed in her ears. She smiled, remembering her mother's unique pitch, "Maryiann-a," rising at the last syllable. Jimmy would always say, "Mare," sounding annoyed even if he wasn't. Robert's voice was huskier, "Marianna," dipping at the end. Her father's voice bellowed, "Marianna, My-Marianna," like it was connected. How strange to hear her old name again.

She'd never tell them that she'd officially changed it to Mia years before; she'd barely told those close to her. Her reasons were too private, too personal to share. She grinned and pushed her emotions away. *I can be Marianna again for the weekend.* She tried to answer the questions being hurled her way.

"So, how've you been? And your brother, Jim?"

"Good, thanks," she finally found space to respond. "Jimmy, he's fine... Working out in Scituate. He'll be around later."

"Is this your dog?"

"Yes, my dog, a Bichon... Mr. French is his name."

"Still living in California?"

"Yes, Lake Tahoe."

"Are you married? Kids?"

"No, not married. No, maybe someday." Her stomach tightened.

"Serious boyfriend?"

"No serious boyfriend."

"Still busy helping people?"

"Yes, Psychologist. Yes, busy with work."

"Do you work with the crazies?"

"No, not crazy, really. Some have tough histories or bad chemistry."

"Well, it was so good to see you."

"Yes, good seeing you, too."

"I'm so sorry for your loss."

"Yeah, it's too bad about my father… Such a shame." *Like he was father of the year.* The little girl in her defended, *he used to be.*

The marriage question hung, and she thought about Rob. *Of course, they remember. I can tell by the way they're watching me, still waiting for me to crack.* Annoyance pulsed. *Their questions are harmless, meant to be polite.* She pasted on a smile and pumped her crossed leg up and down while rearranging the salt and pepper shakers.

Her attention was drawn to the sound of the kitchen door shutting, and she looked up to lock eyes with her aunt. Auntie Rose's face lit up. She set down an oversized metal coffee urn and entered the room, about to take the place by storm. Mia smiled wide as her aunt bounded toward her. Mia's mind automatically flicked to an instant replay of her aunt dropping the coffee pot that last night.

Aunt Rosie's eyes filled with joy and a tinge of something softer. Mia felt a mix of emotions as she walked toward her. Aunt Rose threw up her arms, such an Italian gesture, and embraced Mia.

Same perfume from a lifetime ago.

"Marianna, let me look at you. It's good to see you. What? They don't eat in California? You're so skinny?"

"Aunt Rosie, it's great to see you."

Aunt Rose threw her arms around her again and squeezed hard. "It's been too long." She kissed Mia's cheeks. "Oh, you still got those curls, though? Still beautiful. Got the best from both of 'em. Your mother would be so proud."

Mia's insides burned with affection.

"Marianna's a big shot doctor now," she said to no one in particular.

"Auntie, don't."

"No, don't be so modest. You worked hard, no? Ooh, look at the dog in that sweater." She bent down to make a fuss over

Frenchie. "That hair, it's so 1970's Mod-Squad. Sal, get me a broom handle, and we'll mop the floor." She winked at Sal, standing in the doorway and patted Frenchie's head.

Customers giggled.

"You know I think you're cute, you fluffy thing. How your mother loved dogs." She rolled her eyes to the sky. "Come on."

She stood and took Mia by the waist. *It feels good to be snug against her strong body.*

"We made one of your favorites. You look like skin and bones; we'll change that."

"Hey, kid," Sal greeted. "Good to see you. Sorry about your dad; he was a good guy."

"Hey, Sal. Thanks. Good to see you, too." Mia inhaled deep. "I thought I smelled something good."

Auntie Rose instructed her to sit and brought Mia and Frenchie a heaping bowl of lentil soup. "Just like your dad used to make. It's his recipe."

"He had a recipe?"

"Ain, of course, he did. Whatcha think?" She sat down next to Mia, handing her a loaf of Italian bread.

"Is this Solitro's Sicilian twist?"

"Is the Pope still Catholic? I forgot the grated cheese." She got up from the table.

"It's so good to see you," Mia said, taking in her face.

Aunt Rose patted her hand and nodded. "Hey, it's just you and me today. Caren's little one has an earache—cranky as the devil—and Jo went to help. We'll see them both tomorrow, though. They hope you understand."

"Of course."

"Jimmy still might come by later, but if not, it'll give us a chance to catch up. Just the two of us."

"Great." She already knew he wasn't coming. "This is delicious, really yummy."

"As good as his?"

"Better," Mia mumbled through a mouthful.

"Liar. Your voice still gets high when you lie."

"The place looks good." They'd re-upholstered the old red booths with deep brown. The tabletops were jet black, and the walls were painted mellow tan.

Auntie re-filled Mia's mug.

"Coffee's good. You've always made the best coffee."

"And your mom's coffee… The worst. Like mud."

"Yeah, you and dad used to tell her all the time."

"Cause it was true." Auntie laughed. "She didn't care, though. She wasn't interested in making good coffee."

Mia wished she had known her mother as an adult.

"Come with me." Auntie Rose linked her arm through Mia's. "I want to show you something."

She led Mia to the very back wall of the diner, almost a private room.

"It used to be storage space. It's nice for private functions, birthdays, or events like tomorrow."

Mia inhaled as they approached the back room, near where her mother's last moments had taken place. Her mind spun with the missing details, and Auntie Rose squeezed her arm. Mia hadn't been in that part of the diner since her mother's death.

On the wall was an oversized picture of Robbie, the one from his high school yearbook they always used. He smiled down at her with his familiar face—shiny blue eyes, cocky grin, blonde waves. She scanned the wall, stopping her gaze at a framed letter beside his picture, an acceptance letter from the University of Rhode Island. He'd been accepted into their Environmental Forest Ranger Program.

"The letter came right after you left that summer."

"It would've been such a good match for him." Mia didn't

have words for the sadness she felt. *Rip-off.* Her eyes stung as she fought against tears.

Auntie Rose simply nodded.

The wall had photos of the girls, Mia, all of them as kids and Jimmy and their dad, too.

"Is that The Hill?"

"Yup. In the back, near De Pasquale Square."

There was a photo of the two Aunties smiling and laughing and one of Mia's mom and dad together, looking so happy. *I don't get it.* Mia's eyes pulled to a picture of her aunt.

Mia looked at Auntie Rose. "Is that?"

"Yup, Uncle Rob. We were young then… so in love. Your parents, too."

She looked back at the picture, having only ever seen one other picture of him. She couldn't believe how much Robbie looked like him.

"Saw his face every time I looked at our Robbie."

Our Robbie.

"They finally found him."

"Why didn't you tell me?"

"Ain, you have enough going on with work and now your father… I wasn't gonna bother you."

Mia knew she should've said something but didn't. She froze in place, staring at the massive wall filled with pictures of their family. *What a sad tribute.* Her family had been annihilated, wiped out. Her insides felt numb. She blinked back the tears she'd been fighting while time hung completely still.

"Those were the days," Auntie Rose reminisced. "Had some happy times, huh?"

"Yup, they were fun days."

They stood in silence with their private thoughts.

"Some days, it seems like yesterday," Mia finally offered.

Other days, these people seem like strangers from a different life, one I can barely remember.

"How about dessert?"

"Sure." Mia was relieved to physically move away from the wall. It represented more than their pasts; it documented their loss. She didn't know how to feel about her aunt's sentimentality. *This isn't like her. Has she softened with age?*

Mia excused herself to the bathroom. She shut the door behind her and stared at herself in the mirror. Holding the sink's edge tight, she smelled Rob. Her eyes darted upward.

"Ey, Mare."

Her heart jumped at his voice, and she felt his body against hers.

"Rob." Her eyes started to fill again as she felt him move closer. Their eyes met in the mirror. "It sucks being back here without you."

"Shh, you're doing great."

Her shoulders dropped a smidge, feeling his breath on her ear. She inhaled and dropped her eyes away from his. When she looked back up, he was gone. Disappointment pulsed through her. She washed her face, forcing herself out back out into the diner.

On the counter sat a bowl of grape nut pudding with fresh whipped cream. She attacked it, on a mission. It was more than delicious, and she scraped the bowl clean. Visions of Rob swarmed her mind; she pretended not to notice. Mr. French slumbered next to her on the diner's floor, his body a clump of fur. The last of the late afternoon's customers had gone, and Auntie Rose wiped down the counters and straightened various gadgets.

"Let me help you," Mia offered as she stood. "Anything left to do for tomorrow?"

"We're in good shape, but thanks."

Sal came out of the kitchen, ready to sweep and wash the floor.

"Sal, let me."

Auntie Rose and Sal exchanged a look. "I got it," Sal reassured. "You two beat it." He winked.

"Rosie, see you tomorrow bright and early. Maybe you'll get some work done now that she's finally here, huh? Bye, Marianna. Ey, it's good to see your face around here again. See you in the morning." His face softened.

"See you, Sal, everything was delicious."

The air outside was crisp and refreshing. Mia took a deep breath into her lungs. They walked toward Auntie's house on Tweed Street. It felt surreal to be in the old neighborhood again. She wasn't sure she was ready to see her childhood house up close. A slow dread crept through her, and she silently began counting her steps.

"You okay? Cat got your tongue?"

"No, no, I'm fine."

"The pictures... The wall... It was created to remember all the good. There was a lot."

"I know, it's beautiful. Thank you for showing it to me." She didn't tell her it'd made her sick or that the good memories sometimes felt too far away to remember. She let her eyes sweep the old neighborhood. The tenement houses were smaller than she remembered, but neat and well kept. Several had a pumpkin on the front step, or ghosts hanging from the front shrubs, evidence of young children. The large oak tree on the corner was in full fall display, its burnt orange and red leaves crunched beneath her feet as they walked. The sound pulled her back in time. She and Jimmy hid from the cousins who were scattered about playing hide and seek, he pulled at her arm, "come on, Mare, this way–shh, we can win this." He'd tugged her downward excitedly, knowing the cousins would never find them. It was almost dark outside, but she didn't need to be afraid, Jimmy wouldn't let anything happen. She clocked the house across the street from theirs, a big Victorian style, unlike the others, it had seemed haunted when they were kids. Jimmy, Rob and Jo were dressed as pirates that year, and she and Ca were Tinkerbell. Long johns and gloves peeked from under their costumes.

Jo shone her flashlight on Jimmy.

Jimmy, "the fuck, Jo?"

"We're near your house, your dad's home," she eyed his smoke.

Jim–"yea cause he should talk, or you for that matter."

Jo stomped out her butt, "whatever, don't cry to me when he kills you."

Rubbing her hands together, "I'm freezing, Jim, I'm just going home now."

"Mare, wait, the haunted house has the best candy, full length snickers."

She ran for home, over her shoulder: "just get me one."

Auntie's voice pulled her back to the moment. "Kid, you're just like your mother. Can't lie to save your life."

"Yeah, between Dad's death and being back, it's been a little overwhelming."

Auntie Rose took Mia's hand. "Means you're still normal."

Chapter 17

The lights automatically popped on as they approached the garage. Auntie Rose pressed a button, and the door began to rise, revealing a yellow punch buggy convertible.

"How cute is that! I love those cars."

Aunt Rosie glanced down. "Marianna, we've been together since last winter."

"Who?"

Aunt Rosie looked back up.

"You and Sal!?"

"The car was a present."

Mia had heard it all. *My sixty-five-year-old aunt is having an affair with her recently widowed boss?* Sal's wife of fifty years had just died, and he'd bought her a convertible as a present. Mia bit her lower lip, trying hard not to laugh.

"The car is yours?"

"It is. Don't look so stunned, sweetie. What, you think people my age don't still carry on like fools?"

"No, no, it's not that. I just never knew you to have a boyfriend.

I'm just surprised." She watched her aunt's face, trying hard to compose herself.

"Auntie, good for you. Really, I'm happy for you. You deserve to be happy."

"Thank you, honey; it means a lot coming from you. 'Course, there's not that many people who know. It hasn't been long enough."

"Oh, 'course. I won't say anything."

"Come inside. It's a bit of a complicated story."

Aren't they all.

Auntie's house is quiet, neat as a pin and smelled exactly the same. Looking at the kitchen, she expected to see Rob come around the corner. She exhaled deep and felt Auntie Rose touch her arm.

"You okay? Being here?"

"Course, fine. Where's Ca?"

"She moved back in with him."

"But I thought…"

She poured two brandys.

"Go sit; you look tired?"

Mia sat back on the couch, trying to adjust to being back in his house. She tried to concentrate on her aunt. Between her relationship with Sal and finding Uncle's body, Auntie sure had her own stuff going on. The wall made more sense; she was trying to move on. Mia sipped the brandy, grateful for its strong medicinal properties. Aunt Rosie raised her glass.

"Even though the circumstances stink, here's to your being back here."

"Thank you."

"Mare, I hope you don't think any less of me for what I am going to tell you. You know I hate liars. Me and Sal have had a friendly flirtation going for many years. Now, I know I look like an old lady to you, but things don't change that much as you get older. One day, you'll know what I mean. Anyway, last winter, I got a surprise visit from the State Police. As you might expect, I had been dreading but waiting on that call for many years. Well, anyway, I was at the diner and in stroll two Staties. My stomach sank. One of 'em was Tom McKearnin's boy. Remember him?"

She nodded; he was Jimmy's age. Her eyes pulled toward the hallway that adjoined the two houses.

"They asked me to come down to the morgue to identify the remains of a body. Thirty years is a long time to be all alone. I mean… without a man. I never met anyone that could even compare to him. Over the years, both your mother and your father were dear friends to me. They helped me raise the kids and everything. You remember.

"But it's not the same as having a man. Don't get me wrong, I couldn't have made it without them, though. Really, either one of 'em. But, when your mother died…" She paused briefly. "Your father… He was never the same. The way it happened…"

The way it happened?

"I had no one left to turn to. Sal, he was there for me during those days. First with your mother and then when Robbie died. Those were some lonely days for me."

"I can only imagine how it feels to lose a son." They sat in silence for a beat.

"He was kind and paid attention to me. I knew he was married; we never took our relationship beyond that. We were good friends; it never turned physical. In fact, I thought I proved your father wrong. He thought men and women couldn't be friends without it turning." She made a face. "Guess he wasn't that far off. I really believed we were just special friends that could be there for each other without anything more. And it went like that for years and years. Anyway, when I went to identify the body, Sal offered to come with me. He even told Emma he was taking me.

"You know, after all those years, I figured I'd be fine finally getting confirmation that he was dead. I knew it, anyway. When they pulled back the sheet, he was barely recognizable. All I could see was my life, all of it—the hours at work, coming home sleeping alone, my kids growing up without their father, how that'd affect them. As I stood there, I thought about you and Jimmy, too. No mother, your dad away and no uncle. The loss, the pain–it was all too much. What was it all for? He thought winning was fun, gave 'em a thrill. Stupid ass. We all lost..."

Mia had never heard her aunt confirm the rumors about her uncle's gambling problem.

"I was mad. I mean, really pissed off at him. He missed everything. On the ride home, I crumbled, fell apart, I guess. Sal consoled me. He drove me back to this house, and we were together. You know..."

"Auntie, it's okay. You don't have to explain anything to me."

"Let me finish." She eyed Mia sternly, and Mia tried not to smile.

"It was amazing. I had let myself think about being with him from time to time—you know, imagined us together—but always wrote it off as silly. It was better than I imagined. He made me feel alive. I felt passion again. It had been so long," she whispered. "I didn't know I was so dead inside or that I had even missed anything. Isn't that sad?"

Her words echoed in Mia's head as she watched her foot bop up and down.

"We're in love. I guess we had been for a long time. We both tried to deny it. It wasn't right; he had a sick wife and all. Imagine that, how strange life is?" She smiled for a minute before her eyes clouded over. "What happened with your mother made more sense to me then. The really awful part was the timing. We both knew Emma was dying of cancer. She'd been diagnosed the year before. So there we were. I helped him take care of her.

Poor thing was so sick. Such a shame. We waited to begin our life together. We were waiting for her to die. Doesn't that sound horrible?"

Mia hesitated. "You and Sal are good people. I know that." Mia paused. "The timing part is tough, I agree." Mia was distracted by what Auntie had said about her mother, but she didn't want to interrupt.

Mia let the complexities of Auntie's story set in. After a time, Mia asked, "Did she know about the two of you?"

"No. Why strip her of her dignity? We cut out being physical until after; it wasn't right. We knew better. And, of course, we felt guilty about that one night."

"Emma was a nice lady. She'd want Sal to be happy. The timing might piss her off, but hey, I won't tell if you don't. I think it was respectful to wait."

"You think?"

"Yes, she'd want him to be happy in the end. She may've even forgiven the timing, eventually."

"Would you?"

"Well, I wouldn't go that far. I'm not nearly as nice or wise as old Emma."

"Life is crazy."

"To love and really sucky timing."

They moved to the overstuffed couch. Mia felt relaxed thanks to the brandy, but she was spent. The living room was small and comfortable, just like she remembered. The furniture and flooring had changed, but not much else. The rugs had been ripped out to show the maple hardwoods beneath. The walls were still a pale yellow and went nicely with the cranberry furniture. It felt cozy. It even smelled the same, which made her stomach clench.

Mr. French seemed right at home, too. He curled up in a tight ball in the chair opposite the couch and snored the evening away. He was oblivious to their conversation and the deep sense of nostalgia that burned the back of Mia's throat. Of course, he was an expert at keeping secrets. He'd been present for much worse stories than Auntie's.

"You look happy, lighter." Mia smiled. "Love agrees with you."

"Marianna, I've never felt freer in my whole life. All I can think of is your father and his silly phrases, "What a clear head she has."

Mia smiled. "He did have some unique sayings. I'm glad for you, for both of you."

"I tried to tell the girls, but they don't understand. Or they don't want to. Caren's not right still; her own relationship problems. And with the kids and being pregnant again, she's so busy trying to talk herself into thinking she's doing the right thing staying with their father, she can't handle much else. We tried having them stay next door, but the fights were too awful. She still won't leave him after all he's done. I couldn't watch it. It was easier to rent to a stranger.

"And Joanne, well, you know Jo, her rigid thinking. She's tough, that one; always has been. She thinks it's too soon for him to have somebody... Probably thinks I'm awful. If she only knew... Jo only sees things in black and white. It's her way."

Auntie's eyes clouded.

"I tried to raise them right. Maybe I worked too much, was away too many hours." She patted Mia's hand. "I knew I could tell you. My Marianna, you're just like your mother. I could tell her anything, and she'd never make me feel ashamed."

"Thank you for telling me. I'm happy for you, truly. The girls will come around. Maybe once they see how happy you are."

Auntie sat up straight. "Enough about me, carrying on like an old selfish hag, tell me about you. How's Rory? Is he really gay, or are you guys, well, you know?"

Vintage Aunt Rosie, back in charge. Mia was flattered she'd shown such vulnerability, even for a minute.

"Sorry to disappoint you, but he's still very gay. And he's well. Actually, I don't know what me and Frenchie would do without him."

"Yeah, he's been a good friend to you; that's so important. I still miss talking to your mother all these years later. What a friggin' rip-off to die young. Unreal. When me and Sal started up, I tried to talk to her at the grave. Needed to tell someone. Stupid. It felt empty; she wasn't really there, you know?"

Mia nodded, beginning to dread the following day, the whole charade. A few minutes passed and Mia could feel her aunt assessing her.

"Marianna, I'm so proud of you, honey. With all you've dealt with, you turned out beautifully. They would be proud. I know I am."

"Thanks."

"I have something for you. It's from Robbie."

"A present from Rob?"

Aunt Rose produced a small velvet box. "Listen…"

Mia shifted position, confusion washing through her.

"I meant to give it to you before. Of course, he planned to give it to you himself, but… I didn't give it to you because I thought it might interfere with your future. When you graduated, I thought about giving it to you then, but seeing you and Ror… Well, it didn't seem right."

Mia set down her drink, took the small box and opened it slowly. Inside was a single, heart-shaped diamond. The weirdest mix of feelings settled in her gut as she imagined Rob down on one knee.

"What are you doing down there, Rob?"

"I'm asking you to marry me. Are you gonna answer or what?"

"Marianna," Auntie began. "I hope you understand my

reasons for not giving this to you sooner. I know the timing isn't great, but who knows when you'll be back or if we'll be alone again."

"No, I'm thrilled to have it."

"I had lost one child, and I wanted you to be happy with someone. What happened to Robbie was terrible, tragic. Not something a young girl should see. And after your mother…"

"Where did you find it?"

Rosie looked down. "His coat pocket."

Mia tried it on, the sadness overwhelming. She quickly took it off and stuffed it back in the box.

"Life is crazy, huh." She fought tears.

Needing a distraction, she ushered Frenchie to the slider.

"He needs to go out. I understand, really." Mia shuffled inside her pocketbook and pulled out a stack of papers. "Work, I gotta call Ror; get an update and think about heading back to Providence."

Auntie Rose stood. "Tomorrow's gonna be a long one… No one's staying here, not even me. You can use the car and house until you leave. Ror said your ticket was open… Maybe you'll get to visit? See everyone?"

Anxiety washed through her. "Thanks. I'll go get my stuff from the hotel."

"Good, you can drop me back at the diner. Gotta get some stuff ready." She placed the keys on the counter. "This is for the house, and this here's for the car. We'll be by to get you around 8 a.m." Auntie Rose hugged Mia tight. "I wrote Sal's cell on the pad by the phone."

Chapter 18

Mia dropped her aunt off at the diner and headed to the Westin. She turned up the radio in an attempt to dull the ache that throbbed through her heart. *Rob bought me a ring.*

Entering her room, she began stuffing her papers into an oversized folder and grabbed her packed suitcase. As an after-thought, she grabbed the vase before letting the door slide shut.

Her cell rang while she shuffled through some work papers at Auntie's kitchen table. The number was unfamiliar, but it had a Rhode Island exchange. *If it's Jimmy, I'll see him in the morning.* She'd had enough of the past for one day. Her phone dinged with the voicemail chime, and she pressed play to hear her brother's voice.

"Hey, Mare, It's me. I had to work late. Guess now we're officially orphans. Ha. I know it's bad to joke 'bout the dead, but you know about me and rules… Anyways, seeing how you're always early, and I'm not, maybe you could save your favorite brother a front-row spot tomorrow at church? Unless you're afraid of getting hit by a lightning bolt. Ey, I'm sure you're thrilled being back. I remember how much you love church... See you in the a.m."

"We'll see," she mumbled aloud, all too used to his empty promises. Despite herself, she gave a slight smile at his familiar sarcasm. She pressed delete and then speed-dialed Rory.

"Hey, how the hell are you?" he answered.

"Never better." She felt herself exhale at his voice. "Spent the day with Aunt Rosie."

"Yeah, good ol' Rosie. They don't make 'em like that anymore, huh?"

"I know." She smiled. "Ror, it was so weird seeing the diner again. I'm at her house now."

"Strange, huh?"

"I can't even tell you." She dismissed her thoughts about the ring.

"Your cousins there, too?"

"No, Ca's little one got sick. I'll see them tomorrow at the big service." Her stomach tightened, and she inhaled.

"Did Jimmy surface yet?"

"Sort of... He just left me a message. Says he'll be there. Guess I'll see everyone in the morning. We may get hail, an early snow storm, perhaps."

"Mee, you sound alright."

"I'm hangin' in."

"So, your message said you ran into the guy from the plane?"

"I did. He was with some interesting characters."

"I'm shocked."

"Stop it. One comes from a very well-known family around here."

Costa's name spun in her brain.

"You there?"

"Yeah, what a creep."

"What do you think the plane guy was doing with him? Secret lover's, maybe?"

Mia snorted out a giggle. "No, he's very straight. Said they were business associates… He sent flowers to my room as a sort of apology for the mob guys' bad manners, inviting me for coffee."

"Really, huh."

"That's it? Just huh?"

"Yeah. I'm not sure if it's creepy or sweet? You're not going, are you?"

"No, don't worry. I won't have time. Tomorrow'll be busy, and I'm probably coming home Sunday night."

"That's not even a long weekend."

"Yeah, no. All set with Ghostville."

He laughed. "I guess Rock'll have to find another Adrian… So to speak. God, Rhode Island's such a strange little place. Before you ask, everyone's still as crazy as ever."

"Ror…"

"Mee, they're fine. Good luck tomorrow."

She hung up, feeling slightly less anxious.

A little after midnight, Mia cracked open her suitcase to change into her PJs and an old, oversized T-shirt Rory had given her years ago. She pulled out her navy pant suit and hung it on the bathroom door. She grabbed a blanket and sat on the couch, propping herself up with a pillow. Her mind spun from the day's events.

Providence looks completely different. Auntie's with Sal; she has a VW bug. Mia stifled a chuckle. *"He made me feel alive again. I didn't even know I was dead inside."* Her stomach tightened. *I'm on Rob's couch… I'll see everyone at the service… He bought me a ring… Auntie feels bad for me.*

A few hours later, a streak of sun coming through the window lit her face. Cracking her eyes slightly, she watched Frenchie's furry body rise and fall. Nervously, her eyes darted to her cell. She exhaled. *It's only six-thirty.* She sat up and rolled her neck.

By seven, she'd showered, dressed and was ready to roll. She walked down the street to the diner, knowing her aunt had already been up for hours.

"Hey, we would've picked you up," Sal mentioned as she walked through the door.

"Neh, I need coffee. Felt good to walk."

Auntie emerged from the back wearing a chocolate brown skirt. Her solemn expression caught Mia off guard, but her features softened when she saw Mia.

"Hey, good morning! Coffee's over there."

"Thanks. Let me help set up, do something."

Aunt Rose handed Mia a stack of paper products and nodded toward the back of the room. Glad to have a task, she walked them to a table in a far corner covered in platters of coffee cakes, muffins and bagels. Auntie set down several baskets of rolls, and Sal brought in a tray of homemade biscuits. Mia's lower lip pulled upward.

"He'd really appreciate all this."

"He'd-a done the same thing for me if things'd turned out different."

Mia was amazed she'd remained loyal to him after everything. He'd killed her best friend.

"Let's go," Sal said. "It's time."

They headed to the church in Sal's black LTD, three minutes up the street and around the corner. It was a typical, old-school Catholic Church with marble and stained glass. The all too familiar scent mixed with incense loomed heavy in the air. She'd come to equate it with death. The three were ushered to the front pew. She inhaled deep and breathed out quick, short breaths.

A moment later, her cousins walked in unison up the aisle. Jo squeezed Mia hard in a bear hug.

"Hey, cuz. It takes a cold body to get you back here, huh? Whatever. It's friggin' good to see you."

Jo pulled back. "Rosie." She smirked.

Rosie rolled her eyes at Jo's jeans.

Mia bit down a smile, taking in her cousin's familiar face. Her sapphire eyes crinkled in return. She had short, dark hair and looked years younger than forty-two.

"Good to see you, Jo."

"Ey, sorry about the old man."

Caren touched Mia's sleeve. "Maria— Mia. Sorry about your dad. I took the kids to see him just a few weeks ago. He looked good, seemed healthy. Guess you never know."

Mia fiddled with the hymn book in front of her.

Jo rolled her eyes toward Caren.

"Glad you're here, though." Her bright eyes shone with tears.

"Thanks, Ca."

Caren's belly poked through her print sundress. Her skin looked chalky, and her eyes had dark circles underneath. *Life's been hard on her.*

"Congratulations! How are the kids?" Mia managed to ask.

"Good, thanks to her help." Caren smiled and nodded toward her sister.

"Yeah, yeah. Build me a plaque."

Mia noticed the place had started to fill up, and she scanned the crowd, surprised by the amount of people present. Some looked familiar, most didn't. She'd done this before—too many times. She stared blankly ahead, pushing away her thoughts and feelings. The heavy organ began to play. Men rolled the casket down to the front. *My dad's in there—the one from before.*

During the service, her focus faded in and out. It was fairly short, not exactly sweet. Her emotions only made an appearance at the end of the service when the priest said her father would take his proper spot in heaven because God is all-forgiving. Her mother's face loomed before her. She wondered if her aunt had arranged for the priest to say this. He had to know the circumstances. She looked around, wondering if anyone remembered or cared what'd happened to her mother. *He gets to go to heaven?* Her heart froze and re-broke for her mother. Jo squeezed her hand.

"You're not gonna go all reality show and pass out, are you?" Jo whispered.

Mia shook her head and quickly swiped away the tears leaking from her eyes. For the first time, she noticed an empty spot saved for her brother. *Still empty.*

The priest swayed metal-encased incense near and around the casket as he finished the ritual of death. The official guys rolled the casket out the front entrance. She remembered Jimmy's eyes silently dripping with tears while he and five others carried Rob's casket out that hot summer day. She pushed the image away.

The music switched, and she felt her heart swell with thoughts of her mother. She struggled to find compassion for the father in the box, the one from after, but only found an eerie nothing.

"Think they go get stoned out back now?" Jo heckled. Her face is tear-streaked, too.

They walked out of the church together. Mia started to breathe again once her feet hit the cement. She hadn't noticed she'd been holding it. The fresh air felt good on her face and in her lungs.

"Hey, sis. Sorry, I missed my front-row spot. Was running late."

He hugged her tight. She exhaled into him despite herself and instinctually hugged him back. He smelled like the same old Jimmy—soap, cologne, and fresh air. Stepping back, she took in his face. It was weathered but still handsome. He wore a navy suit that made his eyes pop. *They still twinkle with mischief.* His hair was long and reminded her of Rob's.

"Well, well," Jo started in. "Just glad you didn't sit near me. There's still a chance, though, Mare, move away quick."

Jimmy cocked a half grin and pecked her cheek. "Always good to see you, Joanne. Ey, what's with the hair? Tryin' out for American Idol?"

"Fuck off. I needed a change."

"Come on, I'll drive."

"We actually need to show up, though."

"Yeah, yeah. I'm here, right?"

They followed him down the cement steps and across the street to a beat-up red jeep.

"Sorry, it's not fancy, but she'll get us there."

"Yeah, just how late is the question." Jo slipped into the passenger's seat and rolled down the window to light up a Marlboro Light.

Rob's brand.

"Got a light for your favorite cousin?" Jimmy grinned as he pulled away from the curb.

"Hello!? Pregnant back here."

"Yeah, well… A little too late to change that."

Caren turned to Mia. "Don't mind her; she's cranky. Hasn't gotten stoned in over six months."

"Really? That's great."

Jimmy caught Mia's eye in the rearview and mouthed, "Wow, six whole months."

Jo punched his arm, and Mia smiled back awkwardly.

"Dr. Capaldi, everything going good out West with the whackos and Ror?" Despite Jimmy's word choice, pride shimmered in his eyes.

"Yes, everything's great." For half a minute, he was her big brother again, and her heart swelled with love for him. When the feeling passed, she was happy to be hidden behind her sunglasses.

When they pulled up to the diner, Jimmy stubbed out his cigarette on the bottom of his work boot and threw his suit jacket across the back seat. His dress shirt had white and blue stripes and pulled along his back and arms. He had the build of someone who worked as a physical laborer.

"Pregnant ladies first." He held the door open wide.

He paused briefly before walking into the diner, but once he entered, he instantly became the life of the party. He returned greetings and funny retorts like he was doing standup. Mia had forgotten how likable and engaging he could be when he wasn't drinking.

Jimmy headed over to a table of guys that looked vaguely familiar, but Mia wasn't feeling quite as friendly. Before she could hide in a back booth, Auntie Rose caught her and dragged her around the room to talk to various people who'd known her parents—before. They were all very sorry for her loss. *Original.* She worried that her thoughts were transparent. *My loss happened years ago.* She finally broke away from Auntie Rose and found a back booth. She was enjoying her solitude when Jimmy slid in across from her with a heaping plate of food.

"Aunt Rosie can still cook, huh? I don't think she made enough food, though." He chuckled.

"I know; it's great." Mia's leg swung up and down under the table.

"Weird being back here, huh?"

"It is. Auntie says works going well?"

"It's steady." He took a bite out of his sandwich. "Steady keeps me on the straight and narrow. Well… For the most part, anyways."

"I'm glad for you."

"Mare, sorry I didn't show up for your final graduation. Couldn't get… No excuses, doesn't matter. I shoulda been there, and I shoulda already told you."

Mia sat stunned.

"You guys hiding?" Jo asked out of nowhere.

"Yeah," they replied in unison.

Maybe he's really still under there somewhere.

"So, how's Rory?" Jo asked, setting down her coffee cup. "And your French mutt, we gonna meet him?"

"Ror's great. Sal went to get Mr. French."

"Mr. French, how gay is that?"

"It was your brother's favorite show." Jimmy smirked at Jo, then turned back to Mia. "How long you stayin'?"

"Probably until Sunday night." Jimmy, Rory and Tony were the only people who got the Family Affair reference, but Jimmy was the only one who knew it was Rob's favorite show.

"We should meet for breakfast. Catch up."

"Ey," Jo interrupted. "Don't go making promises you can't keep."

He ignored her. "I'll be there." His voice sounded sincere.

Mia was tempted to tell him she had other plans, but she heard herself reply, "Ok, sure."

He shot Jo a victorious glance and rambled off directions to a small breakfast place in Scituate. Mia couldn't believe she'd agreed to meet him or that he'd apologized for pulling a no-show at her graduation. *It only took him seven years.*

A few minutes later, he scraped his plate clean and excused himself. "Gotta go to work. See you in the a.m., Mare. Later, Jo."

He kissed Auntie on the cheek and shook a few hands on his way out. Auntie caught Mia's eyes from across the room, and her face softened for a quick minute.

Jo got up, grabbed a bottle of wine and set it down on the table.

"Didn't want to tempt your brother. He seemed to be sober today."

"Yes, he did."

Caren plopped herself in the booth. "I wish," she said, eyeing the wine as she sipped her coffee. "I have a few minutes before I have to get the kids. Mia, we'll see you Sunday at 2. The kids will be so excited to finally meet you. Tell Jimmy to stop by, too. I hear you two are meeting in the morning."

"I'll bring dessert."

Jo and Mia helped clear the tables, take out the trash and disassemble the table. Mia placed the oversized picture of her father face down on the countertop. It was one of him standing in front of his rig at their house. She ignored the ache in her heart for that father, that time in her life.

When Jo left, Mia hid in the kitchen, pretending to straighten up. *I'm all done with people. I'll meet my brother in the morning and have lunch with Auntie and the girls on Sunday, and that will be that.*

Mia walked up the street away from the diner, glad to be done with the charade. Once back inside her aunt's house, she changed into jeans and sneakers and threw her suit on top of her suitcase. She needed a change of scenery. It was a warm fall afternoon, so she decided to sightsee for the remainder of the day.

Chapter 19

Adjusting her mirrors, Mia glanced toward Mr. French. He looked like the Red Baron with his fur flying in the wind.

"Ok, Monsieur French, first stop, coffee. And this time, a place with nice wait staff."

She headed to route 10, south toward Cranston. She got off at the Reservoir Avenue exit and found an Italian bakery about a mile down the road.

A nice older man greeted her as she entered the bakery, "May I help you?"

For a second, she thought of Pasquale's kindness. She ordered a large vanilla-flavored coffee and returned to the car. Pulling away from the curb, she switched on the radio and hummed along before easing the car onto Cranston Street. Spotting the familiar gates, her gut tightened. It felt like the Grim Reaper had just exposed himself to her. She exhaled and counted her breaths. Two… Three… Four…

Mia always envied her patients, who talked about how merely being near their church made them feel peaceful and happy. *I wish…*

She rolled in, lowered the radio and held her breath. She eyed Frenchie in his favorite nap position.

"I am coming back as you, my furry little friend."

The creepy, ornate gates loomed in her rearview. She hedged the car along slowly, looking for row G. When she'd first come to the graveyard to bury her mom, she told herself G stood for God or Goddess. She pulled the car over to the curb, thinking it'd be easier to find if she walked. She got out and started scanning the rows. It had been such a long time since she'd visited St. Mary's. There were so many more graves. She tried to remember the last time she'd been here. *It must've been pretty soon after mom died because Jimmy hadn't left yet.*

An anxious, young Mia tried to read the letters of each row.

"There it is! There's G!" She sounded strangely excited.

Her dad's eyes looked vacant, and her brother's were red and hazy.

A sharp sound caught her attention and brought her back to the present. She lifted her eyes to see a crew of men working the dirt across the street from where she'd been walking. *Making more room.*

She kept moving until she found her mother's grave. The gravestone was soft plum with a glossy finish and read, "In loving memory, Mia M. Capaldi. Born June 1, 1950 - Died March 18, 1984. Gone to rest, I did not die. I live with the risen Lord. Rest in peace." She touched the stone's cold surface.

"Mom, it's me, Marianna. I think about you all the time. I'm sorry I don't come to visit; as you know, I live in Lake Tahoe. It's pretty there. When I found out about Dad, it made me miss you and Rob all over again."

Despite the coffee, Mia felt drained.

"I became a psychologist. I love working, seeing my patients get well. It gives me such a good feeling. Auntie thinks you'd be proud. I have my issues, but I think you'd like me and my life, for the most part. My best friend Rory thought I should come home for Dad's service, but I didn't want to. I think you understand that." Her nose burned. "I know I'm not supposed to stand by your grave and cry, but I can't help it."

She dropped her head to see two wet spots where her tears had formed small indentations in the dirt. She fought the urge to count them.

"I wish you were still here. Aunt Rosie's been so good to me, but it's not the same. No one can replace you."

She sat at the edge of the gravestone, silent. She finished her coffee and closed her eyes tight for a moment. The smell of autumn was heavy in the air. The wind rustled through the trees as if her mother were present. The funeral poem floated back to her. Its message clearer but somehow sadder… Then it was gone, too. She opened her eyes slowly as an old disappointment settled in her gut.

"I wish I could hear your voice again, but I know that's not going to happen. Hopefully, Rob's right, and you're out there somewhere." She swept her eyes up to the sky and sighed.

She tried to take in the simple beauty of nature, but like most things, it was fleeting.

"I know it's not going change anything, but I need to know what really happened all those years ago. I don't know why, but it just feels like it's time for me to know the whole truth."

She stood and brushed off the back of her jeans.

"Bye, mom. I still love you more than anyone. And despite the priest's words today, I remember."

She found her way back to the car, and Frenchie's wagging tail felt like a band aid. Tears welled as she pet him.

Mia decided to take the long way back to Auntie's house. She drove aimlessly for a while to let her emotions settle. It'd been a long morning, and her visit to the graveyard hadn't helped her mood. She turned onto Oaklawn Avenue and was pleasantly surprised to see that Del's Lemonade Stand was still open.

The building was still a shack-like structure, typical of seasonal stands in Rhode Island. She parked the car and attached Frenchie's leash. Along with traditional lemonade, they offered several berry flavors. The food menu was the same: hotdogs, twizzlers and pretzels. She ordered the largest lemonade size available, along with pretzels to dunk.

She smiled. Del's had been a part of the before. It was as lemony and delicious as ever. She glanced sideways at Mr. French, who seemed to enjoy his, too.

Not ready to return to her aunt's house, she drove around Garden City, through Dean Estates and finally, Meshanticut Lake. Her heart ached. Being back there made her miss Rob, the way he'd always made her feel safe.

Amazing. The lake looks exactly the same. The trees had nearly reached their peak. The leaves glowed with varying shades of yellows, reds, and browns. The wind blew them to the ground like vibrant dots of paint. Despite the mild day, nature was preparing for the next season. The thought of the winter made her nauseous.

On her way out, she spotted a family of ducks parading up the embankment. As they waddled closer, she threw a handful of pretzels out the window. She watched in amusement as they flocked in a wild frenzy.

She stifled a yawn, emotionally drained. The week had more than caught up to her. She needed sleep.

Chapter 20

Mia pulled the buggy into the garage and sat for several minutes. *Isn't life strange? I'm sitting in Rob's garage, in Auntie's punch buggy.* She never thought she'd return. She let Frenchie out and heaved herself out of the car and in through the side door. On the kitchen table was a note from Auntie.

"Me and Sal left you a few things in the fridge. Call me. Want to talk to you about this morning."

Mia headed straight for the fridge to check out the goods. *A few things?* The fridge was jam-packed with containers and baggies. Unable to resist, she opened each one, tasting it with her fingers. On the counter sat two bottles of wine and a large loaf of Italian bread. *Aunt Rosie.* She dropped a small piece of bread for Mr. French.

She walked down the hallway to Rob's closed door and inhaled as she touched the knob. Swinging the door open, she noticed very little had changed. *Everything has changed.* A picture of them together at the falls drew her to Rob's bureau. She ignored the burn in the back of her throat. Reaching her suitcase, she pulled out her PJs and the ring. She tossed her jeans aside and put on her tee shirt. The ring slid on easily.

Examining it, she walked out to the kitchen to open some wine. She filled a water glass and then walked back into Rob's room, thinking about how things might've been different. She pulled out the top dresser drawer and picked out a few articles of clothing, smelling each piece. Her stomach sank at the faint hint of his earthy aroma.

Enough. She shut the drawer with a slam. *I need sleep. Enough of memory lane; it's been a long day.* She reached for the rest of her wine, sucked it down and placed the glass on the floor beside her before crawling into bed. *Rob's bed.* Frenchie crawled in by her side, did his little circle routine and snuggled up against her. Her last thoughts before drifting off were fragmented and torn. *Being in Rhodey feels shitty. Seeing Jimmy in the morning, ask him details. I miss Rob. Maybe there's an after-life. Mom… What's that sound?*

Ping, clink, clink… "Marianna, Mare, it's me."

She struggled to open her eyes. She glanced at Frenchie. "Where the hell are your instincts, dog?"

He didn't wake from his slumber.

Stupid dog! She threw off the covers as her irritation pulsed and stomped toward the window.

"Marianna, let me in."

She stood frozen in place.

"Marianna, you gonna let me in or what?"

Alright, I'll play along. "Rob? Is that you? What are you doing out there?"

"I didn't want to wake anyone."

"There's only me and Frenchie here." Relief streamed through her. *This is a dream, whew.*

Rob smiled warmly. "You gonna let me in, or you gonna make me stay out here all night?" His eyes danced with amusement.

She walked to the back porch. *Funny, I don't feel like I'm sleeping, though.* She poked at her arms. Unlocking the door, Robert stepped in. She touched his face; it felt prickly but warm.

"I can't believe it's you. You're really standing here. This feels so different from all my other dreams. You never really looked like you."

"You're still beautiful." His eyes were full of emotion as he glanced down at my finger. "You found the ring; I was hoping you would. That night, when I was lying there, I tried to tell you, to say it, but it was too late. I couldn't talk anymore... I mean, I was talking, but no-one seemed to hear me."

"No. Aunt Rosie did... She gave it to me." She stared at him hard. "Who are you?" Fear pulsed through her. "This isn't funny. In fact, it's very cruel."

"No, no. It's me, really." He put his arms out. "It's okay, don't be scared. I'd never hurt you." He moved a curl away from her face. "Our pact... No one else could know about it. Remember? 'I'll love you foreva, even after death,' we said. And if someone tries to take you from me, I'd..."

"Hunt them down." This dream felt too real for her. "Okay, I wanna wake up now. I'm all done with this. Dream over, all fucking set."

"No, Mare. It's me."

She felt outside her own body. "It's you."

He moved closer and hugged her tight to him.

"Please tell me this isn't a dream. You feel so real." She touched his face again. "This is exactly how I imagined being near you would feel." She squeezed her eyes shut. "I've dreamed about this so many times. But this time feels real."

"I'm here, baby. It's me." He kissed the top of her head.

She took a deep breath, inhaling his familiar scent. "This feels too good to be true," she spoke into his chest.

"Oh my God." She pulled away suddenly, her body filled with

dread. *What the hell am I doing? This can't be.* "There's no white light; I feel normal. Was I in an accident? Rory will have to take Frenchie, call my patients. I don't feel any different, though. I don't hurt anywhere. I actually feel pretty good. I don't think I care if this is what dead feels like." Her heart raced. *Maybe I'll get to see my mom again.*

Robert watched her smiling warmly, patiently. She had seen that same look from him so many times. He didn't say anything, just shook his head and held her waist tighter.

"How can this be? You look just like you used to; how is it possible? People don't age when they die? I have so many questions. That last night... You could still hear me? I was so scared; you left me all alone. I felt like it was my fault. If I hadn't used the bathroom or taken so long..." She became overwhelmed by crushing grief.

"No, no." He shook his head hard. "No one's fault. You know I would never choose to leave you... Ever. Never! It was just my time. That's how it works."

"Rob, am I dead?"

"No, sweetie, you're still very much alive." His face looked saddened by this truth. He touched the outline of her face. "Come on, we don't have that much time. Only until daylight." He reached for her hands and pulled her toward his room.

At the bed, she stopped short. "This isn't possible, even though I want it to be."

"You have to trust me... Don't be scared."

She slowly backed away from their embrace.

"Mare, I've watched you for so many years. I'm so excited to be with you, actually touch you. I'd die again just to have this moment, one more chance to touch you." His eyes were filled with love.

"It really is you... I can't believe..."

They embraced, and hot tears stung her eyes as they streamed down her cheeks. Rob's face was wet with tears, too. She felt a surge of joy and pain; it'd been so long. Then, just like old times, her tears and pain turned quickly to a bubbling passion.

She wrapped her arms around his neck. "I've dreamed of being with you like this for years."

"Me too. I'm here now." He lifted her, pulling her tight against his body.

He kissed her face, her hair, her neck, stopping behind her ear. He undressed her frantically, ripping off her t-shirt and pulling her sweats down.

"Still gorgeous." He felt her body with hungry hands, then with his tongue. His lips moved to each breast while his hands worked magic down below.

"Just like I remember," she moaned.

He knelt down in front of her, tasting her with subtle circler motions.

"R-ooob," she ran her hands through his thick blonde locks. "Feels so good." She tore at his clothes. "You need a turn. I want to touch you."

She started kissing his face, then moved down his bare chest. His body felt young and firm, beautiful. She kissed his entire chest, then moved down toward his waist. He was more than ready. She moved back up to kiss him.

"I can't believe this…"

His face was wild with passion for her. He pulled her toward him hard, and together they lay entwined. They were one again, in and out gently, then with wild, unbridled force.

A final thrust sent electric spasms rocking through her entire being. They clung to each other, bodies damp and exhausted.

"I don't want to waste time sleeping. You'll go then, and I can't bear it." She looked into his eyes. "To wake and learn this was only a dream…" One tear slid down her face. "I'm just closing my eyes for a minute. Please, don't go." She felt herself relax, melt into him.

"Mare, whenever you wish for me, I'll come back. Until then, I'll be watching from up there… Never that far from you."

"I just want you to hold me forever."

He kissed her lightly on the lips. "No one could eve-a love you like I do. We're special; you know that, right?"

She was too tired to answer him but knew it was the truth.

"Until the next time, my sweet girl." He whispered her name softly, and she felt a hint of a kiss.

Chapter 21

Frenchie's furry face lay next to Mia's on the pillow. She pushed herself up on one elbow and quickly scanned her surroundings. Her stomach sank. *A dream. Only a dream.* Her disappointment felt like a physical blow. She glanced toward the side of the bed for her cell. It was eight a.m. She dragged herself out of bed. The house felt as cold as her insides.

She showered and put on a pair of faded Levi's with a red fleece sweater. She stuffed the ring back in her suitcase but couldn't get Rob's words out of her head. *"Mare, you found it. I'd die again just to be here with you... Nobody loves you like me."*

She felt the sensation of pleasure from being physically close to him; it left her feeling terribly alone. Her thoughts brought a mixture of sadness and disappointment that made it hard to breathe. She hurried Mr. French out of the house and into the car, knowing full well her brother was never on time.

The Coffee Bean was situated in charming Scituate Village. She remembered it from another life. She exhaled and walked up the front steps of the small country bakery. *One... Two...*

She found a table toward the back, ordered a flavored coffee and waited.

At ten o'clock, the waitress tentatively approached the table for the second time. "Would you like some more coffee? Or to order food?"

Mia had been waiting for her stupid brother for over an hour. She felt annoyed that she'd fallen for his bullshit once again. *Giant, unreliable pain in my ass.*

"I'll have another cup and the chocolate chip pancakes with whip cream, please." She struggled not to sound snippy, mad at Jimmy and herself for believing him again. She struggled to smile back at the girl, felt her leg pump up and down. She felt the disappointment of his no-show like a row of dominos. She remembered all the other times he'd broken his promises to her.

She picked up the newspaper in front of her to occupy her mind. She couldn't call Rory; it was still too early. *Damn time change.*

"Hey, Doc C. Is that you?"

Mia glanced up at the familiar voice, surprised to see Tony towering above her. "Hi."

"What are you doing all the way out here?"

His green eyes gleamed down at her, and she ignored a funny sensation in her gut.

"I was meeting a friend for breakfast, but it turns out he couldn't make it. Had to work or something like that." She fought against rolling her eyes. *I'm pathetic for lying for him, too ashamed to admit that my own brother is an unreliable alcoholic.* She swallowed her aggravation and shame.

His brows creased as he stepped aside for the waitress.

"Hi, Tony! How are you doing today?" The waitress beamed as she set down a heaping plate of pancakes.

"Never better." He smirked.

He wore a pair of faded blue jeans and an oversized

button-down shirt. She could see the gold chain around his neck tucked below his collar. Several of his chest hairs were exposed, and she pushed her gaze back toward his.

"You work up here?" she finally asked.

"No, I come in at least once a week for the food and the smoothies." He glanced toward her plate. "I should let you eat; they're gonna get cold." He checked his watch. "I have time for a quick cup of coffee. If you don't mind?"

Mia shook her head, trying not to roll her eyes. *Do I really have a choice?* "Sure."

The waitress approached with a mug filled with black coffee.

"So, how's it being back here?"

"Good so far."

"Really?"

"Honestly, I can't wait to get back home and the hell away from here."

He remained silent, but she didn't give a further explanation. She wiped her mouth and twirled a sugar packet between her fingers.

"Can I ask how a Rhode Island girl ended up living in Lake Tahoe? I find that most people from here don't leave."

"You're right, most don't. I went away to college and just never came back." She cut through her stack of pancakes and ate a forkful. After she finished chewing, she asked, "What about you, Tony? Have you always lived here?"

"Yes. I was born and raised in North Providence. I was raised by my mom. When she got sick, I helped take care of her. When I got older, I commuted to Roger Williams University to get a degree."

"A lot of young men wouldn't have done that." Jimmy came to mind.

"A lot of men weren't raised by my mother."

She smiled. "These are better than good; you're right. Do you want some? There's a lot."

"It's tempting, but I have a breakfast meeting." He looked down at his watch. "That started about ten minutes ago… And I'm bringing the muffins."

"You late a lot?" she asked, trying to keep the judgment out of her voice.

Tony finished his coffee and stood. "Only when it's completely essential."

Her bottom lip pulled upward. "Essential." *Funny.*

"Yeah, I know you got a busy schedule, and you're not here that long, but I'd love to buy you dinner. Or just a drink if, by any chance, you're free any time before you leave."

Her body unclenched when he changed the ask from dinner to drinks. *He's persistent.* Her mind replayed the day she saw him on the hill with *those* guys. She glanced up at his playful smirk; the tilt of his head relaxed her.

He waited quietly, simply watching her.

"I might be able to meet up for a quick drink tonight."

"Okay, perfect. A maybe-drink later. You have my card."

Mia hesitated; she'd thrown it away since she never planned to call him.

Tony stifled a laugh and shook his head. He dug in his pocket and placed another card down on the table. "Here, in case you can't find it." He made a deliberate face at her. "If you want, text me later, and we'll figure out a place and time." He nodded once quick. "Maybe until later, then."

Mia felt anxiety mixed with something else wash through her. She'd agreed to meet him for a drink. Maybe. *Big deal, it's a drink.* She flagged down the waitress to pay her bill, but the girl explained that Tony had already taken care of it. She tucked a generous tip under the napkin and walked out into the brisk air.

Climbing into the car, she noticed a card under her wiper.

"In case you lose my number again. Looking forward to seeing you later, maybe. Bring Mr. French, too."

She laughed despite herself. She considered calling Rory but decided against it. She didn't want to explain herself to him. *It's no big deal. I'll meet him, maybe, and have one drink.*

Tony hurried out of The Bean, taking the steps two at a time. He hated being late, and the Captain was going to bust his balls. *Wow, she finally agreed to meet me for a drink. Where can I take her where I'm not gonna have to deal with this case? Fuck… Not a lot of options.* He pulled up to the barracks and balanced his bags as he closed the door.

Maybe Hemenway's. Slik had beef with the owner, so it was a good bet. It was a nice spot, too; he wanted to impress her. *If she even texts me.*

"Ey, Anthony. Nice of you to join us," the Captain sarcastically greeted. "Gentleman, feel free to have some food now that Iannucci could join us."

"I caught traffic," Tony smirked wide. "It happens."

"Fuck, man, you're never late. Thought you had an emergency," Detective Williams spoke up.

"Naw, I'm good. Overslept."

"Okay, where are we with the dirt bags?" Captain brought everyone to focus.

Placing down his muffin, Tony briefed the guys on the latest developments. For the next few hours, they discussed the case and next strategies. It was well after two before Tony finally got back in his car and raced to his gym. He wanted to get a head start in case she texted him. He was shooting for twilight, the prettiest hour to see the bridge lit up.

After checking out the sights, Mia stopped by the diner. Her aunt was too busy to talk, and a small piece of Mia was relieved.

"Marianna. Yesterday went good, huh? Big turn out."

"Yes, a lot of people. Nicely done."

Aunt Rosie slid an eggplant special to a customer. "Want one?"

"No, I'm still full from breakfast. Thanks, though."

"How'd that go?"

"Just as expected," she said as she left the diner.

Sitting in the car outside of Minelli's, the sadness of her past became too depressing. She sent a text to Tony before she could change her mind.

He responded immediately. "Is Hemenway's in Providence ok? Its sort of near my gym."

"I can meet you at the gym if you want?" *I don't want to go there.*

"Don't want to put you out. See you at the restaurant if that's ok?"

"Okay, see you there." She threw her cell back in her purse.

She returned to the house in just enough time to get ready for drinks with Tony. She exchanged her sneakers for tan-colored cowboy boots and her sweatshirt for a light green sweater. She ignored the ring in her suitcase, didn't feel like going down that path again. She quickly brushed her teeth, scrunched her curls and applied a small amount of tinted lip balm.

The afternoon couldn't go by fast enough. A client had shown up late, and Tony hated that. The guy had to pick up his kid from school, and the kid was late. The client explained that he'd caught his son smoking pot, so he picked him up every day to remind him that both he and his mother were paying attention.

Tony admired parents who made an effort and showed they cared. Maybe because it'd been just him and his mother growing up, he appreciated men who were actual fathers. It was also why it made him sick to turn a blind eye to the punks he was hanging with while they sold steroids and drugs to street kids. The Captain kept telling him, "It's temporary, and they're going to buy them anyways." It was also going to allow him to work with the kids full-time once the case was closed. He knew the reality, but it still felt shitty.

Finally, around 4:45, he slid the gym door shut and bolted it with a click. He scanned the parking lot and quickly walked to his car. Placing his piece in the glove compartment, he drove fast through the familiar backroads. If she was on time, they'd catch the best time of night to see the bridge. He parked on a side street, almost hoping someone would be dumb enough to try something with him. *Just give me an excuse.* It'd been a long day.

He spotted her putting money in the meter. *Looking hot as usual with her boots and that adorable body.* His grin widened at the site of her puffy-headed dog. They were going to catch the perfect hour. It was stupid, but he wanted to impress her.

Chapter 22

"Hey, hi. You found it okay? Let me help you."

Mia spun around. "Hi, yes."

As he moved closer, she could smell his light scent. For a moment, she's taken to the back yard of Tweed Street. A ten-year-old Mia helped her mother take in the laundry basket after they'd picked the clothes off the line.

Frenchie tugged at his leash, and the memory evaporated. Tony wore an untucked black shirt cuffed just below his elbows. The fabric strained through his shoulder blades as he slid in the last coin. Mia was struck again by his size. Facing her now with his green, glistening eyes, her stomach did a slow roll.

"I'm glad you could meet me." He took Frenchie's leash from her. "You look great! Nice boots; color's great on you."

Frenchie lifted his leg.

"Love your dog. He's a riot. May I?" he asked, offering her his elbow.

His old-school manners reminded her of her father, the one from before, and fresh grief brought tears to her eyes. *This may not have been such a good idea. Just keep walking. I'm that much closer to a drink.*

Mia had never been inside Hemenway's before. It was pretty fancy but in an old-school, Rhode Island way. The waterfall in the foyer had blue flagstone up the entire structure. The main decorative feature, though, was the front bar with an elaborate fish tank that spanned the entire room. The combination of the glass with blue and white granite was simply amazing.

"Wow, this is beautiful."

The hostess greeted Tony by kissing him on his cheeks.

"This is Mia."

The hostess escorted them to a very private back room and into a booth that overlooked an outside deck, Providence River and the River Street Bridge beyond.

"That is a view."

"I had no idea." Tony winked.

She felt Tony's eyes on her. It was twilight, and the bridge was illuminated in front of them. Mia hadn't seen the bridge lit up since she and Rob were together. She absently rubbed her ring finger.

They took in the incredulous moment when the sun seemed to melt into the water.

"And the lady would like?"

Mia looked over to see the waitress had arrived. "I'll have a dirty martini, please."

"You good?"

"Yes, I'm good. I'd forgotten how beautiful this spot was."

The waitress placed a cocktail napkin down in front of each of them, careful not to spill the olive-tainted liquid.

"Thank you." Mia lifted the rim to her lips gratefully, welcoming the burn and saltiness of the olive juice.

"So, how was the rest of your day? You meet up with your friend finally?"

Mia lied about Jimmy, told him she went sightseeing, visited some relatives and then met with her aunt. She slid the olives off the toothpick into her drink and fiddled with the small point on the end.

Tony smirked, and she stopped twirling the toothpick.

"What about you, Tony? How was your breakfast meeting? Were they mad you were late?"

"They were fine; they had some fun with it. It turned out to be a busy day. I worked later than expected. I was anxious for the day to be over so I could be here with you."

Not knowing what to say, she simply nodded.

"Did you spend a lot of time here in Providence when you lived here?"

"Yes, actually, a fair amount. I'd almost forgotten how pretty it was at night." She looked out toward the bridge.

"Can I ask what got you interested in going away to school in California?"

"I had an uncle who lived there." She consciously put down her drink, afraid she might down the entire thing. She popped an olive in her mouth.

"And I'm sure you're one of those people who always knew you wanted to be a psychologist?"

"Pretty much, yes." She knew damn well it wasn't true. "What about you? You knew you wanted to own restaurants and be involved in business? Open a gym?"

"Nope, I can blame my buddy Carlos and his family for that. They owned a local diner near us, and we lived on the same block. His dad gave me a job, afraid I'd get in trouble."

"Was he right?"

"Absolutely, he was. Carlos and I own a place together over near Federal Hill."

"Really? I bet it's something."

"It is, actually."

Seeing the look he wore, she quickly threw out, "and I have a feeling you and Carlos still managed to have some fun, despite his dad."

"Yup, you'd be correct with that statement, m'lady."

"And the gym you own?"

"It gives me a chance to help teenage boys in the neighborhood stay out of trouble. It gives us both a healthy outlet." He hesitated. "Growing up, I needed that."

Mia was much more comfortable listening. She could tell he was sincere by the way he talked. *It's sweet that he cares about the boys in his community.* She liked that about him.

"Alright, enough about me. Tell me about your patients, your life in California, anything?"

She sipped her drink, sad it was almost gone. "Okay, but first, tell me about that colorful crew you were with the other day."

"You're not wrong. They certainly are a crew." He shook his head. "Yup, they're something, huh?" He leaned in and lowered his voice to a conspiring tone. "The really slick one is part owner of Andinos, and I'm pretty sure he does tanning bed commercials on the side." He made a face. "And the two really big guys are sort of his body guards, I guess. The other two I know from my gym. The restaurant owners in Providence get together a few times a year to make sure things are uniform, I guess. It was my turn to host, so me and Carlos sponsored a lunch. Nothing too exciting." He leaned back and took a long sip from his beer.

She seemed sufficiently satisfied and amused by his response.

"Hey, Mia. I know we only agreed to drinks, but do you mind if I order a flat bread or something? I'm starving. Didn't get to eat this afternoon. Was trying to work and meet you here at the best hour to impress you. You know how that goes."

She laughed. "That's fine, of course. I'm gonna use the bathroom."

Upon her return, Tony stood, waiting for her to sit. "Anything you miss about living here?"

She thought about her family and Rob, the *before*... She was grateful when the waitress plunked down a tray between them on the table.

"What happened to a flatbread?" She couldn't help but smile.

"I couldn't resist. The place is known for its seafood... And their wine."

The waitress nervously placed two glasses down and asked Mia, "May I?"

"Thank you." Mia twirled, sniffed, and then sipped the wine. "It's perfect." She looked at Tony. "Thank you, really."

They quietly watched as the waitress poured the light golden liquid into two oversized, stemless glasses and placed the bottle into the metal holder next to the table.

"Bon appetit."

He nodded to the waitress and then turned to Mia. "To being here with you tonight."

They clinked their glasses together and dug into the most delicious seafood tower of fresh, chilled lobster, jumbo shrimp, raw oysters, and fresh little neck clams.

"The food, Tony. The food in Rhode Island can't be topped. That is what I miss." She finished off the final piece of shrimp and wiped her mouth. "Delicious."

"Shall we finish our wine on the deck? It seems the moon is out." Standing, he took her hand. "Oh, I forgot about you, boy. I got him."

Overlooking the bridge, the moon beamed bright and high in the autumn night sky. It smelled like fall, crisp like only Rhode Island could be. It reminded Mia of Rob. She sipped her wine.

Tony leaned in and gently moved a piece of her hair that had blown into her face before leaning in for a kiss. Mia hesitated but leaned in, too. She felt herself stiffen as he moved in to kiss her, but he smelled so fresh, and his lips felt familiar. Everything else fell away. The kiss was magical.

She glanced up toward him and felt her heart start to hammer away in her chest. She was suddenly overwhelmed with the fatigue of the last several days. Tony's hand linked with hers; it was big and warm. She started feeling panicky. *I need to leave.* She placed the empty glass on the rail, ready to make her exit. *Thank him, it's been a very pleasant night. It's not his fault. Being back here makes me feel fucking crazy.*

"Am I scaring you again?"

Catching a glimpse of the concern on his face, she felt bad. "No, you're fine." She pulled her hands away. "I'm feeling the effects of the trip. I think I'll head out. It's not you at all."

"I get it. Glad you could meet up under the circumstances."

She averted his gaze, looking toward the bridge, as he pushed another hair out of the way.

He paid the bill and walked behind her, insistent on taking the dog's leash. At her car, he leaned in and gave her the lightest hint of a kiss. She kissed him back, soft and slow. He pulled back slowly, and their eyes locked.

His voice was barely a whisper, "Did you ever feel like something was destined? Meant to happen, but it had nothing to do with you?"

Her eyes darted to the moon and then back to his. She nodded.

"I feel like that about us. Like I was supposed to meet you."

"Good night, Tony. And thank you for a very enjoyable evening."

She pulled away from the curb. *Meant to happen.*

Chapter 23

It'd been a long time since a kiss had evoked any kind of emotion for Mia, let alone whatever she felt with Tony. It completely unnerved her. Rob's words echoed, *"Mare, we're special, you and me."* She turned up the radio to drown out her thoughts.

Setting her keys down on the counter, she decided the couch would be a better place to sleep. Being in Rob's room was simply too hard. Her mind kept repeating the end of the night, the kiss. *"Did you ever feel like you were supposed to meet someone?" It was a kiss with a man, big deal. I'm going home, and that'll be that.*

Her cell rang, and she checked the time. 1am. It's not Ror. It was a familiar Rhode Island number. She sat up and clicked off the ringer, letting it go to voicemail. She didn't want to hear his empty excuses. She'd heard them all before.

After an hour of failing to get to sleep, she padded out to the kitchen, poured herself some wine and returned to the couch. Unable to resist, she reached for her cell.

"Heeyyy, Mee. It's Jimm. Eyy, sorry 'bout this mornin'. Got stuck at work, didn't have your cell plugged in my phone. An-a-ways, you know I love you, lil sista. Ey, an it's laaate. Sorry 'bout that, too. Hey, I saw little Joey from the old neighborhood. You 'memba him? He felt real bad about Dad. Was asking for you, too.

His voice caught with emotion. "Imagine, they're all fuckin' dead… All of 'em. Can't believe it. Speciaally Robbie… He didn't deserve it. The rest did, not him. He didn't. Even that mob prick's dead. Fuck-king finally. All he put them through… Took 'em long enough.

Her stomach twisted with sadness. *He sounds pathetic.* The beep cut him off. There was another voicemail.

"We was tellin' stories 'bout me and Rob… All of us… The good ol' days. Yeah, he was real sorry 'bout everything, but ey, fuck that. I told'm not to feel that bad, right? Caaall me in the mornin', we'll try'n hook up 'for ya go."

"I don't think so." She deleted the messages.

For a moment, she wished she weren't alone. *I wonder what Tony's doing now? If he stayed at his gym tonight.* Her brain tried to conjure Rob's face but couldn't. She tossed her cell on the floor and laid back against the pillow. She watched as the sky turned from black to gray. She hadn't slept a wink and was exhausted and cranky. She dragged herself off the couch, deciding to visit Auntie Rose. *It might be my last chance to talk to her alone.*

"Come on, Mr. French. Let's go see Auntie." Her stomach growled, and she needed coffee.

Pushing away the pit in her gut, she walked into the diner and sat down at the counter. The place was packed.

Auntie Rose bounded toward her. "Morning, honey. Breakfast is big on Sundays."

"I guess so."

Auntie poured her a cup of coffee, and Mia spooned in sugar and added milk.

"I love seeing your face around here. And you, too, fluffy." She winked at Frenchie.

He nosed the air above him.

"Every Sunday's like this?"

"Mostly. Last week, the Providence Journal did a big write-up on the place and your da— His death and all."

"Rooosie," Sal called.

"I'll be back, just gotta get the rush over with. Stick around."

"Give me an apron. I'll help."

"That's my girl! You want tables or counter?"

"I'll take the counter."

With her old waitressing skills flexed, Mia grabbed the pad and pencil near the register.

"Can I help you?" she asked an elderly man who'd been waiting patiently.

"I'll have the egg special and a double bloody, extra hot."

Mia stifled a smirk. She went to the back to hand the slip to Sal.

He winked. "Hey, you alright with me being with your aunt?"

"I'm glad she's happy."

"She's an amazing lady," he said while expertly flipping eggs.

"Yes, she is."

The morning rush was a blessing. It felt good to be productive and to work with her aunt.

With the rush over, Sal placed down a plate with a ham and cheese omelet and corn beef hash.

"I can see why you're so busy, very tasty."

"Special recipe," Sal confessed.

Her father used to say the same thing... She lifted the fork to her mouth, could see her dad standing by the stove, stirring a pot. He was always cooking something or other. She sipped her coffee, suddenly lacking saliva. She could tell Sal was still watching her, so she forced herself to keep eating.

"The hash is really good, almost tastes like..."

"Yeah, he sure can cook. Reminds me of your father that way." Auntie laughed and glanced over at Sal.

Their intimacy made Mia's stomach ache. *It's sweet to see them so in love, too sweet.*

"Any chance you'll share the recipe?" Mia teased Sal.

Auntie laughed. "No way! He'll take it to the grave, don't bother."

Mia sipped her coffee and faced her aunt. "Tell me about the article they did on my father?"

As if on cue, Sal stood. "I'm going to finish cleaning the dishes so we can actually leave on time today."

"Be right back." Auntie Rose returned carrying a shoebox and plunked it down on the counter, taking out a book. "I wanted to tell you about it over the phone, but I knew you'd be home this weekend." She took a folded piece of paper and a laminated obituary out of the book. "They're for you."

Glancing at the obituary, Mia placed it down in front of her and unfolded the newspaper article.

October 20, 2006: James Capaldi, age 60, died of a heart attack at the Rhode Island Adult Correctional Institute yesterday after killing Gian "Junior" Costa in a prison yard fight. Sources say the fight started after a negative comment during a basketball game. Gian Costa was the younger brother of the infamous Mob kingpin, Anthony Costa. Mr. Capaldi was convicted of killing his wife at Minelli's Diner, 10 Plainfield Street in Johnston, after learning that she and Gian Costa were romantically involved. Capaldi served 21 years of his life sentence and maintained that his wife's death was accidental. The murder weapon was never recovered.

The remainder of the article documented every sad event that had ever happened to their family, linking to the diner's history.

Mia folded her arms, trying to fight a sudden chill. *"He finally got the mob prick." Is this what Jimmy was talking about?* Since her mother's death, the diner held a certain intrigue for people fascinated by the horrors of tragedy. *He killed this man? Unbelievable.* The fact that this had caused a renewed interest in the whole drama made her feel exploited and sick to her stomach.

Aunt Rose touched Mia's arm. "People can't resist a juicy story. They never could."

For a moment, they were both silent, knowing full well that the diner's success had been greatly heightened by the tragic tales that had befallen the families involved with the place.

Mia stared into her mug and tried to re-read the article like a stranger. An image of her mother's final moments unfolded before her. She pushed away the paper and began twirling a piece of her hair.

"She really was involved with the Costa guy?" *The same loser's brother I saw with Tony?* "It sounds like a bad movie."

"She was… I'm sorry."

They had never discussed her mother's infidelity before. She felt herself slip back into the wounded girl of her youth. *A robbery, an accident… The truth was she had an affair.* Mia pictured her mother's pretty face, her innocent expression and easy laugh. She was kind and good… *But not trustworthy.*

"Was she in love with him?"

"He could be very charming."

Mia waited for a real answer.

"Yes… Said he was her soulmate."

"No robbery, no accident; he caught them together. A crime of passion." The convoluted story and Jimmy's anger began making more sense. *Jimmy must've known about the affair.* He had tried to tell her back then, but she hadn't wanted to hear it. What was the point? Her mother was still dead.

Her mother was in love with someone else. The reality was

hard to swallow. She twirled the napkin in front of her, and her foot tapped beneath the counter.

"Rosie, phone," Sal announced from the back.

"Be right back."

Looking over the box, Mia's mind replayed the night everything changed.

"Marianna, wake up." There was urgency in Aunt Rose's voice. "Something's happened. Come on."

She didn't remember how long her father cried that night or how long her aunt had comforted him. She didn't remember how long Rob had held her or how she'd ended up asleep in Jimmy's bedroom. Her memories were fragmented like chards of glass, the feelings sharp but unclear. Time had dimmed a lot from that night, but she could still see the image of Jimmy, Robbie and her hugging out on the curb. Tragedy bound them together in eternal cement.

"Sorry about that," Auntie Rose said, bringing Mia out of her past. "Had to make an order."

Mia was being sucked under by the riptide of her emotions. *"She got in the way." Robbie knew?*

Auntie Rose placed her hand firmly on Mia's shoulder.

Mia stood. "It's okay. I'm going to get going; I need to pack. I'll see you at Ca's house later. Bye, Sal!"

Sal came out from the back, wiping his hands on his apron. "I better say goodbye now. I'm not invited." He hugged her. "Thanks for helping out. Good to see you."

Mia's eyes moved between his and Auntie's. "Good seeing you two together. The girls will come around."

"Yeah, maybe." Sal glanced at the box in Mia's hand. "It's gotta be tough for you, bein' back here."

"Not a picnic, but it's fine." She tried for a half smile she wasn't feeling.

"Marianna, that's bullshit. It's not fine. None of it ever was. But no matter what happened, he loved her more than anything."

Mia stared back, unsure what to say. "Thank you for this," she said, nodding to the box and turning toward the door. "Did Dad know she was in love with the Costa guy?" Mia took in her aunt's face, and time briefly paused. *My mother was protecting him, her lover…* She wished she could retract the question; she didn't want to know any more.

Chapter 24

Mia hurried Frenchie into the car and plopped the shoebox down on the passenger side floor. She reached for her phone and called the airline. After a long hold, the reservations clerk informed her that she had two choices: a three-thirty flight that day or an early flight in the morning. She couldn't pull a no-show; her cousins were expecting her. Annoyed, she booked herself a spot on the 8 a.m. flight.

Back at her aunt's house, Mia stuffed a few items into her small suitcase and placed it by the door. She straightened the couch and wiped down the kitchen and bathroom areas. She let her eyes sweep the place, lingering a moment on Rob's bedroom door on her way out.

Mia headed over to Solitro's Bakery for the dessert she promised to bring as her contribution to dinner. She decided on an apple pie and half a dozen fudge brownies, along with a bottle of wine, to calm the jittery feeling in her stomach.

Heading toward her cousin's house, her cell rang. It was a Rhode Island number.

"Hello?"

"Hi, it's Tony. Just calling to say what a nice time I had last night, and I hope I didn't make it too weird."

There's that openness. "I had a nice time, too."

"And I'm sort of hoping you have good news for me." When she didn't say anything, he added, "Plus, I'm already craving music and ice-cold brewskies later… Had a tough morning."

Despite her foul mood, the smile she heard in his voice was contagious. "Actually, I have both. Good news is I'm leaving tomorrow morning."

"And the bad news?"

"I'm leaving tomorrow morning. But music and beer sound pretty good to me right now, too." *Maybe something stronger.*

"That bad, huh?"

"Yes, but I think I'll live."

"Maybe a night out is just what you need."

"Maybe."

"How's seven?"

A few hours with my cousins and I'll be done with the memory lane, family thing. Her eyes swept the shoebox. "That'll work."

He gave her directions to a tavern in Scituate. "I'm looking forward to seeing you again."

Her stomach dipped at the tone of his voice. For a moment, she was unsure if meeting him was wise. *It's no big deal; I'm leaving in the morning. Besides, we live on different coasts.*

"See you then."

After all this time, it's amazing how being back here still feels the same. Everything reminded her of Robbie as she drove to Caren's, and the worn-out slide show began to spin. She and Rob together at the falls, his body, the deep color of his blood smudged on the street. Her brain wouldn't let her forget any of the details. Memories are weird, especially bad ones. They become part of our DNA.

For the longest time, the smell of ice cream or thinking

about summer time in New England brought her back to that night. She had the strangest pull to see the place again.

Pulling up to the curb, Mia mentally prepared herself and then walked to the front door.

"Hi, come in," Caren said as she opened the door and hugged her warmly.

She followed Caren into the kitchen, where Joanne fed the baby.

"She's absolutely beautiful."

The baby's dark features resembled Jay, her dad.

"Just a little something." She handed Caren a card with a Walmart gift-card inside. Heather, Caren's toddler, shyly held onto Caren's leg with all her might.

"This is Cousin Marianna. But she goes by Mia now."

The little girl smiled a partially toothless grin. "Hi, Mia."

Mia's heart melted. Her skin tone, eye color, and the shape of her forehead were all Rob. The resemblance was uncanny. Mia crouched down and held out a story book.

"It's about a friendly Monster named Tahoe Tessie."

"Tank you." Her eyes lit up when she saw Mr. French. "Can I pet him?"

"He'd love that."

"She looks like his ghost, huh?" Jo said. "She's not blessed with his easy temperament, though… Don't let those angelic looks fool you."

Caren shot a glance of agreement.

"You all packed?" Aunt Rosie asked as she dumped a box of spaghetti into a pan.

"I am."

Jo washed her hands in the sink and then hugged Mia tight. "Come sit. How'd breakfast go with Jimmy? Speaking of challenging personalities…"

"He was an easy baby. I was there," Auntie said with a sharp glance.

"He wasn't able to make it."

"Yeah, well, he's been a dickhead for a really long time now. It's not like you come out here all the time. You think he could make a friggin' breakfast; it's not that fuckin hard."

"Jo, language," Auntie snapped.

Jo handed Mia a glass of wine, ignoring her mother.

The children took up much of the focus that afternoon, and Mia was more than pleased. The dinner conversation pretty much consisted of questions about Mia's work and life out in Tahoe. Jo told funny stories about her late-night customers, and Caren shared that she was hoping for a boy.

After dinner, they all moved to the living room.

"Mom tell you I'm single again?" Jo asked.

"Yes, sorry about that."

"Don't be. He's a liar; I hate that. Fuck him. Something good came out of it, though. I stopped smoking,"

Despite her cousin's words, Mia knows she's still hurting. "You were together a long time. It must've been hard."

"Ten years… Whatever, though. We all got our crosses. What about you, Mare? How's everything out there? "I'm good, pretty busy with work."

"Be right back." Caren got up to check on the baby.

"Speaking of busy…" Mia sipped her wine.

"It's her own fault. What a mess. You'd have a field day with their fucked up relationship. And she can't seem to see any of it; it makes me crazy."

They were silent for a long minute.

"You seeing anyone special back home?"

"Naw, too busy for that. Ror and I manage to have some fun, though." She hated feeling like something was wrong with her when people asked this question.

"Yeah, fuck that. You're better off alone, anyway."

Caren re-entered the room carrying brownies and a coffee pot. "Heather, Cousin Mia brought your favorite."

Heather bounded toward her mother, nearly knocking straight into Auntie carrying the pie. Heather climbed into Mia's lap, a brownie in one hand and her new book in the other.

"Can you wead this Cousin Mia?"

Heather smelled like chocolate and juice. Mia read and then reread the story, and Heather rested her head back against Mia's chest.

"Again!"

"What?! We've already read it four times!" Mia teased.

"Heath, let's let the book rest until tomorrow. It's time to take a bath and get ready for bed."

Heather flung the book at her mom and started to wail, throwing herself onto the ground.

Caren flinched, and something in her look tugged at Mia's heart.

"She's overtired," she said as she retrieved the book from the floor.

"Yeah, that's why," Jo scoffed.

"Heather, we don't throw things," Auntie yelled.

Caren ignored them, picked up the toddler and carried her out of the room.

"Nooo. I hate you. I want daddy." Heather thrashed and screamed.

Aunt Rosie shook her head in disgust. "Happens way too much."

"Kid needs a beat'n. Gets away with murder 'cause my sister feels guilty over that asshole coming in and out of their lives."

About a half hour later, Caren returned holding the baby. "I need to feed her her last bottle before bed."

"Give her to me. You didn't finish your pie," Jo said.

"Thanks."

"You can't ignore that forever, Caren," Auntie said. "It's only gonna get worse."

"I should get going; I have an early flight. Thanks for everything."

She declines her aunt's offer to drive her to the airport.

"I'll leave your car and keys exactly where I found them."

"We'll talk," Auntie said in a bear hug. "It was great having you out here again. Let's not wait until someone else dies, huh?"

"I know… And thanks for everything."

"I'm glad you finally got to meet my kids. Sorry about Heather." Tears glistened in Caren's eyes.

"Don't be silly. They're both beautiful."

"It was really good to see you again, lil cuz. Wish you were here longer. I give you credit for coming back at all."

"Thanks, Jo." This was the part where she should promise to keep in touch or invite them out, but it's not her style to make empty promises. "Thanks again for dinner. It was great seeing all of you."

Halfway to the car, Mia glanced back and waved.

"And don't be such a stranger, Mare," Jo called.

As she got into the car, tears burned the back of her throat. She wiped her eyes. It was still so hard to be near them.

At 6:45, the sky had already turned completely dark. The quickest way to Bishop Hill Tavern was to go up 116 and then cross over to route 6. A familiar fear started creeping up from her toes, and her breath caught. Her instinct was to text Tony that she'd changed her mind. She rolled down the windows hoping the cold air would help calm her mind.

Before she'd had time to give into her fear, she texted Tony.

I'm about 10 min away. See you soon. Looking forward to that drink.

Mia drove, relieved to be going home in the morning, missing her routine. She left Rory a quick message about her flight.

"Hey, I'm flying out at eight; I'll call you when I land. It's been the longest weekend of my life. I can't wait to see you and my patients."

Driving down 116, she turned on the radio to distract her from the hammering in her chest. After two songs, she turned it off with a snap, wishing she'd taken the long way around. *It's time.*

"Okay, Robbie, distract me. Tell me everything will be okay. I won't pass out or lose consciousness. Or my mind... Again..."

She inhaled deep, holding it for a few beats before letting it out and holding the next breath a bit longer. She ignored the sweat on her forehead and focused on her breaths. Every cell in her body had been called to high alert. *Concentrate on the white lines. Stay in your lane.*

Her hands tightened around the steering wheel as she eased the car over into the deserted parking lot. She sat motionless in her car for a minute, resting her head against the headrest.

When she found the courage to look at the last place he'd ever been, she was surprised to find that it looked like the simple, seasonal ice cream joint that it was. Her tears fell, silent and hot.

"Mare, I'll meet you at the stop sign. Ice cream always makes you feel better."

This was the same spot that had so drastically changed her life, forever altering her brain. She sat in her car sobbing, grieving the life that had been taken from them.

I could use that drink about now.

Chapter 25

"It looks like a happening spot," Mia said to Frenchie as she pulled into the parking lot of Bishop Hill Tavern.

She quickly glanced at herself in the mirror, ignoring her eyes, and patted down the sides of her hair before tightening her scrunchy. *Here goes.*

She walked up two oversized stone steps into the tavern. *It's cozy.* Paneled in dark wood, it had old hardwoods and a large fireplace made of enormous rustic stones that took up the entire back wall.

She found a seat at the bar amongst a group of guys watching a flat-screen up in one corner. *Right, the playoffs, almost World Series time. God, I feel like I've been living in a cave.*

"What can I get you?" the bartender asked.

"I'll have—"

"Two ice-cold beers, Teddy," Tony finished.

She turned to face him. His eyes twinkled toward her. *There it is, just like last night.* The air between them felt charged.

"I'm sorry, I ran late at my cousin's. Haven't seen them in awhile."

"Naw, it's fine. I understand. Glad you're here now."

He handed her a beer and quickly scanned the bar.

"It's good to see you. I've been thinking about this all day."

"Thanks." This was the best she'd felt all day. Her stomach did a mini flip, but she was starting to relax.

"You like it?" Tony signaled to her beer. "Or did I talk it up too much?"

"Nope, it's as good as you said."

As if on cue, Bob Seger's *Turn the Page* began to play. It used to make her think of her dad being all alone out on the road. She took a long pull from her beer. *I'm not thinking about him tonight, any of them.* She sat back against the bar stool. *This is exactly what I need.* She tried hard to believe her own words.

"You like Seger, Mia?"

"Who doesn't love Bob? Don't you?"

"Absolutely! What's not to love?"

Her smile made her nose crinkle. He nodded and sang along.

"You smoke the day's last cigarette, remembering what she said."

Here I am, turn the page.

Tony squeezed her hand slightly, and she instinctively pulled it away.

"I give old Bob a run for his money, even though I can't sing."

It was the best thing she'd heard all day. A feeling of familiar comfort washed through her. He reminded her of a straight Rory. *Oh, how weird is that?*

"Do you ever sing Karaoke?" she asked, thinking of Rory.

"No, and it should stay that way." He smirked. "You?"

"Never, but it's fun to watch."

The song switched to a pop song she didn't recognize. The

boys sitting behind them got rowdy, and Tony glanced over his shoulder.

"Come on. There's another room. It's quieter back there. Good for the old guys like me."

"You're not old."

He raised one brow. "It's okay. Compared to them, I'm ancient."

Taking her hand, Tony navigated to the back room. He wore jeans and a thin, black and blue Puma shirt. She couldn't help but notice the arch of his back muscles. *Pretty good for an old guy.* She was still unsure of his actual age. She imagined how it would feel to be close to him and felt herself stiffen. She pulled her hand away from his for the second time.

The back room had a bar up against a wall and two seating areas, one with a love seat and the other with two overstuffed chairs.

"My Lady." He gestured toward one of the chairs.

"Thank you, it's very charming back here. Looks like an old hunting lodge. And we can still hear the music fine."

"So, you had a rough day?"

She didn't know how to answer without telling him everything. She tucked a stray curl behind her ear.

"Naw, I'm just a hopeless workaholic like you." She grinned.

"Here's to work, then." He held his beer up to hers, and they clinked their glasses. "Looks like we need more. I'll be right back. Plus, I promised you cheesy music. It starts at eight."

"You did."

As promised, she could hear someone singing a sorry rendition of Journey's *Faithfully* from the other room.

When he returned, he pulled his chair closer to hers and placed down the beers.

"Hey, why don't you tell me about your day? Or is that your line, Doc?"

"Clever." She fidgeted with the napkin in front of her until his hand rested on hers.

"No, I'm serious. You're going back, and I still feel like there's so much I don't know about you."

"My day wasn't that bad, really. I was just exaggerating before. I went to visit my aunt at work, then had dinner with her family, my cousins. That's it. Really not that exciting or terrible."

Tony sat back and picked up his beer. He hadn't taken his eyes off off hers.

"Look, I'm gonna put it right out there—maybe 'cause I know you're leaving. I'm crazy about you. Have been since the minute we met. I'd like to keep in touch when you go back. See you again?"

She bit down on the inside of her lower lip. He watched her intensely, his jaw clenching and unclenching.

"Tony, I'm flattered. I've had a lot of fun with you, too." She smiled briefly. "I don't think..."

He leaned in and kissed her very lightly at first, almost testing her, his breath a mixture of spearmint and beer. The kiss was packed with an intensity she worried held only a fraction of the energy that'd built between them. The sensation was both intoxicating and jolting.

She finally pulled back.

"You were saying?" The gleam in his eyes and his slight smirk seemed vaguely familiar.

She inhaled deep and sat back in her chair, her heart racing. She saw Rob's face flash, the memory of them making love just before the accident. The channel switched, and the NIKE emblem spun past. Then she was alone, waiting in the hospital.

She sat up straighter, trying to lose the guilt she felt. She wrapped her arms across herself, suddenly feeling cold.

"You come in here a lot?" she asked.

"Only when I'm trying to get away from the city. Ey, don't

mind me. I'm still working on being subtle around you. I didn't scare you too bad, did I?" He grinned.

Damn, his dimple is cute. "I don't scare that easy."

"Come on, let's play some tunes." He winked. "I'll do anything to get the lady to smile again."

Her body began to relax. "I'm smiling, I'm smiling."

The main tavern was crowded and filled with drunken noise. Tony loaded the jukebox up with cash.

"We get four each."

"Okay."

She scanned her choices. Most were older love songs or classic rock and roll hits. The rock ones screamed of Rob, especially Floyd, so she avoided them. Mia chose classic hits from the Eagles and Elton John. Tony chose Angel Eyes and two more Seger tunes before asking her permission to play Sinatra.

Mia and Tony listened to the music while waiting for their picks. She watched, uninterested, as a big guy wearing a dew rag around his head walked toward them. She heard Rory's voice in her head, "*We got ourselves a hero,*" as Tony's arm reached around her waist from behind, pulling her in close. A sensation crept up on her that she hadn't felt in years. She turned her attention back to the music and sipped her beer.

Half a second later, she realized the guy had stopped dead in front of her. Tony's body stiffened, and she reflexively looked toward the guy, catching a full view of his face. She couldn't believe it. In slow motion, her beer did a free fall to the ground.

"Ey, you alright?" Tony grabbed her elbow.

"Ey, I think that's called abuse." Jimmy nodded toward the floor, then back up at her.

They moved slightly to the right as a waitress appeared to clean up the spilled beer.

"Eeeeeyyy, Sis. You're not mad 'bout the other morning?"

The other morning was beside the point. He'd obviously

relapsed again. His blue eyes twinkled at hers, but they were red-rimmed and a little vacant. His balance only slightly wavered. *He's probably hammered but can hide it better than most. He's a trained professional.* Jimmy was the last person she wanted to see.

"Jim, what are you doing here?"

"I live up the road," he said with a hint of a slur. "Who's the thug?"

Mia watched Tony's facial expression change, his eyes flash. She stepped nearer to her brother, who slung his big arm around her waist and hugged her tight. He smelled like cigarettes and booze.

"Tony, this is Jimmy. Jimmy, Tony."

Jimmy kept her in a tight bear hug, seeming to enjoy that his presence was upsetting Tony. To have someone approach a woman who was with someone else was the greatest insult.

"Tony, he's my brother."

"Your brother…"

"Hey, sup?"

He left Tony's hand hanging in mid-air.

"What are you doing here, Mee? Thought you were headin' back?"

"I leave in the morning." She tried to hide her irritation that he was being rude.

"Mare, you could've called me back the other night. And what are you doin' with him?"

Mia eyed him to be quiet, but he ignored her.

"Ey, you hang with that dirt bag Costa? What are you doing with my sister?"

Tony glanced briefly at her but remained silent.

Next thing Mia knew, Jimmy was in Tony's face.

"She don't wanna be bothered with people like you now or ever." He poked Tony in the chest. "You got that? I don't want my baby sister near people like you." Jimmy turned to Mia. "He works for them. Bodyguard thug or somethin'."

"Jim, no, it's fine. I know him." She was embarrassed by her brother and scared of the look on Tony's face.

Tony grabbed Jimmy by his shirt and spoke with quiet intensity, "back off, punk. You touch me again, and I'll…"

Jimmy was significantly shorter than Tony and not nearly as big. She could tell from his lack of fear that he had some kind of death wish. Mia felt fear pulse through her. Tony's facial expression and voice never changed, but something in his eyes transformed.

"You'll what, big guy?" Jimmy taunted. "What are you gonna do? Tell your guys to whack me? Go 'head, bring 'em on. Fact, tell 'em I've been waiting. If it was up to me, his baby brother woulda died seventeen years ago. You can tell 'em that, too."

"Jim, stop it."

Mia's mind flashed to the article. *All the tragedy they caused… Her soulmate.* Her brother's anger and words were more than concerning.

"You're lucky she's your sister, big guy," Tony said, stepping back.

"Tony has restaurants in Providence. That's how he knows them."

"I'm gonna go use the bathroom," Tony tells her. "Good meeting you, Pal."

She stared after Tony, amazed at how well he'd handled the situation.

"Why do you have to act like that?"

"He's one of them, Mee. Fuck that. How do you know 'em anyways?"

Before she could respond, two big guys appeared out of nowhere.

"We're gonna ask you to leave, sir."

"And if I refuse?"

"Then we're gonna make you go."

"Jim, just go."

Jimmy glanced at his cell. "You're in luck. I got somewhere else to be. But I'm gonna say goodbye to my baby sista first."

"In the parking lot," they insisted.

"I have to go get my stuff. It's in the other room." She eyed the bathroom for Tony. *He'll find me, he'll understand.* "I'll meet you out there."

She walked into the other room and glanced around for her purse. *Maybe I left it in the car.* She left out a back door, recognizing Jimmy's profile in the streetlight.

Mia counted her steps as she walked to the car. "I have to let Frenchie out to pee." Jimmy exhaled a stream of smoke. "Cute mutt, huh? Hey, memba how Robbie loved dogs, but Aunt Rosie wouldn't have it? Ey, you should hang around. I played a few Floyd songs for him." Jimmy started to sing. "Heloo, hello, hello, is there anybody in there… Rob used to play that one over and over when we smoked, memba. 'Course you do."

"Are you really going somewhere else?"

"Got one more stop out in Providence. Meeting some friends. Never told me how you know the big guy, Mee?"

"Jim, why don't you just go home?"

"Told you, I got plans."

"Don't you think enough people have gotten killed over them?"

"Only the ones who deserved it. Mare, I'm telling you, the big guy's one of 'em."

Her anger pulsed as she watched him stub out his cigarette on the bottom of his boot. *Only the ones who deserved it?*

"Besides, whatta you know about it?"

"I know the truth."

"The truth, huh? Your motha was a whore, and your precious

daddy was a pussy. That's a piece of it, alright. Ha! The truth... Whatdya think the big guy's gonna say when he finds out 'bout you doin' your own cousin? Fuckin' truth. Overrated, ain't it?"

She looked down, knew Rob would have killed him right there. "You're drunk, go home."

He straightened up. "That an order, Doctor?"

The amused look he wore made her want to slap him.

He pecked her cheek and turned to go.

"Ey, maybe you should take your own advice, lil sis. Be more careful who you... You know."

"I'm going home."

He lifted his brows.

"It's nothing like that," she yelled, angry she'd let him get to her. *And it's none of his business who I decide to go home with... now or ever.* She hated how he made her feel. *He always does this.*

"Mare, I know you... Seen that look before. Did'cha forget he was my best friend? Practically my brother? You think I didn't know... What am I, a fuckin' idiot."

"You know nothing about me, us; you weren't even there." *You left me too.*

They stared at each other for a long moment before he turned away.

After he moved out of sight, her anger was quickly replaced by sadness. *He's pathetic.* She squeezed her eyes shut, trying to block out his words, him completely. A dull throb started above her left temple. There was so much more to say, but she knew he was too drunk and she was too tired.

A piece of her wanted to chase after him, stop him from any further self-destruction, but she knew those wheels had been set in motion years before. She couldn't do anything to stop him. No one ever could.

She put Frenchie back in the car and shut the door with a thump. She turned back to the bar and saw Tony's large silhouette walking toward her in the darkness, holding her handbag.

"Tony, I… My brother," she started to apologize for Jimmy's behavior but didn't know where to begin.

"Shh. It's okay, that's not on you."

Tony folded her into his big body, and a feeling of security passed through her. She closed her eyes and exhaled, letting the comfort wash through her. He kissed the top of her head, and for a second, she wanted to melt into time, like a sunset fading into a warm summer night, slow and long.

After a moment, she pulled away from his warmth, seeing the St. Christopher medal dangling under the brim of his shirt. She stepped back and closed her eyes to get away from the feeling that crept up her spine. Opening them again, she shook off the feel of his body against hers. She bit the inside of her lower lip and opened her car door.

"Tony, I have to go home. I have an early flight."

"I know." He couldn't seem to make himself budge.

"I'll follow you, just to make sure you get home safe."

The hint of a smile started to form on her lips.

"You find that amusing?"

"No. You sound just like Rory."

"I knew I liked that guy." He held the door open for her.

Mia started the car without pause. *"Mare, I'm telling you, he's one of them."*

"Goodbye then. Thanks for everything, Tony. I mean it."

"Naw." He leaned in to kiss her.

She pulled back.

"I hope it's only good night." He winked.

Chapter 26

Tony's brain buzzed as he followed her home. *She's Capaldi's daughter.... She came home for his funeral. No wonder she doesn't wanna talk about her family, can't wait to get the hell away from here. This punk could be our big break. He's the final piece to our case.*

He realized the Captain must've sent Williams to keep an eye on Jimmy. Costa's guys were looking for him. *That must've been "the business" they told me they had when I bumped into them leaving the bar.* He started to connect the dots. *You gotta be fucking kidding me.* He'd spent enough time with Costa and his guys to know they'd find a way to get to Jimmy. He hadn't really cared about the outcome; they'd caught Costa on tape ordering the hit, but now he was *her* brother.

Kid's a loose cannon. Mouth alone's gonna get him killed. He sighed, thinking of her, playing out the various scenarios. He could hear Captain's voice in his head like a skipping record, *"Anthony, nevea trust a lady with the details of an undercover. It's always a fatal mistake; never turns out good, ever."* But she wasn't just some lady. He inhaled deep.

He was tempted to call the Captain to send stronger backup for Williams. *Maybe I'll go myself.* He couldn't change the events that had already been set in motion, but knew staying away from her was no longer an option.

Tony rounded the corner near Minelli's and saw the place from a whole new point of view. *What a nightmare. Her father killed her mother and died in prison. No wonder she moved away…*

He saw Mia wave and nodded back. His stomach tightened. He would've given anything to go inside. He forced himself to keep driving. He thought about the crew, hoped like hell Jimmy would stay away from them. But knowing his type, he wouldn't. *She's his sister… Fuuuck. Costa's had a hard-on for him for a while, feels he's responsible for his brother's death. Kid's a loser looking for a fight with the wrong guys. Our guys won't let him die.*

Tony wished the case was over, wished he could tell her his actual role. He imagined telling her the truth.

"Mia, there's something I need you to know about me, but it has to stay between us. No one else can know; it's life and death kind of stuff. You gotta promise me?"

"Okay," she'd tentatively respond.

"I'm a part of Costa's crew."

"So, you lied?"

"I had to… I'm actually a cop. I've been working undercover with them for over two years. We've been trying to get him on some past… stuff. The less details I tell you, the better."

"You're a cop?"

He imagined her slow surprise switching to betrayal.

"An undercover one?"

"Yeah. I don't wanna say any more. Can't, really… It's for your own safety. These guys are dangerous. Do you understand what I'm saying? You can't tell anybody."

"I understand," she might say.

"They got beef with your brother. We have a shadow on 'em. It's best they know as little about you as possible."

"Why are you telling me this?"

There's the million-dollar question.

"It matters to me that you know me 'cause I'm crazy in love with you. Have been since the moment we met.

"You could get in big trouble for telling me this, detective?"

Yup, and compromise my case. That's why it ain't happenin'.

Tony pulled into his gym parking lot and checked his cell. Williams hadn't checked in. *Where the fuck is he?* After swimming laps for almost thirty minutes, he showered, put on a pair of boxers and headed off to bed.

Still awake after half an hour, their words bothered him. *"I only seen that look once before. You think I didn't know?" "Doesn't matter. It's nothing like that."* That seemed to bother her more than anything else he'd said, and the kid had said a lot. Tony reached for his cell and contemplated calling her. *It's a bad idea, man.* His burner went off with a text from Lil Joey.

"Hey T, we need you, got a situation. I can't say more."

He sat up with a rush of adrenaline. *Fuck.*

He responded, "Send the address. Be right there, my man."

While getting dressed, he dialed the Captain.

"Hey, T, what's up?"

"Sorry 'bout the hour. I'm heading to someplace in Scituate?"

"Scituate, why?"

"I got no idea. Lil Joey just sent me an address. Where's Williams? I saw him earlier tailing Jimmy Capaldi. How do I play this? What's in Scituate?"

"Play it as you've been. You're one of them. I'll get you some answers."

Tony drove as fast as he could without looking suspicious. He had a feeling this was about her brother. Tony ripped his sedan up to the address Lil Joey gave him, 11 Hunting House Road.

Deserted, dark and wooded, it was a duplex. Tony recognized Lil Joey's car, a pimped-out black Benz, in the driveway. Greco's pickup was in the other driveway. A muffled sound came from the left duplex. He put on his gloves and quietly got out of the car. He took the steps two at a time and saw wet, dark stains outside the kitchen door.

He eased the door open, drew his gun, and whispered, "Ey, it's me." He could see Shades, Greco, Jencks and Lil Joey in the shadows.

"Punk had the balls to show up at Costa's card game down on Plainfield," Lil Joey whispered.

"Stupid fuck. Anyone next door?"

"Nope. Why? You hear something?"

Tony shook his head.

"Maybe someone's home now," Shades added. "T man, we wouldn't want them talking, you know."

"Tell me what happened."

"He went after Costa in front of everyone. He was seriously liquored up, my man. He's gonna pay now," he said with excitement.

Lil Joey chimed without taking a breath, "Greco grabbed the punk, they scuffled some. He got a pop off, hit the arm, but this punk's fast, actually drove away."

Tony noticed the swelling on Greco's jaw and eye.

"I popped some other dude in the parking lot," Greco added. "Might be heat. Not sure. Went for the leg; not trying to waste a cop." He wiped the sweat off of his face with the end of his T-shirt.

Tony followed muffled sound to see Jimmy tied to a kitchen chair in front of the TV in the living room. The rag he'd had on his head was in his mouth. Tony felt relieved. *He's still alive.* Jimmy had curly blonde hair that resembled hers.

Jimmy struggled hard when he saw Tony. His large arms strained against the rope as blood dripped from a flesh wound. *He's a scrappy fuck; have to give him that.* His left eye was already a slit, and the guys showed no signs of stopping. Shades swung a punch that landed on the kid's cheekbone. It crunched.

Shades eyes lit up. "Hear that?!" He opened and closed his fists, excited for another turn.

They each took their shots, all for their loyalty to Costa. *The fucking scumbag. Williams, where the fuck are you, man? Hope you're okay.*

Tony landed a punch square in his face, shattering the kid's nose for sure. Yup, in the moment, he was a scumbag just like them, and he would finish this out to the end. Costa showed up, and Jimmy was untied but still gagged. There was no time to think about this punk being anyone's brother. That part of Tony's brain was gone.

The guys all stepped back, pumped up on adrenalin to watch Costa finish him off. After quite a beating of his own, Costa finished with a kick to his head, then looked down at his shoe disgusted.

"We might wanna wrap this up," Tony spoke up. "In case parking-lot-guy was, in fact, blue."

"We should finish off this loser," Shades disagreed. "So he don't talk."

Costa shook his head. "Not yet. Let him bleed out."

Jimmy was face down in a pool of his own blood and looked completely unconscious, all cockiness gone. His left leg was bent at a fucked up angle, and his right arm was bleeding bad. Greco was stationed by the door as instructed, and the sucker punch he'd suffered had not gone unnoticed by Costa.

Tony had come to know the guys as well as you could know

anyone, especially Greco and Jencks. In another reality, he'd consider them friends. Tony could tell Greco was scared that he might've shot a cop and he'd lost face with Costa, or at the very least let him down. He seemed ramped, had a thin layer of sweat covering his dark face.

"You think they got film in the lot?" Greco whispered to Tony.

"Nope, broken."

Greco remained tense.

"It's pitch dark back there. That'll help, too."

"What now?" Lil Joey asked Costa with a twinkle in his eyes.

Costa was still assessing his outfit. *Narcissistic fuck.*

"Yes, we're done here, and we're still on for our run to Jersey tonight as planned." Costa kicked Jimmy's head one more time even though he hadn't moved.

Jencks fought against a wince.

"I'll replace the shoes," Costa said to no one in particular. He took his suit jacket from Greco, shrugged it on, and then straightened both sides to make sure there were no wrinkles.

"Jencks, you can drive me."

Everyone exchanged looks. Costa leaving with Jencks was a giant dis against Greco.

"Wipe it down, but leave him. Make it look like he was robbed. T, school them, will you?"

Tony nodded once.

Costa shook his bloody hand out. It had already started to swell. He grabbed his ring off a nearby counter, tucked it in his suit jacket, brushed himself off and strolled out the door.

The others looked to Tony, and he took a minute to assess where to start.

"Look at you, down here with us wiping shit down," Shades said to Greco.

"Fuck you, man. Shut your psycho trap 'fore I snap your

skinny white ass." He grabbed him by the throat and shoved him hard against the door. The size difference was almost comical.

"Shades, Lil Joe, start out on the stairs and side deck. Get the blood."

Greco let go and backed away, but Shades pulled a knife out of his pocket and moved toward Greco. Tony grabbed him with minimal effort, annoyed, took the knife and shoved him hard against the wall.

"We don't have time for this, you stupid fuck. You trying to get us arrested?"

"You believe his balls? Shit." Greco smirked, took a pair of rubber gloves off the counter and followed him into the kitchen.

He eyed Tony, but Tony just rolled his eyes and smirked. "Suicide mission. He ain't worth it."

He chuckled and started to clean.

"Yeah, I already have one body on me for the night," Greco said in a quiet voice a few minutes later.

"You don't know that."

"T man, I want this time to be different. Be there, you know?"

Tony nodded, knowing he wouldn't be there. He felt a hollowness like when he was young and thought about his dad. He pushed it away and concentrated on wiping down any prints. Lil Joe and Shades came back inside, tipping random chairs. Shades started to unzip his pants and move closer to Jimmy.

"What you doing, man?" Lil Joe asked.

"I have to piss."

"Here? T, can't they trace it to him?"

"Yeah, you don't wanna leave body fluids," Tony responded, hiding his disgust. "Take the stuff out of his wallet."

"You a nasty fuck, Shades. I got it."

Tony returned to his task, pretending not to have seen the obit on the fridge. It was the only thing in the kitchen besides empty beer cans. She was the only thing that seemed to take the empty feeling away.

Half an hour later, Tony got back in his car and exhaled deeply before speed-dialing the Captain to roll an ambo and give him a quick update. Jimmy had been alive when they left, but who knew? They'd done some damage for sure. The Captain told him that Williams was alive but in tough shape over at Fatima Hospital.

Tomorrow, this will all be over. Costa will be arrested for a host of shit. Tony should've felt good, at least a sense of pride, but all he felt was responsible for causing her even more pain.

Chapter 27

Out of a foggy sleep, Mia heard her cell ring. She fumbled for it, knocking over a full glass of wine. *Fuck…* She simultaneously covered the spill and answered.

"Auntie?"

"Marianna, I just got a phone call from the hospital… Jimmy's alive but was rushed to Fatima early this morning. That's all I know. We'll be there in five."

Mia flung off her blanket. *Fucking brother. So sick of this kid's goddamn drama. What the fuuuck.* Their heated conversation spun, his ridiculous drunken behavior, as she washed her face and brushed her teeth. *Stupid ass got himself in a car accident or a fight. Dumb fuck.*

She exhaled getting into Sal's car, and locked eyes with her aunt. They'd been down this road together so many times. Mia stewed in silence. If she'd said anything, her aunt would have defended him like she always did. It was long past old. With every mile they drove, her anger lessened; it was infuriating.

Her thoughts felt disjointed, her memories fragmented. The goofy kid she'd laughed with, the cocky teenager she'd adored, the adult she disliked and avoided. Flashes from the previous night drifted past. *He was on a mission… Careful what you wish for, big brother.*

Almost all her memories of Jimmy from *before* included Rob. Thinking about Rob made her feel strange, almost guilty. *I haven't done anything wrong.* She struggled to categorize her feelings for Tony. *It's pure physical attraction. That's it.*

"Been crazy 'bout you since we met."

She couldn't explain why, but she believed him. It was like he could sense what she needed. The way he'd held her last night felt like a giant security blanket. He was more like a gentle giant than a boxing Champ. No matter what his connection to those guys—and nothing would surprise her—he'd made being back slightly less awful. She imagined what it would be like to be with him. Her pulse quickened, and she tried to focus on the highway signs.

"Rob, I hope you understand how hard being here is. I'll always love you. I'm scared I'm going to let you down, though."

She felt as though she were about to cheat. It's not like she hadn't been with other men before, but this felt different. Fear pulsed through her, and she pushed her thoughts away, counting the exits until they reached the hospital.

Sal pulled up to the front steps. "I'll meet you two inside after I park. Go."

"Frenchie, you stay here." Her fear-noyance for him came back in full force.

That's how she'd learned to explain it, a nasty mix of worry and annoyance. It was such a weighted feeling. *Oh, Jimmy, what have you done? I hope your luck hasn't run out.*

She pushed aside her shitty mixed feelings and dialed Rory, leaving him a message.

"Ror, it's me. I'm not going to make my flight. My stupid brother got into trouble after he was thrown out of the bar last night. He's in ICU in Providence. I am going in now. I'll call you later."

Mia practically ran up the front steps and over to an information desk, temporarily forgetting her aunt, who never broke stride. She hurried down the corridor to wait for the elevator and frantically hit the buttons. They rode in silence. When they finally reached his floor, they hurried down the hall to his room.

Please still be alive. She pushed the door open, her heart stopping while she took in the scene. Jimmy looked practically mummified. The parts she could see were purple and swollen.

"Oh God." Tears stung her eyes as she walked to his side. "Jim…" She touched his hand lightly, and his eyes moved even though they stayed closed.

His head was wrapped in a bandage, and one leg was up in a sling. She tried to regulate her breath, stop her heart from beating out of her chest.

"Let's say a prayer," Auntie spoke calmly.

"A prayer?" she asked as tears streamed down her face. "Really? To whom?" They'd never agreed on this topic.

"It's okay."

"No, really. Who should we pray to? I want to know. I want to feel enlightened like everyone else, to believe in something divine, to have faith in a God. The same one that let all this happen or the one that takes away someone's mother and father in the same year. Oh, wait, or the one that let Robbie brutally die… Prayer, God… Please… You pray, and then let me know how that works out for you. I got nothing."

Mia closed her eyes, her anger sapping every ounce from her.

He's my only family left. If he lives, I'll try harder. I'll get him into rehab again. Call every day. The reality was that even if he lived, he wouldn't change. He never did.

"Jimmy, what did you do, you dumb fuck?"

"Hey, hey." Auntie put her arm on Mia's back.

Mia knew her aunt was thinking about Robbie. *Aunt Rosie had to believe in something, or she wouldn't survive her pain.*

"Hey, you all relatives?"

A large, mahogany woman with graying hair and friendly eyes entered the room.

"Yes, we're his immediate family," Auntie Rose responded.

"I'm Nancy. I'm assigned to Mr. James. You're his…?"

"I'm Mia, his sister." Despite her best efforts, she let out a sob.

"Honey, save your tears. This one's strong. His vitals are good; he's gonna pull through. I can feel it, you hear me?"

Her compassion and surety were comforting, but Mia's doubts circled. Considering her past, she didn't really have a choice.

"He is strong," Auntie agreed. "He is."

"Keep your faith. Sit with him and tell him how much you love him. I've seen it before. They know when people care. They can sense when they're loved."

Mia started to feel a twinge of something. Not quite hope, but a flicker of something when a short, dweeby man entered.

"My name is Dr. Jacobs. And who are you?"

"This is Mr. James' sister and mother."

"Mrs.?"

"Mendoza."

The doctor looked down at his chart. "Your son."

"I'm his aunt. Their mother died when they were young. I raised them."

Mia and Auntie locked eyes. That sentence held so much for them both.

"Your nephew, brother, has sustained some very serious injuries. We're doing our very best. My recommendation to anyone with a relative in his condition is to get his affairs in order and to be prepared for the worst. We are watching him closely, and so far, his vitals are strong, but the longer he's unconscious, the greater the chance of permanent damage to his brain. We've ordered a number of tests to check for permanent neurological trauma, and we're just waiting for the swelling to go down. His heart is also at risk. It seems his blood alcohol level was off the charts. Do either of you have any questions?"

"Not at this time," Auntie assured.

The doctor scribbled something down in the chart and then turned to Nancy.

"Don't let law enforcement inside this room. I will not have a circus. I have other patients to attend to. I'll be back later to check on him."

"Don't you worry about him. He's a good doctor. He's no good with the families, just not his thing."

"Yes, he's an asshole. We get it," Auntie scoffed. "I need to get to the diner. I'll check in in a few. Talk to him." They embraced. "We'll get through this. I'll have Sal leave a car in visitor with Frenchie."

Chapter 28

Capaldi's kid... Un-fucking-believable. Her brother. He could still hear the crunch of Jimmy's bones, see her father's obituary on the fridge. *Wasn't supposed to happen like that, but ey, nothing is.* He turned on the Sinatra station and hummed along to the melancholy tune, "It was a very good year." He got to his condo in record time.

"Was it, though, Frankie? A good year?" he challenged as he got out of the car.

He slid the key in and pushed the door open. He exhaled deep, trying to rein in his thoughts. The adrenaline had worn off.

He unstrapped his holster and placed it down on the table. He knew sleeping was out. He undressed in what felt like slow motion, then turned on the shower. He eyed his clothes on the floor. *If the kid dies, I'll toss 'em.* He stepped in the shower and put both hands against the back wall, exhaling away the night. He let the water pelt him and then washed and re-washed his body a few times. Feeling clean was a thing for other people.

He dressed and stared at his reflection in the mirror. Repulsed, he looked away. *Could she possibly love someone who's done the things I've done?* The look in her brother's eyes as he punched flashed in his mind. *Kid lives, how am I gonna explain that?*

The next morning, Tony arrived at the regular coffee spot to meet with the crew with time to spare. The Captain had said to act normal, so he attempted to follow his usual schedule. He tried to play like it was any other day, but his mind was on her. He could only imagine her face when she saw her brother all busted up or dead.

Tony smirked as Jencks sat down across from him. *It's game time.*

"Tank, what's up, man? Greco mad?"

"Naw, he knows it ain't you."

Tony stifled a chuckle as Jencks ordered chocolate chip pancakes with extra syrup. *Guys got a helluva sweet tooth.* After two years, he was probably one of Tony's favorites—besides Greco. Jencks came into the gym at least three times a week to work out with Tony. Jenks considered Tony a friend, someone who'd do anything for him. Caring too much was a liability; it was Jencks' downside.

He had the typical street story. He'd grown up near Chad Brown and, as a kid, ran dope, stole cars and did other small stuff for guys to make a living. Tony knew he'd never touched the stuff. His brother, JT, had died of an overdose. Jencks named his boy after him. He loved the kid and was going to keep him off the junk at all costs. His kid was his line in the sand, his liability. He was into the gambling part of the operation, mostly. Strip clubs, protection, that sort of thing. He made extra money dealing, like most of them.

"Hey, T…"

Tony followed his gaze to the door to see Dwayne. He was a tall, lanky black kid who showed up a few days a week to represent his boss Toby. Toby had a massive drinking problem and couldn't always make it to the early meetings. Costa didn't care because Toby made him a shit load of money buying and selling drugs up and down the east coast. Toby had no guilt; he saw what he did for work as strictly business. He had kids to support.

"Hey, Dwayne, what's going on?"

"Naw, same shit, different day, Tank."

Snags walked in with Greco behind him. He rolled his eyes about Shades.

Jencks relaxed and smirked. "You good with Costa?"

Greco shrugged his big shoulders.

"Nice threads, my man." Tony didn't mention his face or the fact that, for the first time, he wasn't escorting Costa.

"Those are sweet." Tony nodded to his sneakers. "Nike air?"

"Fresh out the box."

Dwayne whistled long. "What, you got different sneakers for every day of the week?"

Tony smirked and felt his stomach twist. He pushed it down and sipped his coffee.

"Hey, think those'll fit me?" Tony laughed.

"Ain, they don't make 'em in ski-size, man. What you got, like size Sasquatch or somethin'?" He flipped the chair backward, plunked down and opened the menu.

He was the only one who seemed off. He usually never looked at the menu; guy always ordered the same egg white and spinach omelet.

"It didn't change from yesterday, man," Jencks jabbed. "You know you're gonna get the same damn boring thing anyways."

"Nope, not today." Greco chuckled.

Snags jittered in and sat next to Shades, folding his lanky body into the chair. His complexion was pale and pock-marked. He sickened Tony because he was into some nasty child porn. He didn't know they knew. Vegas spun, Snags, Lil Joey and

Shades double-teaming a dancer in the bathroom. She'd looked like a kid.

"What's up, Snags?"

Tony's mind could still see the vacant look Snags wore while banging the girl. And the causal way he'd asked Tony, "Tank man, you want a turn?" He'd held her ass out like she wasn't human. Thinking about it made Tony want to vomit and kill him on the spot, but Snags was Tony's initial connection to these guys, his C.I. Snags had started coming into the gym a few years ago, saying Costa had heard Tony still had connections, heard he retired dirty.

They had access to drugs, and Tony had a clientele. He let them sell roids and other illegal enhancements to customers, some under-age, out of the gym. They didn't know Snags was a lifer who'd turned snitch years before as a trade for old drug and perve charges. He wasn't prison material, so he wasn't going to say anything.

Despite how they made their living, a few of them weren't all bad. Costa was a snake, Snags was a freak, and Tony just plain didn't like Shades. The others were just followers. Limited career choices, "trying to earn a living," was how they justified.

As if on cue, Costa strolled in, all dolled up. His wrist was wrapped in a cast, and Tony pretended not to notice.

Jencks shot Greco a side-ways glance.

Costa was always late, some sort of power trip. He was an arrogant egomaniac. Tony wanted to grab him by the throat and squeeze.

"Mr. Costa, sharp suit." Tony grinned.

"Anthony." He nodded in return. He looked at Greco and nodded once.

Lil Joey had come in behind Costa, his personal bodyguard.

"Look at you, Lil Joey. All fresh in your black get-up," Shades complimented.

Costa snapped his attention to Shades.

Costa ordered toast and coffee and began with his two-bit news. Same ol' stuff—book keeping, minor gambling rings with local college kids and drug sales.

Tony took a quick glance around the table. *They got no way of knowing we have every exchange from the beginning, all on surveillance. That alone's gonna wipe out half the table.* The other half would need something bigger. If Jimmy died, they'd get more time.

He turned his attention back to Costa. Being the one in charge of ordering a hit, or in this case, landing the kid in the hospital might be enough. Tony eyed Snags, who was wearing a wire. Two things Tony had learned over the past two years hanging with Costa: he was as sleazy and vain as they came but smart as a whip—especially if he actually got his own hands dirty. He'd wait and plan. He was meticulous. Taking in Costa's wounded paw, Tony knew emotion had gotten the best of him. Loyalty to his brother had made him sloppy.

Costa stood. "Nature calls."

Tony took a mouthful of eggs when Greco asked Jencks, "Any word about little Capaldi?"

"What about him?" asked Snags.

"He gonna live or what?"

"He came in drunk, actin' all tough," Greco said in a soft voice. "Mouth'n off big time, bad talking Costa's brother... They called him to come down."

"Kid's got balls. He deserved it." Snags rolled his eyes.

"Yeah, we was already told to shut him up permanently."

"All in a day's work, man." Jencks raised his brows.

The table went silent.

"We can't have the kid talkin' junk," said Greco. "It's disrespectful." He cut a piece of his steak and dipped it into his egg yolk.

"What's with the different order?" Jencks asked.

"Never know, man. I'm not feeling no prison food. If this is my last day, fuck my health."

"Man, you ain't going to prison. Stop being dramatic."

Greco rolled his eyes. "Man, you white. Me? Not so much."

"Who was there?" asked Dwayne.

No one spoke.

"Costa did a number at the end, huh? Was the other guy blue?"

Williams. Tony shrugged, and his stomach tightened.

"So, what happened after that?" prodded Dwayne.

"Some guy saw 'em, tried to turn around and leave like it wasn't his business. They did what they had to do, then heard sirens nearby and got the fuck outta there," Tony summarized.

"Kid's in the ICU. Word is, he probably won't make it," Greco added. "He got lucky; they had ta leave."

"They left the big guy there?" Dwayne questioned.

"I'm pretty sure they didn't," Greco said, eyeing Jencks.

"You think the guy was a cop?" Jencks looked to Tony.

"You were there?"

Jencks nodded once and looked toward Greco.

They think he's dead.

"I'll find out," Tony reassured.

"Fucked up big waitin' for Costa." Greco dropped his head. "Kid might've seen the whole thing."

"Ey," started Dwayne. "Kid might not make it."

A hush fell over the table as Costa returned and sat back down. He turned the topic back to other money-making matters. Costa wasn't going to talk about the previous night. They'd fucked up bad. He was already upset that old man Capaldi had been able to get to his brother surrounded by their own guys. It didn't get more personal to him than that. The Capaldi kid might have witnessed them accidentally kill a cop. Tony would call them later with the bad news that he wasn't dead. Mia flashed to his mind for a minute, and he wondered how this was going to touch her. He felt like killing her brother himself. *Stupid fuck.*

With a nod, Costa signaled to Lil Joey that he was ready to leave. They dispersed to their so-called jobs in society.

He wondered how she was doing. He wanted to call her but knew he couldn't chance it. He had to think of a way to explain how he knew her. At some point, they'd realize she was the girl they'd seen on The Hill. He didn't want the crew to think they had anything going—they'd use her against him. Tony climbed into his car.

"Hey, T man, we on for tomorrow?" Jencks asked.

"I wouldn't miss it, man. Could use to blow off some steam."

"I might be 5 late. Gotta pick up JT. It's my day to grab him from the bus. Maybe we can beat Greco's ass with that scratch he's got."

"I think we can." Tony smirked wide and slammed the car door. *JT's gonna miss his dad. Fuck.*

Chapter 29

The next couple of hours for Mia were a blur. The medical staff had come and gone in a busy train. Repairing physical tragedy was their business. Most of them ignored her presence, attending to their tasks. They were accustomed to this. Not her, though; she was used to bruises that couldn't be seen. Nancy would never become accustomed to it. It's what made her different.

If Jimmy dies, who'll really care? He has no wife or children to mourn him. Maybe he has a girlfriend or some close friends. She barely knew him anymore.

A wave of sadness hit her again. She was practically orphaned already. Without Jimmy, she'd be completely family-less, all alone, except for Rory. The empty space where her family used to be was palpable. *And Auntie and the cousins.* But the heaviness didn't lift. She stood abruptly. Despite Nancy's advice, she had nothing to say to him; the silence was deafening. She left him to find a cafeteria.

Minutes later, coffee cup in hand, she decided she could use some fresh air and needed to let Mr. French out. After their brief walk, she returned Frenchie to the car and punched in Rory's cell. When it went to voicemail, she hung up and put her phone back in her purse.

She grabbed the shoebox from the floor and headed back to the hospital. She was glad to find his room empty. She sat in a corner chair and began to read aloud.

"Prison doesn't have clocks, but there's a definite order to things. Lights go out at eleven each night, and with each passing hour, the sounds emerge like the wind on a stormy night. Can't really be sure, but it seems even the toughest sons of bitches get desperate then. I wonder what they cry for, miss? Maybe it's their freedom or the soft body of a woman. I hear rats scratch and move about, they're loud little fuckers. And there's muffled screams unlike anything I've ever heard. This is the time, the dead hour around 4 am in between dark and light, when I miss my life. My Mia, the kids, my rig, my freedom… the way life used to be.

"I can't for a minute believe my life has taken this turn. When I think of her loving him, wanting to be with him instead of me, I'm actually sick. I try not to picture them together, but my mind spins. It's the hardest thing to not think. Some nights I want to choke the life right out of him until his eyes bulge and he's gasping for forgiveness and breath. Neither would I give him. I map it out down to the tiniest detail of what I'd do to him. I want to pretend I'm glad she's dead, that she got what she deserved, but I don't feel it. Sometimes I pretend she's alive. She tells me it's not so, wasn't true. It was all a mistake. I'm the only guy for her, like when we were together.

"To hold her again, touch her again, even for one second… I'd give anything. I might even forgive that she was with him. I miss her so much it hurts to even breathe. I hate myself for still loving her. If I didn't, maybe things with Jimmy and me would be different. He called me a pussy. He's not wrong. I wanna end it all, put myself out of my misery once and for all… at night sometimes I plan it."

Mia stopped reading and looked up at her brother. She continued with another entry.

"Today Rosie took the kids in. Jimmy's eyes are hard with hate for me; they look a lot like the guys I'm in here with. It kills me he's in this, wasn't supposed to be." She reread his words, trying to make sense of them. "It kills me he's in this, wasn't supposed to be.

"They came to visit me today, and my little girl was the saddest little thing I've ever seen. Before they left, Marianna asked me to tell her the truth. 'Tell me you didn't do it daddy. They say you did, but I don't believe them.' She was crying so hard she threw up. She kept saying, 'Tell me you didn't do it… on purpose.' I told her the truth, the one she needed to hear. I loved her mother more than my own life… it was an accident. But I couldn't hold her in my arms, and no matter what I said it didn't change nothing. I'm in here for life and she's out there. This isn't gonna work for her to see me like this. For either of us. My baby girl will be better off remembering me before all this happened."

Mia snapped the book shut and closed her eyes tight. She remembered the nightmare well enough. She didn't need to read about it any further…

Two nurses and a different doctor entered the room. They informed her that they'd have to run more tests and Jimmy would be gone for the afternoon.

"Maybe you want to go home? Eat something, rest?"

Their eyes were kind. They'd seen this all before.

"What if something happens?"

"Miss Capaldi, go home awhile. He's suffered serious injuries, and he's severely dehydrated. We're doing everything we can, but his body needs to heal. Go rest and come back later or tomorrow morning. If anything changes, we promise we'll call you."

Mia walked over to Jimmy. "I'll be back."

She walked through the hallway, counting her steps. Auntie Rose and Sal were just up ahead.

"Marianna, how is he?"

Mia explained his lack of change. "Who would do this to him? I don't get it. What is he involved in?"

Auntie eyed Sal. "I don't know."

Mia simply stared at her, done with being kept in the dark.

Auntie Rose started to walk, but Sal stopped her with his hand.

"We'll talk another time," Auntie assured. "You go, we'll hang around. I'll call you later."

"Listen." Sal looked uncomfortable. "We took the fluff ball for a walk, and there's a care package in your trunk in case you get hungry."

"The house is yours as long as you need it." Auntie hugged Mia tight. Her strong arms felt like a band-aid.

What's she hiding. Mia's throat tightened, and she headed to the car, trying not to think about Jimmy's condition. *I have appointments tomorrow morning. I'm busy, God damn him.* No matter what happened after tomorrow, she was going home. Even if she needed to fly back and forth. She got in the car and threw the shoebox down on the floor. She noticed her phone blinking and speed-dialed Rory.

"Mia, what's going on? What happened?" His voice was filled with concern.

"Jimmy relapsed. I ran into him at a bar last night; he got kicked out for acting like a jerk."

"You were at the same bar?"

"Yes, stupid tiny State."

"Let me guess, the guy from the plane?"

"Yes. I decided to meet Tony for a drink. Turns out he's a nice man."

"I'm sure he's a peach… So, what happened to Jimmy?"

"We had words out in the parking lot. He said he had one more stop to make in Providence. I tried to tell him to go home, but he was wasted. I don't know what happened after that. He looks horrible, really bad."

"That's awful, honey. What are the doctors saying?"

She inhaled and let it out slowly. "Don't know; he's still unconscious."

"Mee, you want me to come out there? We still have Scott."

"No, I need to know you're there. After tomorrow, no matter what happens here, I'm coming home to see my patients."

"Listen, I'm hoping he's still part feline, but I'm pretty sure your patients will live. Mee, you need to stay there until your brother is stable. Don't be ridiculous. I know you hate it there, but still… Come on."

"Yeah, whatever, Ror." After a beat, she felt her defensiveness dissolve. "I know. I just hate how being here makes me feel." The tears started to sting her eyes again, and she felt her anger burn. "There's always a fucking tragedy to deal with every goddamn fucking time. He's such a fucking pain in my ass. Maybe he should die, Ror."

"Mee… I'm bearhugging you through the line, my friend. I get it. I know he's a giant pain in your ass, and I also know you don't mean that."

She started to cry harder. "Part of me does." Hearing Rory's voice made her miss him and her safe life away from all of this. "I'll call you with my new flight time."

"Mee, don't you dare, but let me know how he's doing when something changes."

Chapter 30

Tony pulled up to the back entrance of Fatima, unsure who might be watching. The guys were making the run to Jersey, then NYC, but he didn't want to chance a sighting of him visiting Williams. He could have easily spun his presence at the hospital, but still. *I don't want my crew... Costa's crew to know I'm here.* He seriously doubted they'd go anywhere near the hospital. They weren't dumb.

He dialed the Captain quick before heading in. "Ey, it's me. Kid alive?"

"Yeah, unconscious, probably won't make it. Don't matter to us either way."

Tony's stomach sank, and he hesitated.

"Hey, you there?"

"Yeah. I'm at the hospital to see Williams. Anything on your end?"

"Yeah, we got half those losers in custody already. Were able to raid the truck heading to New York with the roids and fentanyl, exactly where Snags said it'd be. We might be able to flip

Bobby for more info and, now, with the kid, especially if he dies, make it stick. What do you think?"

He was torn. "I'd try him and Jencks. They both got kids. They were together, they got the most to lose, and they think they wasted a cop. Greco went for his leg but really couldn't see cause the kid had sucker punched him in the face before it happened. Truth is, he doesn't know where he hit him. Plus, his girl's pregnant; he doesn't wanna go back in." Tony paused. "Jencks admitted to being there."

Tony thought about the look in their eyes, especially Jencks, when the job was over, and they found out who he really was—his betrayal. It's messed up, but he felt for Jencks. He was just a kid, and he wouldn't be there for JT. He knew what that was like on the other side.

"Ey, you there, Iannucci?"

"Yeah. What about Slick?"

"Costa's lawyered up. Got an alibi, but the time won't stick. You might have to testify. And we got his voice tapped and records of the trucks that directly link back to him, thanks to you, my friend. It's imminent, my man, you're basically done."

"I'll call you later."

"Iannucci, you did good."

Tony took the stairs two at a time, thinking about her punk ass brother—the ramifications for her if he died—they had a better shot at conviction if her brother died. *And I wouldn't have to testify.*

If the kid lives, there'll be no us. Might actually have to tell her. He shook off the thought. *There might not be an us either way… What a fucking mess.* He rounded the hallway, balancing two coffees and a small box of munchkins. He nodded to Dinucci, standing guard outside the door.

"Everything alright with you, Iannucci?"

"Yeah, never been better. Want one"

"Stop it. Poison, my friend."

Tony laughed and handed him the coffee. "Tall and dark. Like your woman."

"Thanks, man."

Williams was alone, one leg bandaged up in a sling. He looked smaller than usual in the bed. Tony sat in the chair to wait until he woke up. He took the lid off his coffee cup and glanced outside, wondering which room her brother was in and how she was doing. He'd check in later even though he shouldn't go anywhere near either of them. He placed his coffee down on the table with the munchkins and leaned his head back.

"Hey, you come here to take a nap or what?"

Tony roused himself. He must've fallen asleep. It was dusk outside. He grabbed the box of munchkins and dropped them on the table nearest to Williams.

"How you feelin'? Took one in the leg, huh?"

"Feeling no pain right now, my man, but it hurt like a fucker."

"Yeah, you look a little too happy."

Williams whacked down two of the munchkins in one shot. Tony couldn't help but smile. They remained silent for a few minutes.

"Capaldi's kid was bombed but could still drive. You know, a real professional drunk. I followed him down to Plainfield to the old post. He knocked out Costa's personal bodyguard, the big black dude. Boom. Out cold for a few, guy was surprised."

Tony smirked, thinking about Greco.

"He fuckin' storms him. I instinctively got out of my car, not sure if I should follow. Thought Costa would kill him right there, but you know the drill. So I wait, listening for any noise from inside. Only yelling. The guy gets up, the kid takes off, so I go to get back in my car, and the bodyguard takes a shot at him. Not sure if he was hit, but he drove off. Guy pops another one off, gets me right in the thigh. Hurt like a mother. Kid dead?"

Tony exhaled. "No. Not yet. "

"I thought he would go home or booty call, whatever."

"Right. You drive here?"

Williams nodded. "Tied it off, was losing too much blood."

"I got a call. Costa ordered us to go beat his ass, take him out at a Scituate apartment. Punk moved, apparently. How the fuck did we miss that? Anyways, he's here, all banged up, unconscious, probably won't make it."

"What's that mean for us?"

Tony tried to downplay it. "Naw doesn't really matter. I might have to testify if he lives."

Williams eyed him. "The parking lot," he began, but the drugs were kicking in, and he drifted off. Tony was relieved; he wasn't ready to explain his situation with her yet.

"I'll be back, man. Be good."

Tony stopped by the nurse's station and flashed his badge at the very tired-looking middle-aged lady, giving her his best smile.

"Good evening, Mrs. Parker," he greeted, reading her name tag. "My name is Detective Anthony Iannucci. Could you please tell me which room Mr. James Capaldi is being kept in? I was instructed to check on his safety."

She made a call and directed him to the eleventh floor, room 305.

Feeling drained, he eyed the elevator but walked past. *Safer to take the steps.*

There wasn't any blue outside his door. Not enough manpower, and it didn't matter if they finished him off. Nobody cared.

No one was in the room, and the kid was out. A total mess. Tony had seen this many times. By the look of him, it'd be a miracle if he made it.

He took a sip of the now-cold coffee and left the room remembering the warmth of the Coffee Bean with Mia.

Chapter 31

Mia sat in her car, trying to compose herself. *Maybe we'd all be better off if he died.* It was a tough reality, but his drama was too much; she couldn't do it anymore. She closed her eyes and put her head back against the seat.

She startled when she heard a tap on her window. *Tony.* She wiped at her nose, which was still drippy from crying and pressed the button to lower the window.

"Hey, what are you doing here?"

"I'm here visiting a buddy—car accident—thought I recognized the car and Frenchie." He patted Frenchie's furry white head. "Hey, boy."

"My drunken brother last night…he got in a fight and is all messed up, I can't even …."

He opened her door and pulled her to him. "Shh, it's ok, I'm so sorry you're going through all this." *And that I'm a part of why.*

His presence, hug, felt like something she couldn't name.

"You want some company? Did you eat?"

If she was honest, she really wanted a drink. Food was an afterthought.

"No, I haven't eaten."

He looked tired, sad.

"Is your friend alright?"

"Yeah. Busted leg, he'll be okay."

"My aunt left some food in the trunk. I'm sure there's enough for ten."

His smile reached his eyes.

"I'm not feeling public right now."

"Me either."

Mia hit the first liquor store she saw on her way to her aunt's house. She bought a six-pack for Tony and a large bottle of Tito's. At the register, she grabbed several vodka nips and two limes, avoiding the clerk's eyes. She thought she had already dealt with her family's ugly truths, but she wasn't sure anymore. They didn't add up.

Back in the car, she uncapped a mini bottle and downed several swigs on the way.

"Don't judge me." She glanced at Mr. French.

Once back on the couch, she drank vodka on the rocks, still trying to soothe her nerves and turn off her brain. Five minutes later, Tony showed up carrying a bouquet of flowers.

"For the lady."

"Thank you, that's very sweet." She riffled through the cupboards, looking for a vase.

"Just put them in a glass for now. Let's sit." He took her hand.

"My aunt left me a ton of food. Want some?"

"Do you?" he asked, clocking her drink on the side table.

"Not really. You want a beer?"

"I do."

She released his hand and retrieved a beer from the fridge. They sat in silence for a long minute.

"What's the deal with your brother?"

"He obviously has a drinking problem. His self-destruction started a very long time ago." She drained her drink and headed toward the fridge.

"Good idea. We should eat something." He followed after her.

She placed the food on the counter and silently handed him a plate. She made herself an eggplant sandwich and returned to the couch. He did the same, and they ate without talking. When they finished, she took their plates to the sink, made herself another drink and grabbed him another beer.

He took her hand, and she rested her head on his shoulder. It felt like the most natural thing to be here, sitting on Rob's couch in Auntie's house with Tony. *Isn't life strange?*

"After our mother died, he was never the same again… I guess none of us were."

"That must've been a very hard time for you."

After a while, Tony could tell she'd fallen asleep. He didn't want to wake her. Knew she had to be drained. He quietly cleared their drinks and draped a blanket over her. He brushed his lips softly on her forehead.

He left a note on the counter.

Hope you catch some much needed z's. Call me tomorrow. Maybe after you visit the hospital I can take you to my buddy Carlos's restaurant for dinner, if you're feeling up to it.

Hope the sleep helps, T

Tony climbed into his car, bone tired. His lack of sleep was catching up to him. Driving home, he couldn't push away the shit show he was entangled in. He switched on some music when his cell rang.

Fuck, it's Slick. Does he know?

His voice was cool and calm. "Mr. Costa, how are you this fine evening?"

"I've been better, T. To tell you the truth."

He slid back into his role—or a darker version of himself. He rested his arm on the armrest.

"What can I do for you, Sir?" he asked nonchalantly.

"Can't say much now, but I think we might have some legal troubles. Have you heard from anyone?"

"Nope, not a word. You?"

"No. Crickets here, Anthony."

The hair on his arms stood erect. Costa knew or at least suspected. Everyone was locked up except for him. It didn't take a brain surgeon.

"Okay, stay close now."

The line went dead, and Tony speed-dialed the Captain.

"Ey, why the fuck is Costa calling me?"

"What do you mean?"

"What do I mean? He just called me, asked about the guys. Thought he was in custody? What the fuck?"

"Let me call you right back."

Tony ripped up to his condo, took a quick shower and laid down on his bed. His thoughts turned to her, her fucking stupid brother and this fucking case that wouldn't seem to end.

His thoughts circled as his eyes grew heavy.

He and Mia were back at Bishop Hill, dancing slowly. His hands were wrapped in her hair, which smelled like apples. He lifted her up on top of the bar and kissed her slowly. She responded, kissing him back. She let out a groan that sent shivers up his spine. The door swung open, and the kid walked in. He was a mess. His head was still bandaged. He limped up to them and poked Tony in the chest.

"Get away from her. You, I told you, you was a scumbag." He turned to Mia. "He did this."

She pulled away from Tony, eyes wide. "Say it isn't true, Tony.

Tell me you're not really friends with them. You didn't do this… You couldn't…"

Costa strolled in. "Go ahead, tell her, Tony, about my brother and her mother. About how you knew all of it. She'll love that."

Her eyes pleaded with his for the truth. He couldn't deny it any longer. Her look was unbearable; she knew his ugly truths.

Tony woke to the sound of his cell with a start. He felt nauseous.

"Ey, this is T."

"Iannucci, he's in custody for now. Delete his contact, throw away the burner. It's over, my friend. The moment you've been waiting for, it's over. We'll meet soon to go over details, but you're officially done with them for now."

For now…

A guy like Costa had the best lawyers. Her safety started to nag at him.

He should've felt happy, relieved. He felt nothing but a slow, burning dread for her. He forced his head back against the pillow. He needed sleep to figure this all out.

I have to tell her some piece of this… My truth. Something.

Chapter 32

Mia woke up with her stomach in knots. *What else is new.* She walked around the empty home and noticed a note on the counter. Tony made it all a little more bearable.

She left Liz a voicemail to set up video sessions with her patients. Then, she planned her day. *I'll head over to the hospital for a quick update, see my patients afterward, then meet up with Tony. Unless Jimmy wakes up…* She wasn't ready to deal with him yet. The sad truth about tragedy was that life moved on. There was no controlling it; she'd have to go with it.

After a quick shower, she grabbed the keys off the counter and hurried Frenchie outside. The hospital parking lot was pretty full, but she finally found a space. She approached the front desk to ask for an update. The nurse checked a paper on a clipboard in front of her and politely informed her there had been no changes with her brother.

After reading Mia's face, she added, "This isn't necessarily a bad thing."

Mia nodded and walked off. She mentally prepared herself

as she rode the elevator up to Jimmy's floor. She let out her breath when she entered his room. She swept over Jimmy, and the reality of his physical condition penetrated somewhere between her heart and stomach.

"Oh my God, Jimmy, what did you do." Tears stung her eyes, and she quickly swiped them away. She couldn't allow herself to cry. She knew if she started, she might never stop. She swallowed her emotions as she positioned herself in the chair near him.

After a short while, she realized she was too antsy to sit. She had nothing to say to Jimmy or to God—who still hadn't shown himself. She'd head back to Auntie's or take a walk.

Back in her car, she fumbled through her purse at the sound of her cell.

"Hey, sugar. Ror filled me in. You doing okay?" Liz's southern drawl filled the air.

Mia's eyes brimmed with tears at the sound of her concern. "Thank you. I'm hanging in, yes. There hasn't been any change, so we'll just have to wait and see."

"I'll say a prayer for him."

Mia stiffened. "Thanks, Liz."

"Okay, Doc, I lined up Jackson, Sara and Caren for this afternoon starting at noon your time. Let me know what else I can do."

"Thanks, Liz, will do." Mia flung her cell on the seat next to her.

Checking her rearview mirror, she backed out and drove to Auntie's on autopilot. She stayed in the car a full minute, bracing herself for the energy she'd need to get through the day. The late morning was brisk for this time of year, and she ignored the smell of autumn. It always conjured her childhood.

She hooked Frenchie to his leash and took him for a quick

walk before her appointments. She walked in the direction of the diner, almost by habit. Her thoughts turned to her brother. She heard the familiar chimes of the diner door as she entered. They were like a wake-up call; every cell in her body felt alert.

"Hey, good morning," Auntie called out. She patted Frenchie's head and hugged Mia close. "Any change?"

"No, he's the same." Mia broke eye contact, afraid Auntie Rose could read her emotions.

"Sit, have some coffee."

Mia envisioned the diner the way it used to be. She pictured her mother on that cold March night all those years ago. There had still been piles of snow outside. Mia remembered her coat with the faux fur-rimmed hood. She remembered watching her mother zipping it up that night before work. Mia still had the coat. Her dad used to say the blue matched her eyes perfectly.

Mia instinctively adjusted her sweater, pulling it tighter to her body. The realization washed through her in an instant. It was finally clear; she knew. It nearly left her breathless. Reality spun and tilted. She was grateful for the counter. She needed to sit.

There was absolutely no way her father could've shot her mother. Even if she'd had a lover, absolutely no way, not the way he loved her.

Auntie Rose poured her a mug of coffee and placed a pepper biscuit in front of her. "Just made them. They're crunchy, the way you like them."

Mia felt a strange remove as if she were outside of herself watching.

"Thanks," Mia managed.

She wrapped her hands around the mug, letting it warm her. She sat stunned, amazed it had taken her this long to figure it out. Jimmy's drunk, angry words, her father's journal entries, even her aunt's comments throughout the years... They all made sense. An old truth bobbed to the surface. *They all tried to tell me, but I never really wanted to know. I accepted their version of what happened because I didn't want to imagine the actual truth. Or maybe I couldn't handle it.*

The truth circled. *It was Jimmy.*

"You okay?"

They both knew she wasn't.

Part 2

Chapter 33

Mia couldn't leave the diner fast enough as her vision blurred and spun. Nervous energy propelled her toward Auntie's house.

They were protecting him this whole time.

She'd lost her entire family because of Jimmy's anger. Fury rose up her spine as reality seeped in. *Did everyone know but me? Did Rob know the truth?* The image of him looking at her entered her mind. There was no way he'd known. He'd been just as perplexed about Jimmy's downward spiral after their mom had died. It all made sense now.

She tried to catch her breath as she approached the house. Placing her keys and pocketbook down with a thump, she scanned for a place to set up her computer and decided on the kitchen table. The lighting was good and didn't remind her too much of Rob. She had scheduled virtual appointments with her patients as she was eager for the distraction. She eyed the vodka, aware of the temporary peace it would bring. She'd never drink before a session, but she couldn't deny that she wanted to.

She set her eyes on the enormous oak tree in the backyard. It would be her anchor, one she badly needed. Its colors, rich in full autumn display, were calming, ablaze with color. She counted its shades. One… fiery red. Two… burnt orange. Three… brown sprinkled with purple veins. Four…

After a few minutes, she moved away from the window and set up her workspace. She moved the note Tony had left, excited to see him again. Tony felt like the only person outside of all her family shit. She definitely was not in the right headspace to meet with patients, but it was too late to cancel, and she selfishly needed an escape.

Mia rolled her neck slowly from left to right, then reversed the motion. She pulled her shoulders back in an attempt to release her tension. *Will Jimmy wake up? Does he deserve to?* The questions started to spin. *Not now.*

She pulled up her emails, ignoring the dozens of unopened messages, and hit the secure link. She focused her eyes on the virtual bookshelves behind her and exhaled slowly, pressing the button to let Jackson into the video chat.

"Hi, Jackson, how are you doing today?"

"My life is falling apart. Emma has moved into Kara's room and hasn't gotten out of Kara's bed since Saturday."

"I'm so sorry to hear that. Can you say more about that?"

"She blames me. I should've gotten someone else to do the surgery."

"Did she actually say that to you?"

"No. She said she wanted to be closer to Kara. She left me all alone."

"Jackson, did you talk to her about how you feel?"

"No. I feel too guilty about everything. I don't blame her for leaving me."

"Listen, she's devasted too, but nothing about her sleeping in Kara's room says that she blames you for Kara's death. It sounds like she's trying to deal with her own sadness. Maybe you can try talking to her about how it makes you feel all alone and that you'd love for her to return to your room."

The session felt long, the topic of grief a little too close to home.

Mia pressed the next link, letting Sara into the waiting room. She slid the chair back and stood to retrieve a glass of water from the kitchen. Her thoughts churned about the pain Jackson and his wife were experiencing and their displaced guilt and anger. She forced her thoughts away from her brother. She felt for them. Sadness and grief are so very private and unique. She felt bad for them as a couple, knowing many couples divorced after the loss of a child. She made a mental note to refer them to couples counseling.

Her internal struggle against hope echoed. They could get all the counseling in the world, but the depressing truth was that they'd never be okay again—ever.

She sat back down and placed the glass next to her on the table. She exhaled and hit Sara's name on the screen.

"Doc C, they said you had a family emergency. Is everything okay with you?"

"Hi, Sara. Yes, I had some family matters to handle in Rhode Island, but I'm fine. Thank you for asking. Tell me how you've been feeling?" Mia noticed Sara looked pale, maybe thinner; she wore an oversized sweatshirt draped off one shoulder.

Sara smiled nervously and started twirling her hair around her finger.

When she remained silent, Mia prompted, "How are things going at home?"

"Pretty much the same. Mom works all the time, and that's fine with me."

"How do you feel physically, Sara? How's the food plan going?"

"It feels impossible. I mean, who eats that much? Besides her, I mean?"

"Who is her?" Mia asks, even though she knows Sara's referring to her mother.

"Sherry."

"Can you tell me what happened?"

"She's just getting fatter and fatter, and she thinks she can tell me how to live and eat."

"Has something happened to make you so upset, angry with her?"

"I was following my program, and then she had to go and say that she felt proud of me for eating like a normal person."

"So, your mom using the word 'normal' triggered you."

"I guess. Doc C, normal people eat too much. They eat like her. And they get fat like her," she whispered, crying softly.

Mia exhaled silently. "Sara, listen. I know your mother's delivery isn't always the best, but do you think she was trying to criticize you or call you fat when she used the word normal? Maybe she was trying to compliment your progress."

"I know it's my mind—that I'm fucked up with the fun mirror stuff—she just always makes me feel like shit, you know?"

"I'm sorry you feel bad. You've learned so much about your triggers and your distorted thoughts about your body. I know you feel abandoned by her, with her work schedule."

"And then you weren't here either," she mumbled as she wiped her nose on the back of her hand.

And there it is. Damn you, Jimmy.

"Sara, I'm sorry you felt all alone."

Sara nodded in response and wiped her eyes on her sweatshirt. "I was doing it. Why does she have to say anything about the way I eat?"

"You tell me."

"Because she's jealous of me—her own daughter. How fucked up is that?"

"I'm sorry it's felt so hard for you and that she's not honest about her motives with you."

Sara was spot on about her mother's jealousy and manipulative behavior. *That's exactly what's wrong.*

"Yes, she's a selfish asshole. What am I supposed to do with that?" Sara replied in a snap.

"You concentrate on yourself and your health, and you see her for who she is, not who you wish her to be. Her capacity isn't your fault. Next year you'll be away at school. A little distance may help."

"I wonder… will it always be this hard with me and her?"

"I hope not, but I honestly don't know."

It hadn't been an easy session. Mia stood and let her gaze find the tree. Changing someone's perception of themselves was very hard, especially when they're so deeply committed and convinced. In Sara's case, she and her mother's relationship was tangled up in deep-rooted self-hatred and craving her mother's affection and attention. Sara's anger toward her mother was healthy; she was angry because she still cared, still desired that relationship.

Mia thought about Jimmy's rage toward their parents and his drinking. She thought about her own denial of her anger toward them all. They'd left her, and she'd carried that pain with her, defended it, even.

She eyed the Tito's bottle quickly before returning to her computer for the last session of the day. Learning the truth about her brother had shifted her outrage. It bubbled right beneath her skin; she didn't like the feeling. She shook her head to shake the thoughts away. *For now.*

She eyed her cell phone, flipping it over quickly to see a message from Tony.

"Checking to see if you're still feeling up for tonight?"

Mia couldn't sit there all alone all night by herself if she'd tried.

"Yes. I am working for another hour than can meet you."

She watched the dots…

"Great! I can pick you up."

"I'll come to you. Would love to see your gym."

"Looking forward to showing you around. My afternoon can't go by fast enough." He sent a heart bitmoji. "112 Mineral Spring Avenue North Providence."

Mia smiled and sent a thumbs-up before flipping the phone back over. The heart warmed her; it'd felt like a band-aid of sorts. He had no idea how much she needed it.

Caren appeared in her waiting room. Mia was not looking forward to this session. Caren's tragedy was horrific, hard to sit with. Mia exhaled once quick and loud to clear her mind, then clicked on Caren's name.

"Hey, hi. Looks like you have quite the view from your room. Nice to see you."

"Hi, Doc C. I'm so glad we have this today; I've missed you being here. Are you home yet?"

"No, some family stuff has delayed my return. Soon, though. And I'll come there myself to check out that view."

Caren's face lit up.

"Are they letting you have visitors yet?"

"Yes, but I've asked them not to come." She looked down, then gazed out the window for a long moment.

Mia sat in the silence with her for a while to let her patient collect herself, her emotions. After a time, Mia gently asked, "Can you talk about your decision to not have any visitors?"

"I can't face them after what I did. After what happened, I can't stop the images." She covered her face with her hands.

The hour was excruciating, her pain palpable. Mia released

a whoosh of breath as she stood, trying to rid herself of the heaviness she felt for her patient. Hearing Caren's suffering was even worse than she could've imagined. She packed up her computer and straightened the kitchen. After freshening up in the bathroom, she grabbed a sweater on her way out and gladly left the house with Frenchie.

Driving to North Providence, her mind returned to her last session. *Poor kid was better off when she didn't remember the rape.* Since they'd spoken last, Caren had been able to fill in some of the empty memories from that night. *Brutal.*

Instead of hating the guy, the act, she hated herself. Her reality was changed forever. Layers of shame and guilt would take a lifetime to deal with. It was outrageously sad and unfair that she'd have to do all the work to feel all right again—whatever that meant.

Mia turned the radio up, trying to push Caren's pain out of her mind. The worst part was that none of it was her fault. Mia knew all too well it was impossible to convince someone of anything when they were wrapped up in emotional turmoil and pain.

Chapter 34

Tony had watched the clock all afternoon. He knew the guys wouldn't be showing up. That should've made him happy, but he just felt weird. The fear he'd seen in their eyes the day before reminded him that they'd just gotten lost. They were the reason he'd got into this business in the first place.

He ran his hand through his hair. *It's all fucked up.* He wanted to help the neighborhood kids find a different route but was arresting them. Is taking them away from their kids a good thing? *Who the fuck knows anymore.*

His mind rewound to working out with Jencks a few weeks earlier. Jencks had pulled out JT's new school picture.

"Ey, is this what you looked like when you had hair, man?" Tony teased.

"Nay, I was never that cute. He's all his mother."

"Now you gonna spot me, or what?"

"Ey, guys. Sup?" Greco strode in.

They both sat up at his entrance.

"What's up with you?" Tony asked as he and Jencks eyed each other.

"Gonna let me kick your asses, or what?"

"What are we so happy about?" Jencks asked.

"My girl... she's pregnant. Seems my guys can still swim."

Tony slapped him on the back, and the three locked eyes in the mirror. "Good for you. You're gonna make a good dad."

"Thanks, my brother. Different than ours. Come on, I'll kick your asses to that, and later I'm buying."

"Wow," Jencks teased. "He's buying, T. Come on, you know he's a cheap fuck. We're gonna let you win 'cause we're happy for you." Jencks slapped Greco on the back. "Man, it's the best thing, being a father. You'll see."

It was almost four, and Tony was completely distracted and edgy. *What was I thinking, having her come here?* His case was over, but he was nervous she'd find out he was a lying sack.

His four o'clock client showed up twenty minutes late. Tony should've canceled his clients for the day, but the captain had instructed him to carry on as normal. *Normal? What the fuck is that?* Her stupid brother was half dead—partially deserved it—the guys were in prison, and Slick knew Tony had been involved in the takedown.

An image of JT spun along with Greco's excitement over his unborn kid. *Fucking normal... WTF. And I'm in love with a woman who doesn't know anything about me or my involvement with her asshole brother. None of this is normal.*

Mia glanced at the time, amazed the drive had only taken her ten minutes. Tony's gym was situated in a high-end strip mall off Mineral Spring Avenue. Swinging the buggy into a front-row spot, she quickly checked herself in the rearview mirror.

Getting out of the car, her eyes swept the strip. There was a bar and grill called Wildfire on the far side, wafting incredible smells of Italian eats. On the other side was a men's clothing store named Spardello's. The clothes in the window display looked imported and expensive. Her mind jumped to the guys she'd seen Tony with on Federal Hill, then to her mother and her lover. She spotted a jewelry store, and her mind flashed to the ring. *Where did Rob get it? How many months did it take him to save up?* Her heart thumped irregularly, and she sped up. Her dream about Rob circled, but she kept moving.

The door had a black mirrored glass front with a simple sign that read, Total Wellness, in sea green. *Chic.* She stepped inside.

An earthy slate brought a sense of calm to the entrance, along with plants and a copper water fountain. Mia watched the water trickle down slowly, admiring the sound. In the far corner was a small fireplace with two inviting, overstuffed chairs. It had been tastefully done with exceptional attention to detail. *This had to be professionally designed. Ror would think so.* The space smelled incredible. She located a Yankee candle sitting on a nearby end table—*Sunflowers* on the label.

For the first time in days, her stomach unclenched. She exhaled and moved to sit by the fire.

Chapter 35

As Tony approached, Mia's eyes darted to his black tank with a NIKE swoosh across the front. Her stomach dipped slightly, and she pulled her eyes away. *I can't do this.*

"Hi, we're almost done. Be about 5 minutes." Tony leaned in to kiss her on the cheek and whispered, "Guy was late."

"Of course."

A few minutes later, Tony's client walked out wearing the hint of a smile. She buried her face deeper in the menu she'd been perusing. Besides the regular gym equipment, the place offered personal training and nutrition, massage, physical therapy, a pool, kickboxing, and a basketball league. Mia was impressed.

As Tony approached, Mia ignored her body's reaction to the familiar logo. He grinned wide in his lopsided way.

"Tony, this is really great. I mean it. I'd like to meet your designer; it's…amazing. So peaceful."

His grin widened. "Thanks," he said as he pecked her cheek. "You look amazing. And you've already met the designer. I was going for simple and comfortable, but I'll take peaceful and amazing. Any word on your brother?"

She shook her head. She didn't want to deal with her jackass of a brother.

She eyed Tony and felt her heart begin to thump in quick little pulses. She glanced away.

"You designed this yourself? Really?"

"Don't look so shocked." He knelt to pat Mr. French.

"Hey, boy, you want to take a dip, huh? I can arrange that."

"Believe it or not, he loves to swim."

"I believe it. And hey, sorry for making you wait. Let me change my shirt and give you the tour."

"I'd love that."

"Be right back." Tony disappeared down the hallway into a backroom, reappearing moments later, wearing a crisp black shirt and carrying an off-white nylon vest. He extended his arm. She was slightly amused at the old-fashioned gesture and linked her arm in his. He smelled nice.

"Did you really design this?"

"Why is that so hard to believe?"

"I'm sorry; you're right. It's just beautiful."

"Like the lady."

Mia's cheeks flushed.

He made a silly face and then bumped her shoulder. "Hey, come on. I didn't mean to make you uncomfortable."

"I've never met a straight guy who could decorate like this."

"Oh, so gay guys have the market cornered on nice taste?"

"Not on nice taste but… sort of on decorating, yes." She crinkled her nose.

"Doc, I think there's a name for that."

"Right." She laughed. "I'm sure there is. You're sure you're straight?"

"I assure you, I'm very straight."

She laughed and handed him a bottle of wine. "This is for you."

"Thank you." He disappeared and returned with two small wine glasses. "A toast." His green eyes peered down at her. "I'm glad you felt like meeting me tonight, under the circumstances."

Their eyes met as they clinked their glasses.

"I think I promised the lady a tour?"

"Let me guess, before you were in business, your past vocation was interior design?" Mia teased.

He chuckled deep. "Not even close."

"You're really good at it."

"Decorating this place was sort of like a hobby for me. It was fun."

She watched as he sipped his wine and smiled up at him. He was so easy to be around. She was enjoying herself despite everything. She placed her glass down on the counter, and their hands brushed slightly. She pulled hers away gently, pretending to scratch her face.

He pulled her forward. "Come on."

After the tour was over, Tony asked, "You wanna hear how this came to be?"

She turned to face him.

"A few years ago, the owners got into some financial trouble. They offered me the place for a song. I knew someone who was looking for an investment, so we went in together. I agreed to run it if the local kids could use it, too. Give 'em something productive to do. That's why we added the indoor hoop setup. They love that and the weights, mostly. The older clientele like the other services and are willing to pay a lot of money. It works."

She admired his commitment. Most men couldn't care less about helping neighborhood teens. "It's nice of you to care."

"Growing up like them made me want to do somethin' good. Give back."

She thought she noticed a certain vulnerability move across his features, but it vanished just as fast.

"Kids need mentors, and adults need trainers to motivate and keep them on track. It's sort of Ror's role in our practice. I am very impressed."

"Only thing missing is a shrink. You know any good ones?"

"That's it, your tour has ended. Is the pretty lady ready to blow this clam bake?" He raised one brow.

Mia attached Frenchie's leash while Tony locked the front door.

"Hope you're hungry. Carlo's has probably been preparing for us all day."

"I am."

Tony drove a black Cadillac sedan with tinted windows. Mia's mind conjured Floridian old men or gangsters in top hats.

"It's a company car," he said as he opened the door for her.

"Thanks."

His arm brushed slightly against hers, and the hairs on her arms stood at attention.

The key was barely in the ignition before Frenchie jumped up on his lap. "I think he likes me."

"Frenchie, off," Mia scolded.

"Nay, leave him; he's fine. You're a fluffy thing." He patted Frenchie's head.

Sinatra wafted through the stereo. Mia was surprised when Tony reached for her hand. She couldn't remember the last time she'd held hands with someone in a car.

"I haven't heard this song in years." She tapped along to Luck Be a Lady Tonight. "My dad used to listen to him."

"Your father liked old blue eyes, huh? Must've been a cool guy."

She nodded, visualizing his casket—the strangers rolling it down the aisle. For years, she'd worried about her lack of emotion with regard to her father; now, she felt anger pulse through her toward her brother. *He took so much that night.*

Her foot bounced up and down.

"I can change the music if you want?"

"No, I like it." She was touched by his concern for her.

They rode the rest of the way quietly, listening to Frank.

She can hear her dad singing the song in his big voice, laughing at her mom. "A lady doesn't leave her escort, and it's not fair, and it's not right. A lady doesn't go off and blow on some other guy's dice." Her mother's eyes shone back at him, and he seemed to melt whenever he looked at her.

The channel switched, and she and Rob drove down the road in his car as he smoked a joint. She was practically on his lap, couldn't get close enough. Rob's warm hand reached for hers, and a feeling of comfort slid over her.

"You still good?" Tony asked, concerned.

"I'm…" She nodded in reassurance, pushing her mind back to the present.

"Just checkin'. I know you got a lot going on."

She watched the corners of his eyes crinkle slightly with the hint of a smile. The strangest feeling swept through her. For a moment, she debated telling him about herself. Some piece of her truth. Somehow, she felt like he'd understand or at least try. Silently, she counted the street exits on the highway. She was on five when they arrived at the restaurant.

Chapter 36

Tony pulled his car around the back of Carlo's Restaurant, located in a renovated house off Broadway right outside the Olneyville section of Providence. He switched off the ignition and turned toward Mia as Mr. French hopped off his lap.

He released her hand slowly, certain he could've sat all night simply holding her. He stretched and then walked around to her side of the car. As he opened her door, he was struck by an impulse to kiss her.

She fumbled with Frenchie's leash.

"May I?" He offered a hand.

She took it and stepped out of the car. Her eyes met his now. Frenchie could wait a minute.

Placing his hands on both sides of her face, he gently lifted it and kissed her. Her lips were full and soft, electric and wonderful. Her gentle grip on his waist made him want to melt into her. His fingertips brushed a mass of her curls. They were wild and sensual, just like he imagined being with her would be. The thought sent bolts through him. He released a breath and gazed at her. His look said it all.

Tony took Mr. French's leash, shut the door with a thump and ran a hand through his short hair. *I need to tell her about me before this goes too far.*

"Are we ready to dine?" he asked breathlessly.

"We are." She grinned.

"Welcome to Carlo's Italian Eatery," he said as he escorted her through the front door.

"You sure he's welcome?" Mia glanced down at Mr. French.

"By the owners." He winked. "Come on."

The foyer was small but elegant. A chandelier softly illuminated the space. A beautifully crafted polished mahogany banister rimmed the stairwells. The restaurant spanned three floors. Directly to the right of the foyer stood a dark-haired hostess.

"Tony." She beamed. "Buenos Noches, que tal?"

"Muy bien," Tony answered, kissing both sides of her face.

"Maria, I want you to meet someone special. This is Mia, and Mr. French."

"Hola, mucho gusto?" Mia nervously smiled.

"Oh, habla Espanol?"

"No, no. Only pequeno."

Maria took Mia's hands, assessing her carefully. "Nice to finally meet you. Tony hasn't stopped talking about you or your perro. Please, go sit. Enjoy some wine; your table is ready. I'll tell Carlos you're here."

Mia followed Tony down a series of steps into what looked like a wine cellar. Bookshelves and stacks of wine surrounded half a dozen tables with overstuffed chairs. The lighting was dark and intimate.

"It feels very European."

Tony escorted her to the very last table, directly against the back wall. The table was almost in a separate room, next to a small fireplace. In the center sat the most beautiful white roses and several small, lit candles. Tony pulled out a cushy chair for her, and patted a nearby ottoman for Frenchie before sitting against the wall.

"Tony, this is absolutely beautiful."

"I am trying to impress you. And take your mind off things." His eyes softened.

"It's working so far."

"So far…" He reached across the table to hold her hands.

Out of a back room came a large, olive-skinned man with thick, shiny black hair wearing a black tee and white apron.

He took Mia's hands from Tony's. "He said you were somethin' special, but I never imagine…" He had the same thick accent as the woman at the front desk.

Tony stood. "The lady's with me."

The two teased each other and hugged.

"Mia, this is my brother Carlos. The one I told you about."

"Can't you see the resemblance?" Carlos smirked.

"Hi, it's a pleasure to meet you, Carlos. Your restaurant is beautiful."

"The pleasure is all mine, pretty lady. I have only one regret: That you're not here with me. But the night is young; maybe I can change that?"

Tony shot him a sharp glance. "Careful of the Latin men. Everything you've heard is all true."

"I'm flattered; thanks for having me."

"This must be the fluffy perro. Tony hasn't stopped talking about either one of you since you met."

Tony eyed him a warning.

"Relax, big guy." Carlos rested his hands on Tony's shoulders. "Maybe I'll join you when the work's through. I'm not like this guy, Mia. I still work to make my living." He smiled wide. "Do I get to pick?" he asked Tony over his shoulder.

"Work your magic, my friend."

"And for the pretty lady?"

"Can Carlos choose your entrée, or would you rather?"

"Oh, by all means."

Before leaving the table, Carlos leaned down toward Mia and said, "We've been praying for your brother's return to good health."

"Thank you."

"Thank God," Tony exclaimed. "I thought he'd never leave. You have quite the effect."

Mia's eyes had glazed over, unaware of his presence, much less his words.

Not knowing what to say, Tony stared at her in silence.

"I'm sorry, I didn't hear you," Mia finally replied, eyeing Tony.

"Are you alright to stay here? It's okay if you can't. I would understand."

She leaned forward. "I can stay. Can I confess something?"

"Of course, anything." A bead of sweat purled on Tony's brow.

"I don't believe in prayer or that my brother deserves compassion. I'm so angry with him. I'm not sure what that says about me..."

"It says you're human." Her honesty made him feel like shit.

A waiter hurried over with a tray of white and red wine and placed the two decanters on the table.

"Which do you prefer?" Tony asked Mia.

"I'll have white." Mia sipped her wine and rearranged her silverware.

Tony studied her from across the table, unable to read her.

"Where'd you learn to speak Spanish?" Tony finally asked.

"I don't really. When I lived in San Francisco, my uncle and his partner were studying it. It was impossible not to learn a couple words here and there."

"Uncle Joe?"

"You have a good memory."

"No, I just listen."

"What about you? How did you learn?"

"I was around Carlos and his family all the time growing up. We met way back." He paused. "We were practically kids. Carlos always wanted to own his own restaurant. His mother's Mexican, but his father's as Italian as they come."

"Really?"

"Oh, yeah. It makes for one hell of a meal. His old man used to own a pizza joint when we were younger. I used to hang around it all the time. I started hangin' with some older guys who were headed for trouble—maybe already there. One night, he came outside, called me in. I was scared, pretended like I wasn't. He was a small guy but tough. He put his hands on my shoulders and said, 'Go home to your family before you get in trouble.'

"I nodded. He didn't understand I didn't have the kind of home you'd wanna be in. I walked back out. The next night, he came outside before anyone else got there. 'Kid, if you gonna be out here hangin' around all the time, I'm gonna put you to work. Let you make me money; teach you to make honest money.' He smiled down at me, nodded like it was settled. 'Show up tomorrow after school.' Let's just say they became my family."

"I'm sorry."

"Don't be. Made me work harder."

The waiter arrived with the first course: pasta fagioli soup.

"This is one of my absolute favorites," Mia beamed.

He grinned at her excitement but didn't miss the compassionate look her face still wore for him.

"When I was a little girl, my father used to make this for me whenever he came back from one of his road trips." She spilled some on her chin, and Tony slid a napkin her way. Her face colored slightly.

"Tell me more about this father. He liked Sinatra and could cook; you got me curious."

"He drove trucks for a living." She paused, and the glazed look returned. "He was great."

Her grief was palpable. He reached for her hands across the table. "I'm so sorry." He felt lousy; he knew the awful story of her family.

Mia finished her soup and drained her wine. "Excuse me, I'll be right back."

With her absence Tony sat feeling torn, he understood logically why he couldn't tell her all that he knew about her family, but the knowledge and pretense made him feel like a dirtbag. To pretend to get to know something about someone when you already knew felt shitty and deceitful, because it fuckin was.

When she returned, a good-sized antipasto sat on the table with fried calamari and hot pepper rings. The waiter quickly approached to refill her wine glass.

"Thank you."

"I hope it's alright," Tony started. "I did the honors."

"Great, thanks." She dug in.

"I love the way you eat."

"I think it's partly my heritage, an Italian thing. I've always had a pretty good appetite."

The wine had obviously taken effect as her shoulders released.

"So, you grew up in Providence?"

Tony nodded and wiped his mouth. "In North Providence. Mom and I lived near her family, just the two of us."

"My dad left us when I was a teenager, around thirteen. I moved out after I finished high school, then moved back in when she got sick." He didn't tell her that's when he completed the police academy. He took a long drink of water. "She got cancer. Wasted away really fast."

"Tony, how sad. I'm sorry."

"Yeah, she had a real shitty life. Life's not always fair, I guess." He sipped his wine. "But tonight, I'm sitting here with the most beautiful lady in the place, so I can't complain."

"That's laying it on."

"Too much?" he teased, thankful for an opening to change the subject. "You like the food so far?"

"It's fantastic. What got you interested in the restaurant business?"

"Where I grew up, there weren't that many things to choose from." *I sure didn't want to wind up like my old man.* "Being a legitimate business owner was my only chance to make money—the right way." He felt dishonest. "You gotta tough job, though." Again, he didn't like the way his stomach felt lying to her.

"It can be. Being here, my brother, I'm not in the right space to work."

The waiter approached, holding a tray of Bolognese pasta that smelled superb.

"This looks unbelievable."

He knew she was in pain. It made him feel shitty that he's had some part in it.

"Tell me one interesting thing about yourself that no one would guess." Tony knew it was time to switch to a conversation more lighthearted—for both of them.

"I'll have to think about that. I'm not really that interesting."

Doubtful. Behind her baby blues, he glimpsed a guarded mix of something. He had a crazy need to find out what made her tick.

The meal was fabulous. Taking cues from each other, they chatted about surface, safe topics. As dinner came to an end, Carlos regaled them with the dessert menu, beginning with the Crème Brulé–

Mia's cell rang.

"Excuse me. It's probably Rory. I have to answer, time change and all."

He nodded in understanding but felt his muscles tense.

Carlos eyed Tony suspiciously. "Who is this Rory?"

"Her friend from back home. They work together."

Carlos lifted an eyebrow. "Her friend?"

After chatting for a few minutes, Carlos returned to work, and Tony felt himself stiffen. *Who is this Rory guy to her? Her face lights up whenever she says his name…* It made him crazy.

"Sorry about that," she said, returning to her seat. "He's a bit of a mother hen and wanted to know about Jimmy. He thinks I should just stay put for a bit."

"Yeah, Carlos was wondering if Rory is really just your work friend?"

"Oh, Carlos was wondering that, huh?"

"Yeah, he doesn't think it's possible."

"He doesn't think what's possible?" she asked with a tone.

"That men and women can just be friends. He's old school and all."

"That's what Carlos thinks? He wants to know about me and Rory?"

Tony clenched his jaw. "Naw, I'll own it. Is he really just your friend or… you know?"

"Rory's been my best friend since we met freshman year. He also happens to be gay. If I could hand-pick a big brother, he'd be it." She reached for the spoon in front of her and fiddled it back and forth before dropping her eyes away from his. "You know, like what you said about picking your own family."

Tony reached across the table for her hands. "Sorry for sounding like a caveman."

He smiled warmly and lifted his glass. "To friendship."

Back in the parking lot of Tony's gym, his face was illuminated by the streetlight above, so Mia could only see the outline of his masculine features.

"Do you know when you're heading back to California?"

"Either tomorrow night or Monday afternoon sometime. My brother doesn't deserve my time; my life is there."

"I get it," he nearly whispered. "But I wish you could stay longer. I love spending time with you."

Mia's foot started to pump up and down. She met his gaze as he leaned in for a kiss, but she pulled back.

"Tony, I had a really nice time. Carlos' place was incredible. Thank you. I really needed that tonight." *Damn, he's handsome.* She was feeling daring, careless even..

"Can I talk you into coming in for a nightcap?"

"I don't think I should."

"I'll walk you to your car."

They were both silent except for their footsteps.

"Get in touch if you decide to stay or if you need anything."

"I will."

He leaned in for a kiss, nearly bending in half to make up for the difference in height.

The kiss was soft but packed with an intensity that made Mia draw in her breath. She felt the strangest pang pull at her insides. Not guilt, desire. With her heartbeat hammering away in her chest, she pulled back nervously and tucked a curl behind her left ear.

"Can I tell you something without freaking you out?" he asked.

She nodded, wrestling her feelings.

"I've thought about kissing you since the minute I saw you sleeping next to me on the plane." His voice was soft, raspy.

She felt slightly drunk. "That's sweet. Maybe a little creepy."

They laughed, and she bumped his shoulder playfully.

"May I?" He untucked her hair from behind her ear and leaned into her more fully.

As he kissed her, his hands moved underneath her neckline. Her knees felt weak, her brain fuzzy, her worries suspended.

Unsure of how much time had passed, she realized she enjoyed kissing him back. She wanted to stay.

"I should get going."

"Why?"

The questions hung between them.

He exhaled and swiped his hand over his head. "Any chance you'll meet me tomorrow night if you're still here? I know this great little spot." He lifted one brow.

"I'll bet you do." She exhaled softly as he brushed her lips with his. His hand was still around her waist; he hadn't let it go.

"Selfishly, I'm with Rory. I hope you'll stay put until you know what's going on with your brother." He opened the door for her. "M'lady."

Judging by the way his stomach danced and the rush pumping through his veins, Tony knew two things for sure: His heart was in big trouble, and he'd crave her taste forever.

He gazed up at the clear autumn sky and inhaled deep. At forty-two, he'd finally fallen head over heels in love. He tried to enjoy the moment but felt like shit with all of the tangles.

Heading back to his car to lock the doors, he noticed her handbag sitting on the passenger side floor.

Chapter 37

Mia followed Mr. French out to the living room, where he stood howling at the door. She heard a soft rap.

"Who's there?" She asked over Frenchie's noise.

"Mia, it's me."

She unbolted the front door and opened it slightly. Her eyebrows arched.

"Figured you would need this." He held up her pocketbook.

She looked back at him skeptically.

"I already missed you, can't lie." He grinned.

His eyes crinkled slightly at the corners, and her heart skipped a beat. He stepped inside, and she closed the door. He lifted her chin to his.

"Sorry, I should've called. I'll let you go to sleep. You got that flight early tomorrow."

He touched the hair framing her face. "Goodnight." He turned to leave.

"Stay, I'm not going. I can't leave." A few moments passed. "I hate him for it, too," she huffed.

"I'm sorry." He stepped toward her.

Their lips touched lightly. Instantly electric, their kissing quickly became harder, more urgent. He pulled his head back to look at her; she was pinned against his body. He kissed her again, and time suspended.

"Hey, we should talk… I want you to know some things about me," his nostrils flared to catch a breath.

"I know you," she said, looking up at him. "Something few people know about me… Mia was my mother's name. I started using it after she died to feel closer to her. My given name is Marianna."

He displayed a mix of compassion and desire. She felt his eyes on her, knew they'd reached a turning point.

He bolted the door, and she took his hand, leading him to the bedroom.

Tony pulled her closer. She watched him pull off his sweat-shirt, then tee.

"You okay with this?" His voice was husky.

She kissed his neck and ears. He reached for his waistband, fumbling with the button before his pants dropped to the floor with a thump. He lifted her, helping her out of her oversized tee.

In what seemed like slow motion, they fell onto the bed. The confines of their clothes were gone, and the skin-on-skin contact felt amazing. He reached for her, moaning deep in his throat. His hands tangled in her hair, he hovered above her. His lips caressed her neck, then moved downward.

She said his name slowly. Gently, she massaged his chest and arms, then moved her hands down his body. He was throbbing, more than ready. They landed on the floor with a thud. He lowered himself into her slowly. He held her gaze and grazed her lips hungrily. They moved in unison, rhythmically. She gasped slightly, holding him tighter with urgency. Everything dropped away at the pleasure coursing through her.

"Mariiaaannnnaaa," he moaned, hugging her body tightly against his.

They lay together on the floor for a long while.

He rolled toward her, leaning up on one elbow. "That was even more incredible than I imagined it would be."

She looked away for a moment. They were in Rob's room. She started feeling anxious, and he pulled her in closer. She relaxed into him. Sweeping her eyes around Rob's room, she closed them tight against Tony's chest.

Chapter 38

From his position on the bed, Tony could see a picture above his head of Mia and a guy in front of a waterfall. He could tell by the way she smiled up at the guy that she was in love with him. His body tensed. *This is* his *room*, his *oversized shirt.*

He knew the story after asking around, but he still had so many questions about the kid in the picture. He feared he couldn't compete with a ghost—especially one that had kept this fine little lady single for so many years. *Tonight's not the night to get into this. She's got enough to worry 'bout; not gonna add my male bullshit to her list.*

He pulled her closer, realizing she'd fallen asleep. He wondered how many times they'd been together in that very room. *What the fuck is wrong with me? I'm jealous of a dead guy. Can't change the past, T. Get ova it!*

He watched her sleep for a while. He touched her hair and moved his lips closer to hers, saying her name softly. Her skin smelled like sweet green apples. He found her irresistible. He'd never believed in love at first sight, but since the first day they met on the plane, it'd been over for him; he couldn't resist her.

She snuggled into him, and he felt his body respond, suddenly acutely aware of her soft skin on his. He let out a moan and kissed her softly. Caressing her lightly, he prayed she'd respond. When she did, he felt excitement like never before. He pulled her toward him. Groggy with sleep, her eyes opened slowly, and she smiled.

"Tony," she whispered sweetly.

His name on her lips made him come undone. They shifted positions, and she moaned as he moved closer. He wanted to stay there forever, locked in the moment. The past didn't matter.

They moved together in their own expert rhythm. He tried to wait for her to climax but was practically panting with desire. His body moved and fit with hers. He felt her hips rise and fall again and again. When her head went back, and she groaned with pleasure, he finally released. She said his name to the rhythm of her own desire. He'd been waiting for her his entire life. An electrical surge pulsed through his arms, legs, groin, landing at his heart's center. He was not going to be able to let go.

Her finger brushed the outline of his St. Christopher medal.

"Hey, sorry I woke you."

"Don't be." She nuzzled against his body.

Mr. French jumped up on the bed's corner and nestled in with them. She felt Tony pull her in tighter.

"Can you keep a secret?" she asked with her eyes still closed.

"For you, anything."

Her voice was just above a whisper. "When I was a kid, my father was accused of shooting my mother… and her lover. He went to prison for it… He died there. This trip back, I found out that Jimmy—"

"Hey." He pulled her to him and continued to listen. His gut sank. How could he tell her what he knew? It'd feel like such a betrayal.

"It was my brother. I think my father was protecting him. They tried to tell me—my aunt, Jimmy, too—but I couldn't hear it."

His grip tightened around her.

She let out a deep breath, and a tear trickled down her cheek. He moved to kiss it.

"It's gonna be alright," he said softly into her hair. "Try to get some sleep."

Her body relaxed a bit as he rubbed her back. He'd never felt more at odds. *She's got haunts.* He was more than happy to stand guard against whatever demons swarmed. *Fucking scumbag brother. I'd wish him dead if it wasn't for her. She's mad, but she doesn't want to bury another family member—even after what he did.*

After a while, he watched her finally give in to a fitful sleep. He resisted the urge to wake her a few times when it seemed she needed him. He wanted to stay beside her and never move, but he needed to go home to shower and change his clothes for his debrief with the Captain in the morning. They were afraid for the safety of her brother and Williams. They'd need a security detail to keep them safe.

He needed to find the balls to tell her about himself. He hoped he hadn't fucked it up too badly. He kissed her forehead gently and patted Frenchie's head, grinning when his tail fluttered.

Love that dog. He looked back at Mia. *And that girl.*

In the kitchen, he found a notepad and scribbled out, Last night meant everything to me. I'll be thinking about you all day. Love, T

He left the note next to her on the bed, trying not to wake her or look around the room.

Chapter 39

Snippets of Mia and Tony's night played through Mia's mind as she woke. Something foreign moved through her. It'd felt natural, good to be with him. She glanced next to her and grabbed the note Tony had left in his place. Pushing the covers off completely, she got up and headed into the bathroom, averting her eyes from Rob's picture.

After showering and dressing in jeans and a fuzzy sweatshirt, Mia couldn't put off her need to talk to her aunt for another minute. She grabbed the journal off the floor of the buggy and shut the door with a thump. The October sky, still dark; she and Frenchie walked to the diner. She rapped softly on the door.

"Marianna, come in. I'm just starting the coffee," she invited as she opened the door. "Any word from the hospital?"

"Jo called me last night, said everything was the same. She'd stopped by on her way home from work. I was supposed to fly back today, but I've decided to wait a little bit longer." She plopped the journal on the counter.

"You got time for a quick cup?"

"I do."

Aunt Rosie poured Mia a mug and refilled her own before sitting down next to Mia.

"Morning, Marianna," Sal greeted as he walked in. "Everything the same?"

Mia nodded. "I've decided to stay here for… Until I can leave." She turned toward Aunt Rosie, knowing she was pressed for time as the diner would open soon. "My father says a lot in here." She looked down at the journal. "Most of it I've already heard." Her heart began to hammer away in her chest.

"I'll leave you two to talk," Sal said, eyeing the journal.

"You can stay." Mia looked back to Aunt Rosie. "If that's okay?"

"'Course, he doesn't need my permission."

The three of them sat in silence, looking at each other for a few seconds.

"A few of the entries didn't make sense to me at first," Mia began. "He said he doesn't know how Jimmy got involved… But later, he says he's upset that Jimmy interfered. Should've let him deal with it."

"I know he felt terrible being gone all those years…" Aunt Rosie wore a pained expression. "I think at the end he wanted you to know his feelings, point of view."

Maybe Jo was right, "He's trying to shed his guilt." Too late. Her foot began bobbing up and down.

"Tell her, Rose. She has a right to know." Sal stood. "I have to prep for breakfast."

"I already know."

Aunt Rosie stared at the ground for a good minute. "Now that he's gone, he wanted you to know."

Mia's breathing changed. She sipped her coffee. "I never thought he did it intentionally. The accident part made more sense to me because I knew he loved her, I remember." She twirled the napkin in front of her.

Aunt Rosie paused and took a deep breath. "He was protecting him." She stopped and dropped her gaze to the floor. "He sort of talks about it indirect like." She nodded toward the book.

"I know Jimmy did it. His crazy behavior makes sense to me now. What I don't understand is why. My brother actually killed my mother… He ruined my entire family." She stood and took a few deep breaths. "He was responsible for all of it?" She felt empty.

The horror of the truth hung between them.

Auntie Rose stood and walked over to Mia. "Yes, it was your brother who found them… together. Not your dad. He wasn't even home yet."

They locked eyes. Mia sat back down, feeling numb.

Auntie Rose rested her hand on Mia's shoulder firmly. "I wish it weren't true. None of it."

Mia's mind unfolded the sketchy details of that day, trying to fill in the missing pieces. Mom's calendar, the newspaper folded to the sports page, the bakery box, Jimmy's unslept-in bed, his angry words that night, dad's strange reaction.

"But why? How did he know to go there?"

"Jimmy knew about them. He confronted your mother, told your father she was planning to leave him. Didn't like his reaction. I don't know the rest; your father wouldn't tell me the details. Didn't want anyone else getting involved. He was sick about all of it. He didn't want you to know until you were older, until something happened to either him or, god forbid, Jimmy." She made the sign of the cross. "He made me promise. Jimmy can still get in trouble. Only person I told was Sal."

Unable to speak, Mia nodded. Her body felt like lead.

"My mother fell in love with someone else, was going to leave him. Jimmy found out… My father took the blame, rotted in prison all those years… Gave up everything—his whole life, me—all to protect him." Jimmy's words spun. *"Your mother was a whore, and your precious daddy was a pussy."* Mia squeezed her eyes shut. *After everything, Jimmy still hated him.*

"Marianna, your dad loved you kids. He wasn't gonna let your brother ruin his whole life. It was between him and your mother. What your brother did was stupid and tragic, heat of the moment. He was barely eighteen; he couldn't handle it, seeing them together. He lost it. No young man should see that. He thought he was doing right by your father... She was my best friend. My sister, really. Despite how she felt, she had young kids; it wasn't right. I told her, too."

Mia felt any illusion of future happiness between her and Jimmy crumble. "I don't get why he hated Dad after everything he did?" *He lost respect for him... He knew Dad already knew and didn't do anything. He was angry Dad didn't kill Costa—maybe both of them—right then and there...* She rubbed her hands together, suddenly ice cold. *So he did.*

"Only he can answer that. Nobody really knows what goes on between two adults. I'm not making excuses now. Sometimes, you meet someone, and things make sense; you can't help who you fall in or out of love with. It just happens. He was away a lot. That's never a good thing. Costa fell hard. He was very charming, believe it or not. And as for you and your brother, she loved you more than anything, and you know it. It had nothing to do with you or Jimmy."

A few minutes passed before Mia was finally able to stand.

"He made it about us when he killed her." She excused herself to the bathroom.

When she returned, she was grateful to see Sal unlocking the front door. She hugged her aunt and said bye to Sal. Before leaving, she turned back.

"Did Robbie know?"

"I don't know," Aunt Rosie whispered.

Mia walked mindlessly toward her aunt's house. The

confirmation felt like a hard slap across her face, waking her up at long last. Her mind almost felt too sharp. She was able to think about her family's saga with newfound clarity. It wasn't a pleasant feeling, somewhere between jaded and manic. She floated as she got into the car, felt slightly akin to how Alice must've felt when she fell down the rabbit hole. Her life changed, distorted. Once again.

Driving along, everything felt different to her. Her reality had been tilted on its side. Her brain chanted, *altered.* Still deep in thought, she turned onto Atwood Avenue. She stopped at the light as the other pivotal moments spun in her mind.

She closed her eyes and rubbed her temples. Her father didn't do it… This new truth hit her straight in the gut. She thought about the journal, knew she'd read it from cover to cover. It was a gift from him.

Chapter 40

Mia turned into the drive and drove through the big, ornate gates. She felt as though she owed her father an apology. She needed to talk to him about what she'd learned. She wished it could have been an actual conversation, that he'd be there, hugging her close to him. She remembered his scent, coffee, cigarettes and soap.

She stopped at the office to ask for directions, knocking on the wooden door.

"It's open."

The small man had grayish, wiry hair with a unibrow to match. Hidden behind wire-rimmed glasses were small, light blue eyes. His face had a tinge of pallid green, like someone with liver dysfunction.

She gave her father's name, quietly saying that he was buried a few weeks ago. *If only I'd known before…* She babbled on about how she was visiting from California and needed to visit his grave. The man moved around the small, neat office to a desk with a computer. Moments after typing in the information, he handed her a piece of paper without saying a word.

As she reached for the door, he quietly said, "His section often goes unfinished."

Mia stared.

"Not a priority."

She pulled the car over onto the grass.

When Mr. French jumped out of the car, she said, "Alright. This is where we end up, Frenchie. Amongst a sea of cement markers, underground with the worms."

He eyed her.

"I know, I'm jaded. I can't help it."

She put him on his leash, and they walked down a path of worn-out grass.

Poor guy. Bad enough to deal with a cheating spouse, but then my stupid brother decides to play Rambo and…

She arrived at his spot, staring in silence for a long minute. It was flagged with a plastic marker, his name and a number. The sight took her breath away. Like prison wasn't impersonal and non-descript enough… There was no date, no scriptures, no father/son/friend, nothing. Mia felt a rush of emotion tinged with guilt for all that might've been.

Most of the graves in the section looked alike. Only a few had stones, and even then, they were inadequate and impersonal. *So, this is how prison families feel? Even in death, our loved ones are less than?*

She'd never given a second thought to what happened to all the men and women who died in prison. Most were there for a good reason, after all. The truth churned. *He spent all those years locked away to protect him. Convicted of premeditated, first-degree murder.* She felt sick. She had a hard time reconciling all that'd been lost, things that often went unnamed. Her blood ran cold as she thought about all the layers.

Mia's heart couldn't stand the lack of respect for the grave marker—closure for him, them. She started walking far away from the sad plastic flags. She couldn't get far enough away.

As she walked, her eyes darted from stone to stone. She started counting them, stopping at thirty. It struck her that someone—a family member, loved one—had deliberately chosen a gravestone to honor their dead. Strange that after all the loss she'd suffered, she'd never been involved in the process. She hadn't understood it before, not personally.

She began looking for the right one for him, deciding it should be quietly dignified, like him.

She finally stumbled upon the perfect one. It was burgundy, respectful, dignified. She thought back to the day he'd died. Rory had made her show him pictures from *before*. She'd been relieved it wasn't Jimmy. Hadn't felt much in the way of loss for her dad, only an old hurt. Her feelings were jumbled.

Before, she'd only allowed herself to miss him. Before, she'd blamed him. Before, she'd hated him. All those years were gone; she couldn't get them back. *Stupid brother.* She shook her head and stood, unsure what to do. She sat on her haunches near the stone, not her father's but the one she felt he deserved.

"Dad, I hope you can hear me. I need to apologize for so much..."

It took a moment for the words to come.

"Not visiting or writing all those years... I blamed you; I was hurt. I thought, prayed it was an accident. I believed it was, but it felt like you'd abandoned me. I didn't know about Jimmy... You should've let him deal with his own stupidity. He should've been the one to go away, not you. Dad..."

A single tear trickled down her cheek, her throat burned.

"I hope you'll forgive me for saying this... I don't have a son, so maybe I can't understand, but you gave up your whole life for him; I don't get it. He didn't deserve it. I guess I don't understand that kind of love?"

The name on the stone in front of her read Anthony Piccolli. She rubbed her fingers across the name and dates of his life.

"Thank you, Mr. Piccolli, for letting me talk to my dad."

She wiped her eyes and nose on the inside of her jean jacket.

"I'm going to buy you the stone you deserve, Dad. Maybe move you and Mom together. I know you'd want that. Dad… I know about Costa. I'm sorry you had to go through that. After everything, I know you still loved her. I get that. I hope you're together."

"Reunited in God's kingdom." Up there.

"Up there," she repeated aloud. "I'm hoping there's an up there, a heaven. I stopped believing such a long time ago… It's just too hard. I miss you and Mom and Rob so badly. Being here brings it all back. It feels… painful doesn't quite cover it. I know you'll be disappointed with me for this, but I don't think I can forgive Jimmy. It's one thing to ruin your own life, but he ruined everything for all of us… I don't have it in me."

She couldn't continue; felt like her lungs were on fire.

"Honestly, maybe it'd be best if he doesn't, you know… make it. He's not my worry anymore. I don't care what happens to him now. I came to apologize and say thanks for the journal. I read every line. Thank you for telling me the truth. It means everything to me. I have a few more things to take care of while I'm here, then I'll go back to my life. It's much better for me there.

"Dad, I know I'm far from perfect; in fact, part of why I came back this time was to try to put some of my past behind me, but I think you'd like who I turned out to be. I think you and Mom would be proud, or at least I hope you would. I love you both. Always have."

She whispered, "You broke my heart when you went away."

Mia stood and walked back to the car, Frenchie following quietly. Leaves crunched under their feet.

She returned to the cemetery office, unbothered by the fact that she probably looked like a wreck. If the man noticed, he didn't give a sign. He was probably used to the many faces of grief. How interesting humans can be. Given enough exposure, we grow accustomed to almost every awful scenario.

Mia handed the man a piece of paper with the number of the stone she wanted for her dad. He eyed her curiously.

"This is the one I want for James Capaldi." *The State of Rhode Island can throw his little dinky one away or stuff it up its ass.*

The man continued to stare at her.

"I also want a quote on moving his body to be with my mother's, if that's even possible." She grew impatient, eager to get the hell out of there. "Look up the price to order the stone; I'll pay for it now."

He leafed through a book and gave her the price. She scribbled out a check and filled out numerous pages of paperwork.

"To exhume a body often involves a lengthy process," he informed her.

"Then it's good we're starting today," she replied sharply.

Mia felt lighter after leaving the office. For the first time in a long while, she felt she was on the right path. *Rory might be right. Maybe I need to visit my ghosts and put them each to rest, one by one, once and for all. I probably won't admit it to him, though.*

It was late afternoon by the time she returned to Auntie's house. She'd spent almost the entire day at someone else's grave, talking to her father. As crazy as it sounded, she felt a bit better.

She desperately needed a shower and some food. Cold soup straight from the fridge and a glass of strong cabernet was easiest. She turned the water temperature up, and her mind flipped through the last few weeks. Being back had been painful as hell, but she was starting to feel like it might turn out to be a good thing after all.

She stepped out of the shower, suddenly exhausted. She walked into Rob's room and placed the picture of them face down on the bedside table. Her mind flashed to Tony. She pulled out Rob's top drawer to look for socks, feeling a pang of guilt or some emotion she couldn't name. The picture of the two of them at the Falls sat on top of the dresser, next to the small velvet box. She picked up the ring box and rubbed her fingers over the smooth material before opening it. *What a shame things turned out the way they did for us… Poor Rob. He could've done so much with his life.* She snapped the box shut and returned it to its spot.

She sat back on his bed, lost in her thoughts. Slowly, an idea emerged. She knew what she needed to do. She smiled. *He was so fond of nature, especially "our spot," as he used to call it. It's the perfect place to visit him, our memory. Maybe I'll pack a cooler, take music and everything, just like the old days. I'll bring the ring. Say my piece to him there. No more guilt. Maybe it'll feel good to see the old spot.* She was all set with graveyards for a while.

Mia reclined back on the bed, looking up toward the ceiling. *Closure.* The word swirled around her brain. It was a simple enough word, but the process of getting it always proved to be more than complicated. Her plans would have to wait until the morning; there wasn't enough light left in the day or energy in her body.

Her mind swirled as she drew closer to sleep. The gravesite, those poor families, she and Rob holding hands as the Falls crashed loudly around them. Tony's strong arms holding her protectively. He smirked, and they kissed.

She woke with a start, looking around the room. Frenchie was snoring. She used the bathroom, grabbed her phone and returned to bed. She scanned her messages, finding two texts from Rory and a voicemail from Tony. She hit play.

"Hey, when you didn't call me back, I figured you were tired and all. I really enjoyed our time together last night. Maybe tomorrow night we can meet at the Oaks for dinner if you're up for it. I'd love to see you. Call me back when you get this."

Chapter 41

Mia cracked one eye open at a time; the sun streamed in through the window. She reread the note from Tony, still on the bed and felt as though she was smiling from within. She pushed herself off the bed, remembering the day's mission.

After getting ready, she realized she hadn't packed a jacket. She had nothing warm enough to traipse through the woods near water. She slid open Rob's closet and pulled out his leather jacket. Just the feel of it gave her nostalgia, and she cringed. Placing the jacket back in its spot, she grabbed an old flannel instead.

After packing up everything she needed, she and Frenchie loaded into the car.

"Okay, Monsieur French, we're off like a prom dress."

Trepidation grew as she approached the familiar road she still didn't know the name of. She looked for a street sign, there wasn't one. She turned off the radio and slowly eased up the winding road.

There it is: our spot. She cut the engine and took in the scenery across the way. The water expanded on each side of the rock wall, just barely contained. The waterfall was still out of sight; she'd have to walk to their regular spot to see it. She eyed the clock; it was almost noon. *"It's five o'clock somewhere."* She'd need sedation for this.

She got out, went to the back to open the cooler, eyed the wine but grabbed water, returned to the front seat and let her mind drift.

"Maybe I didn't think this through..."

Mr. French wagged his tail, ready to roll.

She sighed and got out of the car. *I'll come back for the stuff.*

She walked Mr. French along the outskirts of the Falls. He couldn't have been happier peeing on everything from twigs and grass to littered soda cans. He looked at her adoringly.

Mia sat for a long while watching the sun dance over the water. She pulls at her plastic bottle, noticing it's empty. Her overeducated brain whispered in a pejorative tone her need for meds at some point in the immediate future.

Quit being a drama queen; you're dealing with a lot...

Maybe you're not that different from your brother...

She took Frenchie back to the car and returned to their spot, ignoring any further internal debate.

Scanning the area, she could have sworn she smelled Rob's earthy scent. Despite all that had happened, she tried to be grateful for what she had. *Ror, Frenchie, my patients, Tony...*

She retrieved her stuff from the car and followed the path until it felt familiar. *I'm here.* The spot had meant so much to her, to them. She had mourned there, fell in love, laughed, cried, and gotten very drunk. It was where they'd given their bodies to one another, free and unencumbered. *This is where it all happened.*

She turned on the radio to 92 PRO-FM. They used to sit and listen while Rob smoked. She liked the smell but not the effects; they made her feel worse. The grief-stricken girl who'd landed in San Francisco after that awful summer, couldn't bear to think about any of the silly details that'd once made up her life. Her sanity depended on burying them deep. She was finally able to glimpse some of those details and reclaim them as her own. Marianna and Mia met at long last.

She laid back on the blanket, looking to the sky. Sara McLaughlin's "Angel" played over the radio, and Mia hummed along. "Spend all your time waiting for that second chance, for a break that would make it okay. There's always some reason to feel not good enough, and it's hard at the end of the day. I need some distraction; oh, a beautiful release. Memories seep from my veins. In the arms of the angel, fly away from here." She felt far away, like she was floating.

She turned to her right and saw Rob smiling at her. He broke off a piece of cheese and nibbled, handing some to her.

"You look good," he said as he reached over and touched her hair. "Still curly, soft."

It felt good to be near him. His outdoorsy smell surrounded her.

"Rob, I've missed you." She felt an overwhelming rush of emotion. "Everything… All the things we used to do together. The things that made you *you*."

Their fingers intertwined in the most natural way. His skin felt masculine, warm.

"Mare, you met someone. He's crazy for you, cares a lot."

"I did."

"Tell me all about him."

"His name is Tony. He knows about my family. I guess he cares for me enough… But he's not you."

He touched her face gently. "No, he's not."

His eyes penetrated hers; they were still the bluest eyes she'd ever seen, clear and beautiful.

"You could still have something special with him. Mare, you deserve to. You should at least try."

Her tears felt weighty. "I don't really want to, though. What if something happens? I can't take any more…"

"It'll be alright. You're just scared." He squeezed her hand. "You're stronger than you think. Don't avoid living."

Mia put her head on his shoulder. She felt so damn comfortable she could've stayed there forever. He kissed her. It was a long, seductive kiss. Her lower stomach flipped. *He's the only man who has this effect on my body. Until recently…*

They lay in silence for a while longer.

"Not that you need it, but you have my permission. You can be happy with him; he'll love you. Who wouldn't?" He looked away.

For a split second, Mia thought she read sadness in his face.

As they sat listening to nature, Rob rubbed her forehead. Mia closed her eyes for a moment; the gesture was intimate. *He used to do this all the time. I almost forgot.*

When she opened her eyes again, he was gone.

"Rob, you here?"

I'm alone. The reality pulsed through her, echoed.

Gathering her stuff, Mia walked to the exact spot where they had been together so many times. She opened the box and put the ring on her finger one last time. Fiddling with it, she wondered what he'd want. *The water races with motion, with life. He'd want me to decide. "Mare, you should try. Don't avoid living 'cause you're afraid."*

Mia stood at the water's edge and tossed the box in first, then the ring. She watched as the water swallowed them.

"This is for you, us. I'll love you always."

She could have sworn she heard his response. "Love you, too. You promised."

However crazy it seemed—and she was sure it was crazy, like certifiable—she answered, "I promise to try."

The force of the water curled and crashed, causing white

caps along the surface. The sun shone down on the water, making it look as if it were dancing with diamonds. Nature was simple, beautiful. *Maybe Rob was right all along. Maybe we do come back into nature.* The tree-tops swayed, and a hawk soared high above. Her senses were alive. For a moment, she could feel Rob's presence.

Heading back through the path, she laughed when she caught sight of Frenchie's big round head, his paws resting on the steering wheel.

"Hey, boy."

Dusk was approaching, and she watched the pretty layers of yellow, orange, faded gray and brown spread across the sky. She had a love-hate relationship with this time of day. Part of her dreaded the coming of night, the misery the dark could bring. But the new day promised a do-over, another try to get it right tomorrow. It symbolized possibility, offered hope. Mesmerized by the sunset, her only thought was how utterly beautiful it looked. She waited for the moment when the ground and sky intimately met.

Mia was almost in Cranston when her cell rang.

"Hey." Her stomach dipped with anticipation.

"Hey back, m'lady. I left you a voicemail earlier; figured you were busy… Can't stop thinking about the other night…"

"Oh, I didn't check my phone yet." She wondered what he'd say about how she'd spent her day. "I was just thinking about my next meal."

"Hungry, huh? You want to meet at Twin Oaks?"

"I'd like that very much."

"Did you have a good day?"

Mia couldn't find the words to respond. Rob's words came to mind instead: "*You should try.*"

"You there?"

"Yes, yes, right here. Just trying to decide between the veal parm or a steak sandwich."

"Come on, everybody knows the veal trumps the steak there."

She laughed. "Okay, decided."

"I'll meet you there." In a rough voice, he added, "I wore the same shirt today... It smells like you."

Her heartbeat quickened. "See you in a little bit then."

Chapter 42

Twin Oaks was a Rhode Island Institution. Mia hadn't been there since she was a kid, and her father had taken her there for lunch. She remembered the loaded steak sandwich on the heel of an Italian bun, the crunchy kind that could break your jaw; she could almost taste it. She stood outside the front door, lost in her thoughts. She smelled Tony's distinctive scent and felt the warmth of his mitt-like hand on her shoulder.

"Hey, gorgeous. Green's definitely your color." He looked her up and down approvingly before kissing her forehead and engulfing her in his body. "Couldn't wait to see you," he whispered into her hair. Pulling back slightly, he asked, "Everything alright? You sounded funny on the phone."

"Yes… I was just remembering one of the best steak sandwiches I've ever eaten in my whole life. It was around a hundred years ago with my father. I was a kid."

"Nice. That's good stuff right there."

"It sure is."

"You had a good day then?" He looked into her eyes.

"I did." *How can he tell?*

Tony led Mia into the foyer, holding her hand tight.

Talk about stepping into a time warp. Twin Oaks still looked like an old man's study. The foyer was packed with people. Pictures of the owner's family scattered the walls. An older woman with jet-black hair and penciled eyebrows stood behind a counter selling keno tickets and homemade sauce. The maître d' took names from behind a dark wooden pulpit. The floor was made of dark blue slate, and the bar sat directly in front, still paneled in dark wood. The booths and chairs were burgundy and navy with dark gold studs. They were rimmed in dark walnut, leather-bound along the sides.

Tony gave a nod to the maître d', and they were escorted to a back room. Tony duked him for the quick seat. Glancing at the patrons, Mia wondered if she was underdressed. The place was filled with dark-haired men dressed in expensive suits wearing gold rings on their pinkies. The women ranged in age and dress, but they all seemed to don lipstick, big hair, and hooped earrings. It felt like a scene from an old gangster movie. Inwardly, she reminded herself to tell Rory about the place. *They could do a reality show here.* A window expanded across the entire back wall. It was dark outside, but lights illuminated the water beyond. The pond was called Speck's. For a moment, her day returned.

"This was my mom's favorite room," she told Tony as they sat down.

"Really? The water view?"

"Yes. The rest of the place is too dark for her taste."

"Do you agree with her?"

That's a loaded statement. "Not really. The dark, old-fashioned style fits the place. She was from California. I think it reminded her of her childhood. The part she didn't like." Mia paused, thinking about her. There was so much she didn't know about her mother.

"Do you resemble her?"

"No, but I wanted to. She was blonde, stunning. But my name… it was hers, as you know."

They locked eyes, both remembering their intimate night.

"I like that you told me," Tony finally said.

She fiddled with her silverware.

He smiled and took her hands in his.

"My father couldn't handle it—the name change—so I waited until I moved away to legally change it."

"I think it's a very pretty name. Mia." He hesitated. "Can I be blunt?"

"Yes, of course."

"I think Marianna suits you better. Maybe it's that great hair, I don't know; I just love your real name… Are you mad?"

"No. Thank you for the compliment." She paused. "There's a lot I never learned about her." For a moment, her emotions nearly consumed her.

"So, you look like your father, then?"

"Not really. Maybe his coloring? He was a big guy when I was a kid. Milk-man, I guess." She half smiled, suddenly aware he was watching her. She dropped his hands and began fiddling with her napkin.

He buttered a roll for each of them.

"They said I looked exactly like my grandmother, father's side. I never met her, though."

"That's the first time you talked about them to me like that."

"Being here… Sorry."

"No, don't be. I wanna know everything about you, them."

The server arrived almost immediately.

"You must know some pretty important people in this place," she whispered.

"It's one of the benefits of my past career." He winked. "And between you and me, I train the owner's grandson."

The server brought out two massive platters of veal parmigiana. Mia was ecstatic about her meal when a description out of her father's journal started to spin.

She saw Jimmy as a young man, a senior in high school, only months away from leaving for the service. Jimmy had confronted their mother about the affair. She said she was going to end it but then changed her mind, saying she couldn't do it.

Mia imagined Jimmy walking into Minelli's, searching for his mother. She had been late getting home, not typical for her. What he saw horrified him. In the back storage room, he found them together. She was crying. They were yelling at each other, his mother and some strange man.

Maybe he thought she was in danger, being sexually assaulted. Mia tried to imagine his reaction. Serve, protect, eighteen-year-old brain and all. She couldn't imagine how he must've felt. To see with his own eyes… He realized they were having a lover's quarrel.

Mia wondered what had gone through his head after he shot his own mother—killed her. How does one handle a truth like that? She wasn't in danger. She had made a decision to be there with her lover.

Their father knew, and he'd asked her to make a choice. She told him she'd tried to end it… Jimmy ended it instead. He'd wanted their father to kill the guy, but he wouldn't make that choice for her. He didn't want to live like that.

She saw Tony watching her.

"Hey, you alright?"

She nodded.

"Being here makes you miss them? Your parents?"

"A little bit." Her leg started to pump up and down.

Tony continued eating. A few minutes went by before he spoke again.

"It's your brother." He put his fork down and wiped his mouth. "Naturally, you're worried about him."

"As much as I hate myself for it, yes."

"I was trying not to bring it up, but how is he?"

She couldn't pinpoint her feelings about Jimmy. Knowing that Tony knew the truth made her feel better.

"How'd you know I was thinking about him?"

"It's all right there in your eyes. I can tell when you go away… Plus, you barely touched your food. Now, that's not like you." He smirked. His expression grew serious, thoughtful. "You don't do it as much as when you first got back here, though. The way I see it, that's a good thing. I think in your world they call it progress?"

She smiled. *He can read me, amazing.*

Tony walked Mia to her car, smiling wide when he saw Frenchie.

"Hey, boy." He opened the door for her, doing a little bow as she got in. Always the gentleman.

"I'll follow you. For safety purposes, a course."

"Of course." She yawned.

"I might get to tuck you in." He brushed his lips to hers. "Give a guy at least a maybe?"

"At least a maybe." She paused. "She would've really liked you."

A smile spread to his eyes that twinkled back at hers.

Chapter 43

Five minutes later, Mia pulled up to her aunt's house to find the lights on.

Tony pulled up next to her. "Expecting company?" He stepped out of his car, weirdly alert.

"No, it's probably my aunt." She was slightly irritated, she just wanted to be alone.

She looked back toward Tony. *Maybe not completely alone…*

"I'll wait here." Tony stood with shoulders puffed.

"I'd tell you not to bother, but I know you won't listen."

"Smart lady. I'll be right here."

Auntie, Sal and the girls were sitting at the kitchen table.

Joanne stood to greet Mia. "Marianna, sorry to barge in unannounced."

"Mare." Auntie Rose stood up with a look in her eyes that said this wasn't a social visit.

"Caren needs a place to stay," Jo blurted.

Caren turned towards Mia. Her face was swollen, one eye severely bruised shut and her lip was red and purple. It was tough to look at her.

"Oh my God! What happened?"

Tears clung to Caren's open eye as she stood, slowly moving toward Mia for a hug.

Mia tried not to wince when she saw Caren up close. In her gut she already knew what had happened.

"Were you in an accident?"

"Accident, pah," Joanne chimed. "It's called Jay. He relapsed, beat her up, again. Someday he's gonna kill her, and we're gonna be crying graveside with their kids tryin' to explain why their stupid mother couldn't leave him!"

"Alright, that's enough." Auntie Rose's face showed she feared the same.

"Enough? Look at her face! What kind of loser hits a pregnant lady? She looks like the elephant man, for Christ sakes." Jo stormed out the front door. "I need a cigarette."

"That's awful, Caren." At a loss for words, Mia stayed silent for a long beat. "Ca, I had no idea he was hurting you... I'm so sorry." She turned to Aunt Rose. "Did you already call the police?"

"No. My stupid sister won't let us," Jo spat walking back into the kitchen.

"What?"

"Marianna... He's got a prior; he'll go to jail. I can't do that to my kids." Caren started to silently cry.

Mia was sure she hadn't been able to disguise her look of disgust.

Aunt Rosie broke the silence. "She'll need to stay here tonight. He won't come near her here, with us around."

Mia felt a twinge of guilt. Despite all the sadness and horror that happened here, she'd been able to leave this reality. They hadn't.

"I'll book a room in the city."

"Don't be an asshole," Joanne's chided. "We have enough room."

"I would be closer to the hospital." The truth was, she couldn't handle any more family pain.

"Hey, you got company." Jo swept her eyes toward the front walk.

Tony was still standing by his car. *He's probably worried.*

"Look at the size of him!" Jo's eyes were wide. "He looks like a friggin' bodyguard, for Christ sakes."

"He's a friend of mine." Heat rose to her cheeks.

Jo smirked. "Maybe he can help us." She nodded toward Caren. "Have him beat him up or somethin'?"

"Don't say that." Caren turned away.

"Don't say that? Go look at your face, you dumb shit. Turn away all you want, I'm gonna tell you somethin' right now. If this doesn't end soon, I'm gonna kill him. Literally. All by myself. You have my word, Caren, this ends tonight. Now."

"Where are the kids?" Mia asked.

"His sister, Beth, has them." Caren hesitated before continuing. "I knew he wasn't right a few days ago when he went off on a bender," she mumbled through her fat lip, barely intelligible.

Mia looked back and forth between her cousins, thinking about all they had gone through.

"I'll be right back," Mia assured before stepping outside.

She explained the situation to Tony.

"I'll be tied up for a while."

"He'll probably show up, cause trouble. I've lived this scene too many times to count." His demeanor changed.

She eyed him, unsure what she was reading on his face.

"Do you want to come inside?"

"Question is, do you want me in there with you? Them?"

It was another turning point, they both knew it. Did she want him to meet Rob's family? She paused, frozen.

"My cousin thinks you look like a bodyguard." Her lips pulled upward but her stomach fluttered.

"I've been called worse." He took her hand.

A pickup truck pulled up and screeched to a halt. Tony stiffened and dropped Mia's hand.

"Go inside, you don't wanna watch this. And don't listen to whatever he says. They all lie when they're desperate." Tony pulled out his cell.

Mia remained planted, not fully understanding. Seconds later, Jay stood on the lawn, disheveled.

"Ey, Marianna. Your cousin in there? Go get her for me. I gotta talk to her, please. There's been a big misunderstanding. She fell—hit her head, her lip. They think I did it. Mare, you know how much I love her. I'd never hurt her on purpose. We got in a fight, shit happens. You know how she is."

He was on the verge of tears.

"Hey, 'member that time we all had that barn party out at Frankie's house in Scituate? She got all toasted up, punched me in the lip? Eey, Robby was there, too. We laughed our heads off." He shook his head. "Those were the days, huh?"

She stiffened at the sound of Robert's name. "Jay, listen…"

Tony was off the phone and her words fell away. The look on Tony's face said he meant business. *Did he just say "Detective Iannucci?"*

She looked at him, stunned.

"You're a cop?"

"I am. I can explain later; go inside." He turned toward Jay, his jaw tight.

She turned away from Jay and tried to ignore his pleas. *He lied to me.*

"Mare, you'll tell her I'm out here, right?"

She felt bad for him even though she knew better.

Jay moved closer to her.

"Don't take another step, my man." Tony's voice was sharp. He positioned his body between them. The swift movement caused the fabric of his shirt to bunch, exposing metal for a quick instant. "That's his gig. He wants you to feel bad for him; they all do. Go look at her face." His voice softened. "Ey, I'm still me… crazy about you."

Tony reached for her arm but she instinctively shrugged away from his touch.

"Why did I think you were different? I don't know what I was thinking…" She turned away and hurried up the walkway, her heart was pounding out of her chest. Sirens sounded down the street.

"Who the fuck are you?" Jay yelled at Tony.

"I'm your worst nightmare, punk. You won't be hittin' any women where you're goin'. Save your breath; I already heard it all."

Mia shut the door behind her.

"Your friend's a cop?" Jo sounded impressed.

Mia simply nodded in response.

Slam. Mia winced as someone hit metal, hard.

He's a detective… Why didn't he tell me that?

Because they're all liars. Every last one.

"Ey, I'm still me… Crazy about you."

I can't believe he left that out after last night. How could he do that? Why?

You already know why, Mia.

She felt something deep down in her slide shut. She wrapped her arms around her midsection for support.

A few minutes later, Jay was cuffed and being led away by two uniformed, Johnston police officers. None of it deterred him from calling to Caren through the window.

"Ca, tell 'em to let me go. You know I love you. It was an accident, come on!" he screamed. "What are the kids gonna say?"

Caren had to be restrained by Aunt Rose. It was hard for Mia to witness her pain as she watched Jay being dragged away like it was her fault.

"Take her in the other room," Aunt Rose asked, out of breath.

They pulled her up and silently watched as Jay was shoved into the back of the cruiser. The spectacle was over. All that remained was a deafening silence.

Chapter 44

"What a fucking horror show," Jo spat.

"Stay here with the kids, Caren. We'll help you," offered Sal.

Caren cried into her hands.

Sal patted Aunt Rose's hand. "I'll be at the shop if you need anything."

After a few minutes, Auntie cleared her throat. "Who needs coffee?"

"I need something stronger than that," Jo shot back.

Ignoring Joanne, Aunt Rosie poured each of them a cup.

"Joanne, what about what Sal said…"

"It's the best idea I've heard all night."

Caren's face was still buried in her hands. Jo put her hand on Caren's shoulder.

"Marianna, your thoughts? Professional now, forget she's your cousin."

Mia was still lost in the fact that Tony was a cop. *Nobody but Rob will ever be trustworthy or honest.*

"Ca, I think it's a good idea. There's programs that can help you feel different. Stronger." Mia didn't have enough distance to give appropriate advice. She felt sick, wondering how they'd all ended up at this point. The feeling carried a weight she couldn't bear and she leaned on the end of the sofa to sit, lightheaded.

Caren looked up at Mia then, tired and resigned. "I don't know how I got here."

Mia touched her arm as Caren blinked back tears.

"I feel like it's my fault."

Auntie shook her head and stood abruptly. She riffled through the freezer for a bag of frozen peas. "Put this on your eye."

Moments later, Tony stood at the front door, his face tight.

"Officer Iannucci?" Mia couldn't hide the snide in her voice. She thought about all she'd told him the other night.

He hesitantly smiled, an expression of remorse crossed his face. *Good, he should.* He had compassion in his eyes. *It's too late. He can't be trusted.* She reached for the door.

"I'll walk you out."

Tony reached for her, but she pulled away.

"Mee, you're not gonna let him in? Introduce us or what?" Jo raised a brow.

"Naw, now's not a good time," Tony answered for her. "You have enough goin' on. Anotha time."

Jo looked confused. "Thank you, we appreciate it."

Tony nodded and he and Mia stepped outside.

"Marianna, I've—"

"You lied."

"It's complicated. I didn't want that for you…*us*." He looked away. "I thought you had enough of that already."

Her eyes met his as she stiffened and wrapped her arms around her waist.

Tony lightly touched her arm. "Come here. I'm so sorry. Let's do this somewhere else. Let me explain."

"Don't." She flinched. "I don't need any more explanations or excuses from the men in my life." Mia started to walk away.

"Ey, tell your cousins he'll be in lockdown by tomorrow morning. Besides violating his restraining order, he was caught driving drunk on a suspended license again. It's enough to put him away for at least a few months. We're lookin' into some old priors. Longer he stays away the better. Easier for her, you know?" He paused. "It'll give her time to get stronger. Maybe get away from him for good."

Mia turned toward him. "Thanks, Detective. I think we both know the pathetic stats on what happens to these women..."

"You got every right to be hurt. Meet me later to talk. There are things I couldn't tell you. I swear it's not what you think."

"There's nothing to talk about, Detective. I mistook you for someone else. It won't happen again."

"Wait. I wanted— "

The door opened and they both turned to see Jo step out.

"Mare, sorry to interrupt. It's Ror. He's all in a tizzy, hasn't talked to you in a whole day, I guess." She handed Mia the cordless phone.

"It's fine. We're done here." She took the phone. "Hey, Ror."

"Mee, what the fuck? Where the hell have you been for two days?"

"Everybody's alright." She continued with a rundown of her day.

"Mee, you gonna tell me what the hell is going on or what?"

"Later."

Mia hung up feeling like shit. She had avoided talking to Ror about anything except work since her father had died. She needed to tell him so much, but didn't know where to begin.

"Sounds like he's worried about you," Tony said, interrupting her thoughts.

"That's none of your business."

"I deserve that." He looked at the policeman standing by his cruiser. "He's gonna need to talk to her."

Mia nodded.

Tony started down the front walkway, then stopped. "You and your fur ball need to crash somewhere, my condo's open. We can talk; then you don't need a hotel room. I'll be at the gym for a few if you need me for anything. I'm sorry I didn't tell you sooner..."

Mia turned away still trying to untangle her web of emotions. She counted her breaths as she reentered the house.

Chapter 45

Caren gave her statement to a sympathetic officer while Joanne and Mia sat with her at the kitchen table. Aunt Rosie moved about the kitchen, cleaning everything in sight. Caren's account of what happened was sad and typical of domestic abuse victims. She felt responsible for his violence and drinking. She downplayed her injuries, more concerned about his punishment. Aunt Rosie left the house, slamming the kitchen door shut behind her.

About an hour later, Mia and Jo sat in the living room mindlessly watching television. Caren had gone to bed. Glancing at her cell, Mia decided it was time to find a hotel. She wasn't in the right space to stay with family. She blamed work and excused herself for the evening.

"You serious about the bodyguard or just fucking around while you're here?"

"I was just passing the time. That's done now."

"Does he know that?"

Mia was still thinking about her cousin's words as she passed the Downtown Providence exit and headed to Tony's gym. She'd check into her room later.

She found him doing laps in the pool. Sitting on a lounge chair, she watched him swim. His strokes were clean and strong. He was in a zone.

Frenchie ran laps with him along the side of the pool. Tony noticed him and glanced around. He hopped out in one motion and wrapped a towel around his waist as he walked toward her.

His muscles flexed with the forward movement. Her body betrayed her at seeing him. *This was a mistake.* She averted her eyes away from his.

She thought back to the previous night—them together. She'd completely lost her instincts. She should've known better.

"Ey, I'm glad you came." Tony reached for her hand.

"I shouldn't have." *Forget this.* She walked quickly. "Frenchie, come on," she snapped.

She pushed through the front door and it nearly closed on her dog. All the men who'd disappointed her swam through her mind. First, her uncle, who'd disappeared out of thin air. Her father, too weak to tell the truth and stay. Robbie, taken too soon—not his fault but still felt like a betrayal. Her brother, the ultimate lie responsible for her family's complete demise. And Tony... *Forget this. I don't have the energy for another.*

Her tears burned, falling down her cheeks in silent streams. She ushered Frenchie into the front seat and slammed the door shut. Starting up the car, she used the back of her hands to wipe her nose and eyes. After a few deep breaths, she edged the car forward. She looked up to see Tony standing in front of the car and slammed on the breaks.

"Move."

"I won't. No," he panted. "Hear me out."

"No! I don't care what you have to say. Move, or I'll run you over. What's one more death? Move!"

They locked eyes.

"Detective, I don't have the energy for this. Please. Just move. Go." The underbelly of her anger was dangerously close.

"I have a good explanation. Marianna, I'm not like them. It's not the same. I get that you've been hurt and that you're tired. Open the door. Let me say what I have to say. If you decide I'm like them, then you can go. This, us, ends."

Mia took a few deep breaths to calm herself but she couldn't stop the tears. She put the car in park and lifted her eyes to his.

Tony slid into the passenger seat next to her.

He moved to wipe away her tears with his hand.

"Don't, please. Talk. You've got about two minutes."

He shivered, still wet from swimming. She turned the heat on full blast and sat back against the seat, exhaustion settling in.

"The reason I became a cop was to protect and save people."

"Get out."

"I thought I could protect my mother from guys like Jay." His voice became low and soft, "And save their scared, broken kids."

She exhaled, annoyed by her compassion. She was used to hearing confessions and heartbreak.

"I learned quick that most people don't want saving, though, and that some aren't worth it. Not in the way the law offers it, anyway. But protection I can still offer. I got involved in special cases about 10 years ago. Deep assignments because I felt that's where I could make a difference in this shitty, fucked up world we live in. I didn't tell you because I'm not allowed to share that part of myself with anyone. It puts them in danger and compromises the case. Until now, I simply didn't have anyone to protect from that world."

They locked eyes.

"I'm sorry I didn't tell you, I really am. And truthfully, I can't say any more because I won't jeopardize your safety. Ever."

He was allowing her a glimpse into his broken pieces. She knew how hard that was for him, how rare it was for anyone to be vulnerable. She was scared for him; he was taking a chance on her. She wanted to bolt but felt his hand squeezing hers. He rested his head on hers and exhaled deep and slow. Her fear paused, almost subsided, with his breath.

"How's your cousin doin'?"

"She's guilt-ridden, ashamed. Blames herself. You know how the shitty layers unfo…"

"Unfortunately, I do." He kissed her slow and then leaned back against the seat.

She wondered, as she often did with her patients, what he'd been like before he was hurt by his father's violence, who he would have been without all the pain and fear. She felt a stab of sadness for him. *Funny how the people closest to us hurt and shape us the most.*

"Would you look at that?" He pointed toward the sky. The moon was full and bright. "Makes you want to believe there's still good out there."

She smiled for the first time in hours, wanting to believe. *Maybe the pain that shapes us isn't all bad. Maybe it's the thing that gives us dimension, the ability to go on, the possibility of hope. Maybe…*

"Let's go inside, you must be freezing."

Chapter 46

Back inside, Tony turned on the shower and the bathroom filled with steam as they undressed each other. They stepped inside, his body blocking her from the hot water. He positioned her against the opposite wall, his giant body engulfing hers. He soaped himself, then her, tenderly framing her face with his hand. There was a soft tenderness to his touch that she was unsure what to do with.

She tried to change positions but he persisted, barely breaking eye contact. Passion overtook them and he explored every inch of her body with his mouth and hands. While the water pelted against his head and back, he pleasured her. With her head thrown back, she gave into the thrill and sensation exploding inside of her.

They were barely dry when they tumbled onto the bed. He lifted her down onto him.

"I loved you from the second I saw you," his voice was barely a whisper.

Her heart stopped briefly, and her body went weak at his

touch. She escaped into her bodily sensations. He was skilled. He aimed to please her; she let him. Eventually, they tired.

He pulled her closer to him, and she could feel his heartbeat thumping against her back.

"Tony, I should go…"

"It's late. Stay with me," his voice was thick.

"I don't think I… can." She turned to face him. She was going back home, back to her life. She didn't want to get used to this, used to him.

When she glanced back at him, he was watching her, fiddling with his charm. The tenderness and understanding in his eyes melted her anxiety.

He held her tighter. "Sure you can."

She closed her eyes against him, her body as heavy as lead. Her mind was at peace, however fleeting.

Jimmy was surrounded by dark blue velvet. *He's in a casket.* She watched herself kneel beside it, crying softly. It was his funeral; she had missed the wake. Robert stood in the front pew, waiting for her. After she was finished, she slipped into the pew beside him.

"You knew and you didn't tell me," she said incredulously.

"You're with him now."

"No. I'll always be with you."

"Our pact is broken."

"You told me to. You made me promise…"

"Mare, I didn't mean it. Didn't think you would really fall for someone else. Someone besides me."

The pain in his voice penetrated her heart and she squeezed her eyes shut. *Jimmy's dead and Rob's not here for me anymore…* It felt as though a dentist had accidentally hit a nerve. Re-opening her eyes, she noticed Rob was only wearing one sneaker, the other swirling through the air. She smelled ice cream and blood, heard the vacuum-pack sound of a casket clasping shut. She bolted upright

"You have a bad dream? I'm right here, it's okay."

She wiped at her eyes. "My brother and…" She couldn't tell him about Rob. "Was dead. It was awful to see him in a casket. It felt so real… Sorry." She went to the bathroom to wash her face and take a few deep breaths. A few minutes later, fully composed, she re-entered the room and began pulling on her clothes.

"Don't." He sat up and pulled her to him. He kissed her entire face. He smirked at Mr. French watching them with a bored expression. "I think this is your job, boy."

She tried for a smile. Since her father's death, her dreams had been brutal. She was embarrassed.

He reached up and kissed her lightly on the lips. "It's okay."

One kiss became another until comfort turned sensual. She was reminded of the fine line between pleasure and pain. Her jeans fell in a clump to the floor.

"You okay?" he asked.

She lost herself in him.

"Tony?"

He rolled toward her.

"I want to tell you something, but… I don't know if it'll put you in a legal bind."

"Hey, I can handle whatever you've got."

She propped herself up on one elbow and told him about her father's journal. "I'm not sure what I'm supposed to do now… He's still unconscious, I don't know if it was on purpose."

"Don't do anything, yet. Wait until he wakes up, talk to him then. Come here."

"Rory doesn't know." She glanced away, felt his arms hold her tighter. She relaxed into him and he kissed the top of her head.

"You'll tell him when you're ready. He'll understand.

Safety washed through her.

"I'll stand guard," he whispered as she drifted to sleep.

Chapter 47

"Morning, gorgeous. How'd you sleep?" He pulled her closer toward him.

"Good, actually." She checked on Frenchie, still fast asleep.

Tony noticed her foot moving a mile a minute under the sheet. He pushed a mass of curls away from her face.

"I already took him out. We did a few laps. French pooch loves the water. Went to get coffee and muffins, too. He's a cool little dog."

"If your gangster friends could see you now…"

His stomach twisted. *It's on them, doing illegal fucked up things.* He tried to convince himself. *We all do fucked up things when we think we don't have a choice.* He knew about it firsthand.

Tony's earlier conversation to the captain spun.

"Hey, it's T. I got new info on the Capaldi kid."

"I'm listening."

"I know two things: He's got a sister that came home to bury the dad and the old man wasn't responsible for the mother's shooting, he was."

"Costa could use her against the kid."

"Yup I would."

"How'd you get this?"

"Overheard some things from the guys about that night before the kid was knocked unconscious. He'd bragged, the dumb fuck."

"Okay, what's our angle?"

"We get two douchebags at once. Costa and Capaldi. The sister's innocent, got nothing to do with any of it."

"You sure? You looked into her?"

"She's clean. She deserves protection, the truth." *Some peace of mind.*

"You got a plan?"

"Maybe I get to know her better. Offer to keep her safe from Costa, explain a small piece of it. Maybe if the kid wakes up, she'll find out what really happened to her mom."

"You think you can get that?"

"I do."

"Iannucci, you sure? I thought you were done with all this."

"She deserves protection and the truth."

"I can get Dinnucci on it."

"Naw, it's still mine. I won't be able to rest."

"Stop in tomorrow, we'll talk details."

He looked across at her. *I'll make it up to her by keeping her safe from both of them. She deserves at least that much.*

"Tony, I was kidding."

"No, you're fine," he answered, snapping back into the moment. "I got a few days off, thinking of heading to the White Mountains... Was wondering if you'd like to join me for the long weekend? I'm just going to say what I need to, don't want to lie to you, you don't deserve that. I was working undercover with those guys. They're not really my friends, it was work."

Even as he said it, it felt strange. He imagined JT's face when his dad failed to pick him up at the bus stop. Tony knew the feeling. He exhaled deep.

"Listen, most of them are away for a while, but the most dangerous, Costa, might not stay that way. And your brother pissed him off. They might try to take it out on you. I literally can't tell you more than that or your safety could be in greater danger. I refuse to put you in jeopardy." *Any more than I have,* he thought.

A mix of emotions crossed her features.

He held her hands tighter and she pulled them away.

"You don't have to decide now. Just think about it. I know it's a lot to take in. I got some clients I have to train. I'm sure you have family stuff. I'd like to help keep you safe. And I swear, I would've told you before." *It felt good to tell an almost full truth.* "I know you understand that with your patients."

She nodded. "I have to go visit my brother."

He watched a shadow flicker across her face and reached over to gently touch her cheek with the back of his hand.

"I really need to go."

He flinched at her withdrawal. "Hey, I'm sorry you're involved in any of this."

"Tony… Is there more I should know about you?"

He put his hand up. "You have a right not to trust me; I get it. Come here." He pulled her toward him. "I know how it seems, and I don't blame you, but you do know me." He kissed the top of her head. "Now smile. You don't want me to do my hulk move on you, do you?" He flexed, sending a single muscle twitching in his right bicep.

"No. How'd you do that?"

"I got all sorts of hidden talents, Doc." He winked. "Until later, then."

He rolled over and stood up in one motion. He kissed her hand.

"I'm glad you decided to stay."

"Me, too."

He lifted her chin slowly. "It's all gonna be okay. You'll see."

Chapter 48

Mia called Rory on her way to the hospital and was instantly relieved when his voicemail picked up after the first ring. She smiled as she replayed the previous night… Bits and pieces floated past. By the time she approached the hospital's parking lot, her thoughts had returned fully to her brother. *I need to talk to him.*

She was more than disappointed when she got to his room and he looked almost the same as he had the week earlier. Her stomach sank. From behind her, she heard Nancy, the kind nurse. An image of Glenda the Good Witch flashed through her brain. *I must need drugs.*

Mia darted her eyes away from Nancy. She hadn't been there in almost two weeks.

"Dr. Capaldi, you of all people know that people handle things their own way. There's no right way."

"Thank you." She was still trying to convince herself.

After Nancy left the room, Mia walked up to Jimmy's bed and took his free hand.

"Jim…" Her anger momentarily faded. "I have so many

questions about what happened… But why? I was thinking about your drinking. There's this place right by my house; it's a hardcore program. I think it'd be good for you. It'd do you wonders to get away from here." *It did for me.*

She wondered how her life might've turned out if she'd stayed all those years ago. It was futile. She knew she could have never lived there without Rob. *Altered paths…* Mia imagined Jimmy on the West coast. Why not? She had plenty of resources. Her house wasn't big but he could fit comfortably. For a little while, anyway.

Who was she kidding? She couldn't have lived with him if she'd tried. She looked away, frustrated. *How can you love and hate someone at the exact same time?* A piece of her thought it best if he'd just stopped breathing. She winced at her thoughts. *Should I lift the pillow now? Do it myself?*

Despite the harsh reality, she wanted him to live. In her heart, though, she wanted her real brother back. The one from her childhood, from before. She sighed and counted out her breaths. *That's never going to happen.* Even if he did wake up with any brain cells left, he'd go right back to being him.

"I hope you prove me wrong." She wished desperately that he'd say something, anything. "Wake up, if that's the plan. We have some things to figure out. I'm not so good at talking to you when you're like this, I'm sorry. I'd make a bad nurse. Maybe I haven't been the best sister, either."

She closed her eyes and lowered herself down onto a chair.

"Mare, don't worry," Robbie's voice comforted her. "He's got at least five more lives left."

"Maybe he doesn't deserve them."

"He's sorry for what he did… I talked to him."

"Sorry doesn't change much. I'm not sure I believe in forgiveness on that level anymore."

"Mare, you'll do the right thing. You always do."

"Don't be so sure."

He brushed his lips against her cheek and inhaled.

Her stomach flipped and fell as she felt the hair on her neck rise. Before her thoughts or emotions could catch up, he was gone again. The only evidence he was ever there was the hole in her heart and the bile she fought to swallow every time he left her again.

Irritated, she opened her eyes and tried to push off the blanket of sadness over her heart.

"You sleeping, honey?" Nancy asked quietly.

"No, just resting my eyes." Mia stood in one quick motion.

"You need more time alone?"

"No." *What's the point?*

"Remember, sometimes they do wake up. He's been moving his hands, his eyes–that's always a good sign. What happens after that is God's plan. No one else's."

Mia nodded, not believing a single word. She hadn't seen God make an appearance in a really long time. And when he did, she didn't usually like his plans.

"Nancy, if anything changes with him... Will you call me?"

"You know I will." Nancy took the card Mia held out to her and tucked it inside her pants pocket before excusing herself.

Mia glanced back at Jimmy. "Auntie and the girls are expecting me at the coffee shop. This weekend's Thanksgiving."

Tom Turkey, that's what her family had called the Holiday as an inside joke.

"Do you remember all the fun we used to have on Thanksgiving when we were kids?"

Her father worked on the actual holiday so they celebrated Thanksgiving on Saturday. He could never resist the time-and-a-half pay. Adults at one table, kids at some assembled card table they'd brilliantly named the "kid table." Mia's dad would sleep all day Friday then wake up "with the chickens", as Rosie used to say, Saturday morning.

He'd prepare everything from the antipasto to the nuts. Auntie and Mia's mom made the pies and sweets. He'd get the meats and cheeses from Vitos on The Hill. Crunchy bread, too. His soup had to have mini meatballs with raviolis, escarole, just a hint of boiled egg, and special grated cheese. That was followed by homemade pasta and sauce, then turkey and vegetables—which her dad and his friends referred to as the *A'medigon* part of the feast, slang for the holiday without pasta. They would eat into the night, the kids drinking orange soda with a splash of red wine. The memories made her smile.

"I wish things had turned out different."

She kissed his cool check. The reality of all that had happened rushed back. *He caused this... All of it.*

She couldn't wait to get the hell out of there, away from sickness, away from her memories. She suddenly craved life. Images from the previous night played in mind. *It's a little late for peak foliage, but the scenery will still be pretty.* What's more, she had no ghosts in the White Mountains.

Chapter 49

Heading back toward Minelli's, the scent of the air came straight out of Mia's childhood. The weather teased snow, gray and still, almost heavy. Thinking about her brother, Mia slowed the buggy and brought it to a stop directly out front of the diner. She exhaled as she watched Frenchie jump down from her side. Pushing through the front door, the familiar chimes sounded, her pulse quickened. Every time she entered the place, it felt like a step back in time. Caren and Joanne sat at the counter.

"Hey."

Caren's face had gotten worse. The swelling around her eye had gone down some but the surrounding area had turned purplish green, and her lip was crusty and split. Despite the physical reminder, everyone seemed to be in better spirits.

They were both eating soup. Mia sat next to them with Frenchie at her feet.

"Look who the cat dragged in," Jo threw out. "Monsieur puff ball."

He wagged his tail daintily.

"How's Jimmy?" Caren asked.

"Seems exactly the same. Nurse said there was more movement in his hands."

"That's good, right?"

"Supposed to be."

"How's the bodyguard?" Jo raised her brows.

"His name is Tony."

Jo threw Mr. French a piece of bread. "Somebody's rested, huh?"

Mia and Caren rolled their eyes in unison. It was funny how easily they'd fallen back into their set dynamics, scripted and set in stone by families everywhere. *I'm still her little cousin.* Sitting there, it was as if time hadn't passed at all.

"So, you got it bad then?" Jo slid the basket of bread toward Mia.

"No," Mia shot a little too quickly.

They eyed her and then each other.

She took a piece of bread and started to butter it.

"That might work out in Cali," said Jo. "But don't even try it here. We know you too well, Doc."

Mia's foot started bobbing up and down in quick little movements. She dipped a piece of crust in Jo's bowl and then popped it in her mouth.

Jo smirked.

"It's really no big thing… We're just friends."

"Yeah, I haven't seen that look since…"

Aunt Rosie bounded into the room and placed a bowl down in front of her. "I'm gonna need some help cleaning out that back room over at the house." She nodded toward Caren. "You'll need it, closet space and all. It's time, anyway." She returned to the kitchen, the double doors swinging back and forth in her wake.

They stared at one another, unsure if they'd heard correctly.

"Sir, yes, sir. Reporting for duty, sir," Jo whispered.

They all started to laugh. Caren winced in pain, trying hard not to smile as she giggled.

After so much time, Rob's room was finally going to be cleaned out. Mia's heart tugged and she ignored it, spooning escarole and bean soup into her mouth.

When they finished eating, they carried their dirty bowls into the back. The diner was filling up with locals hungry for lunch.

Aunt Rosie stopped Mia on her way out.

"Rory called me last night. He's concerned about you. You do look tired. He's got some questions I think you should answer... It's time."

Mia pushed open Rob's bedroom door. The last time she'd been there... Her eyes moved to the bed.

Coming up behind her, Joanne handed her a glass of wine, poured one for herself, and then placed the bottle on the bureau. She looked toward Caren.

"Sorry for your troubles, ol' prego one." She handed her a chocolate biscotti. "Next best thing."

Mia picked up a large garbage bag, giving it a quick snap, and opened the top drawer of Rob's bureau. None of them looked at each other for a long while, each keeping to their chosen tasks. Joanne tossed things into a box from the top of his closet while Caren was on her hands and knees, going through his shoes.

She separated underwear and socks from pictures and other tchotchkes, moving quickly through her task. The girls also seemed to work quickly. Caren's kids were getting dropped off the following day and they were all secretly a little scared of Rosie.

"Hey, you gonna actually bring the bodyguard around us this weekend?" Jo asked, breaking the silence.

"You already met him."

"Last night doesn't count… How'd you meet a cop, anyways?"

"On the plane."

"Could he even fit in the seat?"

"Barely."

"So?"

Mia sighed. She'd forgotten how relentless her cousin could be. She opened the last dresser drawer while telling them the edited version of how she and Tony had met. It was a slightly amusing story—her bad mood, first impression, a windstorm, getting trapped in Boston with Frenchie and all.

She didn't tell them that when he held her tight, she felt safe, as if everything was going to be alright for the first time in forever. She also didn't tell them how scared she was to feel anything for him. She told them about his invitation to New Hampshire for the weekend and instantly regretted it.

"… As friends."

It felt strange to be telling them about Tony as she tossed Rob's old tee shirts and work socks into a garbage bag. Being there with them reopened an old feeling in her heart she didn't want to name. She reached for her wine desperately trying to dull it.

She placed the empty glass down next to the bag of Rob's stuff. "Hey, how 'bout a refill?"

Jo poured. "He must have, what? Fifteen years on you?"

Mia drained her glass. Standing, she carried a small box of pictures and an overstuffed bag out to the kitchen. She told herself that she and Tony were temporary and decided to decline his offer.

Jo raised her brows as she walked by. "Nice of him to ask his friend to spend the holiday away with him…" She hefted a bag in each hand. "We'll send these to Big Sisters. Especially the coats."

Jo glanced over at Mia's small pile of things she couldn't let go—a few pictures, an old flannel shirt and a pair of socks she used to sleep in. Without saying a word, Jo placed his leather coat down on Mia's pile. Jo had a small box of her own—some CD's, a few t-shirts, a baseball hat, and his glove.

"You sure you don't want this?" She held Pink Floyd's "The Wall" out to Mia.

"It's yours." Mia didn't tell her that it was the soundtrack to most of her nightmares.

Chapter 50

Mia and Jo heaved the rest of the boxes and bags out to the garage. When they returned to Rob's room, Aunt Rosie was observing from the doorway.

"I got tied up. It looks… Clean."

"Sure, show up when all the work's done. I see how you are." Joanne touched her arm and winked.

Rosie shook her head and smiled through cloudy eyes. "I left food on the counter." She eyed Mia's empty glass. "You should eat." She left them to finish up, leaving out the front door without a goodbye.

"All these years later, it's still so fucking hard." Jo closed the door to Rob's room behind them.

Mia sunk into the overstuffed chair in the living room, watching Frenchie jump up and curl into her. She absently stroked his fluffy head. Caren was already sitting with her feet propped up, as she ate a piece of homemade apple pie. They sat in silence for a long while.

Jo slid the wine toward Mia. Her head was still a little foggy from the first glass, but she couldn't get rid of the ache in her chest.

They covered a range of topics, starting with Rosie and Sal's relationship to Rory's sexuality.

"It must suck being back here." Jo offered. "Your father, now your brother… What the fuck is with him anyway?"

"Love your wording." Mia chuckled.

"Yup. She always had a way with words." Caren rolled her eyes.

"You didn't answer my question."

Mia met her gaze.

"Mare, cut the bullshit. What the fuck is up with your stupid brother? Fangool. How'd he really end up in the ICU? The wrong guys, right? You think I'm a shmo?"

"Jo, what is with you?" Caren asked.

"I don't know where to start…" Mia shook her head.

"And you're the shrink…" Jo chuckled. "How many years was your training? Fuckin' fifty or something'?"

"Eight. I've learned that it's a hell of a lot easier to ask the questions then answer them."

"Ain't that the truth." Jo refilled her glass. "Tell us about Jimmy?"

Mia struggled with what to say first. She admitted her frustration with Jimmy's alcoholism, lack of consistency, empty promises and her eventual withdrawal.

"Okay. Now tell us something we don't already know?" Jo pushed.

Mia sat up straighter, felt her mouth go completely dry. In not more than a whisper, she told them about their fight at Bishop Hill, her questions to Rosie about her father's journal and the truth she'd learned about that night. She didn't tell them about Tony's undercover involvement with Costa.

After all their questions had been answered and they'd had time to acclimate, Mia pivoted the conversation.

"Hey, did Aunt Rosie tell you about the ring?"

"What ring?" Caren looked confused.

As Mia exclaimed, Jo's eyes immediately began to fill.

Mia stopped. "I'm sorry. I thought you'd want to know."

"I already know."

"You did?" Caren and Mia asked simultaneously.

Jo nodded.

Mia turned to Caren. "You didn't?"

"No, but it doesn't surprise me. I knew he loved you more than anything, but I didn't know he got you a ring. I can't believe you never told me," she said to Jo.

Jo reached for her cigarettes.

Caren's eyes brimmed with tears. "Rosie'll kill you, smoking in here."

"Don't cry, you fucking idiot. It'll hurt your face. She should've cleaned his room herself then. Fuck her." She got up to fill a glass with water.

They watched as she struggled for composure. She flicked her ashes in the glass, eventually tossing the cigarette inside.

Jo wiped her nose with her hand.

Mia stood and riffled through her bag for a tissue.

"He was so in love with you… It was so fucking sad."

Tears sprung to Mia's eyes and she struggled to stop them. She took a deep breath, counting out slowly.

"He showed it to me the night before he… He planned to give it to you that night. He planned it… but he never got the chance. Me and Rosie both knew."

They sat in silence.

"At the hospital, we asked them to look for it. They found it in his jacket pocket… You were so bad… We didn't have the heart to tell you, or anybody. I'm sorry we— I've felt like shit about it for a long time. It doesn't change anything, just adds more fucking sadness."

Mia touched her arm. "I understand... It's okay." *It wouldn't have helped, nothing could have.*

Caren whispered, "You could've told me."

"I know; you're right. Every time I tried; I just couldn't get it out."

"I dream about him a lot."

"Are they good or bad dreams?" Caren asked.

"Since my father died, they've been bad." *Brutal.*

She didn't tell them she was considering meds again. It'd been over a month since she'd slept right and her nightmares seemed to be getting worse.

"Do you still think about it? ...That night?" Jo asked. "I've wondered if it comes back to you. Still don't know how it happened, it's not something you can ask..."

Caren stared at her sister. "Jo."

Mia was silent for a minute. She took a deep breath and glanced down at her unsteady hands.

"You don't have to talk about it," Caren said.

"I know I don't... Lately, I think about it all the time."

She shared how hard it was being back.

"I see his face a lot. Like that night before... It's still beautiful, with that crooked smirk of his. But then his sneaker appears and all I see is the weird angle of his foot and it's like being back there."

She explained how she knew something was wrong even before she'd left the bathroom. She told them how the trucker had never seen him coming. She left out the details they didn't need to hear. She didn't tell them the smell of his blood, her vomit, and the sugary scent of ice cream filled the air.

"Aunt Rosie dropped the coffee pot and ran to the car when

I told her." She turned to Jo. "Rosie must've thought I was there to share the good news…" Her stomach twisted with sadness.

Jo took a long pull of her wine.

"Should you be drinking like that?" Caren questioned.

"I gave up smoking, not drinking… What am I, a fucking nun?"

They turned their attention back to Mia.

"Sometimes, in my dreams, he gets up, takes my hand in his, and we walk away together."

She didn't tell them how his head had been smashed into the street. Or how her vomit mixed with his blood had created a deep reddish, almost purplish brown color. She saw his blood on her hands for a long time after… Still hates those colors; can't stand to look at raw meat.

She didn't tell them how she still hears a wild animal's scream in her dreams. Or about holding him, half his head missing. The image was still too horrific for words.

"His touch feels so real I forget he's dead… Sometimes it's like I'm actually with him."

She didn't tell them how it felt when she'd wake up to realize he was still dead—how it'd rip at her soul.

Startled by Caren's sobs, Mia stopped.

"Mare, it's so awful you were there. Had to see that."

Mia eyes dripped with tears she hadn't realized were falling. "I'm sorry, you didn't need to hear that."

She'd never shared the details with anyone but had always wanted to talk about it with them. They were like her sisters. She looked at them, reminded that she'd lost them, too, that night. It had been too painful to be with them after he'd died.

"No, we did." Jo's eyes sparkled with tears and gratitude.

Mia drained her wine glass, feeling slightly woozy as she stood.

"I think in your world, that's progress." Maybe seeing them

didn't have to be a bad thing. She excused herself to the bathroom where she washed her face with cold water and blew her nose. As strange as it was, she felt as though a load had been lifted. She was surprised by the lightness she felt, deciding it had to be the wine.

When she returned, they were sitting quietly. *They really know me. All of me. The good, bad and ugliest parts of me.* Gratitude washed through her.

"I'll tell you both a secret," Caren began. "I fell in love with Jay because he made me feel so safe and sure. Like he accepted me, really loved the 'me' underneath what everyone else saw. I don't know when that changed…" Her eyes brimmed with tears. "After dad left… and then Rob, I really needed that feeling. I felt like it was even more special 'cause he and Rob were friends from when we were little. Does that make any sense?"

"Sure it does," Mia comforted.

"He got really bad a few years ago. Started drinking all the time. Not like when we were younger, I mean alcoholic drinking, in the morning even." She whispered, "Right after we had kids… I think he's jealous of them, of me loving them. I can't pay as much attention to him maybe… Isn't that awful?"

"Yes, it's fuckin twisted and awful, but it's not your fault and you don't have to put up with it." Jo took her hand and they stared at each other.

"The other day I thought he was gonna kill me, he got so mad. I thought, what will they do if something happens to me? I don't want them to grow up like us…"

"It's different, though. You have a choice; you can get away from him. Trust me, I know it's hard. When me and Frankie split, I was high twenty-four seven for a while." She looked at Mia. "I tell people that I caught him in bed with our neighbor. All the signs were there… that I was stupid…truth is he caught me in bed with our neighbor, and not Mike in case you're wondering. I've known who I am since I have memory. I didn't want to admit it, It's still really hard. I had my head buried up my ass, I guess, for a long time I tried to pretend." Jo picked at her fingers and bit at her lips. "It made me take a good long look at myself… Wasn't crazy about who was looking back. I'd been hiding myself for… practically my whole life. That's when I stopped smoking. Fuck it, you know, bring it on fully–not feeling wasn't working for me.

"Right after I quit, I started getting this familiar pit right here in my stomach. It reminded me of the same feeling I used to get as a kid whenever I missed my father and then when your mother died, too. You know the feeling like when you're young and your hand lets go of some prized possession, like a carnival balloon or an ice cream cone? Kinda like panic and fear and humiliation all mashed together? It would happen whenever I thought about him just disappearing, puff, right out of the fuckin' blue. I know it's stupid, but I would actually look up at the sky and think, where the fuck did they go? Wonder if he was gone because of me, like I made it happen, because of how I am somehow…"

"It's not stupid at all." Being with Tony felt like she'd found her childhood security blanket stashed away in a drawer. *What eases pain isn't ever logical.*

"After a while, the feeling, that shitty empty pit, and fucking self-hatred I realized is what I had to learn to deal with. And it sucks, but if I do something else—anything, really—to take my mind off things, just as long as I'm not getting stoned, it'll get easier… Right? Please tell me the shitty black feeling will go away."

Pain's not always bad. "I used to see your brother that night over and over when I first got to California. Uncle Joe sent me to a therapist, and they had to put me on medication so I could sleep. But it numbed out my thoughts of him—at least that's what it felt like. After a while, the nightmares stopped and I could sleep again. That night stopped replaying, but I couldn't see his face either. I couldn't stand not seeing him, so I went off the meds. As crazy as it was, I needed to remember him, all of it, even the painful parts. You learn to live with the pain." "And you can learn to accept yourself and stop inflicting pain that you think you deserve, you're a good person, it doesn't matter who your attracted to, that didn't cause anything." Mia was officially shit-faced.

"That's fuckin' great," Jo slurred. "Something to look forward to…you guys should've seen Frankie's face..."

Caren, "fuck him and his big ugly face."

They all cracked up.

Glancing at her watch, Mia stood, amazed she was steady on her feet as her head swam. "I need to go while I can still drive."

She kissed Caren and wished her luck with the kids, watching as she waddled down the hall into the bathroom.

After gathering her things and the small box that contained what was left of Rob's belongings, Jo attached Mr. French to his leash and walked them back to the diner. It was freezing outside so they moved quickly.

"I'm glad to see you, little cousin," Jo said as they embraced. "I know it's hard for you being here… Talking about all that."

As they pulled in front of the house, Jo asked, "Hey, what should I tell Rosie about you and Tom Turkey Day?"

"That I'll be at the hospital with Jimmy."

Jo snorted. "Yeah, right." She exploded into a fit of laughter that confirmed she was as wasted as Mia felt.

"Make something up for me."

"Tell the bodyguard I was asking for him. Friend? Pah." Jo winked and chuckled again before getting out of the car. "I want details about that body. What? I'm bi–wait, new word is pan."

"I love you Jo, don't care which neighbors you're doing." They both cracked up, Jo shut the door with a thump.

Chapter 51

Mia watched her cousin disappear into the house and immediately speed dialed Rory before she lost her nerve.

"Heyy, mmyy long lost friend-d, what's shakin'?"

"Mia? You sound… Weird."

"Naw, bad connection."

"No. You sound drunk. What time is it there?"

"A lil bit." She broke into a fit of giggles that quickly turned into a sob.

"Where are you? You okay? Tell me you're not driving."

"I'm not driving… You in with anybody?"

"No, what happened? Why are you driving like that?"

"I just left the girls. We cleaned out Rob's room. Jo and I drank some wine…"

"You want to pull over to tell me about it? We can call someone to come get you."

"Ca's kids are moving in there with her tomorrow."

"That must've been terrible. I'm so sorry. Why aren't you staying there?"

"Ror, I'm a bad person. I can't stand being near them. Isn't that awful? And now they expect me to be around, like for holidays and all the things we didn't do for all these years. I can't. I..." She started to sob again. "I just can't do it."

"Mee, it's normal, it's okay. Did you pull over?"

"I did," she lied. "Listen, I—I didn't want to do it over the phone but... Ror, it's really bad stuff I need to tell you," she spoke through sobs. "I feel such shame..."

When she didn't continue, "Mee, please. I'm a gay man, I know about shame. You can tell me anything. You know I won't judge you."

She almost missed Tony's exit.

"You there?"

She forced out the words. "Ror, my father was in prison when he died. Had been there for almost twenty-two years."

"Okay, why?"

"For shooting my mother. She was involved with another man. It was supposedly an accident, not meant for her. The jury didn't buy it, he was convicted of premeditated murder."

"Mee, that's awful. I'm so sorry. If I could bear hug you through the phone I would."

"Nope, I'm not done yet. Rosie, my lying sack of an aunt, gave me his journal. His words were confusing, so I asked Rosie about it. Turns out, it wasn't him, Ror. He didn't do it. Maybe you already know this, too. Maybe she already told you." Mia knew she was being mean, unreasonable, but she couldn't stop her words.

Driving up to Tony's condo, she saw him standing at the front door. Her stomach got the strangest sensation looking at him. He waved to her, and she waved back, motioning to her cell.

Her voice was just above a whisper, "It was Jimmy who... Who shot my mother. My father took the blame... for him. Ror, it changes everything." *My entire existence... again.* "Everything could've been different. I fucking hate him for it. Part of me wishes he was dead!"

"Mee, you were blindsided. You have a right to be upset, that's a lot. Are you wherever you were going?"

"I am. I'm sorry to dump all that on you."

"Don't be stupid. I'm here for you always. Should I catch a flight out and put a pillow over Jimmy's head for you?"

"Actually, yes." Mia snorted, blew her nose and set her head back.

Tony stepped back inside to give her privacy.

"I should've told you a long time ago. I just…"

"It's okay. Take a deep breath."

"I love you, Rory. Thank you. I'm going to go try to compose myself. I'll call you later."

"Love you, too. Please sober up and don't drive anywhere, please."

Her tears burned the back of her throat. Her anger dissolved back into sadness as the weight of the day hit.

Tony checked on her through the door. She craved the secure feeling she got when near him. She tossed the crumbled, soggy napkin on the floor and wiped away her tears with the back of her hands. She took deep breaths and then pushed herself out of the car. She couldn't believe she'd finally told Rory.

Chapter 52

Tony watched Mia pull into the lot and scanned the area for any danger. He didn't trust that Costa didn't know about her. He was both thrilled and relieved that she was there but his cop radar buzzed. He tried not to look too eager. He wasn't sure with her ambivalence and his reveal that morning if she'd even show tonight. He didn't want to scare her but there was no way they wouldn't use her against her punk brother. *Or me.*

He swung the front door open and could see she was talking on her cell. He watched a black sedan roll by slowly. The car had tinted windows, and he couldn't make out the plates. He stood alert. When the car passed without stopping, his breath resumed and he went back inside.

About fifteen minutes later, he peeked out to see her just stepping out of the car. No one was around, it was quiet. She seemed unsteady on her feet, and he quickly walked out to greet her.

"I was talking to Ror. I told him about Jimmy."

He could tell she wasn't right, not herself. Her words sounded sluggish at the ends. He brushed her lips, took her suitcase in one hand and her hand in the other.

"You okay?"

She shook her head. "But I will be."

"Hey, I would've picked you up."

"I know. Not my proudest moment."

"I'm just glad you're here now." He pushed his worry aside.

Together they walked up the three steps leading to his front door. In the foyer, he dropped her bag with a thunk and pulled her into him.

"Been waiting to do this all day." *So much for not acting too eager.* He pulled himself away, trying to get a read on her. She looked pale and her eyes were glassy.

"I had to tell him… About my brother, what's going on here. He called my aunt concerned. Don't worry, I didn't say too much about your job."

Her words hit him right in the stomach. *My job…* "It's been a lot."

He moved a curl away from her face and wondered how long she'd been drinking.

"I was afraid you wouldn't show tonight."

She leaned her head against his chest. "Yeah, here I am, though."

"Your cousin's okay?"

"She'll be all right, she has a good family."

He wrapped his arms tightly around her waist. "It helps." He kissed the top of her head. "Still no change with your brother?" He felt like an asshole for asking. He already knew the answer.

She nodded, her posture stiffened. He could tell she didn't want to talk about him.

"Forget all that." He lifted her chin to his.

Her mouth was warm, inviting, sensual… The previous night

had left him craving more. He rubbed her back as excitement surged through him. He forced himself to break away.

"Come on. I made you some eats in case you're hungry."

"That's sweet."

Tony eyed her again, fighting the urge to be with her.

"It's very modern and very clean," she observed as they walked into the kitchen.

"Does that mean you like it or not?"

"Very much so."

On the counter sat a platter of olives with a variety of cheeses, roasted peppers, and dry sausage. Next to the platter was a loaf of Italian bread, a tray with chocolate dipped fruit and a bottle of wine.

"You did all this?"

"I was hoping you'd be hungry. I like to cook."

"And I like to eat."

He saw something cross her features, wondered about her day but didn't get to finish his thought before she wrapped her arms around his waist.

"Tony, this is too much. Thank you, really… For everything."

"Don't thank me. I'm just trying to impress you." He winked and dropped a small piece of sausage for Mr. French. "Him, too."

"You already have… I'm practically drooling."

Me too. He handed her a plate.

"I don't know where to start though. They're all my favorites."

He helped her make a sandwich of cheese, sausage and peppers.

"It's delicious."

He loved to watch her eat. She wasn't self-conscious about it like most broads. He loved to watch her, period. He could feel the corners of his face pull upward in a giant grin and rolled his eyes at himself.

"We've decided to join you this weekend… If the offer still stands. Although, I could care less about my safety."

"'Course the offer still stands. And don't say that."

"I'm half kidding. The White Mountains sound perfect."

He saw the same shadow cross her features then quickly disappear.

"I got a buddy who's got a hunting lodge up there. Nothing fancy, but it's over in Jackson. Me, you, and Frenchie'll fit fine. I promise to make it holiday-ish." He noticed her plate was empty and tried not to smile. "You good?"

"For now, yes. Fat and happy, I think, is how you described it to me once."

He grinned wide. "May I show you to your room, Madame?"

Chapter 53

Tony's condo was nice but not like his gym; his heart wasn't there, Mia could tell. She followed behind him, slightly disappointed when they stopped outside the guest room.

His eyes swept toward hers. "Figured in case you need privacy or space for anything. Didn't want to assume. There's a bathroom there if you need it. I got one, too... Whatever you want." He kissed her lightly then excused himself to firm up their plans.

Mia glanced around the spacious, tidy room. It was pretty but non-descript. She sat on the edge of the bed, thoughts of her day starting to hedge. Her eyes darted to her cell and she thought about checking in with her patients. *Not in this condition.*

She stretched back on the bed and closed her eyes. *Just for a minute.* Despite her buzz, her thoughts hummed. Her father's grave, the truth... *"Some things are hard to say out loud."* Her brain was fried. She pushed herself upright, didn't want to think about it. She went to her suitcase and started rifling through it, not looking for anything in particular.

Her heartbeat raced faster as her fingers touched the metal of the picture frame. She scanned their young faces. *"Mare, I have a surprise."* She placed the picture back underneath her clothes, sensed she was no longer alone.

She turned to see Tony in the doorway watching her.

"Hi." Mia noticed for the first time that his shirt has a small Nike emblem on it. The hair on her arms stood up and she averted her gaze.

His eyes sparkled down at her. *How incredibly handsome he is.* He took up the entire doorway and she was once again struck by his strong physical presence, her attraction to him. She forced her eyes back to his.

"You want to talk about it?"

"Nope."

"Okay. I got good news and bad news. which one—"

"Bad first… Always save the good for last."

"What's that, shrink 101 or somethin'?"

"I guess so, yes." She leaned against the door's frame, arms folded.

"My buddy's place is being used this weekend for hunting. He invited me along; I never told him I might have company."

"I understand. You should go hunt."

"I don't want to hunt. Don't you want the good news?"

"Of course. Yes."

"When I explained I was bringing a special lady guest with me, he offered us another little place. Real small, cottage like, right at the foot of the mountains, right over the line outside of Jackson. No one's using it, his girl's away, warm weather–Caribbean or somewhere–If you're still interested…"

"I'm still interested." Her heartbeat quickened as she held his gaze. "Sounds great. When do we leave?"

He stepped closer to her and wrapped his arms around her

waist. "I can't tell if you're relieved or excited. You need to dodge some haunts?"

"Both. I'm excited to go. Happy about spending Thanksgiving away from here." She felt him hug into her and nod his understanding. His grip tightened and her mind jumped back in time.

For a minute, she found herself sitting with her family at their favorite table at Angelo's, Every table adorned with a small paper turkey in the center. She thought they were the cutest little things but Jimmy kept flicking theirs to make it twirl around. She pretended not to be amused but secretly thought it was hysterical the way the fake chin bobbed up and down. Brother-sister relationships are complicated.

She saw her father beam over his glass of wine at her mother—his lover, his wife. *Groooooosss. Luckyyyy.*

"He said we can pick up the keys whenever we want," Tony spoke. "I was thinking early in the a.m."

Mia forced herself back to the present, hating that her demons might hurt him. "Sounds good."

"Come on, let's sit." He reached for her hand. Frenchie followed them down the hallway.

He led her to the couch and put on a CD.

"A little music, a splash of wine… Or maybe not."

She was still buzzed but felt a little less light-headed after eating. She watched Tony retrieve two glasses from the wet bar and disappear into the kitchen for a bottle and the tray of fruit. He placed the tray before her and she plucked up a strawberry, popping it into her mouth.

"Delicious."

His muscles flexed as he popped the wine's cork. He poured a small amount in each round glass, then sat down close to her, sliding his arm around her shoulder. His scent surrounded her.

"Here's to you and our weekend together."

"And to you. Thank you, you've made my time back here… Easier."

"I did?"

"Yes. You're sweet and funny and…"

"And?" He grinned. "Don't stop there."

You make me feel safe…

He moved closer to her. "And I'm very much in love with you."

She dropped her gaze. "And I just want to say thank you." She exhaled, twirling a piece of her hair.

Their chemistry was undeniable. She felt it loom like a separate entity, and although she wasn't quite ready to name her feelings for him, she couldn't deny their presence. Her pulse throbbed with anticipation and fear.

He raised her chin to his. "You know I'd give anything to make it all better for you." He grazed her lips lightly.

"To our weekend, then… Away from here, detective. Away from gangsters and my stupid brother."

He pulled back from her and picked up a strawberry, inspecting it for a minute.

"Marianna, tell me about today. What happened?"

She was surprised by the question, his sudden shift. Her foot started to bob up and down.

"I can handle it."

She was unsure of what to say. "I went to the hospital, didn't stay that long… Couldn't. Then I met my cousins at the diner. We spent the afternoon cleaning out their brother Rob's room… He died a long time ago. Caren's kids need his room." She fiddled with the rim of the glass. "That's it, my day."

"That must have been difficult."

"Jo and I drank some wine. A lot of wine, actually…"

"Feel like talking about it, Doc?" He raised one brow.

"Not really, no."

She liked the way his hand felt warm around hers. He lifted her hand and started kissing each finger, slowly, softly. He lifted her chin to his and their eyes met. He folded her into his arms and kissed the top of her head. His hands reached behind her neck, tucked under her ponytail. Laying side by side, her hands were on his lower back. Feeling his mouth on hers, everything else dropped away.

It wasn't long before they landed in the middle of the living room floor with a thud. Intertwined in each other, they pulled at each other's clothes, kissing and exploring. He caressed her, it felt so good to be there with him. She moaned his name.

"Want you so bad," he whispered into her hair that had fallen out of its elastic.

Her body glistened with a thin layer of sweat as they moved in unison. Sinatra crooned in the background, somethin' about it being a very good year.

Their eyes locked.

"Mariaaanna…"

Laying side by side, her body was slightly numb. She had just experienced almost indescribable sexual pleasure. He was incredibly attuned to her. Her stomach dipped in fear. *He's in love with me.* She felt hazy but couldn't ignore the look in his eyes. *"No big thing… Just friends."* An image of herself and Rob in his room flashed for the briefest of milliseconds and she closed her eyes.

"Ey, that was incredible."

She opened her eyes as she felt him slowly trail his hands over her body. His eyes studied hers as he touched her, like he was trying to commit her to memory. Her body responded and they moved toward each other like magnetic pieces. She moved down his body, kissing him slowly. He was very much aroused and she caressed him gently. He responded with a suddenness that startled her as he shifted his position and pulled her face to face.

They were passionate. She wiggled underneath him as he shifted his weight. He placed both hands over hers, his body swallowing hers.

"Wanna make me happy back?" he whispered into her ear.

She nodded. Their passion had taken over and his breathing was choppy.

"W..ant you to want mee..ee back. Need you to sa..y it. Te.. ll me."

They were grinding hard, near their grand finale.

She glanced at him and moaned. She was close, he was too. They were lost in lust, the sensation other-wordly. He slid his hands through her hair, resting them just behind her neck. He continued slowly, gently, deeper. Her hands on his lower back pulled him downward.

She whispered in his ear, "Waaant yoouu too."

For about five seconds, he stopped moving. Mia was confused as she scanned his face. He dangled his body above hers, she clung to him, arching upward.

"Say we have a real chance," he whispered back. He began moving again and she moved with him, closing her eyes. Her voice took him there and she finished with his name.

For a few minutes, they were completely together. He held her tight.

Chapter 54

Mia opened her eyes slightly in a squint, bringing the unfamiliar room into focus. Mr. French laid at her feet and Tony sat beside her. She couldn't remember the last time she'd felt this hungover. Her drunk confession to Rory played.

"Hey, gorgeous." Tony's voice was raspy. "Figured you'd be more comfortable in here."

He sounded tired; she wondered if he ever slept. A glow shone from the corner fireplace, softly lighting the walls.

"Sorry, I fell asleep." She yawned and stretched. "I'm dying of thirst."

He grinned. "You must've needed it."

"I don't remember moving in here."

"You didn't. I carried you in after..."

She bit down on her bottom lip.

He handed her a bottled water.

"Tony..." she whispered. Their night had felt incredible but she couldn't remember all the details. "I hope I didn't say... Jo and I drank too—"

"Shh, you didn't say or do nothing wrong."

Mia cringed at the thought of driving in that state. "Okay."

"Okay, ain't exactly the word I'd use to describe… Every time I even think about it, or you, Charlie here wants another go." He touched her chin softly.

"My memory of last night isn't exactly clear," she admitted. She looked away from him as her mind spun.

"Come here. You wanna hear something?"

"I don't know, should I be scared? Is this Charlie involved?"

"Charlie aside, I'm honored you're here with me now and are gonna spend your holiday with me." He leaned over and kissed her. "Don't worry about the rest. Although, I gotta say, last night was something to remember. We'll have to repeat it again when you're sober." He grinned and took her hand in his.

She punched his arm playfully but felt her stomach tighten. It wasn't his words that bothered her but what wasn't being said.

"I'll be right back." She tucked a mass of curls behind each ear.

"I'll be right here waiting."

Anxiety started creeping up her spine as she walked to the bathroom. She counted out her breaths, suddenly unsure that going away for the weekend was the best choice. She knew him only as well as she'd allowed herself to, but her desire for him still made her feel lightheaded.

She sat down to pee, suddenly seeing Rob sitting across from her on the edge of the tub with a familiar smirk.

"You startled me."

"Sorry," he apologized as he touched her cheek. "You aright?"

"What do you mean?"

"You know, with the big guy?"

She scanned his face. "Rob… Nobody could ever take your place or even come close."

"I know that. But you're falling for him."

"No, I—I only like him. I don't know what I feel yet." As soon as she spoke the words, she knew she was lying. She stood and walked over to the sink.

"You don't wanna know. You're scared."

Their eyes met in the mirror.

"He's not you…"

His scent surrounded her as he hugged her into his chest. "Wish I could still be here with you."

"I know." His words tore at her heart.

He turned her around and kissed her. She felt his body tense, could feel his breath on her neck. "Mare, you taste like him…"

She closed her eyes to escape the pain in his voice.

"Ey, maybe you don't know him good enough to go away with… A conflict of interest."

"And my safety." She slowly opened her eyes, unsure he'd still be there.

"Naw, you're safe," he breathed into her hair. "He's the one in danger, not you."

"Stop. Don't." She pulled back. "You told me to do this…"

He silently watched her.

"You made me promise to try…" Her eyes filled with tears.

"I know I did." He looked away. "I didn't mean it though," he admitted just above a whisper.

She touched his face. "I'm going to throw up."

He stood behind her holding back her hair. "I'm sorry, I know I'm being selfish." He handed her a warm face cloth.

She stood slowly in front of the mirror and wiped her face. It was puffy and slightly flushed.

"Mare, the big guy's crazy in love with you…"

"It doesn't matter. I am going home soon."

"You're gonna crush him."

She put her hands over her ears and shut her eyes. "Stop.

You're making it worse. Please, go. I want you gone when I open them. Please… I can't do this anymore."

A minute later she opened them to find that she was alone. She exhaled as another wave of nausea hit.

Tap. Tap.

"Ey, are you all right?"

She flushed the toilet. "No…" She stared at herself for a beat. "Be right out."

Through the door, she heard her cell ring. *It's got to be Ror.*

She popped her head out the door. "Can you answer that for me? It's probably Ror. Just tell him to hold on for a sec, please?"

"Rory, this is Tony. Marianna'll be right with you…"

After a few deep breaths, Mia splashed cool water on her face and rinsed out her mouth. For half a second, her reflection reminded her of everything that'd ever gone wrong in her life. She forced herself into the present, focusing on Tony's conversation with Rory.

"She's in the bathroom, um, not feeling well at the moment. She didn't want to miss your call, though… Yeah, I think she had a hard day. I guess they cleaned out her cousin's room. Must've been tough… Will do man. Ey, she tells me you're going to Mexico… Rory, heard all good things about you, man. Good to finally talk to you. Hope you enjoy your holiday."

Opening the door, she inhaled deep, walked back into the bedroom and crawled into bed.

"You all right?" He asked again.

"No." She nestled up against him. "Got sick."

"Was that Ror?"

"Yeah, just checking to make sure you made it here in one piece."

"I was stupid to drive like that." *I should've trusted him with my truth sooner.*

"Yup." He hugged her to him. "But I'm glad you're here."

Her head still hurt but being near him felt good. Her brain spun another scene from the previous night. Saliva returned to her mouth and her heart no longer raced. *The White Mountains will be fine for a few days. Getting away from here is just what I need.*

She exhaled, feeling Tony's arms tighten around her waist. Her mind flashed, *"Say you want me."* She did, couldn't deny it. *"Say we can have a real chance."* Her stomach twisted with unnamed concerns until she finally drifted into a fitful sleep.

"Hi, mom." Her mother sat next to her as the warmth of the sun radiated down on her.

"Marianna, don't feel too bad. If he makes you feel better... I know all about that."

Mia opened her mouth to respond but no words formed.

She woke with a start and felt big arms tighten around her. She exhaled slowly, wrapped in her giant security blanket.

She started to drift off again, could see herself asleep in Rob's room.

It felt so natural to be with Rob, like it was where she was supposed to be. She inhaled deep, never able to get enough of him. She felt his arms around her tight until she was snug against him. The realization hit her slowly and she awoke for a moment. She was with Tony... Her thoughts spun back toward sleep.

She held onto Rob tight as they rode his bike. She felt herself shiver as they approached Suzy Q's. The air smelled of burning leaves. *We're in the wrong season.* Rob dropped her off out front like he always did.

"We're in the wrong season," she kept repeating before reluctantly getting off his bike.

"We'll meet at the corner," he said before revving off.

Alright, but I'm freezing.

When he glanced back to wink at her, his face wasn't right. She blinked hard as his face slowly morphed into Tony's.

As a scream started to build, she felt someone squeeze into her. The touch was warm and woke her up long enough to pull her out of her crazy unconsciousness.

She sighed into the warmth radiating from Tony's body.

Chapter 55

"Morning, sunshine," Tony sang as Mia tossed in bed.

Mr. French sat by the door amidst a duffel and other bags. Tony was packed and ready to go.

Mia pushed herself up onto one elbow, then got out of bed, wincing.

"You ok?" Tony asked. There was more worry in his voice than he'd intended.

She yawned. "Just need a shower."

He'd watched her battle her demons all night long. At one point, she said some things out loud, even seemed to have the chills. He hoped getting away would do her some good, let her finally rest.

Selfishly, he had plans. He couldn't believe he'd have her all to himself for the entire weekend.

After she had showered, Tony placed her suitcase into the crowded trunk as she plopped a bag in the backseat and slid in next to Frenchie.

"Sorry to keep you waiting."

"No problem. We already got the keys." Tony leaned over to kiss her. "You feel better?"

"I do. I'm starving, though."

"I'm on it."

As they sat eating their breakfast at The Coffee Bean, Tony couldn't have been any more in love with her. He'd take a bullet or kill for her, without blinking. His mind replayed his conversation with the captain.

"Costa knows Jimmy's got a sister and that she came to Rhode Island."

"That makes her a target on a few counts."

"We got him on his prison cell asking questions about her whereabouts, her name…."

"Does he know anything?"

"Costa suspects she was seen with the punk at a bar in Scituate, maybe the night he was put in the hospital—they were heard fighting out back. He knows she's a shrink out in California. He's waiting on confirmation from his people, though."

Tony stiffened. He had suspected as much but the confirmation made it real. If Jimmy lived, she would be a natural way to keep the punk quiet. If he died, she was still guilty by virtue of blood—two counts. His stomach dropped. *Third count is that she's with me now.*

This was on him. Tony wasn't sure how to play it yet. In no time, the captain would know and he needed time to get ahead of it. At least he was getting her out of there for a bit. He wished both Costa and Jimmy dead.

Coffee in hand and belly full, Mia's mood had improved three-fold.

"Now I'm ready to head north," she told him as he closed his door with a thump. She dipped her chocolate biscotti in her coffee.

He watched her sideways, trying hard not to laugh as he sipped his shake. "For a skinny dame, you sure can eat."

"Ror teases me about it, too."

"You didn't call him back yet?"

"No. And I owe him an apology for driving in that condition."

"He cares about you." Tony grabbed her hand off the seat.

"I know he does." Mia stared out the car window and took a long breath and she dialed Rory.

"Hey, Ror, it's me. You have every right to be mad at me, I shouldn't have driven like that, I have no excuses. And I should've told you sooner—well, the part I knew, anyway. Enjoy your holiday. In case you talk to Rosie, I've decided to go up north for the long weekend... With some friends... I'll be back on Sunday night. I haven't told her, I didn't want to hurt their feelings. They wanted me there with them but... I just couldn't."

Tony stiffened, staring straight ahead. *Some friends? She hasn't told them anything about us...*

"Hope to talk soon, Ror." She turned to Tony. "He's just over-protective and not used to me going away with—"

"Strange male friends?"

"Yes. With everything else, it just seemed easier not to tell him about the weekend. Yet. I'm sorry."

He felt slightly better but all the stuff that brought her back to Rhode Island hung between them for a few awkward moments. He felt like a hypocrite with all she still didn't know about him... *I've got some nerve.*

"He'll forgive you." He took her hand in his.

Tony tried not to let her conversation with Rory bother him. They'd be together for the entire weekend.

After an hour of driving, Tony noticed she was quiet and watched her head bob, finally giving in to sleep. With her eyes closed, her face looked peaceful. He pictured her cleaning out *his* stuff, then needing to drink away the sadness. It bothered him bad, though he knew it shouldn't have. It had nothing to do with him.

After the previous night's performance, he'd already promised himself he wasn't going to go all crazy about things like her leaving. She was a professional woman with a life elsewhere. It'd work itself out. His priority was to make everything right and keep her safe until the Costa-and-Jimmy thing was sorted out.

Chapter 56

A gentle rocking motion shook the car and woke Mia.

"Hey, sleepin' beauty. We're here."

She winced. "Sorry, I didn't exactly keep you company."

"No worries, you needed it. Plus, I had Monsieur Puff here." He patted Frenchie's head. The dog wagged up at Tony, looking more than infatuated.

She looked out the window at the most amazing view. Possibly even comparable to Lake Tahoe. She squinted her eyes into the sun, then glanced back at the cabin. It was small, as promised, but set right at the foot of the White Mountains.

"Wow."

Stepping out of the car, she was awestruck by the view. She and Tony seemed small in comparison. The mountains looked majestic, already capped with snow—an inch covered the ground.

"This is amazing." Mia whispered. "It almost resembles home."

"Good, you won't feel homesick."

"Really, it's like a New England version of Tahoe." She pulled her arms tighter around her waist, it was at least twenty degrees cooler in the mountains. "Did I tell you that I work out of Sacramento in the wintertime because it's too cold where I live?"

"No." He chuckled. "Figured you liked the snow and cold."

"Nope. Hate it."

"Come on, before you freeze, then."

The inside of the cabin was adorable. It looked exactly the way you'd expect an old hunting lodge to look—dark and manly, pretty much a one-room design. A kitchen and living room space made up the first floor. Directly in the center of the room sat an overstuffed couch. It was blood-red suede, she decided as she rubbed her hand against the seat cushion.

The fireplace was made of field-stone and adorned with stuffed animal heads. She wondered how the animals staring back at her felt about being used as wall art. She was far from an animal rights nut but stuffed heads were just too much for her. She darted her eyes toward Frenchie, who seemed unconcerned.

On the floor lay an enormous bear-skin rug. It was a little unnerving to think he had once been a local around these parts. She raised her eyes upward to the dark pine walls, then noticed the open-beamed ceiling and loft. The stairs were off to the side near a small mudroom connected to the bathroom. Except for the dead animals, it was perfect.

"Be right back." Tony retrieved their things from the car and carried them up the wooden staircase to the loft.

When he returned, she said, "Look at that."

Out the side window was a glorious view of the mountains. Their attention was pulled away when they heard a strange scratching sound. They turned to see Frenchie sniffing and rolling on the bear rug.

"Too real for me, too, boy. But it matches the place's charm," Mia offered.

"Want me to move the rug while we're here? I don't think I can move the heads, but I can try?"

"No, of course not. Frenchie, stop it right now."

Mr. French sat up with his head high looking away from them.

Tony moved toward the back door. "We'll need a fire to keep us toasty."

She watched him from the window, working in his short-sleeved t-shirt. For a second, she felt like Karen from Frosty the Snowman when he melted so she could be warm. Gratitude washed through her. Her eyes fixed on his flexing muscles and for a moment she replayed their previous night. The hairs on her arms stood up. She was pulled out of her thoughts when he kissed her lightly on her lips. She hadn't heard him re-enter the room.

"Hey, you in there?" he teased.

"I was just enjoying the view."

"Good. Go sit by the fire, get warm. I'll be right there."

From the couch she watched him unpack a cooler and a few bags of groceries.

He glanced over at her and winked.

"Let me help you with those."

"Nope, you're my guest. Plus, I know just how to stay on your good side."

"You do?"

"Damn straight." He grinned. "Remember, I've seen you hungry."

In an orderly fashion, Tony placed the items into the small fridge.

"Come here, I got something to show you."

Mia stepped out back with him to see a hot tub nestled on the far side of the cabin.

"Perfect spot to catch the views." He turned to her and sniffed into her hair.

"This whole spot's too good to be true, isn't it?"

He pulled her into him. "That's how I feel about you."

She felt the warmth of his body radiate through her and she stirred with desire. She stepped back.

"Let's go in. I don't want you freezing yet."

"Yet?"

"Then you'll regret coming here with me… Come on."

She kissed him once quick before they re-entered the kitchen.

Chapter 57

Tony and Mia passed the afternoon talking.

"I have a surprise," he said, getting up from the couch.

Mia watched in amusement as he produced a giant red portable eight track player and a bag of clunky tapes.

"I borrowed them for Carlos."

"I can't believe he still has one of these. And check out the color!"

"This thing's rare, and he's Latino. The loud-color stereotype is true; he'll tell you himself."

"My brother had a yellow one."

Her stomach tensed with nostalgia as she fumbled through the bag of classics. Boston—the old one with the spaceship—the Commodores, Diana Ross and Marvin Gaye, Elton John, Billy Joel's Piano Man, Santana…

"Let's start with something you… know?"

She eyed him curiously, realizing he was referencing her age. "I grew up with all of these, too. Pick whatever and I bet I know it."

He took her face in his hands. "I know but you do realize

this was how we actually listened to music. I'm more than a decade older than you."

"Is that a problem for you?"

He grinned and riffled through the bag, finally pulling out Tom Jones and Marvin Gaye, shaking his head, *Not a problem for me.*

She watched as he prepared what looked like an indoor picnic. He returned with a tray of an oversized sandwich on an entire loaf of Ciabatta bread, a bottle of gourmet pickles and a bag of Cape Cod Salt and Vinegar chips.

"Traditional Italian Sub… I'm on vacation."

She bit into an end piece and tasted salty Italian ham, sharp provolone cheese, tomatoes and spicy mustard. The bread was crunchy.

"Yummy."

They watched the fire while they ate. The crackle and blaze were almost hypnotic. The music of Tom Jones crooned in the background. "What's new, pussy cat… ooh, ooh, ooh?"

She grinned and crunched a chip. "Okay, I might be a little too young for this one."

He smirked. "I'll change it."

"This is great; I'm officially spoiled."

"Good, it's all part of my master plan."

She glanced at his face, wondering why he was single at his age.

Sitting back down, Tony bit into his sandwich. "You got something to ask me, Doc?"

Her foot began pumping up and down. "You don't have to answer if you don't want to. I mean… if it's too personal."

"I got nothing to hide from you."

"I know… How come by now you're not already taken, married? You seem good at this."

"Good at this?" He seemed slightly amused.

"You know what I mean."

He wiped his mouth with a napkin, eyeing her. "I could ask you the same thing, right? You're at least 30?"

"Thirty-two."

Her face turned neutral. She felt she had already met her one, *Rob.*

He rotated the tape after the first side had ended. When he sat back down, his voice was serious.

"You wanna know why I don't have a lady by now?"

"Well, I'm sure you've had lots of ladies."

He lifted one eyebrow.

"Okay, I'm curious, I guess."

"First off, you should know... I practically work all the time, or I used to. It makes for bad company. Not attentive enough, I've been told."

"Huh, you seem very attentive. Bad company? No way, I don't believe it."

He leaned in close. "You want the real truth?"

"I don't know, do I?"

"Haven't found the right person. Until now."

She smirked. Poor Tony, how could she be right for anyone with all her layers of crazy. She heard Rob's voice: *Mare, you're not crazy, just sad.*

"I'm dead serious." Tony's voice pulled her out of her memories. "Since we met; I got the feeling like we're supposed to be... together."

Her foot started bobbing again, she wasn't sure what to say. Marvin Gaye's smooth voice filled the air between them. Again she felt she had already had her chance with destiny, it was Rob, and it was over. Sadness stabbed her heart's center.

"As I mentioned, my parent's marriage was no picnic. I didn't want any repeat performances."

"I can understand that."

There was silence for a few minutes.

"You believe in destiny and all that?" he quietly asked.

Her eyes darted away from his for a moment. "I do, actually."

Her mind flashed to Robbie and the strange sensation returned. Looking at Tony, it was like something within her had shifted. She couldn't explain it. Her feelings were both surprising and unnerving. Her heartbeat hammered away in her chest.

"Be right back." She walked to the bathroom. *It's just a weekend.*

When she returned, Tony said, "M'lady." He handed her a glass and took her free hand.

"Where are we going?"

"It's approaching your favorite hour… The hot tub awaits."

He remembered. "I don't have a bathing suit."

"Me either." He smirked and dropped down to his boxer shorts.

She snorted out a giggle and flashed him a sheepish grin. "When in Rome."

"You mean New Hampshire." He gawked as she undressed and handed her a towel.

"Yeah, yeah." She giggled, following him outside.

One quick stride and he was already settled, waiting for her. He held her wine as she dipped one foot at a time, then her entire body into the steaming, bubbling water. After adjusting herself and glancing around, she decided it felt liberating to be partially naked outdoors. It had been years. She leaned back against the side of the tub.

"It feels great, and the view is unbelievable."

"I was just thinking the same thing. And I gotta feel this… Can't help myself."

She rolled her eyes as he caressed the front of her bra. A shiver passed through her spine. He kissed her lightly.

"Silky, nice." He pulled away. "Look at that." He pointed toward the sky.

It was streaked with the most beautiful colors she'd ever seen. Blues, browns, oranges, and pinks stained the horizon.

"It's stunning." Mia's eyes were wide.

"Unbelievable," he agreed, placing his arm around her shoulders. "To be here with you."

They watched the colors eventually melt away into the earth. It had been too long since she'd felt this peace.

"You ready to go in?"

"I am. I'm pruned." She stepped out and let Tony wrap her in a giant towel.

"Yeah, me, too."

In the darkness her eyes explored his handsome features. She took in his broad shoulders, chest, abdomen… He took her hand and led her inside. Climbing the steps to the loft, his towel fell away and she noticed he was already excited.

She peeled off her wet garments and Tony hung them on a nearby hook.

They practically fell into bed, his arms wrapped around her waist. From their angle, they could still see the fire burning. She felt his body up against hers and her lower belly dipped with desire. She'd missed being this close to someone.

He slid his hand down her flat stomach and her breath caught.

"Hey, tomorrow's Thanksgiving. I thought we'd go into town to eat, celebrate a little. I got a surprise for you. I think you'll enjoy it."

"More surprises? You're good to me."

He kissed into the back of her neck. "Still hoping to get you to fall head over heels for me."

She liked the feel of him next to her. She snuggled into him, excited for the following day.

"I can't remember the last time I didn't dread a holiday." Her eyelids drooped as she drifted off. The nothingness in her mind was refreshing. She felt her body give into it, welcoming the black that followed.

Chapter 58

Mia woke the next morning feeling refreshed; a feeling that had been a stranger to her since her father had died. She looked over and noticed Tony wasn't in bed. Her stomach sank. She scanned the area for Mr. French, but he was missing, too. The two of them being together made her feel better.

She dangled her legs over the edge of the bed. *It's freezing in here.* She grabbed her sweater, then spotted Rob's long johns and stuff on the side of the bed. She pulled his shirt over her head. It smelled like him. She tugged on the pants, rolling up the hems several times while her stomach twitched slightly. She slid the jacket over the make-shift outfit. *That'll do for now. I'll go out tomorrow to buy some warmer things.* As she padded down the stairs, the smell of coffee surrounded her.

"Tony, you are the man."

She helped herself to a steaming mug of coffee, then shuffled over to the fridge to find the milk. She scanned the room for sugar, relieved when she noticed sugar packets in the center of the kitchen table. She added three packets to her cup, stirring absently as she sat down by the window.

The view is amazing. I should call Ror, tell him how great this is. She reached for her cell but after two attempts she realized she had no signal. Despite how cold the cabin felt, a fog rolled up toward the mountains, inches from the ground. The snow glistened like diamonds against the early morning sun. The colors splayed out almost resembled a rainbow.

The sound of footsteps made her turn toward the front door. Mr. Frenchie paraded inside, bolting quickly up the stairs.

"Hey, boy. I'm down here."

His head swiveled as he reversed his direction, arriving by her side in record time. She patted his head as he wagged vigorously.

"Morning. We went for a run, brought you some chow."

"Really? No wonder he's so happy."

Tony plopped down a brown bag that smelled like warm sugar and chocolate. He brushed her lips with his and placed an oversized box that looked professionally wrapped directly next to her.

"A present for the lady… Happy Turkey Day."

"It's Thanksgiving, not Christmas."

"I didn't know." He rolled his eyes. "Just open it already!"

She eyed it hesitantly, afraid to ruin the paper. It was glittery, the kind that sparkled in the daylight. It was a silvery purple with a giant matching bow.

"The paper's beautiful. What's even open at this hour? On a holiday?"

"I had an appointment… And it's almost nine thirty." He clocked her outfit. "I'll start a fire…" He moved toward the stone mantel and started building a pyramid with the small wood. He crunched up some paper and tossed in a match.

"I've haven't slept this late maybe ever."

Tony lifted the package, placing it down in front of her.

Mia's excitement built as she reached for it. She peeled back the fancy paper, then the tissue wrap. She looked on in amazement.

He leaned in to kiss her again.

Slowly, she lifted out a beautiful sapphire colored ski jacket lined with silver white fur. The eskimo-style hood was completely made of fur. She ran her hands up and down.

"It's real?"

"It is. Are you offended?"

"Offended? No, I love it, it's... It's just too much. Tony." She dropped her gaze back to the box. Underneath the jacket was a matching pair of ski pants—the second skin kind—and boots the same stunning color as the fur trim. "Tony, this is way too much."

"Stop it. You won't be cold on my watch."

"Thank you, really." She stood to face him. "I really love it but can't accept this."

"Don't insult me. Go try it on. Please? I wanna see if it fits like I imagined it would."

She couldn't resist his expression. "It's beautiful, thank you. I don't know what to say..."

"Don't say anything, just go try 'em on. I'm dying to see your fine little ass in those."

Moments later, she returned wearing the entire outfit.

"It fits perfect. Just right," he admired as he spun her around for effect.

"You don't think the pants are too—"

"They're perfect." He looked her up and down. "Check the pockets."

Without taking her eyes from his, she peeled a mitten out from each pocket.

"What's this?" Tony pulled a hat out of the center of her hood.

She smiled wide, approaching him. "You, my friend, are just way too much." She placed her arms around his waist and kissed him. "Thank you."

"Friend…" His eyes changed to a darker shade of green and he glanced away.

"I didn't mean it like that… I'm sorry."

He brought his eyes back to hers and wrapped his arms around her lower back, pulling her in close to him. Their lips met and for a few minutes everything else fell away.

"How come you didn't tell Rory about us… This weekend?"

She didn't know how to explain.

He touched her chin softly. "Marianna, I don't want to be your friend."

"I know." Heat rushed to her face. She wanted to tell him that she hadn't been in a real relationship since Rob. That it all felt too complicated for words.

"Hey, stand back, let me check out the colors. They match your eyes and hair just right. I know, Ror is usually your fashion guy. Think he'd approve?"

She paused. "Don't tell him, but I don't think he could've hand picked a better outfit for me… He'd definitely approve." Their eyes met and held before she glanced away. "I want you to know it has nothing to do with you."

He nodded into her and she could feel him exhale.

"Besides, a good looking, straight guy with fashion sense is very rare."

"That's a little wrong."

"I know it is." She sat down, split open the brown bag and started eating. "I'm starving." She took a bite of a croissant. "It's delicious, but…"

"But what?"

"If I keep eating like this, the pants aren't gonna fit me for long."

"I got some plans to put in motion, some people to call. Be right back."

"I'll go shower." She popped the last of her pastry into her mouth. "How should I dress?"

"Warm. Both of you."

Chapter 59

Mia had no idea where they were heading as Tony had insisted on keeping it a surprise. She dressed warm in a black turtleneck and jeans, along with her new jacket and boots. Mr. French wore his red Coach sweater.

Tony suppressed a chuckle every time he glanced toward Frenchie.

"What is so funny?"

"How's he supposed to have any dignity wearing that?"

She rolled her eyes. "I know. It was a Christmas present from Ror… You tell him."

Tony pulled off to the side of the road behind a long row of cars.

"Where are we?" She asked as she got out.

"It's our first stop." He popped open the trunk and pulled out a neatly folded wool blanket, a stainless-steel thermos and a huge poster board.

She grinned; it was the cleanest, most organized trunk she'd ever seen.

The air felt like snow and the smell reminded her of

Thanksgivings past. Holding the leash and the thermos, she walked beside Tony. The thermos was warm in her hands. She was thankful for the new gloves tucked into her pockets. After a few minutes of waiting in line, she realized they were being herded into a high school football game. Tony looked back at her, waiting for a reaction.

"Can't have Thanksgiving without football, right?"

"Right." She nodded in surprise.

"I hope you don't mind. My buddy's girl, her son's playing. He's away… Kid's real dad's a jerk. He asked me to come by, show my support for the kid."

"Of course I don't mind." Even those who aren't big into football have to admit that there's something magical about a Thanksgiving Day football game.

Her eyes were drawn to the packs of teenagers greeting each other self-consciously. Her mind drifted to her patient Caren. *I wonder how she's doing today.* The stands were filled with excited voices, rivaled only by the school's marching band down in front. It was a festive atmosphere and it felt good to be swept up and pulled outside of herself.

Being there gave her nostalgia, the good kind. She remembered back to when she was a kid, way before tragedy struck, when she and all the cousins would go to the Thanksgiving Day game. She glanced up at Tony and caught him watching her. Her lip pulled upward in a grin as he held up a GO CHARGERS sign. Tony had made friends with some local boys sitting near them.

When she looked down at Mr. French, she nearly burst out laughing. He was looking away from the game with his round fluffy head tilted, letting her know he wasn't at all interested. Her attention was drawn back to the game when a giant cheer erupted from the crowd. Tony and his new friends high-fived each other.

When the game ended, they met the boy and his mother. Tony patted the boy on the back, congratulating him on his touchdown.

When Tony and Mia back from the crowd, they shared a knowing look. They both knew how it felt to grow up fatherless. *If it wasn't for Jimmy, I could've had a relationship with my father.* She pushed away her futile thoughts.

"That was fun," she said when they got back into the car. "I haven't been to a football game on Thanksgiving in years."

"Glad you liked it."

"I did, thank you."

He placed his hand on the top of her thigh. "Good. Are you ready to feast?"

"That's a silly question. Are you going to tell me now where we're going?"

"Nope!"

The sign read, "Historic Jackson Village." They pulled up a long winding drive to Nestle Nook Inn and Farm. It was something out of a story book, acres of farmland tucked away in the hills. On one side was a skating pond complete with benches and a fire pit. Next to it sat an enormous gazebo completely decorated with autumn flowers showing off the season's brightest colors. Directly in front of them were huge baskets full of pumpkins of all sizes and acorn squash. It was stunning.

In keeping with the old New England farm style, ski-chalet condominiums had been built into the mountains. The cross-country trails up ahead were peppered with people. From Mia's view in the car, it seemed like they were pieces in a miniature village. Some of the trails crisscrossed at the bottom, leading in and through the woods, while others led down to an embankment. Her mind flashed to the falls. Her visit there had seemed so long ago. For the second time that morning, she felt the stab of something hit her in the gut.

"It's post-card pretty." She made a mental note to send one to Rory. She folded her mixed emotions away. "Absolutely incredible."

"You'll want to take all your gear. Supposed to get even colder later."

Her excitement started to get the best of her. "We're going cross–country skiing?"

"Nope!"

"Ice skating then?"

"Not today, no."

She sighed. "Just tell me something. Anything."

"Nope." He smirked. "He'll be happier in the car." He nodded toward her dog. "The barn will block the wind, keep him warm enough." He grabbed the blanket from the trunk and placed it down near Frenchie. "Just in case."

He grabbed a brown shopping bag with his other hand and their eyes met.

"Nope!"

Mia followed him into the barn. "This must be historic."

"It is." He pointed to a plaque that indicated it had been built in the early 1900's.

"It's in such good shape." She looked around at the old farming equipment and tools hanging on the walls. "It feels like we've stepped back in time."

"They must've recently renovated."

As they traipsed over the hay-covered floor, the smell of farm animals hit Mia hard. They were greeted by an older gentleman wearing snow overalls, the rubber kind that Mia's father used to wear in really bad weather.

She heard his loud voice calling, "Mariiiaaaannnnaaa, Jiiiimm, come ova here a minute. Throw this around while I chip away some'or ice."

Tony touched her arm and she tried to re-focus on the

farmer. His hat covered almost his entire face but his eyes twinkled blue and his smile was wide.

"You must be Mr. Iannucci." He pumped Tony's hand. "Davey told me about you. And this must be your new Mrs. What a nice way for two newlyweds to spend Thanksgiving. It seems the snow'll hold out 'til later."

She eyed Tony questioningly.

He whispered out the side of his mouth, "I had to tell 'em that to get them out on a holiday. You alright?"

"You're shady, Iannucci. Very shady."

"Just amuse me." He winked. "A guy can dream."

She blushed deep and looked away.

A minute later, they stood beside a horse drawn carriage.

Her eyes widened. "A carriage ride?"

"It's our ride to dinner."

"Okay, I'm completely surprised. A carriage ride never entered my mind. Hey, big guys," she said to the horses. "You're right, Mr. French wouldn't like this one bit."

The horses were attached to an open-air style carriage. Tony lifted her up in one sweep and then climbed in himself. The bench seat was velvet of a rich, ruby tone, trimmed in ornate gold.

It was snug, room enough for two. Harp music played.

"I feel like an underdressed Cinderella." Under her breath, "I hope it comes with a fairy Godmother."

Tony popped open a bottle of Champagne.

"I thought you didn't like Champagne," she whispered.

"It's our honeymoon."

"Oh, right. I forgot."

He pulled out a Tupperware container with sliced cheese, crackers and grapes and winked. "How's it feel to be married to me?"

She rolled her eyes. "What's with the food?"

"I've seen you drink on an empty stomach." He raised one brow, his dimple popping when he smiled broad.

"It's so romantic. I feel like we're characters in a book."

His face turned serious. "Only if I get to write the ending…" He reached over and kissed her softly, tucking a curl under her hat.

She bit down on the inside of her lip.

"Where'd you go back there?"

"Nowhere. Was just taking it all in. I've never done this before, have you?"

"No."

The only sound was the horses' click-clacking feet on the pavement. It was old New England charm at its best. The feeling settled in her chest told her for certain what Jimmy and Rob already knew. Her stomach dipped with fear.

The light clink of their glasses together made her ears ring.

Chapter 60

A short time later, the carriage slowed, pulling off to the side of the road. Mia noticed a small inn, the Scottish something or other. It looked like a cross between an old family estate and a farm. The outside was reddish with oversized windows lit with small white candles. Out in the pasture were horses, sheep and cows. The driver dropped them off near the front door of the Inn. A carriage house was tucked down low, right into the landscape.

"Amazing! There's a restaurant down there? How'd you find out about this place?" She turned to Tony.

If possible, he looked even more handsome than usual. His thin, heather gray sweater highlighted his eyes and light complexion. Even under the loose-fitting style, his athletic build was obvious. He wore faded jeans, work boots and the hint of a five o'clock shadow flecked with specks of gray.

"Can't give up my sources." He smirked.

"Well, I'm impressed. You really did your homework, detective. Went through a lot of trouble?"

"Trouble?" He lifted her chin. "I love planning stuff for you." He kissed her for a long moment.

Moaning softly, he stepped back, never taking his eyes off of hers. He brushed his hand through his hair and shook his head.

"Be right back."

Mia watched Tony's broad shoulders from behind. From someplace deep, she wondered if she'd miss being physically close to him.

As Tony tipped the driver, Mia reminded herself that Monday she was going back home. "Come on."

She followed Tony down a winding staircase that wrapped around eight or nine times.

Wow. The climb down had been well worth it. Mia took in an oversized dining room with eight round tables elaborately done up for the season. They were draped in soft copper toned linens with fancy gold colored place settings. The centerpieces were gilded cornucopia-style baskets with brilliantly colored dahlias and softly lit tapers.

The floor was dark cherry hardwood and each table had its own oriental rug. The room was softly lit by an ornate sparkling chandelier. The chandelier and the walls were trimmed with the same polished wood as the floors. The back wall had oversized, French-stye doors that led onto a sprawling deck.

Located directly in the center was a flag-stone fireplace that reached from floor to ceiling, its raised hearth a black and cranberry granite speckled with gold. Above the mantel hung a historic picture of Jackson Village surrounded by several pictures of local covered bridges.

Tony gave their reservation to the maitre d' and seconds later wait staff appeared, eager to take her coat. They were quickly escorted to a table toward the back left of the room with a spectacular view.

"And I thought Tahoe was something special," she whispered to Tony.

"I'd love to see it with you sometime." Their eyes held for a quick minute. His flashed all the uncertainty they chose to ignore. He grabbed her hand and squeezed and her body relaxed. "Listen to that."

The doors leading out to the deck were open just enough to hear water. It was as if mother-nature and the builders had co-conspired. The waterfall was tucked in between rocks and ledges in the woods. The soft yet elegant ambiance of the room coupled with the rugged New Hampshire scenery was simply breathtaking.

As they approached the table, Mia counted eight other couples already seated.

Tony slid out the chair. "For the lady." He winked.

On his left were two older couples who'd been coming together for years. Mia smiled warmly toward the silver-haired lady who held Tony's arm admiringly.

"It's more fun than sitting with a bunch of old people." She laughed.

Tony nodded his agreement and attentively listened to the foursome.

Mia smirked, noticing two middle-aged men to her right. They were dressed in designer, ironed jeans with matching cowboy boots. They looked impeccable. She suspected by their coordinated looks and good-natured bickering that they were a couple. The one closest to her welcomed her and engaged her in their discussion about the décor. Mia bit down on her lower lip as they continued to bicker, trying hard not to laugh.

The Matre'd cleared his throat. "All the guests have arrived. They'll be starting the holiday festivities pronto."

Her new friend whispered, "How very punctual of them."

A parade of waiters began circling the table.

Mia whispered to Tony, "They must've been waiting for us?"

"And here we are, right on time." He glanced at his watch.

Her new friends eyed Tony, then each other, smiling approvingly. She introduced him to her new friends, Randy and Tony. Randy's Tony blushed deep and Tony and Mia smiled at each other.

Mia whispered to Tony, "I think you just blushed."

"I don't blush," he retorted, kissing her nose.

He introduced her to the silver headed foursome. They were a fun group full of stories. Mia relaxed amongst the chatter, sipping her wine. The sun glistened off of the water at just the right angle.

Tony noticed it was *her* hour. "Ey, come on. Bring your wine."

They stepped out onto the deck and she inhaled the fresh air deep into her lungs. The scenery and the hour had drawn others outside, too. Despite its spacious design, the deck was crowded with patrons.

"This is fantastic."

Tony pulled her close to him.

She warmed to the heat of his body against hers. They stood for a long while, not saying anything. The last shred of daylight crossed the sky, a three-tiered painting of reds and grayish-blues winked briefly before turning to the all familiar night sky.

Mia felt Tony shift and darted her eyes to his. He smiled, his green eyes crinkling slightly at the edges.

"A toast… Here's to you and a perfect weekend." He touched his medal and something flickered across his face.

"Thank you for all this. I know you'll downplay it, but I'm impressed with your planning. It really means a lot."

He took her hand in his. "You're worth it."

The look he wore made her heart hurt. She knew a permanent relationship with him was out of the question. She swallowed her guilt, didn't want to hurt him.

Once they returned to their seats, a deacon cleared his throat and said a blessing. Mia turned her attention toward him but her mind drifted to Jimmy. He used to make faces when her father said the blessing on Holidays. His bruised face circled in her mind. *Forgiveness…*

"Amen," the crowd chanted in unison.

The waiters warned with smiling faces that they were in for a charming New Hampshire dining experience. They began by shaking out the linen napkins of each patron.

As if on cue, another tier of waiters appeared carrying large silver trays with delicious smelling holiday foods. The soup was brought out first, a rich creamy pumpkin bisque that smelled incredible.

Tony smiled wide at her expression. "I love that you get excited about food. Never seen a lady eat like her," he told his seatmates.

Mia felt the lady's eyes on her as she smiled self-consciously, staring down at her bowl.

After the soup was cleared away, individual turkeys were rolled out to each table, hand carved by a chef dressed completely in white. The sides were gourmet and fantastic looking, placed in the center of the table.

"This is unbelievable."

His smile grew with her approval. "I 'm glad you're happy. Was sort of hoping to impress you." He leaned in close and whispered in her ear, "So later…" He raised his brows.

"Well… It worked."

Completely full, Mia glanced around the table.

"You analyzing the guests, Doctor?"

"Nope. Just curious."

There was a couple who they hadn't interacted with that seemed different than the others—something pretentious about them.

Mia whispered, "You think his name's Biff or Spencer?"

"Yeah, the third." He chuckled.

Mia excused herself to the ladies' room but when she returned, the pretentious lady was sitting in her chair, flirtatiously chatting with Tony. Mia froze, she couldn't remember the last time she'd felt like this. Mia met Tony's gaze, and he smiled warmly.

He stood and kissed her.

"Hi, I'm Mia." She extended her hand to the woman.

When the woman remained silent, Tony said, "This is Monica."

"Glad to meet you."

The woman mumbled a hello and quickly scampered back to her seat.

"Come on, gorgeous. Let's get dessert."

She felt relaxed again and very silly. *What am I, fifteen? He can talk to anyone he pleases.*

They shared a piece of cheesecake. Mia sipped on an apricot brandy while Tony sipped a beer.

After they were finished, Tony retrieved their coats. "Our chariot awaits."

Chapter 61

She's beautiful, he thought as he took in Mia's profile illuminated by the moon. The *clickity-clack* of the horses' hooves broke through his thoughts.

"Let's go home," he said as they settled into the carriage.

"I really enjoyed myself today." She leaned against him. "This feels like something out of a romance novel. And dinner was unbelievable, too. It was a great day, thank you." She reached up to kiss him.

Back in the car once again, Tony smiled as the furball settled on his lap to look out the window.

"Hey, boy."

Looking around in the darkness, Tony wondered what kind of calls came in. It was probably all the same bullshit.

Glancing over, he noticed that Marianna had fallen asleep, her head propped up against the window. Mr. French trotted beside him as he carried Marianna inside. He carefully placed her on the couch and draped a blanket over her.

Stepping back, he decided to light a fire to take the chill out. After the fire was lit, he grabbed a six pack and sat next to her on the couch. He popped open a can and watched her chest rise and fall. Frenchie jumped up and snuggled between them. With his free hand, Tony patted Frenchie's head and rewound the day.

He wished they could've stayed there, playing house indefinitely. His stomach muscles tightened with uncertainty. He thought about waking her but didn't have the heart. An hour and almost a six-pack later, he was half-cocked and horny as hell.

Mia slowly opened her eyes. "All that delicious food I ate… Too much." She stretched and sat up to face him. "Sorry, I feel like a bad guest."

"Don't be silly." He slid closer. "Here's what I care about." He inched closer to her and took her head in his hands. He began kissing her slowly, wrapping his hands behind her neck. Within minutes, they became intertwined in each other.

"I think today was the best Thanksgiving I've ever spent," she whispered.

"It's just starting… You wanted a sober replay of the other night, right?"

She nodded.

His warm mouth covered hers and he lifted her to her feet.

They fell onto the bed. "I've been waiting all day for this."

"I told Randy and Tony you're definitely straight."

"They questioned it? Me?"

"Yup."

He tried to feign upset but her lips on his body felt incredible. His hands twirled in her hair as he listened to her breathing.

He moaned deep. "I love you so much."

She squeezed his hands.

He imagined that she'd whispered the same to him. He was almost there.

"You're beautiful."

She moaned his name and his body took over, shaking with pleasure.

"That was unbelievable," his voice was thick as he reached for her.

He pulled her on top of him and she moaned his name. He continued kissing her, neither of them able to get enough. He trailed his tongue around each ear and down toward her neck, watching her body tremble. They flipped positions and he continued trailing kisses downward. His mission was to drive her wild. She massaged his back, moving her hands down near his buttocks, pulling him downward. They moved together, her voice saying his name drove him wild.

His mind flashed to her ghost. *He knew what she liked, too.* He pushed the thoughts away. *What is wrong with me?* He felt their bodies dancing with fire. She fell into him, their bodies dampened by sweat. There were no words for the pleasure he'd felt.

He could feel her breath, her heart, *thump-thump, thump*. Then slowing, *thump…thump…thump*. He loved this lady.

"You're right, that was better than okay."

"Told you." He paused. "Today one of my thoughts was how great we are together."

"We are." She traced her finger over his charm and rolled onto her side.

He pulled her in close. "Tell me what's in your heart right now."

She looked away. "I always feel incredibly safe near you… I like the feeling."

His grip tightened around her waist. He had so much more to say but couldn't keep his eyes open. *Damn beer.* That's why he tried not to drink a lot, it fucked with his edge. He smiled to himself. *She feels safe with me. Who is gonna keep guard if she has bad dreams tonight?*

He tried to fight it but couldn't. His eyes grew heavy, his thoughts started to swirl.

Her words came again, "Best Thanksgiving."

"I love you."

Silence.

"How was it with him? Being with him?"

"Tony... What are you talking about?"

He loved the way she said his name, especially when they were together... He reached over and touched her wild hair. *Fuck am I doing?* He rolled over on his side so they were face to face.

"Tell me about you and him. I want details."

Her body stiffened, and her face lost color. She suddenly looked smaller.

He rubbed his hands through his hair. *What am I doin'? I'm too buzzed for this convo right now...*

"Tony, don't do this. Not now." She looked away.

He grabbed her chin, harder than intended. She wouldn't look at him. Their faces were inches apart, he couldn't stop squeezing.

"I gotta hear about him and you." He imagined her touching him, riding him. She loved being with him. *She loves him, not me.* Jealousy ate at his insides. "How come you can't say you love me? Is it because of him?" He shut his eyes, trying to lose the images of them.

"You're hurting me." Her voice sounded far away, muffled.

His father's face flashed and he thought he might throw up. "I gotta know. Is it as good as fuckin him? Do my moves compare?" As soon as the words were out, he regretted saying them.

He moved to hug her, apologize, but she slapped him hard across the face.

"I have to go. Shouldn't have come here with you to begin with. Knew this would happen."

Her words echoed. *"Shouldn't have come here with you. Should've known this would happen."*

"Don't deny it! You're holding back with me because of him! Not being honest with either one of us. You're not over your dead boyfriend."

"Let go of me, right now!" She pulled away, afraid.

He had her by the arms, pinned against him. She was still naked, looking sexy as hell. He began spinning out of control.

Despite her wishes he held her tighter.

"I won't… I can't. I didn't mean to say it like that. I'd never hurt you. I didn't mean it. I love you; you know it." He wrapped his arms around her.

"Why are you acting like this then?"

"I can't stand to think of you still wanting him more. I want you to love me like that. To not hide things from me."

She went limp. "Let go of me." Her voice was so even it scared him.

He knew if he let go, she'd evaporate into thin air. He held tighter.

"Pretend I'm him…"

"Get off."

He started kissing her, moving his body slightly up and down.

"Stop," she spat. "I'll never love you like that. You're nothing like him… Let go of me!"

Her words felt like a physical blow. "Don't say that. You don't mean it, I know you don't."

"Let. Go."

"I can't. I don't know how…" His voice was pathetic.

What am I doing? Get off of her, what the fuck? He didn't move.

"Do you think about him when you're… with me? Wish it was him instead?"

"Why are you doing this?" Her eyes brimmed with tears.

He kissed them, tasting the salt. "I just need to know the truth."

He felt desperate. He needed her to look at him.

I can't take it.

"I'm sorry." He kissed her. "Sorry." He planted kisses softly all over her face. "Didn't mean to hurt you or say those things. I'm just jealous."

Her body responded to his and relief washed through him. She looked up at him like all the times before and she moved with him. Her chin had started to swell, turn purple. He looked away with deep shame.

"Tony, it feels gooood."

"Good, baby. I'm glad you feel good."

"You want me to tell you the truth?"

He was almost there, she was too, he guessed by her breathing. They locked eyes, her baby blues staring at him through the darkness.

"I am always going to wish you were him. I'll never trust you."

Tony bolted upright in bed, reaching for his heart. He expected to find a hole. His heart beat a mile a minute, and he'd broken out in a cold sweat.

He saw Mr. French curled up tight on the corner of the bed.

"Whoooo," he exhaled. *A dream. Oh, a dream. A fuckin' dream, thank you God.* He touched his St. Christopher medal and squeezed his eyes shut.

He was tempted to wake her up, needed to touch her. She was turned away from him and he brushed her back softly. She snuggled into him. *I'm nothing like my father.* He couldn't imagine being without her, or the hurt he was going to cause when she learned about his involvement with her brother. He kissed her cheek, inhaling her scent, and stared at the ceiling, waiting for morning.

Chapter 62

"Hey."

Mia glanced at Tony as he pushed a mass of curls away from her face.

"You're up early." He gently reached over and kissed her. "Morning, sunshine."

Her stomach protested with a growl.

"It must be feeding time?"

"I know, sorry. I'll get up and come out with you."

"No way, you're still my guest. Stay in bed."

Her stomach flipped watching him get out of bed. She needed to be honest with him, he deserved it.

"Tony, wait." She pulled him to her, peering into his eyes. "I just want to say thanks and that I… Just want to tell you I'm having a great weekend."

"I wish it could last forever." He shot her a crooked grin. "Come on, boy."

Frenchie leaped off the bed like there was a fire.

"Hey, you little traitor."

She pushed her anxiety away and rolled onto his side of the bed. She woke to a soggy cheek.

"What the…" Frenchie was licking her face. "Stop. You'll drown me."

Tony chuckled.

"You find that amusing, do you?"

"Gut bustin', actually." He placed a cup of coffee and a bag beside her on the nightstand.

"Thanks. I actually fell back asleep."

"That's shocking," he teased. "I'm gonna start calling you Rip for short."

"I know. I haven't slept this soundly without…" She regretted her words instantly. "This smells great."

He sat on the edge of the bed. "Chocolate swirl. Without what?"

"I don't want to spoil the weekend. It's been so great."

"You're not gonna spoil nothing."

She looked at him tentatively. "Without nightmares."

"Yeah, I noticed… Have you always had 'em?"

"On and off for years."

"That's awful. What are they about?"

Death.

It was a simple question but she didn't know how to answer. Her brain scanned through the list: *my mother, Rob, my father, and now Jimmy—he's not even dead yet… Yet.* She pushed away the thoughts and reached for her coffee.

"I have nightmares about how they…" *Left me.* "Died." She bit into the scone.

"I'm sure your brother's situation hasn't helped either."

"No."

He sat, listening.

"I still have a hard time talking about them. What happened

to my mother, no matter the circumstances, was…" She eyed him. "My cousin, too."

"I know you were together—not really related—it's alright. It must've been terrible for you to watch that." He touched her cheek. "Sorry you had to go through all that."

She nodded, done with the subject.

He excused himself to the bathroom.

His kindness and genuine compassion struck an emotional cord, one she wasn't equipped to deal with. She shouldn't have been surprised that he knew about Rob, but she was. She sipped her coffee and continued eating her scone, trying to re-group.

"Today is lady's choice. We'll do whatever your heart desires."

Her eyes focused on his, her lip turning slowly upward as her left leg moved up and down. She was grateful for a change of topic. *He's perceptive, sweet.*

"First, I have something to show you. Come with me."

They gazed out the window. The ground was covered in a fresh blanket of snow.

Mia sipped her coffee. "It's beautiful."

"I thought you hated snow?"

"Yes, but it's still pretty."

He wrapped his arms around her from behind. "Listen. It makes everything so quiet, like an extra layer of insulation or a giant blanket."

She turned to look up at his face, and could see the view reflected in his eyes. They were pale green.

"Do you know your eyes change color?" she asked.

"My mother used to tell me that when I was little… Well, you know how a cat has nine lives?"

Mia nodded, thinking of Jimmy.

"She said I had nine eye colors to match my moods. Silly, huh?"

"No, I think she was right. They're sort of like a mood ring."

She smiled and pecked him on the cheek. "What does this color mean?"

"I bet you can guess. The snow is supposed to end by noon… What will it be?"

Vulnerability crossed his features but was gone just as quick. She could have sworn the color changed again.

"You said it was lady's choice?"

"I did."

"I haven't ice skated in years. How about that? Can we?"

He rubbed his hands through his hair and the stubble of his beard.

"We can do something else if you'd rather not… It's okay."

"No, no… I never learned to ice skate."

"Really? You? You're so athletic. I'm shocked."

He hesitated. "I never got the chance when I was a kid. By the time I was interested, I was too old and embarrassed to learn. But I'll give it a whirl."

Sometime around noon the snow tapered off, finally stopping altogether. She was excited to skate, but in the back of her mind she knew in a few days she'd be back in Rhode Island. The thought of seeing her brother made her sick. She tried to push her thoughts away and spotted Rob's clothes in the closet. For the first time in days his face appeared.

His eyes were sad. Her heart tugged with a guilt she felt she deserved. She let his image linger before dragging herself downstairs to take a hot shower. She hoped the heat from the water would burn away her memories, numb her feelings.

Her past was too complicated for a future with Tony… Or anybody. Secretly, she'd known this her entire adult life. She'd accepted it as the price of loss. She'd traded that piece of herself for work long ago. It was easier.

Tony came in from shoveling and walked upstairs. Moments later, he passed her on the couch wearing only a towel. He winked. Leaving the bathroom door open, he turned on the shower. Her mind replayed the scene from his condo the night before their trip. At least what she remembered of it. Her mind had been hazy from drinking but something he'd said came back to her. *He wants us to be permanent, said he needed that.* She couldn't remember how she'd responded.

He came out of the bathroom and smiled, wearing black puma sweats and a white mock-turtleneck. He'd shaved his stubble into a mini goatee. Her stomach did a flip. *He looks handsome.* He tied up his boots and put on a black vest. She averted her eyes from the Nike symbol.

"What?" he asked, concerned.

"Nothing. Just checking you out."

His smile returned in full force and wiped out her heart's ambivalence.

Tony bowed as he held the door for her. "M'lady."

It was bitter cold but bright. The sun had made its appearance, making the snow-covered landscape sparkle like glitter.

"Thank you for taking me skating." Her excitement built as they pulled up to the pond. "Once, I talked my mother into letting me skip school and we went ice skating. My father was away driving. She couldn't skate, either... But we had a lotta laughs. She talked a worker into letting us use chairs until we got our legs. With her looks, it didn't take much convincing." It was her favorite memory of her mom, but even the good memories came at a cost.

"How old were you when she died?"

"I was eleven."

"It must've been terrible for you."

"My entire life was altered that day, nothing was ever the same... For a long time, I wanted to be with her in heaven—wherever that was." She slid on her sunglasses.

He took her hand in his. "I love it when you let me in."

She inhaled the cool air deep into her lungs and followed him into the giant barn.

The farmer greeted them, "Hey, how are the newlyweds?"

She blushed deep, feeling like an imposter.

"Great! Thanks." Tony beamed and squeezed her hand. "Today the Mrs. and me are gonna try ice skating. It's my first time, it oughta be interesting."

They walked back outside with their skates to a wooden bench by the fire pit. Without a word, Tony knelt in front of her, lacing up each of her skates. She felt a pang of gratitude and guilt.

"You're good to me."

"You say it like it's a bad thing." He lifted his face to hers.

"No, it's not bad." She felt undeserving.

"You know what I dream about?"

She shook her head.

"Someday coming back here with you as my real bride." He stood.

She felt emotionally unequipped to be doing whatever it was they were doing. She was more than grateful when he didn't wait for a response.

"Come on, my little lady. Let's do this."

Moments later, they stood on the pond's silky surface.

"You alright? We don't have to do this."

She giggled. "You're the one who can't skate. I'll be fine, just a little rusty."

Mia glided away from Tony who seemed even more imposing on skates. The feeling of gliding on ice was exhilarating. In no time, she was twirling around like she was ten again. The sun and wind felt a part of her. She looked at the tree line and the mountains above.

She tried to impress Tony with an elaborate twirl. Next thing she knew, she'd landed on her ass, sliding toward a group of children like a bowling ball. Tony lifted her up, brushing the snow from her ski pants.

"Ow." She rubbed her rear end. "That hurt."

"Come here, I'll rub it for you." He smirked.

"I guess I got a little too comfortable."

"As long as you're havin' fun. That's all that matters."

She watched as he tried not to laugh. His facial features had become so familiar to her.

They spent the afternoon intermittently skating and warming by the fire. Tony turned out to be a natural. Mia wasn't surprised.

Chapter 63

They stopped at the White Horse for dinner, drinks and a round of darts before returning to the cabin for a soak in the hot tub.

Once back inside, Tony added a log to the fire and they headed upstairs. He lit candles on the side tables and set up the ancient eight track player, playing a duet by Diana Ross and Marvin Gaye.

"I didn't peg you as a romantic…"

"I'm not, really. It's all because of you." He pulled her near.

"I think you like sappy love songs."

He pulled off his shirt and lifted hers up over her head.

"It's only half true." He grazed her lips.

"Half?"

"I'm still trying to get you to fall hopelessly in love with me, but you're not easy, doc. Tonight, I'm pulling out all the stops. That's the full truth."

"T, you don't have to try so hard."

He eyed her curiously, unsure if he's heard her right.

Their eyes met before she glanced away.

"Don't be afraid. Everything's gonna be fine."

She kissed his neck.

Why does she look so sad? His thoughts faded as his body took over. He wrapped his arms around her waist, and they fell onto the bed while the classic sounds of Diana and Marvin serenaded them.

Long after Marianna had fallen asleep, Tony lay wide-eyed. She hadn't had any nightmares. *Yet. Not on my watch.* Looking at her sleeping next to him, he'd never felt happier or more content in his whole life.

She loves me back.

Chapter 64

Tony drifted somewhere between wake and sleep. He called it resting, he didn't know any other way. Between his years as an undercover cop and his alcoholic father, his guard was never completely down.

He pushed himself up on one elbow, careful not to wake her. The moment his feet hit the floor he heard a loud *thud, thud, thud* on the door. Mr. French let out a low growl. Tony's adrenaline pumped. *Who the hell is out there at this hour?* He grabbed his sweats from the floor and slid his Glock off the nightstand. He was down the stairs in record time, his French sidekick at his heels.

He went out the back door, slowly creeping around to the front. Standing at the front door were two New Hampshire State Troopers.

"Gentlemen, how can I help you?"

They turned to face him, eyes stopping at his gun.

"I'm Detective Tony Iannucci. My ID's inside, didn't really have time."

"We know. We're here as a favor to your Captain."

"My Captain." He tucked the gun into the back of his waistband, never taking his eyes off them.

One of them passed him a hand-written message. URGENT, GET HERE ASAP. CAPALDI AWAKE.

"Awake?" *Fuuuuck.* After almost a month.

"Never seems like we get to deliver good news. Sorry."

Tony extended his hand. "Naw, thanks guys for taking the time. I appreciate it."

Tony stood alone in the darkness, note in hand.

Jimmy knew Costa ordered the beating, saw them pop Williams. He thinks he's dead, they all do. Maybe we can use that… When Costa finds out he's awake… Maybe I let him… What would that do to her? To lose another family member might destroy her. We can try to make a deal with Capaldi, details of that night for something he needs… My silence that he killed his own mother and attempted to kill Costa's brother.

He exhaled sharply, trying to get a grip. Reality was that the kid was a loose cannon with an attitude and a severe substance abuse problem. Maybe he didn't remember that night. *Please God.* Tony knew one thing for certain, Jimmy wasn't going to want to help them. But did Tony really have it in him to use the information she'd offered him against her brother? If it kept her safe, made things right. She didn't have to know it'd come from him…

The pit in his gut grew. He knew the best thing for her was to go back home. To be far away from her brother, Costa, and him.

Tony sprinted back up the stairs, cursing silently when he realized she was awake.

"What happened?"

The color had drained from her cheeks.

"Tony?"

"Honey, it's your brother…"

Her eyes widened, brimming with tears.

"No… He's awake."

"Really?"

Seeing her relief, Tony sat on the bed and hugged her into him before quickly explaining the message.

"I hate that I care."

"Hey, no matter what, he's still your brother."

She was silent for a minute. "Why are they telling you this in the middle of the night while you're on vaca… What does this mean for you, detective?"

"That I love you and would never let anything happen to you." *And, yes, I also reentered a case to do just that. And I don't regret it.* "When Costa finds out your brother's awake, Jimmy's gonna need our protection."

The line in her forehead creased. "Tony, do they know about us?"

"Not fully, no. Don't worry about that." He touched her face. "That's on me. With regard to the case, we don't actually know each other. The night at Bishop Hill, I was working. That's what they know."

She stared at him.

"Listen, let's not worry about all that now. Please, don't take this the wrong way, but I never expected him to come out of it… I'm glad for your sake, now you get to speak your piece."

She shook her head. "It might've been easier, though."

"I know that's emotion talking. It's a good thing he woke up," he lied.

"Why help him?"

Million-dollar question. Tony took a deep breath, didn't want her involved any more than she already was.

"Unconscious, he's no threat. Alert and talking, he's the biggest threat they got. It's partly selfish… He saw something that could actually help keep them away longer than we hoped."

She stood. "What does awake even mean?"

He took in the oversized t-shirt she'd worn to bed—his. His eyes were immediately drawn to her exposed shoulder. He forced his eyes back to hers.

"I don't know yet."

She slipped on her jeans and he pulled her close to him, craving her. He inhaled her scent and kissed the top of her head.

"We need to go."

Their eyes met. They both knew they'd be stepping outside the cabin as different people than when they arrived.

Chapter 65

Mia allowed herself a final glance as Tony edged out of the gravel drive. Being there had been like a retreat.

They drove through the sleepy town and out to the turnpike without saying a word. Tony turned onto the highway at a speed only a cop could get away with. Mia watched the strobe effect of the light attached to the dash.

With each passing mile, her thoughts pulsed, spinning in a manic mix of confusion and anger toward her brother. She counted the lights on the highway, trying to calm her anxiety.

"Ey, Cap. Iannucci here. I got your message and I'll be there in about two and half… I don't know her locale yet, probably away for the holiday… I know."

She watched his face darken.

"I'm on it… I'll find out. Is the kid mentally there? …Think he'll cooperate? … I'm on my way."

Mia glanced at him as the call ended.

"Doctor's say there's no permanent damage."

She nodded.

"They're concerned you haven't been to the hospital yet.

Wanna make sure you're safe, know how long you're staying in Rhode Island."

"Tony, isn't being with me going to get you in trouble?"

He shot her a quick sideways look and reached for her hand. "You don't need to worry about that, or us. You got enough going on."

At the mention of *us*, Mia's stomach did a free fall. She exhaled. "I don't know what to say to him, know if I even want to talk to him at all... I still can't believe he was... Responsible."

"I'm so sorry. Maybe you should try to rest. We got at least two hours before we get back. It's gonna be a long night for you."

She nodded, feeling the warmth of his hand, the illusion of security. Mia found comfort in the steady motion of the car. Her eyelids grew heavy and she started to drift off.

At first, everything was pitch dark and ice cold. She was walking through the woods at night but couldn't remember why. Her stomach was tight with fear. She stood completely still, trying to decide which direction to go, when she saw a hint of light. She followed it down a steep hill as prickly bushes tore at her clothes.

Her heart raced. She stumbled out of the woods, relieved when she spotted his familiar, lanky shape. Rob waited for her. His smile felt like the sun, instantly warming her. He stepped toward her and her stomach danced with excitement.

"Mare, I've been waiting days for you. Welcome home, baby."

They embraced and her fears instantly dissolved.

Eventually, Rob pulled back.

"Hey, it's time for me to go but I'll come back. I always do." He touched the side of her face.

"Just a few more minutes. Please?" A tear slid down her check, he kissed it away.

"Mare, you'll wait for me?"

She nodded.

When he moved to leave, the thought of being away from him made her desperate and raw.

"Rob, wait. Don't leave me here alone. What do I say to Jimmy?"

She startled awake, immediately aggravated.

"Ey, you alright?"

"Yes, fine." She tried to push away the image of Rob walking away and the crushing hole it'd left burning through her heart.

Tony pulled up in front of Auntie Rose's house.

"I'll walk you in and check things out. It looks quiet, like everyone's sleeping." Once inside, he whispered, "I'll be right back."

While Tony checked out the house, Mia poured a glass of wine.

"Want one? Something?" she asked when he returned.

"No, I can't."

They were silent for a long minute.

He inhaled deep, brushing her lips with his. "I have to go to the hospital. Call me if anything seems out of place. They have someone outside to watch you, make sure everything's okay."

Her instinct was to pull away from him but she couldn't seem to do it. "Tony, I want to thank you—"

"No need." He exhaled as he folded her into him. "The weekend was better than great."

"You'll be careful?"

"Don't worry about me… I got too much to lose."

Uncertainty hung between them.

He pulled back. "Bolt and lock the door. The hospital has cameras in the front lot. When you visit him, park there. They'll issue you a pass."

An hour later, Mia headed to the hospital. *Why put it off*

any longer? When her feet hit the pavement, her legs felt like lead and her heart began to thump wildly. She paused at the door briefly before forcing herself inside. She felt the presence of her ancestors like familiar pieces of herself that had gone missing for a few days. Back in place, her parents lead the way, Rob behind them.

He reached for her hand and together they stepped inside.

Chapter 66

"Excuse me, miss?"

A short man dressed in a black security shirt blocked Mia at Jimmy's door.

"Immediate family only. Those are the orders, request of the family."

"I'm his sister."

"You'll need to show an ID. I've never seen you before."

Mia riffled through her bag and pulled out her wallet. She slid out her driver's license and handed it to him.

"Just doing my job, Dr. Capaldi."

"I understand, Sir," she mumbled. The security guard types she'd treated in the past came to mind. Such a strong desire for respect.

The room was quiet, dimly lit. Mia approached the bed slowly, Jimmy' eyes were closed.

"He's just sleeping now. Had a busy few hours."

Mia turned toward a nurse sitting in the corner with a novel on her lap.

The young woman hesitated. "You're…?"

"I'm his sister, Mia." She walked over to her. "Glad to meet you."

The book fell to the floor with a loud thump as they shook hands.

"Sorry." She bent to retrieve it. "I'm Laura. We've been expecting you, weren't sure if you went back home."

Mia leaned against the wall and exhaled slowly. "Not yet."

"Sometimes it happens just like that." She snapped. "And they wake up. He'll need physical therapy, some TLC for a while, but he's lucky. Seems okay otherwise."

Lucky… Mia noticed the book Laura had been reading, *The Bridges of Madison County*. She remembered it well. After the main character died, her adult children found letters from her true love. Someone they never knew existed. They learned that their mother had only stayed in her marriage because it was the right thing to do, her duty. In essence, she gave up the love of her life for her family. The true romantics hated it, couldn't deal with the notion that love, like many aspects of life, had many shades of gray.

"You've read it?" The nurse followed her stare.

"Yes, a long time ago."

She hedged back over to Jimmy, feeling relief when the woman excused herself.

Mia noticed Jimmy's bruises had started to heal. He looked better, more like the brother she remembered. Despite all that had happened, she felt her heart soften. Annoyance pulsed through her. *He doesn't deserve it.* She touched his arm gently and gazed past him. In the window, Rob's reflection stared back at her.

"You got something against true love?"

She looked back toward Jimmy, trying to ignore Rob. She wasn't in the mood to talk to the dead. He moved closer and his smirk grew.

"Mare, I missed you this weekend... Did you get it, him, out of your system?"

The hair on her arms stood up; she resented her body's reaction to him. She kept her eyes on her brother. Her head started to thump directly behind her left eye. She massaged her temples with her hand.

She felt his warm breath in her ear as he whispered, "I'm here now... You're just tired, you'll see. We'll figure it out together, like we always do."

She stiffened at his words, wishing they were true. His breath lingered and then he was gone. Disappointment and something else settled over her. *Why do I allow myself to have a relationship with a memory?* She squeezed her eyes shut, trying to make her thoughts go away.

Instead, her brain spun a list of her aggravations. She wished he could hear it.

I hate that you left me here, and that I let you keep doing it. I hate that I can't have a normal relationship with a living guy, and I hate that I still love you.

She took a deep breath.

And... and I really hate the way it hurts every time you leave, and that I'm standing here alone, talking to myself.

She glanced at Jimmy, it was torture being near him. *How could you?* She stood at the edge of the bed trying to reign in her emotions.

Laura returned. "I brought you coffee. Are you okay?"

"Yes, just tired." Mia took the cup. "Thanks. It's been a long night."

She noticed for the first time that Jimmy was still connected to a heart monitor and an IV.

"They're just being cautious. But you already know that. You're a doctor, right?"

"I'm a psychologist."

"Good, he's going to need your help more than ever. Those bruises are the easy part."

Mia watched her leave, glad to be alone with her thoughts. She plopped down in a nearby chair and thought about the nurse's words.

Tony pulled his car around to the far side of the hospital building, scanned the empty lot and cut the engine. Once inside, he headed toward the stairs, descending two at a time. He flashed his badge across the safety bar and entered when the door beeped. He mentally prepped himself as he slid into a backroom where the captain and a few guys were already sitting.

"Gentlemen." He nodded as he headed to the coffee station. With his back still turned, he heard an unfamiliar voice.

"Nice you could join us."

Tony turned to face them, his eyes hard as he sized up the kid who'd spoken. He was small, cocky. Tony knew from experience that having a badge and a chip was usually a bad combo.

"Made excellent time, Anthony. Didn't expect you for another forty-five minutes," the captain said. "Didcha relax? Kill anything?" He smiled, telling Tony to ignore the kid and chill.

"Not yet, no… The roads are empty at this hour. Castelli, always a pleasure." His eyes rested on the twerp with the mouth before turning back to the other two men. "Fill me in."

"Yeah. First, meet Detective Joseph Testa. He's got a big mouth but he's harmless. Good at his job, that's why he's here."

Testa smiled and nodded. "I was just playing."

He nodded back, unsure. The Captain motioned to the chair beside him and Tony flipped it around before sitting and crossed his arms over the back. They began bringing him up to speed. Tony had worked with Castelli before, he was a good guy, excellent cop. The kid seemed like a piece of work, a legend in his own mind. Tony would wait, try to reserve judgment.

They didn't know he'd been with her by the questions the captain threw his way. He was used to being evasive in the name of a case.

They strategized for the following hour.

Chapter 67

Beeeeep. Beeeeep. Chirp, chirrrp.

What is that annoying sound?

She heard a soft chuckle followed by a snicker, immediately recognizing the voice.

Jimmy's silhouette entered the bathroom on one leg. On his way back, he hobbled past her and she felt the blood leave her face.

"You look like you've seen a ghost, sis."

Before she could respond, his room filled with doctors and nurses. He winked at her.

"They must've fallen out in the night," he said convincingly. "Besides, I'm sure you're tired of cleaning this thing." He held up a bed pan and smiled at a nurse nearby.

"This one's a charmer," the nurse replied.

Their father's voice echoed in her head, *"Can't bullshit a bull-shitter." Well, he's still him.*

"Thanks for thinking of us, darling. Next time, call us to help." Nancy smiled at Mia. She saw right through his bullshit.

Mia was unsure what to make of Jimmy, not able to

understand the emotions moving through her. Part of her was thrilled, relieved her brother was alive and well. She heard Rory's words, *"Maybe you two can figure something out."* Another part of her was angry. Couldn't understand or forgive what he'd done all those years ago. His reasons didn't matter. Her head spun with contradictions.

"Glad you got my message, sweetie. We gonna check his vitals now. Maybe you want some coffee or somethin'."

She glanced toward her cell to see several voicemails.

"Mare, there was no white light, but I talked to Rob."

She nodded. "I'll let them work." Her ass and legs were painfully stiff. The ice injury came back to her and she thought about Tony.

Tony heard machines buzzing and beeping. He followed the sounds over to a grouping of TV monitors in the far corner of the room.

"What's that?"

"That's Capaldi's room," Castelli answered. "Sonofabitch. Look, he unhooked his monitors. Guess he had to go bad."

They watched him hop out of the bathroom.

"Kid's a real piece of work, huh?"

"You got the room on camera, good move." Tony walked up to the monitor and scanned the room. "Yeah, he's a piece of something, that one."

"Yeah, speakin' of a piece… Take a look at her." Testa smirked.

Marianna was standing in the back of the room.

"That's the sister. Arrived about an hour ago," the captain informed.

"I heard she's a big shot doctor from California but didn't think she'd be so hot," Castelli mused.

Tony's body tensed.

"I'll volunteer to tale her anyway she wants me to." Testa mimicked a humping motion.

Tony saw red, had to refrain from grabbing the little prick by the throat. He remained unmoved but felt every muscle in his body pulse with adrenaline. *I'll fucking smash your big mouth in right here.*

When Tony didn't laugh, Testa said, "Hey, I was just kiddin', big guy."

Tony eyed the kid, careful to keep his face straight and his voice even. "That's strike two and it's been less than an hour. Show some class."

"Why don't the two of you go get us some real coffee," the Captain suggested.

Tony saw Marianna leave the room and wondered where she was going. He ran his hand through his hair, inwardly still trying to get his anger in check and figure out his next move.

The captain cleared his throat.

Tony turned to face him. "The kid's a punk. I didn't like him the minute I stepped into the room."

"He's got a big mouth but he's harmless. Got good instincts, trust me."

"Okay, but he needs to keep his mouth shut."

"I'll talk to him. One of you needs to interview her—see how long she's staying, if she knows anything about that night. One of you needs to tail her until she leaves…"

"I'll put Castelli on it, brief him. You think Costa knows he's awake?"

"I don't know. I do know that the best thing is to get him out of here and into a locked rehab somewhere far away. I might be able to pull some strings to have it happen asap."

Tony paused a beat too long. "I'll talk to the staff, immediate family, keep a lid on the situation."

The captain eyed him. "Already did. Her and the brother are the only two left."

"I'm on it. You think he'll talk to us? Agree to rehab?"

"What aren't you telling me, Anthony?"

"Naw, it's just… Kid saw me the night Costa ordered us to take care of him. He might recognize me. I was thinkin', we let him confess to her about their parents after his near death and all. She'd need to know the room is on camera, though. We can make sure of that; prep her, maybe."

"Anything else I should know about?"

"No, except that she doesn't know about my undercover—completely."

"Meaning?"

"Nothing." He wasn't sure if he was protecting her or himself anymore.

"Jo?"

"Hey, my long-lost cousin. How was your Turkey Day with the bodyguard?"

Mia dropped her voice. "Do me a favor? Don't tell anyone where I went or who I was with. I'll explain later, okay?"

"Okay… You do know your asshole brother's awake?"

"Yes, I'm at the hospital now. Does Rosie know?"

"Of course she knows, they called her late last night. Is he with it or drooling on himself?"

"I think he's still him. What did you tell Rosie about me and Thanksgiving?"

"What's going on? Why all the drama?"

"I'll explain later."

"I told her you were spending it local with friends. That it was still too hard for you to be around us 'cause of Robbie."

"Thanks, Jo. I'll call you after."

Mia dialed Rory, getting his voicemail. "I'm back in Rhode

Island. My brother's awake. I plan to talk to him at some point, hopefully this morning, and then get the hell out of here. Hey, I hope you're having fun."

She grabbed her coffee. The quicker she confronted him, the quicker she could get back to her own life. She rehearsed her words, outlining her questions as she counted the lines in the linoleum floor.

Chapter 68

Jimmy's room was quiet; Mia approached the bed slowly.

"Mare, that you?" His eyes were shut.

"It is. How are you feeling?"

He reached out his hand to find hers. "I'm sore, tired. I can't believe I was out of it for that long. Crazy, huh?"

He sounded fatigued, more fragile than she'd expected. Her throat constricted with emotion. "I know, almost a month."

He opened his eyes. "You were almost the sole survivor, kid." He squeezed her hand. "Robbie thinks it might be my last chance to get it right."

She squeezed back and the past fell away. She fought tears.

"What do you think, Doc?"

"He might be right."

His eyes closed and his voice was soft, barely audible, "No matter what happens, kid, I love you."

A few minutes passed before she realized he'd nodded off. For a while she watched him sleep, she knew he needed to rest. She felt disappointment burning behind her eyes, but feared that if she allowed the tears to come, they wouldn't stop. Sometime around ten, Auntie Rose stopped in for a visit, her large frame filling the doorway.

"Thank God he's alright." She pulled Mia into her.

"And he was doing so well. Maybe this is what he needed… a wakeup call."

Mia didn't say anything.

"How does he seem? You know, up there?" She pointed to her head.

"He seems like him, just tired."

"Guess that's normal after what he went through." She paused. "What now, kid?"

"I'm not sure." Mia averted her gaze out the window.

"Too soon to tell." She patted Mia's hand. "We're all just glad he's gonna be okay."

Mia was grateful her aunt didn't bring up Thanksgiving.

"I know you got a busy schedule, but I'd like us all to spend Christmas together. Even Rory. He can bring his new friend… I don't know, maybe it's your dad's death, or Jimmy's near miss, but I don't wanna put things off anymore. It's been long enough."

"I'm not sure—"

"Maybe you can pull off a long weekend. Christmas falls on a Saturday this year. That way you wouldn't miss any work."

"Auntie, I'm not sure I can forgive what he did. It's not okay with me, never will be."

They stared at each other for a long while.

After a few minutes, Rosie stood up to leave, pecking Mia on the cheek.

Chapter 69

After the morning's incident, Jimmy's room had remained fairly quiet. Tony watched her as she sat next to him. Watching her from a distance was more difficult than he'd imagined. He wanted to be with her. He knew she had a lot going on, but he couldn't help but wonder if she'd thought about him at all. His undershirt still smelled like her.

He was pulled out of his thoughts when a heavy-set woman entered Jimmy's room. Mia hugged her, it was Aunt Rose. Marianna left the room once to get food from the cafeteria before her aunt left for work. Her food was untouched and she eventually slid it into the trash bin.

Castelli entered the room, and they talked for a little while. After he left, she rested her head back against the chair. Despite her tired posture, her foot moved up and down.

Around suppertime, Tony left the hospital for a short while to grab a shower. He decided to drive by the aunt's place, pulling up to the patrol car.

"How's it going? Anything?" He was relieved to see Sulli.

They had history, went way back. He felt himself exhale knowing she was in good hands

"Hey, T man. Just living the dream. Quiet, boring, actually. A pretty pregnant lady and two kids were picked up a few hours ago, that's it. I heard we're dealing with Costa's crew? I'd love a chance to bust his head open. Haven't seen anyone, though."

"That's good, man." Tony scanned the area. Costa was a shady fuck, had eyes everywhere.

Tony entered the house through the back door. His body felt tense, overtired. He needed a release. He was disappointed the house was undisturbed. He patted Frenchie's head and left a note. He scanned the parameter thoroughly before heading back to his car. He planned to call Castelli, tell him he'd secured the place. He gave a salute to Sulli on his way out.

When Tony got back to the hospital, Testa was watching the screen with a large container of DD coffee and a bag.

"It's black and egg sandwiches. Didn't know if you had time to eat and I didn't peg you for a donut guy."

"Thanks."

"Still quiet up there. I guess that's good."

The kid had been amazingly respectful since their last conversation. "Listen, you're free to go. Castelli will stay outside the aunt's house overnight and I'll be here. Go get some rest. See you in the morning."

"I'll look around first, check in later."

Glad to be alone, Tony reclined in the chair, his eyes peeled on her. Around ten thirty, a small, dark-haired woman walked in and sat beside her. Jo, he recognized her. He was surprised when they left a short time later and didn't return. He assumed she would've stayed.

He speed dialed Castelli. "Ey, any activity there?"

"The sister was dropped off by a female, mid-thirties, fucked hair, in a blue Buick, older model. Woman stayed about five minutes and then headed north on Fletcher. Want me to go inside? Make sure?"

He wrestled with his paranoia. Reality was, it was unlikely Costa knew about them.

"Go in if you suspect anything out of the ordinary." He didn't want to alarm her for no reason, he trusted Castelli's instincts.

Tony must've dozed off because when he heard a beep, chirp coming from the punk's room, the clock read 3 a.m. He scanned the monitors but they were black. *Fuuuck.* He speed dialed the Captain, the 911 would signal both Castelli and Testa.

After bolting up two flights of stairs, he checked on the uniform laying on the floor in front of the kid's room. His pulse was faint. He clocked blood droplets on the floor… *Fuck.* Entering the room, he looked toward the bed. Empty. *Fuck.* The tray was tipped over and he raced to the bathroom to find it empty.

Tony raced down the hall looking for anyone or anything that didn't fit. He followed the blood droplets to the service elevator and took it to the ground floor, scanning the parking lot. In the darkness, he saw two guys pushing a wheelchair down the ramp and toward a van.

"Hey, stop right there." He broke into a run.

Jimmy turned to face him. Recognition and fear flashed in his eyes. Tony heard footsteps next to him. Testa and another guy he didn't know were keeping pace with him. They spread out between cars and Tony ran faster, almost catching up. Despite his feelings about the punk, his tangles, he doesn't want it to end like this for her. She needed him alive.

They got Jimmy in the van. *They leave, he's dead for sure.* Tony started to list the facts: two guys, dressed in black; the van was moving, a third guy, a driver; he wore a baseball cap and gloves. Tony noted the make and color of the van. *No plates, fuck.*

They struggled with the wheelchair briefly and Tony and Testa ascended on them at once. Testa drew his gun and let out a pop, hitting one of the guys. He winced and yelled out in pain. The van swerved but righted itself quickly. *Driver's done this before.* The van started to speed away as the other guy prepped for the shot.

Tony dove, covering Jimmy with his full body's weight. He felt two things at once: his body collapse and a burn somewhere in his left side. *Motherfucker.* He started to lose consciousness.

"T, you hit?"

"Get him inside. Check on her." His world went black.

Mia was thrilled to see Mr. French curled up in a dog bed. Hearing her enter, he ran over, wagging his rear end off as she patted his head. She immediately saw a folded-up piece of paper.

"Marianna, hope today went well and that you could feel me there with you. I'll have to stand guard from here tonight, still dreaming about our weekend. I miss you. Know I'll miss you even more tonight. Love Tony. PS. See you in the morning.

After a quick shower, Mia ate half a cheese sandwich and headed to bed. She tried to sleep but thoughts of Jimmy keep circling. She got up and headed to the kitchen. Standing at the sink, she chugged down a glass of wine and returned to bed.

She drifted off into fragmented sleep, waking often wanting to be engulfed by her giant security blanket. Her stomach sank with the realization that she was alone, but she pushed herself upright.

She dug through her suitcase for her father's journal and gathered her belongings, heading for the hospital.

Chapter 70

By the time Mia walked up the front steps to the hospital, the sun was just making an appearance. Her brain was foggy from lack of sleep. The kind detective she'd met the day before and a shorter, younger man stood near the elevator.

"Dr. Capaldi," Castelli said.

She nodded. "Good morning."

They escorted her down two flights of stairs and through a long, sterile corridor. She scanned for Tony. *He said he'd be here.* She felt the familiar burn of disappointment.

"Please have a seat," offered Detective Castelli.

He sat across from her while the other man stood, arms folded across his chest.

"Dr. Capaldi, this is Detective Testa."

Mia nodded a hello. Something seemed off.

"I'll cut right to the chase. It's our job to make sure you and your brother remain safe until he leaves the hospital and you return home. I suspect he'll be here for another week. We're waiting for a bed to open up in a Cape Cod treatment facility.

It's a locked rehab program, excellent for someone with his background."

"His background…"There was a tightness in Detective Castelli's face that she hadn't noticed before.

"Is everything okay, detective?"

"Yes. His priors are consistent with someone who has a strong alcohol and drug abuse history. Is that correct?"

"Yes. He's struggled for a number of years with addiction, mostly alcohol. Detective, even after what's happened, I'd be surprised if he agreed to enter a locked treatment program."

"We're hoping he'll think of it as extra protection and a shot at recovery all at once."

She already knew the answer but asked anyway, "Why would he agree to that? And where's Detective Iannucci? He said he'd be here."

"We believe your brother witnessed something the night of his attack. If the men involved find out he's still alive, they may try to alter things to their advantage. They don't want him talking–and this is unlikely–but you being related… We just want to be cautious. Do you understand?"

"I think so. You didn't answer my question." Alarm rose up her spine.

"I'm sorry, we're not at liberty to speak with you about Detective Iannucci. Do you know how long you'll be staying in Rhode Island, Doctor?"

She tried to ignore the nausea rising up to her chest. "I'm hoping to leave later today, after I speak with my brother."

Castelli and the other man exchanged a look.

"I need to get back to work," she said defensively.

"Did you see your brother the night he was involved in the altercation?"

"Yes. I was in town for my father's funeral and met some old friends at a bar that night. I ran into him there."

"Sorry to hear about your father."

"Thank you, I barely knew him."

"Detective Iannucci was at Bishop Hill that night working a case."

"I don't remember seeing him but, as you can imagine, that weekend was a bit of a blur for me."

He nodded. "What kind of relationship do you have with your brother? Are you close?"

Her stomach tightened. "We used to be. He can be very charming when he's sober, but when he drinks, I don't like him very much."

"Our sources say you two had words, a fight that night, out in the parking lot."

Her foot began bobbing up and down. "He was drunk, said stupid things, said he had another stop to make in Providence. I told him to go home… He doesn't like to be told what to do."

"Did he tell you who he was meeting?"

"No, he only said he had some business to take care of."

"Did he talk about that night when you saw him yesterday? Can you tell me what you argued about that night?"

"No, and I don't remember. It's almost a month now."

He waited a long beat.

"He drinks too much, he often doesn't make sense."

"Thank you for your time. If you remember anything you'd like to add, here's my card. One of us will be by his room later to ask him some questions."

"Can you at least tell me if he's okay? Tony, I mean."

The door opened and an imposing older man strode in.

"Captain."

He averted her gaze. "Have a seat, Dr. Capaldi. Gentlemen, you can sit too, sounds like you had a long night. These fine men were instructed to wait on my orders. They didn't know of Detective Iannucci's condition."

"His condition?"

The captain patted her hand. "I won't mince my words. Tony just got out of emergency surgery. He saved your brother's life last night with the help of Detective Testa. They'll both recover."

Detective Testa seemed to suddenly look his young age and nodded in gratitude.

"Simultaneously, Detective Castelli was responsible for taking out a threat against you at your aunt's house early this morning. Thank you both, good work. The threats have been eliminated, for the time being, but, as you know, these are very dangerous men your brother has crossed."

Mia was speechless.

"Testa, please get Dr. Capaldi some water."

Mia tried to process all that had happened, her heart beating out of her chest. She stood despite the fact that her legs were shaky.

"Thank you for everything," she finally managed.

In the hallway, she let her breath out slowly and deliberately.

"He's asking to see you, before you speak to your brother."

She eyed him gratefully, tears spilling silently down her cheeks. He handed her a tissue but remained silent for the elevator ride up.

"I'll be out here if you need anything."

She entered Tony's room and slowly approached the bed.

"Hey, you good? I heard Castelli worked his magic. Don't cry, I'm gonna be fine. Shhh, it's okay." Tony wiped her tears.

"I heard about what happened with Jimmy…" She squeezed his big, warm hand. "Thank you. I'm relieved you're okay. He's not even worth it; we both know it."

"Listen, I did it for you," he said just above a whisper. "Not a big fan of your brother, but he's still your brother. I just want you to know I love you no matter what he says."

She bent her head closer to his, letting her tears flow freely.

"After you talk to him," he whispered. "You should go back home. You're not safe here."

Mia fought the urge to kiss him. As his grip lessened, she realized he was drifting off.

"I love you," she whispered. Then, barely audible, "Please be okay."

Chapter 71

"Morning, sis. I've never been this tired before. All this action is catching up to me."

Her heart ached thinking of Tony laying in a hospital bed because of Jimmy. After everything, it was unbearable.

"I heard about last night, Jim. Thankfully the detectives were there."

He snorted. "I would've been fine. I can hold my own."

"Listen—"

"Morning," Castelli greeted as he walked in. "I was hoping to talk to you for a few minutes, Mr. Capaldi."

Mia stood and slipped the journal back into her bag. "I'll give you two a few minutes alone."

"It's up to your brother."

"She can stay; why you here?"

"My name is Detective Castelli, I'm here in place of Detective Anthony Iannucci, the one who saved your life last night. Remember that? I just want to remind you both that we have a camera watching the room for your protection… You're on tape."

"Detective? No kidding… Undercover fucking snake, wow." He turned to Mia. "You know your lover broke my jaw and smiled? I think he enjoyed it. In fact, I know he did."

The detective's face turned hard.

"I'm here now to talk to you about a few things, Mr. Capaldi."

Jimmy ignored him. "You knew he was a cop?"

Mia looked at the detective.

"Yes, she's been very cooperative, and worried about you."

"I don't need or want your protection, big guy. Your buddy's the reason I'm here."

He used me.

"Until you leave the hospital, you got it."

"What do you need, detective?"

"I know who's responsible for landing you here in this condition."

"No shit. Besides your friend, you mean?"

"I was wondering if you'd talk to us about that night. About Costa and what you saw."

"Why should I tell you?"

"They nearly killed an innocent man. You can help us keep them locked up. If Costa finds out you're still alive, he's going to try to kill you again. Doesn't matter if he's in prison."

"I'm not afraid, detective. I can fight my own battles."

"Right, like last night. If Special Agent Iannucci wasn't there, you'd be dead right now. I watched the film."

"You think he's a hero? Just doing his job? Naaw, he fell for her and feels guilty cause she probably don't know about him. He used her to get to me, that's my guess." Jimmy grinned when her look confirmed his words.

"Do you have any interest in a long-term treatment program out in Cape Cod? Top notch, difficult to get into. We can pull some strings, give you a second chance."

"Not interested in helping you, Detective. You can tell Costa, too. Or you can ask his other buddy, I'm sure they still talk. If his goons didn't jump me from behind, he'd be the one in here, not me."

"If you change your mind or decide to think about someone other than yourself, let me know." The detective backed away without looking at Mia, closing the door shut behind him.

"Mee, the other guy's an undercover cop! Fuckin' kidding me?! Did he tell you?"

He made a choice. Jimmy and Tony.

"You're judging me?" She slid the journal out of her pocketbook. "He kept a journal. Wrote about that night and many others."

"Where'd you get that?" His face froze.

"How could you?"

"I found them... She moved, got in the way." He looked away from her as tears shone in his eyes. "She was going to leave us for him... Dad knew and did nothing. What the fuck kind of man is that? Lets his wife just walk away from her life with someone else?" He wiped his eyes with the back of his hand. "I had to do something."

Mia felt her throat constrict, it was hard to swallow. She wanted so badly for it not to have been true. For a minute she could barely breathe.

"I thought the details would make me feel better, help me understand..." Mia was losing control. "They didn't change anything..." *Even my love for you somehow remains.* "Their fate wasn't for you to decide. That was between them. Dad knew that Costa also had two kids and a wife at home. He was the kind of man who considered other people. Even *you!* After what *you* did, accident or not, you killed her, and he paid for it."

"I wasn't trying to hurt her, or you. I thought it was the right thing. Was trying to save our family."

Heat rushed to her cheeks. "What you did that night *wiped*

out our family. Hurt all of us. Like a chain of events all connected. It changed *everything*. Your choice altered our fate and its shadows still remain."

"You're going to tell me about living with shadows, doctor? You think yours can compare with mine? My sentence was way worse."

She shook her head. "That's the worst part. Your decision destroyed the brother I knew... You chose this, we didn't." She opened the journal and read it aloud. "December 23, 1992. This was a bad day, haven't had one of these in a long time. I know she's out there feeling all alone when she should be blowin out her candles like any other girl her age. She's 12 today. To think of her with no mother, father or brother around to speak of is too much for me to handle.

"I know now in my grief and despair I wasn't thinking straight. My only wish for her is that someday she understands. Sometimes parents'll do anything for their kids, even if later on it turns out not to be the right thing. Maybe someday she'll fall in love, be a mother. Maybe she'll forgive me for leavin her all alone."

She leveled her eyes on Jimmy.

"I remember my twelfth birthday. It remains one of the worst days of my entire life. It was the first birthday and Christmas I spent without any of you. Rosie filled a stocking with all sorts of stuff, but nothing could fill the hole I felt as I looked around that morning and only saw her family. Mine was gone. Later, I tried to blow out candles but was so grief-stricken I threw up and went to bed. Rob snuck cake into my room and tried to make me feel better. He played my favorite music on his 8-track player and told me every joke he knew. He tried so hard to make it better, it was impossible not to love him for it."

She took a deep breath, trying to push away the awful feelings that remained from that day so long ago.

"I still hate the wintertime, Christmas and my birthday suck, and I have nightmares that should be medicated but I'm afraid I'll forget them, never see their faces again. While you were away drinking, I was left an orphan trying to survive... I still am."

"Mare, he deserved it. They both did, really."

She shook her head in disgust.

"Here's a glimpse of the man who loved you so much he did your sentence; the same one you robbed me of my relationship with; the same one you judged and hated because you couldn't comprehend that kind of selfless love. He didn't want her to stay if she didn't want to be there with him. And yes, she was flawed. She fell for another man, she was human.

June 1, 2000

Today there's no sadness, I'm angry. The world feels red like my mood. From the minute I got up I hated everything and everybody. My eyes look weird, empty, like they're not mine nomore.

"I started a fight with the Mexicans, wanted them to put me out of my misery so I could join her on her birthday. Instead wound up in solitary for a week with broken ribs. They still hurt like a mother fucker. She would've been 52 today... I dream about her still. about us having one more minute together, even after what happened. I wonder if Jimmy's thinking bout his mother today, regrets his actions. She and I might've worked it out. I was no angel either, people go through things. Deep down I blame myself for everything. I wasn't around enough. I still wish I got there sooner..." Mia's eyes were clouded by grief and tears, she could no longer read his words.

She brushed her tears away with the back of her hand and looked at Jimmy.

"You made a conscious choice to show up with a gun and

kill. We all did your time…" Her anger had been replaced by agonizing sorrow.

He was quiet for a long moment. "Two words, Mare. Murder. Weapon?"

They locked eyes, his glinting, playful.

"That's quite a story, Mare. Wow! And I'm the one whose fucked up on pain pills, barely know what I'm saying. What's your excuse? And hey, I didn't mean to hurt you, but the me in that wild story would probably do it again. I'm not sorry, Mare."

She watched her tears drip onto her jeans as he reached for her leg. She searched his eyes, they were both empty and haunted.

"Don't," she spat.

Chapter 72

When Mia reached the elevator, she felt someone gently tug on her sleeve. She recognized Rob's familiar scent. Stepping inside, Rob took her hand in his. She leaned against him as they rode the elevator down. She had one final thing to do before she finally went home.

"That must've been hard," Castelli comforted.

She nodded without eye contact. "It's over, I'm heading home. You'll tell the other detectives for me? I want to catch my flight." She reached inside her bag. "Here. This will help solve an old case. I hope…"

Rob whispered behind her, "Mare, you sure?"

"It was my father's."

The detective gave her a quick nod and touched her arm. "You need to do anything or see anyone before we head to Green for your flight?"

"No, I'm ready now."

Chapter 73

"How are you feeling, Mr. Capaldi?" Tony asked.

"What's it to you, detective? Pah."

"I was wondering if we could talk."

"Save your breath. She already knows."

"Your sister gave me something of your dad's." Tony watched Jimmy's face closely, saw the armor drop back into place. "I won't tell anyone what's in here under two conditions: You stay at the treatment center until you complete the program, a full year, and you tell me everything you remember about the night Williams got shot. He's dead. His wife and kids deserve justice."

Jimmy grinned. "Or maybe I say, 'Fuck you'. Start at the part where you and my sister were together, detective. You used her to get to me?"

"Or I could hand this over to the right people and you can spend the rest of your life in prison for murdering your own mother. It's not your word against hers, it's proof. They love cases like this."

"If that's true, it was an accident."

"We both know it wasn't."

Jimmy paused. "How do I know you'll keep your word, detective?"

"Because your sister's happiness means everything to me."

"Your word is as good as mine." He smirked.

It'd been almost three weeks since Mia had returned home. She was acutely aware that it was almost Rob's birthday. Like every year since his death, her nightmares had returned.

We often peel back one thin layer to uncover another than another deeper one underneath. The layers come with coping mechanisms that serve us until they don't. The thing no one talks about outside of therapy is that sometimes pain becomes so familiar, we don't know how to function without it. We've not only grown to accept it but, in a way, we cherish it. And we often don't know how to do it any other way.

Christmas was everywhere—toys, wrapping, decorations. Mom and dad sat on the couch sipping light brown liquid from mini wine glasses. Mia and Jimmy excitedly played with their new toys as the lights from the tree twinkled behind them.

Like someone had accidently hit the remote, switching the channel, it was the day before Christmas. Rob's birthday. The familiar tune played, "Is there anybody in there? Just knock if you can hear me. Is there anyone at home…" Rob and Mia were intertwined on his bed, kissing long and slow. She felt goosebumps rush her as he slid his hand up her back. "There is no pain we are receding, a constant ship is on the horizon, you are only coming through in waves, your lips move but I can't hear what you're saying," Rob hummed as they kissed.

The song grew louder. The sounds of metal and the music became deafening. The channel switched again and she started to scream. She was outside of Suzy Q's. "I, I, I have become comfortably numb," the song blared. She vomited on Mr. Pezzullo's shoes, ending up immobilized in the hospital.

She bolted upright and felt Tony's arms around, safe and warm.

"Ey, what's happenin'?"

"Bad dream." Silent tears streamed her face. She was embarrassed.

He held her tighter. "How 'bout some milk or a drink?"

She nodded and his large frame left the room, returning with a mug of wine.

They exchanged a long glance. "Thanks."

"I'd understand, you know. You can talk to me."

She followed his gaze to the picture of her and Rob on the nightstand. She looked away. "I know."

"You know they have good drugs for that, Doc?"

"I have an appointment after the holidays. It's my New Year's resolution." She didn't tell him she was terrified that meds would erase the good as well as the bad.

"Sounds like a good one. Come here."

She laid back against him, trying to get back to sleep. Everything still loomed way too close to the surface. Every time she shut her eyes, the music started humming.

"You wanna talk about it?"

I don't know where to begin…

"Try a piece of it."

"Rob's birthday is at the end of next week. The nightmares start about a week before, then eventually go away." She exhaled into him. "But then the rest of the time… He's sort of with me. Like he's not dead."

"You *see him*, see him?"

She started to pull away.

"Can you ask him not to visit you?"

Rob whispered, "Tell him, Mare, about our pact…"

"I can't. We've always been there for each other. He's always been there for me…"

"But it's hurting you."

"No, not always."

His arm tightened around her.

"Sometimes it's nice. He keeps me company when I'm sad or alone."

"I could do that for you," he said in a low voice.

"I wanted that. But then you—"

She bolted upright, her heart beating out of her chest.

Chapter 74

Tony tapped on the Captain's door.

"Hey, Anthony, come in. How you feelin', big guy? I like the beard. Sit, sit."

Tony pushed the door shut and sat with a heaviness as he exhaled his breath. Tony looked up at the captain. The compassion he wore convinced Tony he was doing the right thing.

"Cap, you've been more than a boss or leader to me… A father."

"Hey, you dyin' or retirin'? Just fucking tell me, what the fuck, T? With the drama?"

Tony sat back and looked away, welcoming the pain that shot through his ribs.

"What is all this?"

"I need to retire; I'm done with the life. I'm burned out; that's all, really. Tell the guys for me?" He stood to leave, knew he was being a coward not telling him the whole truth.

"That's it, huh? No real reason? I'm gonna make shit up for you now? Be a man, T. Own your own shit for once, don't hide behind hero bullshit."

"You think he's a hero, Mare? Naw, nope."

He turned back to meet his gaze. "You're right, I owe you more than that." He let out a deep breath. "I met her on a plane before I even knew she was his sister…"

The hint of recognition ignited in the captain's eyes. "Okay. And?"

"And I fucked it all up… bad."

"I'm listening."

"I just fell," he admitted after spilling the whole mess. "I compromised everything, everybody. Her safety… The punk deserved what he got, and fuck Costa, but I didn't walk away. I don't know how I got here, shit is so fuckin' blurred."

"Shit gets blurred all the time. What, you forgot that all of a sudden? You're a detective, for Christ sakes! We got 'em, they're not getting out."

Tony stared at the ground thinking about Greco.

"The rest is fully on you. Fuck were you thinking?"

"I take full responsibility, sir, I do. But I don't regre—"

The captain cut him off with a hand and they sat in silence.

"Who knows?"

Tony stared.

"Who?" his voice grew louder. "I have to do damage control, I gotta know everything, for fuck's sake. You left me out, now I gotta figure out how not to make me, us, the department look like a bunch of… I don't even fuckin' know."

"Her family here, including the brother. And Castelli. He saw a note I wrote to her the night her brother was taken from his room… He gave it back to me in the hospital after she gave him these." Tony handed him a stack of journals.

"Anthony, are you kiddin' me? And what are these?"

"They're her father's. They back up what the punk confessed to her before she left. They implicate the kid. He shot them, his mother and Costa's brother, not the old man."

The captain sat back. "Jesus fucking Christ, Tony. You sat on this for some broad? Some piece of as—"

Tony stood. "Sir, respectfully, she's no piece of ass and I'd do that part all over again. I love her."

The Captain stood. "Hey, I recommend you sit back down and think very carefully about what comes out of your mouth next. That case you sat on is a fucking famous case around here. That man spent his life in prison. Died there. If anyone finds out that we had information going back over a month because of you… Do you know how bad that makes us look? We could all lose our jobs. This is an election year, we could lose funding and a lot more."

Tony sat, his anger replaced by guilt. "She told me when we were in New Hampshire. No one else knows, sir."

"Well, we have to play this exactly right or the brother'll get off, and we'll get sued for fucking god knows what…What did she say when she found out the truth?"

"Nothing. She left, went home."

They locked eyes.

"I know you gotta do what you gotta do. I deserve whatever they want to do with me."

"Save your remorse. I can't tell them that, we'd both get fired. Here's what we're gonna do. You're gonna fix this, Iannucci. You're going to re-solve a very famous case. Got it?"

Tony stared, confused.

"Think with your fucking brain for a minute."

"No. She can't come back. It's not safe, she needs to be done with all this, and you know that. I won't do it. No. Fire me. I can't do that."

"Look, you'll do what I tell you to do. That case won't stick against the brother without her. There was no murder weapon and confessions don't always stick. We both know the punk'll walk free without her testimony. We get her in and out in a fucking day and you or Testa or fucking Castelli better keep her safe. I don't really care who. But the father's case deserves to be turned and you're going to fix this. That's what needs to be done, so get yourself together, big man."

Tony stood. "Castelli'll have to handle it. I can't, sir. I need to be done."

"Anthony, you're a detective, a damn good cop. Best I've known, blue through and through. You'll be lost and all alone without the badge."

"Sir, I've been lost and all alone with the badge."

Chapter 75

Mia counted her breaths in small bursts before pulling open the door to Dr. Gonsalves' waiting room. The last time she saw him was when she lived with her uncle. Dr. G was kind and seemed to understand her sadness, loss and need for medication, even later respected her hesitation to keep taking it. He didn't, however, understand or agree with her desire to discontinue talk therapy.

"Marianna, hello. Come on in; it's nice to see you."

Mia followed him into his large, sunny office and sat on the navy couch.

He picked up his clipboard, resting it on his lap. His hair had lightened at his temples, but otherwise he looked the same.

"How have you been? It's been a while." He took a short pause. "What brings you here today?"

"Yes, it has been a long time." She wanted to say she was good but he'd know it was a lie. "I was in Rhode Island for a few months. Originally for my father's funeral, then my brother had some… medical and other… complications." Fury for him rose in her. *Messy and layered.*

He nodded, waiting for her to continue. When she didn't, he said, "Sorry about your father."

Mia's typical response bubbled up; *I barely knew him.* "Thank you."

"When was the last time you were back there?"

"I haven't been. It was the first time."

"That must have been very difficult for you on many levels."

"Yes, it was." She didn't want to talk about the levels, she wanted to get sleep meds and be on her way. "I think it's time for me to go back on medication for my sleeping problems."

"What's happening at night that's making it hard to sleep?"

"I'm having nightmares again. I think his death and being back there brought everything back for me." Mia's eyes filled and spilled over. *Damn it.*

"It's okay, take your time."

They sat in silence for a beat as she tried to gather herself. This was part of why she had stopped therapy all those years ago. It was too hard to say out loud. It was still too hard..

"Help me to understand. So, the nightmares you had all those years ago had stopped, and now they've come back?" He paused. "What can you tell me about them?"

"They actually never stopped… They seem worse now." She searched for the words. "So much has happened, I don't really know how or where to start."

He smiled warmly at her. "I find the very beginning is a good place, "so how did you learn about your father's death, Marianna?"

Mia filled him in on the details of that initial call and some vague explanations of what it was like to go back, and the trouble Jimmy had gotten himself into. She didn't share the new information about her mother's death or anything about Tony.

"Our time is up for today. It's so nice to see you again. I imagine that was very hard for you, trauma and loss aren't easy to talk about. It's painful, maybe opening up feelings of vulnerability or anger… I know you came here today for medication to help you with your sleep, I agree sleep is essential, but I'd like to set up another session to talk.

"We've known each other a long time. I think if you could access and process your feelings around all that has happened, maybe you could move forward past the traumatic losses. Maybe we can understand and treat your nightmares better than simply medicating them."

Mia got back in her car, resting her head against the seat rest. *Access and process…* She exhaled out a loud breath and looked in the rear-view mirror.

"You going to continue, Mare?" Rob asked from the back seat.

"I don't want to… but I know I have to."

Mia stopped for breakfast at one of her favorite spots, The Diner. She had just finished paying her check when she heard her cell ring.

"Hello, Dr. Capaldi?"

"Yes, speaking…" Her stomach dipped, she recognized the soft-spoken voice.

"Hi. This is Detective Castelli, I hope I'm not bothering you?"

She was silent for a beat. "No, I'm just surprised to hear from you. Everything okay?"

"I'm calling because… We need your help with your dad's case."

"My help?"

"Yes. To wrap it up we need to ask you some follow up questions about his journals, on the record. It's called a deposition or hearing. The court has to rule if there's enough proof to move forward in this case to prosecute Jimmy. Then he can't dispute it."

"Are you kidding me right now?"

"I'm sorry. I'm not."

She waited a beat, felt herself getting heated. "And we both know I don't really get to say no, do I? My brother got a lawyer?"

"One will be provided to him if he doesn't. We both know he won't cooperate with us."

"Wooo, un-fucking-believable." She laughed, shaking her head, despite not feeling the humor at all. Her outrage was building. "No, he certainly won't," she snapped.

"Dr. Capaldi, I'm really sorry. The case is more complicated than we could've known."

"We both know you're not. You gave them to Tony and this is what he came up with?" It felt like his biggest betrayal.

"If it's better for you, we can try after the holidays. We'll make it as quick as possible. I really am sorry. It's the only way to clear your father's name."

"I— Fuck!"

"I can't imagine how hard this must be for you. We'll try to accommodate your schedule. If I can do anything to make it less shitty for you while you're here, please let me know."

"I don't want detective, whoever Iannucci involved. I don't want to see him. I can't."

"Detective Iannucci… He's not working this case in any way."

Good, he deserves it. "I'd rather do this as quick as possible and be done with it finally. I'll get the next flight and send you the information."

Chapter 76

Boom, boom, boom.

Before he even cracked open his eyes, Tony sensed that someone was in his room. He rolled to his right, grabbing his gun off the bedside table and standing up in a flash. He pushed the figure hard against the wall, his gun against the middle of a forehead.

"T, T. It's me, Jencks."

"Tony! Hey, stop, let him go, it's us. The fuck?" Bobby's voice shouted from behind.

Tony released Jencks with a shove and set his gun down on the side table.

"The fuck, guys? You don't knock?"

Greco held up Tony's keys. "We've been calling you for three days, left you about five messages. We gotta go; today's the day. We got about two hours. Where have you been?"

Bile rose in Tony's stomach. *She's coming in today…*

"I–I didn't know you were out?" His mind spun.

"Please, we're untouchable. You know that. And now Costa wants revenge."

"Yeah. I called Shades and the guys." Bobby smirked. "Just in case… You look like Casper. You good?"

"Yeah, of course. Let me grab a quick shower." Tony glanced at his gun.

Watching him, Bobby grabbed it first, quickly raising it to Tony's head. Bobby's eyes were empty and hard.

"You fucked us over, we know it," Greco spat. "Little man waited that whole afternoon, not knowing where the fuck I was."

"My girl won't talk to me," Bobby chimed in. "Don't matter that I'm out or that I'm the father, she doesn't want to see me no more, said she's done."

"And I can't go back, they got me for killing blue. I'll fry for that. Thanks, my friend, for that. So, your girl's done, too. You'll watch us do her like her brother. It'll be fun to tie her up. Shades will help, he'll love that." His eyes gleamed.

Tony struggled for his gun. An explosion sounded. He braced himself for the burn. *Better than them getting to her…*

Tony bolted upright. *Whoa, it's a dream, just a dream.*

Chapter 77

"Hey, Jo."

"Hey, you land yet?"

"Yeah, just waiting to deplane. Are you already here?"

"Yup! I said I would, besides, you know I'm not about to let you face those motherfuckers alone."

Mia chuckled. "Okay, see you soon."

She gathered her belongings and Frenchie's crate and moved awkwardly down the aisle with the other passengers. She counted her steps as she walked up the ramp, the cold air hitting her like a bitch slap of reality.

Rob whispered, "You're good, I'm right here. Give me your hand."

"Dr. Capaldi, not sure you remember me, I'm Detective Testa, part of your security team. Let me take that for you."

Rob had disappeared in Testa's presence, and she was alone again. This hit her hard. *He's a memory, Mia.*

In just a few moments, she was surrounded by three other men. She nodded to Castelli.

"Hello, Dr. Capaldi, thank you for coming. These are special agents Reed and Izzo, they're part of our team."

"Hello," she greeted coolly, incredibly uncomfortable to be surrounded by them.

"After we leave the airport, we'll be around in case you need us, but we'll stay in the background."

Her stomach dipped at Tony's absence. "I have one suitcase."

They followed her down to baggage claim and she exhaled relief when she saw Jo.

"Relax, guys. I'm her cousin. No threat, back down." She hugged Mia. "Hey, how was your flight?"

"Long. I'm starving and need to use the bathroom."

They started walking, trailed by their entourage.

Jo rolled her eyes and handed Mia a bag. "Here, I grabbed these from the diner."

"Thank you," Mia gushed as she stuffed it in her handbag.

"We'll watch the dog," offered the blonde agent.

"Thank you."

"He might have to pee, too," Jo said not so politely.

"I'll take him and meet you outside," Testa replied.

After finishing in the bathroom, she returned to her mission. Being surrounded by three giant men all dressed in black shirts and jeans felt surreal.

"Hey, little man," Jo said to Frenchie once they caught up to him outside. "How was your snooze? Mommy give you good drugs?"

Testa held the car door open for them and they slid in while the men loaded her luggage.

"Everyone comfortable?" Castelli asked after they had all loaded into the SUV.

"Fuckin peachy, sir."

Mia opened the bag Jo had brought her. "Yum, mini calzones." She bit into a roasted pepper and cheese. She'd finished two by the time they pulled off the exit toward downtown Providence.

"The hearing will begin in an hour. They're aware that you'll only be here for a few days."

"Ms. Mendoza." Testa turned toward Jo. "We ask that you not mention your cousin's visit. It's best to keep it quiet for many reasons."

"Sir, yes, sir."

Finally alone with Jo in her hotel room, Mia began freshening up.

"Ey, you missin' your bodyguard?"

"Nope. He's the reason I'm here," Mia snapped. She knew Jo meant well, but still…

As ready as she could be, Mia hugged Jo—she wasn't able to attend the rest of the party.

"Should I wait?" Jo asked.

"Nah, I'll call you later."

"Okay. See you tomorrow in between this shit show… And hey, maybe he didn't have a choice."

"There's always a choice." *For all of us.*

On the way to the courthouse, Mia took in the city. It was fairly busy for a Thursday afternoon, but it was the week between Christmas and New Year's. She spotted an ice rink and an image of skating with Tony flashed. A couple crossed the street holding hands and the sight made her stomach tighten. She caught Castelli's glance in the rear view before quickly averting her gaze.

Chapter 78

The three-hour deposition was straight out of a bad legal movie. One where she was cast as the craz-erita for defending a convict. They made him out to be the bad guy instead of a man who loved his wife and son even after they'd betrayed him.

During a short break, she accepted a coffee, gagging into the cup. Her nerves were shot.

"Ey, you okay?" Castelli asked, concerned.

"Great. I'm great."

She returned to her seat to continue answering the same painful, pointless questions that the team of attorneys had been tossing at her all day. Dr. Capaldi, how do you know that these are your father's journals? Can you be certain? How did you come to possess them? Is it possible that someone else wrote them? Can you walk us through that night again? How long after your mother died did you move to California? What was your state of mind when you learned about the journals, hadn't your father just died? Aren't people who have severe trauma and compounded grief susceptible to blurred reality? What was your state of mind the night your brother was hospitalized?"

Mia answered their questions void of emotion. They didn't deserve access to her pain. Their words were twisted and cruel, and they demonized her mother, but the worst part was that they were trying to imply her trauma and grief had confused reality.

"You can rest assured that I am completely sane and lucid. I'm not confused in the least about the sadness I have experienced. My brother, however, has been bending reality since we were kids and has apparently continued this unhealthy pattern."

The Providence skyline looked beautiful from her angle at dusk and she allowed herself to tune out for a minute.

"I'll ask the question again. Who was Robert Mendoza to you? How do you think watching him die affected you?"

They were trying to poke holes in her sanity, wanted her to lose it.

Rob whispered, "Mare, you got this. Fuck them."

She stiffened, sitting up straighter. "He was my cousin, not by blood. He was my friend… He became my everything."

He squeezed her hand.

"Yes, I've had a tremendous amount of traumatic loss, but my reactions have been appropriate."

Castelli stood up. "We're done for today."

She stood with the two agents and Castelli in silence waiting for the elevator to ding, hot tears falling silently down her cheeks. They stared straight ahead, giving her space. She counted her breaths, trying to soothe herself.

She was silent on the short car ride back to her hotel.

"I want you to know this wasn't Tony's idea." Castelli looked at her in the rear-view mirror, ensuring that she was listening. "He tried to stop it, it's not what he wanted for you.

He resigned, felt it was the right thing to do, the only thing. The Captain wanted him in charge, wanted him to resolve the case, go out with a bang. He said no."

Whether he'd wanted this or not, she was right back in the middle of her family's shit show.

Chapter 79

After eating a steak sandwich and fries, Mia got into bed. She sipped a vodka rocks as she watched *Casablanca*. Her mother had loved it but Mia never really understood why. She watched for a while, not really paying attention. When her eyelids grew heavy, she welcomed sleep.

Suddenly, she was tumbling through the air, endlessly floating. She saw ocean waves which quickly turned into an infinity pool. She braced herself but was caught right before she hit the water by a pair of big, warm hands. She was anxious to see Rob again, hated when he disappeared into thin air.

"Hey, you."

She turned to see Tony's eyes staring into hers. She felt his smile like the sun, saw him lean back to take in her face. His grin widened, his dimple deepened and his green eyes twinkled. She felt so light. She basked in his warmth.

"I caused you so much pain, I didn't mean to. I've missed you, missed *us*."

She leaned into him. "Me too."

He was right, though. He had caused her a tremendous

amount of pain and she was still angry and hurt. Yet, somehow, her heart still felt less broken in his arms. She yearned to be comforted by him, the very person who'd caused her pain.

"Forget him," Rob gaffed. "Stay with me."

She leaned into the feeling, letting it happen. Tony pulled her into a kiss and she felt a longing for more. She closed her eyes as he pulled her closer.

"I love you more than anything," he whispered into her hair. "Can you forgive me?"

"I feel… I feel… Alive and safe. Because I…"

Mia's eyes popped open and disappointment hit. The ringing of her cell had pulled her completely out of her dream and she resented it.

"Hello?"

Mare, hey. How was yesterday?" Jo asked.

"It was horrible. They tried to make me seem crazy because of everything and made my mother out to be a whore who deserved what she got."

"Fucking ass-wipes. You near a TV?"

"Yeah, why?"

"You better get your minions. The diner is swamped with reporters. Someone must've leaked the story about your brother, the journals… all of it."

Mia froze, processing the lunacy. "Jo? Why is this happening to me?"

"This is not you. People are fucking twisted and nosy; they want to hear the scoop on the drama from 20 years ago. This is not you. Get your bodyguards to drive you to Boston and get the fuck out of here. It's fucking ridiculous."

"I can't. I still have one more morning of court in… What time is it?"

"It's 6 a.m. Mare, it's on every station. The courthouse will be swamped with reporters. What time do you need to be there? I'll meet you."

"At 9." She turned on the TV, horrified when she saw the reporters lined up outside the diner. There were at least half a dozen lined up the walkway out front.

"I'll see you there."

Aunt Rosie appeared on the screen at the front door wearing her apron, a cloth napkin tossed over her shoulder.

"Please, we're trying to run a business here. No, she's not here. No they were not blood related. No further comment."

Mia's eyes started to fill.

She wrestled on a pair of blue jeans and pulled a pink turtleneck sweater down hard over her head. She gathered her toiletries and stuffed the rest of her clothes—shy of an off-white pantsuit—back into her suitcase, sliding it out into the hallway along with the crate.

Castelli greeted her with a quick, "Morning." He glanced toward her suitcase. "As you know, there's been a change of plan. You're leaving out of Boston after court."

She ignored him, walking down the hallway toward the elevator.

"My cousin called me. Thanks for keeping a wrap on this, I appreciate it, detective."

"We have no idea how word got out. And where are you going? We need to leave. Court starts at 9."

She stopped and turned to face him. "I know. I need to walk, grab a cup of coffee."

"There's a Brewed Awakenings next door. We'll try the back way. I could use a cup."

Stepping out of the back stairwell, she froze when she spotted the circle of reporters lining the sidewalk. Castelli blocked the door and ushered her back up to her room. The other agents were standing outside her door.

"We'll leave as soon as you're ready. We'll need the extra time."

Chapter 80

Castelli pulled the car around the front of the hotel and a group of reporters descended, blocking them and the street. Castelli's jaw clenched and he glanced at Testa, then at Mia in the rear-view mirror.

"Don't respond or listen to anything they say." He shifted the car into park and got out in one motion. "You need to move out of the way. Now."

The reporters circled the car in a flurry, firing questions and snapping pictures.

"We understand she had an affair with her cousin before he died. Is that when she lost her mind and moved?"

A special agent appeared, picking up the guy by his shirt to remove him. The other agent joined him, pushing the line of reporters back so they could drive through.

Driving to the courthouse, the questions fired away in Mia's head.

"Is Dr. Capaldi staying here? Is it true she's romantically involved with a detective working on her father's case? What is it like to learn that your father wasted his entire life in prison? Did she know her brother allegedly killed their mother?"

She felt Castelli's eyes on her through his glasses.

"You hangin' in there?"

"Nope." She felt Rob's hand tighten around hers.

They pulled up to the courthouse into a storm of reporters. Mia felt lightheaded. *Can't believe this is happening…*

"I'll park and meet you in there, they're going to escort you inside. You're almost there, the reporters aren't allowed inside the building. We won't let anything happen to you."

"We got this," Rob assured her.

Her door was opened, and in a blur, the two agents hurried her out of the car. Sandwiched between their big bodies, Mia moved through the crowd into the courthouse.

Inside the hallway, she spotted her cousins huddled together. They waved and she smiled back. Ror and Vince stood off to the side, making her heart swell. Seeing all of them woke an old emotion she'd been missing since her mother died. Her ability to hope for her own future had all but disappeared. Healing comes from letting others in but also in being brave enough to hope again.

Before approaching the conference area, Castelli returned to her side. She exhaled and quickly realized he wasn't alone. Her heart stopped for a beat, and her eyes brimmed with tears.

"Mare?" Rob whispered.

She ignored him. *It's time to gravitate toward the living.*

She locked eyes with Tony. It felt as though he'd seen her exchange with Rob. He saw her fully and she let him. Time stood still for a beat and the world went quiet.

"Ey, thought you might need a hug."

She inhaled his familiar scent as his warm arms surrounded her. Love may be the only way to truly inch toward healing.

ABOUT THE AUTHOR

Lia Cooper is a Rhode Island-based author and licensed psychotherapist in private practice. Her writing is grounded in emotional realism and explores grief, resilience, and the lasting impact of relationships. Deeply influenced by the landscapes and communities of Rhode Island, her debut novel *Ripples* and its prequel, *The Before*, trace how loss and connection shape who we become.

www.ingramcontent.com/pod-product-compliance
Lightning Source LLC
LaVergne TN
LVHW010555100826
845148LV00014B/2729